# THE
# CAIRO BRIEF

## POPPY DENBY INVESTIGATES

### BOOK 4

## Fiona Veitch Smith

LION FICTION

Published by
**Lion Hudson Limited**
Wilkinson House, Jordan Hill Road
Oxford OX2 8DR, England
www.lionhudson.com

ISBN 978 1 78264 249 7
e-ISBN 978 1 78264 250 3

First edition 2018

A catalogue record for this book is available from the British Library

Printed and bound in the UK, August 2018, LH26

*For my granddad, Horace Hawkins,*
*who first gave me music,*
*and*
*my beautiful Ruby Tuesday, faithful friend and*
*furry companion during many writing hours.*
*I'll miss you curled up at my feet.*

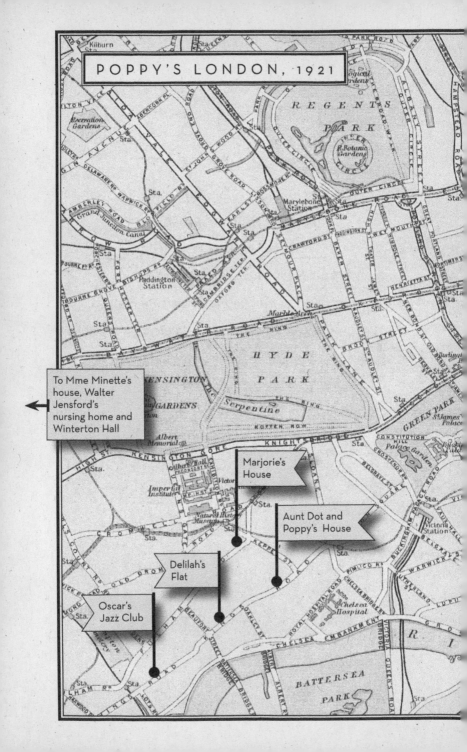

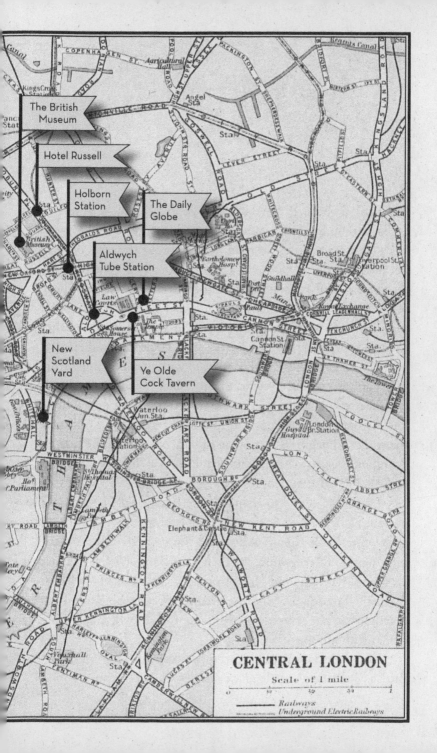

The British
Museum

Hotel Russell

Holborn
Station

The Daily
Globe

Aldwych
Tube Station

New
Scotland
Yard

Ye Olde
Cock Tavern

**CENTRAL LONDON**

Scale of 1 mile

0           ¼           ½           ¾           1

Railways
Underground Electric Railways

# ACKNOWLEDGMENTS

It's hard to believe the flapulous Poppy Denby is about to embark upon her fourth adventure in so many years. That girl has a far more exciting life than her author, who spends most of her time in slippers. However, I do occasionally get out and have a chance to put on some glad rags. Most recently that's been for the Newcastle Noir Crime Festival. I had a fantastic time meeting readers, listening to other authors, and having a chance to introduce Poppy and her friends to a whole new audience.

But it's the readers that have been with me and Poppy from the beginning whom I would like to thank now. I can't tell you how heartening it is to receive emails from readers desperate to know when the next Poppy Denby will be out. To know that the stories I imagine as I'm lying in bed, or walking the dog, or riding on the bus – and then type up in my slippers – actually make a difference in people's lives, is humbling.

I would also like to thank all the kind people I meet – in person, or virtually – during the course of my research. Firstly, to my Facebook friends who are a font of trivial but useful information: ta very muchly. Then, to the experts I've plagued at various museums and institutions. I would particularly like to thank the London Transport Museum who were able to tell me exactly what bus Poppy would have got, from where to where, on her trips around London.

My appreciation also goes to the very kind guide at the British Museum who helped me one day when I swooned – more accurately it was shaking, sweating, and needing (very quickly) to find the nearest toilet. I didn't get the lady's name, but she was very supportive. Fortunately, that was the only bad experience I've ever had at the British Museum. In doing research for this book I have spent many an hour wandering through its halls, pretending I'm Poppy, and imagining what it would have been like back in 1921.

Thanks as always goes to my indefatigable editor Jessica Tinker, who has simultaneously trained for and run a triathlon(!) while preparing for her upcoming nuptials. I am delighted to hear that Poppy has inspired her to wear a 1920s themed gown. I wish Jess and Mr Jess a glorious wedded life. My thanks too to the ever-supportive and eagle-eyed Julie Frederick, as well as the rest of the team at Lion Hudson. In addition, I would like to thank Blackwell's Bookshop in Newcastle upon Tyne for hosting the last two Poppy Denby launches and look forward to our next shindig.

Finally, I would like to toss some bouquets towards my wonderful family. My husband Rod and daughter Megan are my rocks. They put up with so much from me while my mind is wrapped up in my writing. I love you both with all my heart. Thank you too to my dad Dougie and cousin Shirley who both, in their own ways, encourage me to keep on doing what I'm doing. In the words of Maisie the flapper from *The Boyfriend*, "I love you all!"

# Character List

## Fictional characters

**Poppy Denby** – arts and entertainment editor for *The Daily Globe*. Our heroine.

**Rollo Rolandson** – senior editor and owner of *The Daily Globe*.

**Daniel Rokeby** – photographer for *The Daily Globe*. Poppy's beau. Has sister, Maggie, and two children, Arthur and Amy.

**Ike Garfield** – senior journalist at *The Daily Globe*. Has wife, Doreen.

**Ivan Molanov** – archivist at *The Daily Globe*.

**Delilah Marconi** – actress and socialite. Poppy's best friend.

**Yasmin Reece-Lansdale** – barrister and former solicitor. Legal adviser to delegation from Cairo Museum. Rollo Rolandson's on-off sweetheart.

**Marjorie Reynolds** – MP and Minister to the Home Office. Has son, Oscar, who owns Oscar's Jazz Club.

**Dot Denby** – actress and former suffragette. Poppy's aunt.

**Grace Wilson** – bookkeeper and former suffragette. Dot Denby's companion.

\*

**Sir James Maddox** – adventurer, antiquities collector, and amateur archaeologist. Baronet of Winterton Hall.

**Lady Ursula** – wife of Sir James.

**Fox Flinton** – actor and cousin of Lady Ursula.

**Grimes** – butler at Winterton Hall.

**Wallace** – footman at Winterton Hall.

**Booker and son** – the gamekeeper and his son.

**Lionel Saunders** – reporter, *The London Courier.*

**Harry Gibson** – photographer, *The London Courier.*

**Dr Giles Mortimer** – Head Curator, Department of Egyptian & Assyrian Antiquities, the British Museum.

**Dr Faizal Osman** – Director, Egyptian Antiquities Service, Cairo Museum. Brother of Yasmin Reece-Lansdale.

**Kamela El Farouk** – assistant to the Director, Egyptian Antiquities Service, Cairo Museum.

**Herr Dr Heinrich Stein** – Director of Antiquities, Museum of Berlin.

**Herr Dr Rudolf Weiner** – assistant to the Director of Antiquities, Museum of Berlin.

**Dr Jonathan Davies** – Director of Antiquities, Metropolitan Museum of New York.

**Jennifer Philpott** – assistant to Director of Antiquities, Metropolitan Museum of New York.

**Albert Carnaby** – auctioneer for Carnaby's Auction House.

**Madame Minette / Minifred Hughes** – spiritualist medium.

**Walter Jensford** – retired journalist for *The Times.*

**Freddie Waltaub** – former assistant to Dr Ludwig Borschardt at El-Amarna archaeological dig.

**DCI Jasper Martin** – chief detective for the murder squad of the Metropolitan Police.

**Sergeant Barnes** – desk sergeant at New Scotland Yard.

**Constable Jones** – police constable at Henley-on-Thames.

# HISTORICAL CHARACTERS

**Sir Arthur Conan Doyle** – author, physician, and metaphysicist.
**Lady Jean Conan Doyle** – second wife of Arthur Conan Doyle, spiritualist medium.
**Emmeline Pankhurst** – founder of the Women's Suffrage and Political Union. In this book she is a friend of Dot Denby, Grace Wilson, and Marjorie Reynolds.
**Howard Carter** – archaeologist, Egyptologist, and (in this book) special adviser to the British Museum. In February 1922, three months after the fictional events of this book, Howard Carter discovers the tomb of the boy king Tutankhamun, grandson of Nefertiti.
**Dr Ludwig Borchardt** – archaeologist and Egyptologist. In 1912 he discovered the famous bust of Nefertiti at El-Amarna. In this book he also discovers the (fictional) death mask of Nefertiti in 1914.

\*

**Nefertiti** – wife of Pharaoh Akhenaten who ruled Egypt from 1353 to 1336 BC. Together they founded the city of Akhetaten (Horizon of Aten) whose ruins are at modern-day El-Amarna. They were considered heretics because they abandoned the pantheon of old gods and declared only one god was to be worshipped – the sun, Aten, who created the world. Nefertiti and Akhenaten had six daughters, one of whom he also married, and with whom he incestuously fathered Tutankhamun. After Akhenaten died it is believed Nefertiti may have ruled as pharaoh queen, before abandoning the city and returning the capital to Thebes, where Tutankhamun became king and returned Egypt to the old religion. Akhenaten was buried in El-Amarna. Nefertiti's body has never been found.

## OZYMANDIAS

I met a traveller from an antique land
Who said: Two vast and trunkless legs of stone
Stand in the desert. Near them, on the sand,
Half sunk, a shatter'd visage lies, whose frown
And wrinkled lip and sneer of cold command
Tell that its sculptor well those passions read
Which yet survive, stamp'd on these lifeless things,
The hand that mock'd them and the heart that fed.
And on the pedestal these words appear:
"My name is Ozymandias, king of kings:
Look on my works, ye Mighty, and despair!"
Nothing beside remains: round the decay
Of that colossal wreck, boundless and bare,
The lone and level sands stretch far away.

*Percy Bysshe Shelley, 1818*

# CHAPTER 1

## 10 APRIL 1914, EL-AMARNA, EGYPT

Two brown-cloaked figures picked their way through the half-filled trenches and incomplete excavations of the ancient city. Without its centuries-old shroud of desert sand, Akhetaten lay shivering and exposed in the shameful moonlight, filtering down from the carved cliffs to the east. From the cliff face, hacked and hewn, the likenesses of the heretic pharaohs Akhenaten and Nefertiti stood sentinel over the valley where, three and a half thousand years before, they had built a city to worship Aten, the golden sun.

But tonight it was Iah, the silver moon, that ruled the shadowlands below, where the city of the dead was being reclaimed by the living. To the west of what the foreigners called "The Dig", the Nile snaked through fields and farms, an artery of life to the villages dotted along the plain.

The cloaked, trespassing figures were a twin boy and girl of around seventeen who lived in one of the nearby villages: Et-Till Beni Amra. At least they used to. Now they were at boarding school in Cairo, far, far to the north, and only came home during the holidays. Their parents were the only people in the village able to afford to send their children away to school, an enormous expense and – so the villagers whispered as they tilled their crops – a wasteful one, particularly on the girl. But the twins' illicit family business – secretly passed down from generation to generation – had been doing well in recent times, thanks to the Europeans swarming over the carcass of Akhenaten like pale flies. The children with whom the twins now shared dormitories in Cairo talked behind their backs and called them graverobbers. But their father preferred the title "antiquities dealer" and now, since he had been so well paid by the German professor, his children were able to write his profession in German, English, and French.

The girl had been reluctant to come on the moonlit adventure. It had been fun to dig around in the ruins when they were children, but now she understood the consequences of being found with reclaimed artefacts. She'd heard stories of locals being beaten and imprisoned for theft. The Egyptian Antiquities Service issued licences to excavators on a seasonal basis. For the last seven years the licence had gone to Professor Ludwig Borchardt and his team. No one else was allowed to dig there – no rival European archaeologists and most definitely not a pair of young Mohammedans. Never mind that the girl's family had been digging and selling the fruit of their labour for a hundred years before Borchardt came. Her father had been hired by the German as a consultant and had sworn to stop his own black-market business in return for a substantial salary. But her brother refused to adhere to the agreement. "It's our people's heritage," he had argued, "like the crops of the field and the fish of the Nile."

So, on this weekend which the Christians called Easter, when her father was in Cairo with his German employer, her brother had coaxed her to join him in a little subsistence looting. "For old time's sake," he had grinned. Reluctantly, she agreed. After she helped her mother wash up and read her younger siblings a bedtime story, she donned her cloak, preparing to join her brother for an evening walk.

The mother assessed her twin children. The boy looked as cock-sure as always. But the girl... there was something bothering her. "You don't have to go," the woman said to her daughter. "Not if you don't want to."

"I – well – I –"

Her brother interrupted before she could finish, putting his arm around her and ushering her to the door. "Don't worry, mother, I'll look after her. She's just a bit out of practice, aren't you?"

The girl couldn't deny this. She nodded half-heartedly.

"Hmmm," said their mother, wiping her hands dry on her apron. "If I didn't know the Europeans were away I might be more worried."

"Worried about what?" asked her son, as he too pulled on his cloak. "We are just going for an evening stroll. And if we happen to walk past the old city... well..." he grinned and kissed his mother on her forehead.

"Watch out for Mohammed and his dog," said the mother. "He's usually asleep on the job, and he owes your father half a dozen favours, but you never know..."

"We will," said her son as he and his sister picked up their sacks – containing ropes and tools – and headed out into the night.

Half an hour later the twins were at their preselected destination: the remains of an ancient workshop that had belonged to a man called Thutmose, the personal sculptor of Pharaoh Akhenaten and his wife, Nefertiti. Two years ago the German team, guided by the twins' father, had unearthed the ruins of the sprawling facility and found a bust of the beautiful queen, with only one eye. The sculpture had now been sent to Berlin. But it wasn't the only work of art retrieved. There were dozens of half-finished statues and bits of broken limbs in a series of storerooms and trash piles. And – so the twins knew – a secret underground chamber where the sculptor had kept his most precious work. Their father had declined, so far, to tell his new employers about the chamber. But rumour of its existence had been passed down in the family from generation to generation.

"I still don't understand why Papa hasn't told the Germans about it yet," said the girl.

"Perhaps they haven't paid him enough," observed the boy. He struck a match and lit a small hurricane lantern he'd taken from his sack, then ranged the lamp in a wide arc over the trenches and roped-off squares of earth. "But it's only a matter of time until someone finds it."

"And you think you know where it is?" asked the girl.

The boy nodded. "And so do you. Do you remember that rhyme Grandpa used to sing?"

The girl's face lit up in the light of the lamp. She smiled, remembering fondly the old man with skin like dried parchment. "One palm, two palm, between the trees, there's Old Tut's treasure, so please don't sneeze!" She giggled, just like she used to when she was a child.

The boy grinned. "The thing is, I don't think it was just a rhyme." He pointed to a small copse of palm trees about thirty paces west of the perimeter of the workshop dig. A pair of trees were set slightly apart from the rest. "What do you think?"

The girl's almond-shaped eyes opened wide. "That's a bit of a stretch."

The boy shrugged and walked towards the trees. "Worth a dig, though, don't you think?"

The girl scanned the horizon, looking for any sign of the old watchman and his dog. It was all clear. She sighed, shifted her sack from one shoulder to another, and followed her brother. "Can't do any harm, I suppose..."

"Hey! Looks like someone's already been here," called the brother. The girl broke into a run and joined her sibling under the palms. He ranged his lantern over the area to reveal a hole in the ground, which had previously been hidden by rock and scree. The siblings both knew that this is how the entrance to Thutmose's workshop had been found: under a pile of rubble. But around this entrance were footprints in the sand – human and animal. The girl got down on her knees and peered into the hole, gesturing for her brother to shed light on it. He did and the girl could make out a steep tunnel, wide enough for a medium-sized man to squeeze into, angled down into the darkness. "Do you think someone's down there now?" she whispered.

"I doubt it," said the boy. "If the Europeans had found it already, they would have blocked the area off and put guards on it until they came back from their Easter break."

The girl nodded her assent and cocked her ear, trying to pick up any sounds that might be emanating from the underground chamber. "I agree about the Europeans. So that means it must be one of our people."

"Yes, but I doubt they're still there. Look, these footprints don't look fresh. He poked at the faded tracks with his sandal, then grinned. "The Europeans wouldn't be able to get a clear print from these," he said, reminding his sister of the graverobber who had been caught and convicted on another dig by the famous archaeologist Howard Carter, who photographed footprints leading from the scene of the crime and matched them to a suspect.

"What do you want to do then?" asked the girl.

The boy put down his lantern on a nearby rock and shuffled

his sack off his shoulder. "Go in, of course. Even if someone's been here before us, there'll still be lots to see. And good luck to them if they have! Better one of our people than a foreigner."

The girl couldn't disagree with that. So, with one more scan of the area above ground to prove they were most definitely alone, she helped her brother tie a rope securely to a palm tree and thread it down the hole. From experience, she knew that in all likelihood the entrance was not above a dead drop and was most likely a steep ramp. But also from experience – and family stories – she knew that the ramps could be treacherous. Great Uncle Kadiel had lost his footing at one of the tombs on the cliff face forty years ago and broke his back in the fall. So they tied a second rope and knotted it around her brother's waist – as their father had taught them – and made him lean back to see if it held his weight. It did and before long he slithered through the hole and made his way down, using the first rope as a guide.

The girl waited in the company of the twin palms, standing sentinel beneath a canopy of stars.

"It's too tight to stand," a muffled voice called after a few moments. "But I can crawl. I'll give three tugs when I reach the bottom. If there's anything to see, I'll give another three tugs; if there's nothing here, I'll only tug twice."

"All right!" called the girl as loudly as she dared. They appeared to be alone, but old Mohammed and his dog were still unaccounted for...

It must only have been five minutes, but it seemed like twice that before the rope between the tree and the hole jerked... three times. The girl let out the breath she hadn't realized she'd been holding. *There's something there... he wants me to come down...*

She looked around once more – still no sign of the watchman and his dog. She wasn't surprised; he was a known slacker. The heavens only knew how he managed to keep his job. Some said he knew secrets the Europeans wouldn't want divulged – secrets about questionable practices on the dig that didn't quite align with the terms of licence granted by the Egyptian Department of Antiquities in Cairo.

She tugged the rope three times to indicate to her brother that she'd got the message, tied another rope around the tree, and securely fastened it around her waist before approaching the entrance to the underground chamber. On her haunches she pulled up the hood of her cloak and tucked the stray hair from her plait behind her ears. She'd only just washed her hair that morning and didn't want it full of muck from the tunnel. Then she sat on her bottom and worked her way, feet first, into the hole. There was no need to go head first; her brother had traversed the route before her and wouldn't have called her down if there was any obstacle in the way. And besides, she was more confident keeping her head up, rather than down, just in case she needed to pull herself back up the rope with no one above ground to help her.

She held her breath and shimmied into the hole, then down the tunnel, which had sufficient clearance that the ceiling only intermittently brushed the top of her head. She stopped a metre or two below the surface, braced her ankles against the sides, and felt around with her hands. Someone, a long time ago – Thutmose himself perhaps? – had lined the tunnel with timber and overlaid it with compacted clay. The clay lining had cracked and crumbled in places but remained largely intact. The girl mumbled a prayer of thanks for the ingenuity and industriousness of her ancestors.

"Are you coming down?" A call from below.

"Yes," she answered and continued her downwards shimmy, pushing herself up onto her hands and propelling her bottom forward to her knees in a caterpillar motion. "How far?"

"About twenty metres! Can you see my light?"

Yes, she could; there was a dim glow below her. Her brother had lit the lamp he had taken down with him. "Yes!" she affirmed, then: "What can you see?"

"Piles of loot!" Her brother's voice bubbled with excitement. "It's not a tomb –"

"Didn't expect it to be."

"No. But it looks like this was where old Tut stored his funerary artefacts. The ones that would be used for burial."

"Of Nefertiti and Akhenaten?"

"Possibly. We'll see when you get down. I haven't gone too far in… Ah, there you are. You're getting slow in your old age." The boy held out his hand and helped his sister upright at the bottom of the ramped tunnel. She took it then gave him a playful punch on the shoulder.

"You're fifteen minutes older than me!"

"And always fifteen minutes ahead of you too!"

She punched him again.

"Ow!" yelped the boy but didn't retaliate. Here, surrounded by vases, chests, sarcophagi and amphora – with who knew what kind of treasure inside – they put their sibling high jinks aside.

The girl took the lantern from him and traced a wide arc around the chamber. She let out a long whistle. "It looks like there are other chambers leading off from this one."

The boy agreed. "At least one; there's an entrance over there. I haven't been through yet. Thought we could start here."

The girl nodded her agreement, put down the lantern on top of a carved stele leaning against the wall, and started to investigate. The stele – possibly a grave marker – was inscribed with hieroglyphics. The twins were learning to read the ancient script in their Classical civilization classes at the academy. The girl traced her finger over the shapes, mouthing the words as she went: "The sun and the moon, the day and the night, wed forever in celestial splendour. Akhenaten and Nefertiti shine on your people, divine ones, shine." The girl gasped and raised her face to her brother. "It is them! This will fetch a fine price on the black market!"

The boy grinned. "Of course we can't take too much… we'll never get away with it… but I don't see why we can't take a couple of small pieces and then let Borchardt know when he gets back with father… we'll have to leave the stele, too heavy… besides it identifies the find… but something smaller…"

He lifted the lid on one of the painted wooden chests. Inside, in a bed of straw, was a set of gold-plated amphora, perhaps intended to hold sacred oil. "Hang on," he said, his fingers raking through the straw, "this is fresh… it's fresh straw!" He reached for the next chest and it contained statuettes. These too were neatly packaged in fresh straw.

"Why's it fresh?" he asked.

The girl's stomach clenched. "Oh no…" She too opened a chest and came face to face with a burial mask of gold leaf, blue enamel, and black jet that looked very similar to the bust of Nefertiti, discovered elsewhere on the dig two years earlier. But what struck the twins more than the exquisite beauty of the pharaoh queen was the nest of fresh straw and modern linen wadding in which it lay. "Someone's been here before us," the girl whispered.

"Yes," agreed the boy, "and it looks like they're packed and ready to go."

"We need to report it," said the girl. "This doesn't look like a casual looter. It's organized. It's… pssst! Where are you going?"

The boy was picking his way through the treasure-filled chests heading to the back of the chamber. "I'm just going to stick my head in here."

The girl stood up and put her hands on her hips. "I don't think we've got time. What if they come back?"

"Just a few minutes more," said the boy and continued on his quest. As there was only one light the girl had a choice of staying there in the dark or following her brother. She sighed and, with a humph, joined her sibling. They had been right – there was another chamber, this too filled with chests, vases, statues, stele, and amphora. And in the middle was a stone sarcophagus. It was incomplete, with only the first layer of chiselling evident in what would eventually be an intricately carved design. The twins weren't surprised. Thutmose had abandoned his workshop when the city was evacuated after the death of Akhenaten. Much of the finds on the dig to date had been of unfinished or discarded pieces, though still of immense value to historians, antiquarians, and collectors of ancient art.

The boy took hold of the lid and heaved. It shifted slightly but didn't budge. "Give me a hand, will you?"

The girl snorted. "You won't find a mummy if that's what you're looking for."

"I know!" said the brother. "But I'd like to see where one might lie. I've never seen inside one, have you?"

The girl admitted she hadn't. There were a couple at the Cairo Museum, but she had never got around to visiting. When you lived a stone's throw from an archaeological treasure trove, seeing the artefacts in the musty confines of a museum wasn't quite so enticing. So she shrugged and leant her strength to her brother's effort. With a few heaves and pulls the heavy stone lid began to pivot. When they'd moved it about 45 degrees they stopped and the boy picked up the lamp from the floor. He held it aloft and gasped. There, staring through the opening, was the grimacing face of a dog, its teeth bared, its eyes wide and lifeless. The muzzle was matted with blood. The girl knew that if she reached out and touched it, it would still be sticky to the touch – it looked that recent. "It's the watchman's dog! Who would do this?"

The siblings stepped back from the sarcophagus and drew closer together. The girl slipped her arm around her brother's waist. She was not a sentimental girl, but the thought of a poor animal being killed and hidden like this made her feel sick. Hidden… hidden… "And why would they hide it?"

"And where's Mohammed?" The boy's voice was hollow. He took a step towards the sarcophagus.

The girl knew immediately what he was going to do. "Don't! Let's call someone. The police at El-Hag Kandeel…"

But the boy was undeterred. He passed the lantern to his sister, then climbed up onto the edge of the stone coffin and positioned his backside on the rim. He pressed his heels against the edge of the lid and used the strength of his legs to push. The lid gave way and fell to the earth floor with a deathly thud. And there, as the siblings both feared, was the body of Mohammed the watchman under the corpse of his faithful dog.

The twins screamed, their voices merging as they had on the day they were born, and they ran from the chamber as fast as they could. The girl had the presence of mind to snatch up the lantern and was a step or two behind her brother as they fled towards the tunnel. But waiting for them, in the outer chamber, were two men, one an Egyptian police officer, the other a European.

"Mohammed! The watchman! His dog!" the boy cried in Arabic.

"Arrest them," said the European in English.

"But we haven't done anything!" cried the girl. Her protest was met with a blow to the head and the last thing she heard was her brother calling out her name.

# CHAPTER 2

## LONDON, THURSDAY 8 DECEMBER 1921

"Miz Denby! What do you know about Queen Nefertiti?" Poppy looked up from her Remington typewriter – where she had been bashing out a theatre review – to see her editor stalking towards her with what looked like a press release in hand. Since returning from a trip to New York earlier in the year, the diminutive newspaperman had taken to walking around with a noxious Cuban cigar clenched between his teeth, adding to the already foul atmosphere of the fourth-floor newsroom. He clambered onto a spare chair near her desk, his short legs dangling a foot off the ground.

"Nefertiti," he said again, pronouncing it "Nay-fur-toy-toy" in his New York accent.

"Hold on," said Poppy, then swiped the carriage return twice, typed ENDS, and turned her attention to her editor.

"Who or what is 'Nay-fur-toy-toy'?" she asked, reaching out her ink-stained hand to take the sheet of paper Rollo passed to her.

Rollo grinned at her attempt at a New York accent and then, in affected Queen's English, articulated "Ne'er-for-tea-tea," before slipping back into his usual drawl. "She was some Egyptian broad. A pharaoh queen. Married to a fella whose name I can't pronounce."

Poppy scanned the press release.

*Dear Mr Rolandson, you are invited to report on the auction of the death mask of Queen Nefertiti at Winterton Hall, Henley-on-Thames, on Saturday 10th December. The auction will be part of a longer clay-pigeon shooting weekend – weather permitting – and will be attended by luminaries in the world of antiquities and archaeology, both local and international. Your readers might also be interested to know that on Friday evening, a séance will be held, led by Sir Arthur and Lady Conan Doyle, at which an attempt will be made to contact the spirit of Queen Nefertiti.*

The release then went on to give a brief history of Nefertiti and to state that the mask had just recently come to light, the general consensus being that it had been stolen from a dig in Egypt in 1914, under what were described as "murderous circumstances".

Poppy raised her eyebrows. "Murderous circumstances? What does that mean?"

"Damned if I know," said Rollo, and stubbed out his cigar in the soil around Poppy's precious potted begonia. She glared at him. "Sorry," he offered, then picked out the stub and plopped it into an empty tea cup. "You really should get an ashtray, Miz Denby."

Poppy bit back her *you really should respect other people's property* and said instead, "So, are you going?"

"It's short notice, but yes. And I think you should come too. Technically, it falls into the art and entertainment brief – particularly with Conan Doyle in attendance; you might be able to get an interview."

"What's this about a séance?"

Rollo rolled his eyes beneath his shaggy red brows. "Another one of his spiritualist stunts, I suppose."

Poppy pursed her lips. "Quite. I wish he'd stick to his detective stories. They're far more sensible."

Rollo grinned. "But not half as newsworthy. Which is why this Maddox fella thinks we'll be interested. And he's right."

"Well, I'm not interested in the least."

"Hocus pocus not Christian enough for you?" asked Rollo with a grin.

Poppy swivelled in her chair and looked Rollo squarely in the eye. "There are two ways of looking at this. Either they're a hoax and people are being duped, or they are actually talking to the dead – which, in my book, is a very dangerous thing to do. Dabbling with the spirits can lead down sinister paths."

"Spirits that don't exist."

"You have no evidence of that."

"Neither do you."

They held each other's gaze. Poppy and Rollo had been over this ground before. She believed in God. He did not.

"Well, Miz Denby, hopefully you can admit that whether it's a hoax or real, anything involving Conan Doyle is newsworthy. And you would be professionally remiss to ignore it."

Poppy lowered her eyes. He was right. She had a job to do. She cleared her throat and then scanned the press release again. It was signed by Sir James Maddox, Baronet of Winterton. "Do we know anything about Maddox?" asked Poppy, indicating that she was most firmly back "on the job".

Rollo leaned back in his chair, his plump belly straining between the parallel lines of his scarlet braces. "I've heard the name. Yazzie has mentioned him before. He was a friend of her father's, I think. Some kind of maverick archaeologist collector type. A bit like that Carnarvon fella."

"The one that's looking for King Tut's tomb?"

"That's the one," said Rollo and took the press release back from Poppy. "I think I'll ask Yazzie to come as well. She might be able to give us some insight into the Egyptian angle. And she might want to bid on the mask… She's got quite the art collection, as you know."

Poppy brushed a stray blonde curl behind her ear and avoided meeting Rollo's eyes.

"What?"

"Nothing. I just thought you and Miss Reece-Lansdale were no longer – er – well – no longer stepping out together." She straightened a pile of notes on her desk.

Rollo cocked his head to one side. "I don't know if we were ever 'stepping out together'. But no, whatever you've heard, Yazzie and I are still friends. She's a fine lady."

What Poppy had heard was that the famous female barrister, the Anglo-Egyptian Miss Yasmin Reece-Lansdale, had been forthright enough to ask the editor of *The Daily Globe* to marry her. And he had turned her down. But it was none of her business. What was her business was a possible story involving Arthur Conan Doyle and a valuable Egyptian artefact that was somehow associated with a murder… A shiver ran down her spine. "Apologies Rollo. Yes, I'd love to come on the weekend with you and Yazzie – in a professional capacity, of course." Annoyingly, she felt a slight blush creep up her neck.

Her editor laughed. "Goodo. And I'll ask Danny Boy too," he winked. "In his professional capacity, of course." Rollo heaved himself off his chair and stood at Poppy's side, his head barely reaching her shoulder. His eyes expertly scanned the typescript in her machine. "Is this the Ivor Novello / P. G. Wodehouse collaboration?"

"It is," said Poppy. "At the Adelphi."

"Any good?"

Poppy whisked out the sheet and passed it to him. "Very funny, as you'd expect. Jolly music too."

"I might give it a go. If you're finished with this why don't you go down to the morgue and pull some jazz files on the main players at the Egyptian weekend. And I'll telegraph Maddox to expect a group of us from the *Globe*." He paused, his eyebrows furrowed. "Bet we're not the only press he's asked."

"Lionel Saunders from the *Courier*?" asked Poppy as she stood up and straightened her calf-length Chanel grey skirt – all the rage in office wear for the working lady – and shrugged into the matching jacket.

"You can bet your bottom dollar on it," observed Rollo. He wagged a finger at Poppy. "We'd better make sure we get the scoop on him. Do as much research as you can, Miz Denby, and I'll see if Yazzie knows anything about these 'murderous circumstances'. Her brother Faizal is with the Egyptian Antiquities Service, did you know?"

Poppy didn't. She didn't even know Yasmin had a brother. The editor and reporter parted ways, promising to touch base later in the day.

Down in the morgue, Poppy hung her jacket and matching cloche hat next to a huge black greatcoat, which had previously seen action on the Western Front. The coat belonged to Ivan Molanov, the archivist of *The Daily Globe*. Ivan was a refugee from communist Russia who had met Rollo Rolandson in a military hospital in Belgium during the war. At Poppy's request, Ivan had dug out the jazz files on Arthur and Jean Conan Doyle, James Maddox, the archaeologist Howard Carter, and his backer, George Herbert, the fifth Earl of Carnarvon. Poppy didn't know whether Carter and Carnarvon were going to be at the shooting weekend, but as they were currently the most famous Egyptologists in the country, she thought their files might contain some useful background material. She also asked Ivan to look beyond the jazz files – which contained mainly celebrity gossip – to the subject clipping files.

"Do you have anything on Egypt in general? Or this Queen Nefertiti?"

"Nay-fah who?" asked Ivan.

Poppy wrote down the name on a piece of paper and gave it to him. Ivan held it in his huge paw-like hand and grunted. "Thees ees not a library, Mees Denby. Go to the British Museum. Beeg library there. Lots of Egyptian artefacts too. You ever see a mummy?"

Poppy admitted that she hadn't. She was a frequent visitor to the British Library, but in the eighteen months she had lived in London she had never ventured into the bowels of the museum which shared the same premises. History did not interest her that much, and most of her time – work or leisure – was taken up attending art exhibitions, book launches or theatre and cinema shows. She was, after all, the arts and entertainment editor of the *Globe*, not a historian. However, this new story, which she had labelled "The Cairo Brief" in bold letters at the top of her notebook (she had initially called it "The Pharaoh Brief" but wasn't confident she could spell it), was about *ancient* art. She felt a little out of her depth.

"Yes, that's a good suggestion, Ivan. I'll head over to the museum when I'm finished here."

Ivan left her to her research. First off she opened the file on Arthur and Jean Conan Doyle. Actually, it was two files in one, as the file of Jean Leckie, long-term mistress of the famous detective fiction writer, was slipped into her lover's when they finally married, the year after the death of Conan Doyle's first wife. Sir Arthur, Lady Jean, and anyone close to them denied that they'd had a physical affair, but no one denied that they had been in love for at least a decade while the first Mrs Conan Doyle became increasingly infirm with tuberculosis. It was partly due to Jean, apparently, that Arthur became embroiled in spiritualism, which avid readers of the Sherlock Holmes stories struggled to understand. Conan Doyle had previously been a doctor and gifted his scientific mindset to the forensic genius of Holmes. However, as Poppy read on in the file, she realized that this was just a veneer. The real Conan Doyle was just as interested in the metaphysical as he was in the scientific, having become a Freemason thirty years earlier. He had also written articles on psychic phenomena, which he claimed to have observed in his children's nanny. When he married Jean in 1906 and she professed to have the gift of contacting the dead and communicating their messages to the living through automatic writing, Conan Doyle became increasingly active in the spiritualist movement. Poppy noted that his first published work on spiritualism was in 1916, the year after one of his nephews was killed in the war. Poppy swallowed hard. That was the same year Christopher died...

Poppy's brother Christopher had been a voracious reader of the Sherlock Holmes stories and had used his pocket money to buy *The Strand* magazine and kept it hidden under his mattress. Knowing their parents would disapprove of wasting good money on what they would have thought "bad literature", he swore Poppy to secrecy. A few years later, when Christopher died, she felt she needed to continue keeping his secret. But when she went to his room to retrieve the stash, their mother was already there. She had pulled the mattress off the bed for beating and found the collection of story magazines. They now lay around her as she knelt on the floor, her shoulders heaving as she sobbed. One of the magazines was clutched to her breast as she wept out her anguish for her lost child. Poppy did not speak; she just turned around and left her mother to her private grief. Later, she returned to the room, but the magazines had all gone.

Poppy closed her eyes to suppress the tears that were beginning to well. *Pull yourself together, old girl; there's work to be done.* Poppy turned a page in the file to find a clipping from *The Strand* dated December 1920. The article, written by Conan Doyle, was in defence of the girls from Yorkshire who claimed to have photographed fairies at the bottom of their garden. Poppy smiled as she looked at the whimsical photograph, considered a hoax by experts and academics, but widely believed by the general public. This article by the author of Sherlock Holmes had much to do with the popular acceptance of the fairy hoax, as the public seemed to struggle to differentiate the unimpeachable fictional detective – who could never be fooled – from his more fanciful creator.

The next page in the file held an article written by Rollo Rolandson, lampooning Conan Doyle for his defence of the photographs and quoting Daniel Rokeby, *The Daily Globe*'s resident photographer, who explained how the photographs had been staged and faked. Poppy remembered Rollo and Daniel working on the piece last December. *Golly, had it been a year already?*

Poppy trailed her finger along Daniel's name. Last December Poppy had believed she and the handsome photographer might soon be married. But here they were, twelve months later, and there was still no ring on her finger. Their relationship ebbed and flowed like the tide, and for three whole months, when Poppy was in New York with Rollo, she thought it might be over forever. But on her return Daniel had been waiting for her... Poppy pulled herself up again: *Stop daydreaming!*

She read through her notes on Conan Doyle and decided that she had enough to go on for now. She was fascinated to meet the man in the flesh – as well as his wife; although the idea of speaking to someone who spoke to the dead was a little troubling. *Claims to speak to the dead*, Poppy reminded herself. Surely, the whole thing was a hoax. Not to mention un-Christian! Nonetheless, she was intrigued to see what actually happened at a séance. Despite her qualms, Rollo was right: it would make for a fantastic article.

The next file was on Sir James Maddox, whom Poppy had never heard of before. There wasn't much in the file, as Maddox appeared to spend much of his time abroad or on his country estate, Winterton, and did not come up to London much. There was, however, a photograph of Maddox and his wife, Lady Ursula, at the opening of an exhibit at the British Museum. He was a beefy, balding man, sporting a moustache and wearing one of those curious Ottoman hats – a fez, Poppy thought it might be called. His wife was more conventionally dressed, her unsmiling face giving nothing away. The notes added little to what Rollo had already told her. Maddox was a gentleman archaeologist and world traveller, with an extensive collection of Egyptian, Roman, and Greek antiquities. There was, however, one newspaper clipping that gave a hint of something slightly controversial. It was from *The Times*, dated August 1914, reporting that Sir James Maddox had been asked to step down from the board of the Egyptian Exploration Fund. A representative of the board had told *The Times* it was due to concerns that had been raised about Sir James' "methods of procurement of certain antiquities". The representative declined to give more specific details and Sir James was "not available for comment". It was a short article, covering a mere three column inches. Poppy was very surprised the journalist hadn't dug deeper. There was clearly a story there… but, perhaps the outbreak of the war that very same month had caused the story to be spiked – or it had been longer and the sub-editor had cut it for space. She checked the byline on the article – Walter Jensford. She'd never heard of him but made a note of it.

Poppy closed the file and checked her watch – nearly one o'clock. *Time for a spot of lunch then I'll head over to the British Museum.* She hadn't had a chance to read the Carnarvon and Carter files. "Ivan," she called out to the archivist. "Can I take these with me please?"

Ivan said she could and made a note in his meticulously kept record book as Poppy slipped her jacket over her white silk blouse. "You should wrap up warm, Mees Denby. I see it is starting to snow." Poppy glanced out of the third-floor window, overlooking Fleet Street. Down below, horse-drawn vehicles jostled for space with motorcars, and pedestrians pulled up their collars against the cold. Ivan was right; it was starting to snow.

# CHAPTER 3

Poppy stopped by the newsroom to pick up her heavy winter overcoat and umbrella before popping her head into Rollo's office to tell him where she was going. He was on the telephone and waved her off. So she asked Ike Garfield, the senior journalist, to let him know when he was off the phone. She took the lift down to the entrance foyer, watching the brass arrow tick off the floors one by one. At the second floor she wondered for a moment if she should stop in to see Daniel in the photography department but decided against it. She didn't have much time to get to the British Museum and do the research she needed. Besides, if Rollo was asking Daniel to accompany them to Henley-on-Thames, she would see him for the whole weekend. Yes, they'd be working, but still... Poppy smiled to herself at the thought, remembering the last time she and Daniel had travelled west of London, on their way to Windsor: he on a motorbike and she in a sidecar with the wind teasing long strands of hair from under her leather helmet. That was before her flapper friend Delilah had got hold of her and given her a jazzy makeover, including a fashionable bob. Poppy pulled her hat firmly over her cropped curls. There would be no wind in the hair today. And hopefully not too much snow...

The lift shuddered to a stop on the ground floor and Poppy stepped out into a black and white marble foyer, lined with Egyptian-inspired art deco statuettes in alcoves. London designers were afroth for all things Egyptian or Oriental at the moment, and as the owner of the *Globe* was romantically connected to one of the city's most prolific antique art collectors, it was no surprise that that was the chosen design motif. Poppy was looking forward to seeing Yasmin Reece-Lansdale again; she was a woman the young journalist greatly admired. Rollo was a fool to turn her down. But, Poppy reminded herself as she waved to the receptionist Mavis Bradshaw, who was signing in a visitor to the building, it was none of her business.

Out on Fleet Street Poppy was absorbed into the throng of pedestrians, shoulders hunched, brollies up, picking up their pace before the snow really set in. Across the street, Poppy saw the door to Ye Olde Cock Tavern open and close as it sucked in more clientele, while to the right of the pub, an alleyway leading down to Temple Church and the law courts was like a cave mouth, beckoning black-cloaked lawyers and clerks like bats at sunrise.

Poppy joined the bedraggled queue waiting for the number 68 bus as the wind picked up and lashed icy gusts at her face. So as not to impede on other people in the queue, she held her brolly at a jaunty angle, but then pulled it down as it was doing no good. Instead, she tucked up her fur collar under the brim of her hat, contracting her neck like a tortoise retreating into its shell. After a few minutes she realized that even if the bus did come before she froze to death, there was no guarantee that it would be one of those new double-deckers with roofs. If it was one of the older buses – or a pirate bus – the bottom floor would be full and she'd be forced to sit upstairs, open to the elements. It was only a quarter of a mile to Aldwych tube station so Poppy decided to go underground. She slipped out of the queue and put her brolly back up, chastising herself about how soft she was getting living in London. She was a northern lass, and back home in Northumberland they would have laughed at the southern softies bleating about a few snowflakes. Poppy straightened her spine and trudged on.

She passed Chancery Lane, then the Royal Courts of Justice, and turned right into Aldwych Crescent. The snow was turning to sleet, leaving wet streaks on her stockings and splodges on her shoes. She picked up her pace and half-ran into the station entrance. The station had been built on the site of an old theatre and her lovey friends had told her that at night the ghost of an actress walked the tunnels. Poppy chuckled to herself and wondered if Lady Conan Doyle had ever chatted to her.

Poppy joined the queue for the ticket office and bought a single to Holborn. She didn't bother with a return, as she would head home to Chelsea afterwards and just telephone in an update to the office. She had already arranged to get off work early as she was going out with her aunt Dot and her companion Grace for a farewell dinner with friends. The pair were heading off to France in the morning to join the Orient Express for a three-month return trip across Europe.

Fortunately, the journey to Holborn was only one stop up the Piccadilly line. Poppy did not like enclosed spaces – particularly tunnels – so when at all possible travelled around London above ground. But as time – and the weather – were not on her side this afternoon, she bit the bullet and joined the other commuters spluttering their way through the smoke- and steam-filled corridors to catch the next train.

Fifteen minutes later, Poppy was spewed from the bowels of the city into the relatively fresh air of Southampton Row. The rain had won in the battle of the sleet, and the pretty white dusting – which for a moment had transformed the grey Bloomsbury streets into a picture postcard – was washed away. Poppy, like the rest of the commuters emerging from the station, popped up her umbrella and ploughed on. Right down Southampton

Row, past Baptist Church House, then left at Victoria House and onto Vernon Place, before a quick shortcut through the park at Bloomsbury Square.

The museum was on the far side of the park. She crossed vertically through it, via an avenue flanked by aged oaks, planted in the days of mad King George, and whose leafless branches did nothing to shelter pedestrians from the rain. Sheets of water spilled from the roof of the bandstand where, Poppy remembered, she and Daniel had come the previous summer with his two children to listen to the Salvation Army brass band.

But there was no time to reminisce now: the rain was getting heavier and Poppy picked up her pace, hoping to get into the shelter of the museum before her black leather Mary Janes were completely soaked through. She soon reached the grand Greek Revival-style building and slipped gratefully through the black wrought-iron gates. In the summer there would be queues of people lined up; today, there was only the gatekeeper huddled in a shelter and a young mother unsuccessfully trying to keep her toddler out of puddles. Poppy hurried up the wide stone stairs, past the giant Ionic columns, and into the museum proper, where she joined a huddle of dripping visitors, shrugging out of their overcoats and shaking their brollies in the museum's cloakroom.

Finally free of her sodden attire – and regretting not keeping a pair of galoshes in the office – Poppy endeavoured to ignore her squelching stockings and shoes as she checked out a map of the museum. The exhibition space was a giant quadrangle with a circular domed reading room at the centre. The reading room housed the British Library, where Poppy had spent many an hour researching and reading for pleasure. But she had never ventured into the galleries of the quadrangle nor the wings to left and right that housed the museum's treasures.

She checked the board to see where the Egyptian collection might be and discovered that it was to the left of the reading room, in galleries 22–26. She headed off in that direction and soon found the entrance to the main Egyptian and Assyrian gallery. As she was about to enter, pondering what wonders she might see, she came face to face with a familiar figure: Marjorie Reynolds, one of the country's first women members of Parliament and minister in the Home Office. Marjorie was a good friend of Poppy's Aunt Dot and, it was rumoured, an undercover member of the Secret Service – although she would never admit to that publicly.

"Mrs Reynolds! Fancy seeing you here!"

The older woman's intelligent grey eyes lit up with recognition. "Poppy!" A leather-clad hand reached out from the tailored cuff of her houndstooth jacket. "This is a surprise!"

Poppy took Marjorie's hand and shook it firmly. Next to Marjorie was a large man in a crumpled brown suit. His fulsome belly strained against the buttons of his waistcoat, putting excessive pressure on a pocket-watch chain. He peered down at Poppy over a pair of half-moon spectacles.

"Giles, may I introduce Miss Poppy Denby from *The Daily Globe*. Poppy, this is Dr Giles Mortimer, Head Curator of the Egyptian and Assyrian collection here at the museum."

Dr Mortimer reached out his hand and took Poppy's. Like most men when shaking the hand of a lady, he didn't apply any pressure – perhaps out of fear of breaking it – holding for the briefest moment before withdrawing.

"I'm very pleased to make your acquaintance, Miss Denby. Are you here on behalf of the *Globe*? The press office didn't tell me they'd set up an interview..."

Poppy shook her head. "No, nothing official, I just want to do some background research on a story I'm working on."

"Oh?" his eyebrows raised in two arches over the half-moon lenses.

Poppy detected a hint of suspicion in his tone. In the eighteen months she had worked at the newspaper she had become accustomed to two broad reactions when people heard she was with the press: the first was surprise that such a young woman would be doing a "man's job", followed by curious questions or suggestions of stories she might be interested in. Nine times out of ten the "stories" were either blatant self-promotion or scurrilous gossip. Poppy would listen politely, say she would keep it in mind, and then get out of the conversation as quickly as she could. The second kind of reaction was more disconcerting: a hooded look, a suspicious stare, and defensive body language, followed by the person, instead of Poppy, shutting down the conversation as quickly as possible. Dr Mortimer's reaction fell halfway between the two. Here was a man, Poppy thought, wary of journalists but needing to keep them on side. Marjorie's introduction of her as "from *The Daily Globe*" had immediately charged the air between them; they were instantly polarized, a power dynamic at play. Poppy was rushed for time, uncomfortable in her wet clothes, and not mentally prepared for it. She wished Marjorie hadn't said anything.

However, she had, and the curator's expression made it clear that he was expecting a fuller explanation for her presence. There was nothing top secret about the Cairo Brief, but at the same time she knew Rollo would expect her to find some kind of angle to scoop the rival papers. It was best if she didn't let too much out. On the other hand, it would be common knowledge in the circles Dr Mortimer frequented that there was going to be an auction of an Egyptian artefact. In fact, hadn't she seen the British Museum on the guest list...?

She smiled politely at the curator. "You're probably aware that there's going to be an auction of a mask this weekend. The *Globe* – along with other papers – has been invited. I'm just doing some preparation for that."

"Ah, the Nefertiti mask."

There was a fleeting exchange of glances between Marjorie and Mortimer. *Hmmm*, thought Poppy, *what interest does the Home Office – or possibly the Secret Service – have in this mask? Or did I just imagine it...*

"Yes, I'd heard Maddox was inviting the press to his little soirée," continued Mortimer, his nose twitching slightly in what Poppy suspected was disapproval.

"I assume Rollo will be going too," observed Marjorie, with a twinkle in her eye. "I heard Conan Doyle will be there – I'd love to be a fly on that wall after Rollo's pasting of him with the fairy story."

Poppy smiled back at the older woman, noting to herself, not for the first time, how such an apparently severe exterior covered such a warm personality. "Yes, he's packing his bags as we speak!"

"And you'll be going with him?"

Poppy nodded. "I will. We'll head down tomorrow afternoon after I see Dot and Grace off."

Marjorie turned to Dr Mortimer, who was beginning to look like he wanted to be somewhere else. "Poppy is Dot Denby's niece, you know, Giles."

This seemed to draw the curator's attention back to the young woman in front of him, appraising her with an iota more respect. "Is she really? Your aunt is a remarkable woman, Miss Denby." He paused and raised a sardonic brow, "... as is Mrs Wilson. I assume they are going to be – erm – *convalescing* after Mrs Wilson's – erm – recent *ordeal...*"

Poppy smiled tightly. Rumours about her aunt's friendship with Grace Wilson had been splashed over all the city's rival newspapers. It annoyed her no end that that's what the gossip columnists focused on rather than the very serious issues that both Grace and Dot had brought to light the previous year, resulting in the exposé of corruption at the highest levels. She pulled back her shoulders and looked Dr Mortimer directly in the eye. "They are taking a trip on the Orient Express." *He could make of that whatever he pleased!*

Marjorie, perhaps sensing Poppy's annoyance, interjected: "And they're going to be having a fabulous time! And now, I must dash. Work to do at the Home Office. I'll see you tonight at Oscar's, Poppy, for the dinner. Giles, send over those documents by courier will you as soon as you get them?"

Mortimer said he would and then turned as if to leave. But before he could, Marjorie chipped in: "Perhaps you could show Poppy around the exhibit, Giles. It might be helpful for her to get an expert's perspective on everything."

Mortimer considered this for a moment, then nodded. "Yes, I suppose I could do that. If Miss Denby would like my input..."

His tone suggested that perhaps Miss Denby might be too irked to spend any more time with him. He was right – she was. However, she also had a job to do, and getting a personal tour from the most knowledgeable man at the British Museum would definitely give credibility to whatever article came out of it. She very much doubted Lionel Saunders at the *Courier* would have such an opportunity... an image of her weaselly rival flashed across her mind... and she made up her mind: "Thank you Dr Mortimer; I'd be honoured."

Marjorie and Mortimer exchanged another brief look – which Poppy filed away to ponder later – and bid their farewells.

"After you, Miss Denby." With a wide sweep of his arm,

Mortimer gestured for Poppy to precede him through the giant pillared entrance of the Egyptian gallery. Poppy stepped into the graveyard of another world. Giant amputated statues, their limbs hacked and hewn, lined the walls of the exhibition space. The style was brutal compared with the European Renaissance statuary of Michelangelo and Donatello that Poppy was familiar with from perusing her aunt's books on art and, in her opinion, lacked the emotional beauty of the exquisite creations of the Frenchman Rodin that she had seen in Paris on her first trip abroad.

But she nodded politely as her guide enthused about the origins of the statues, liberated from temples, tombs and abandoned palaces in the deserts of North Africa. Then, when they stood in front of a black granite slab, protected in a glass cabinet, his face all but shone. "The Rosetta Stone," he announced. Poppy peered through the glass, trying to make out the tiny carved writing, as Mortimer explained how this stone – inscribed in three languages – was the key to understanding so much of the archaeological finds of Egypt. "It's unlocked a lost world."

Poppy asked if there were any books he could recommend so she could read up on it all. He said there were and gave her a few titles by Egyptologists such as Flinders Petrie and Ludwig Borchardt. "Speaking of Borchardt," Mortimer said as he led Poppy from the sculpture gallery into a far more colourful room filled with painted panels, jewellery, and exquisitely decorated coffins, "he's the one who found the original Nefertiti bust. You can read all about it in that book I recommended. There's one in translation in the library."

"The original bust?" asked Poppy as they stood for a moment and peered into an open sarcophagus containing the mummified remains of an ancient Egyptian. Poppy shuddered, and wondered at the callousness of displaying someone's dead body for public entertainment.

"Yes," answered Mortimer. "It was found at El-Amarna in 1912."

"Do you mind if I take a few notes?" asked Poppy, and reached into her satchel for a notebook and pencil.

A flash of self-importance crossed Mortimer's face. Poppy had seen that look many times. When a journalist starts to take notes the interviewee feels valued and respected.

"So that was Ludwig Borshart, Excavations at El-Amarna."

"Borchardt with a c-h and a d-t," corrected Mortimer. "He's German. Petrie – our chap – excavated the royal palace of Akhenaten." He spelled the name for Poppy. "He was Nefertiti's husband. She may have become pharaoh after he died. Petrie talks about it all in his book. The Egyptians themselves did the cliff-side tombs. We thought that was all the treasure there was. But then the Germans got a concession to dig down in the valley and they uncovered an abandoned workshop of a man called Thutmose. He was Akhenaten and Nefertiti's official sculptor. It was there, in 1912, that Borchardt found the Nefertiti bust. I'll show you a picture of it if you like. There's one in the library..."

"Oh yes, please," said Poppy. She looked around the treasure trove on display. "Do you have the original here somewhere?"

Mortimer laughed, a paternal look settling between his mutton-chop sideburns. Poppy was familiar with this look too. It implied: *the pretty little thing doesn't know much after all.* Poppy didn't mind. She knew what she knew and knew what she didn't. If people thought less of her for it, then that was their problem, not hers.

"No, my dear. It's in Berlin. It emerged last year."

"Emerged?"

"Yes, it disappeared during the war. There was some controversy back in 1914 about whether or not the Egyptians should keep it. You see, there's a deal with Cairo that anything found by foreign expeditions must be split fifty-fifty with them. And Cairo have first dibs. No one understands why the Egyptians didn't demand the bust. It's exquisite. But Borchardt insists they didn't. The Egyptians, though, claim that they were duped – but they would. Can't trust them now that the whole place is run by natives."

"And it's now in the Berlin Museum?"

"Yes, and the Egyptians are furious. Which is why this new find – Maddox's mask – is causing such a hoo-hah."

Poppy's newshound nose began to twitch. "There's a hoo-hah?"

Mortimer led the way past a cabinet labelled "Book of the Dead", displaying colourful papyri. *How fascinating*, thought Poppy. *I'd like to have a look at that, but I don't want to distract Mortimer. Not when there's some hoo-hah afoot...*

"Indeed there is," the Egyptologist answered. "Apart from the gossip that someone was murdered in its acquisition – which I personally think is a poppycock story made up by Maddox to gain publicity – no one really knows where the mask has come from, or even if it's authentic. It's not on any official dig manifest."

Poppy absorbed that, then remembered something she'd read in Maddox's jazz file. "Maddox is a little unorthodox, isn't he? I believe he was asked to step down from the Egyptian Exploration Society in 1914."

Dr Mortimer's face registered surprise and then relaxed into a smile.

*He's warming to me*, thought Poppy. *Good.*

"He was indeed, Miss Denby, I'm impressed. Let's just say his methods are not what we approve of here at the British Museum."

"Oh?" asked Poppy, probing for more.

"You never know quite what you are getting with James Maddox, which is why we are sending along our best man – Howard Carter, the gentleman who's hunting for King Tut's tomb – to have a look at it tomorrow night. *If* it's authentic, we'll put in a bid – but so will the Germans and the Americans. And of course the Egyptians are saying they want it back – that it must have been stolen and taken out of the country without their permission – which wouldn't surprise me, actually..." He chuckled. "It's going to be worse than an assembly of the League of Nations!"

"Golly," said Poppy, jotting down Mortimer's words in shorthand.

Mortimer's eyes twinkled through his half-moon glasses. "Golly indeed, Miss Denby."

# CHAPTER 4

Poppy stepped out of the piping hot shower of number 152 King's Road, Chelsea, and wrapped herself in a large, soft, bath towel. She still could not get over the wonder of having such a facility en suite. Her family home in Morpeth – the manse of the Methodist church – did have indoor plumbing, but nothing as fancy and modern as a shower. She had once thought a bath in a separate bathroom was the lap of luxury, knowing that most of her father's congregants only had a tin tub in front of an open fire, but not any more. Her aunt's three-storey townhouse in the fashionable London borough was fitted with all the latest mod-cons. There were showers, a telephone, a stairlift, electric lighting throughout, and even one of those new-fangled thingies to clean carpets: a vacuum cleaner, Poppy had heard it called. And it was going to be all her own for the next three months. Fortunately for Poppy, Aunt Dot's charlady, Violet, was going to be kept on in her mistress's absence, so Poppy didn't have to worry about learning to use the sucking machine herself.

Poppy stepped into her bedroom – decorated with pale blue wallpaper and a peach blossom motif – and headed towards the white and gold gilded dressing table. The decor was not quite to Poppy's taste, but it wasn't her house and she had no say in its fittings. In the spring, when Dot and Grace were back from their trip, she intended to move into a place of her own. She had been living with her father's sister for the last eighteen months, but now, with a steady job, some savings and a growing sense of independence as a fashionable working woman, she felt it was time to step out on her own – just like her friend Delilah. Delilah had a flat further down King's Road. Poppy didn't think she'd be able to afford anything quite as plush, but something perhaps in Pimlico or Shepherd's Bush might be within budget.

Poppy was looking forward to finally getting her own place. For a while she had thought that she might move straight from Aunt Dot's house into Daniel's – when marriage was on the cards twelve months earlier – but now that didn't seem likely to happen. Oh, she still loved him, and she knew he loved her, but his children, and his sister who looked after them, continued to pose an obstacle. Maggie was now – against all odds for a woman of thirty-five – engaged to be married to a diamond mine manager from South Africa. He was a widower and had a daughter who was in boarding school in England. But the girl was unhappy and he had come to fetch her home. While visiting her, he had met Maggie. The mine manager wanted Maggie to move to South Africa with him after the wedding; and she wanted to take the children – his and Daniel's – with her. Since Daniel's wife had died of the Spanish Flu, "Aunt Maggie" had been the only mother his children knew. And she too considered them her own. But Daniel, naturally, did not want to let them go. So for the last few months – by mutual consent – Poppy and Daniel had put the brakes on their relationship while he sorted things out with Maggie and her fiancé. As time went on, Poppy began to wonder if it would ever get back on track. She would be seeing him this weekend at Winterton Hall, so she hoped they could find some time alone to talk.

Poppy sat down and pulled off her shower cap. *Oh fiddlesticks; it still got wet.* Her naturally curly hair was now more frizz than wave. She assessed her damp blonde mop, blue eyes, and heart-shaped face. She looked like a half-drowned Pollyanna, not the sophisticated career-lady-out-on-the-town look she was hoping for. She sighed, opened her dressing table drawer, and pulled out a wooden-handled hair iron, which she then poked into the hot coals of her bedroom fireplace. She checked the carriage clock on the mantelpiece: half-past seven. *Not much time...* Aunt Dot and Grace were already out, having pre-dinner drinks, and she had arranged to meet them and the other guests at Oscar's at eight. Fortunately, the club was only a ten-minute walk. Still, it wasn't much time to do her hair. She had been planning on coaxing her dry curls into some flattering Marcelle waves, but now that it was damp and frizzy, she'd have to think again. The coals were hardly glowing... She gave them a poke; there was a splutter and a spark, but not much else.

With a sigh, Poppy gave up on the hot iron idea and instead selected a jar of Brillantine from the array of potions and lotions on her dresser. She'd always thought the hair product was for men, until her visit to New York earlier in the year introduced her to some young flappers who used it to slick down their hair and create perfect little kiss curls on the forehead and temples. Yes, that's the look she'd go for: slicked down and kiss-curled. And if she wore the new Gustave Beer-inspired gown, she could also wear the matching headband, which would help calm the frizz. Poppy got up and opened her wardrobe, selecting the sky-blue calf-length frock, embellished with silver embroidery. It was a sleeveless number with brocade straps – might it be too cold to wear it? Oscar's was always hot inside, but it had been snowing... She reached towards the back of the wardrobe and found a silver-fringed shawl with similar geometric patterns to the metallic embroidery on the gown. Another imitation.

Although she had had a wage increase since her return from New York, she wasn't quite able to afford the Parisian couture originals that her friend Delilah wore, and had to make do with off-the-hanger copies from Milady's or John Lewis on Oxford Street. She did have an original Charles Worth, but she couldn't wear it to *every* swish do, now could she? No, definitely not. She looked at the clock again: *Oh diggety dog! Shake a leg old girl – time is ticking!*

Oscar's Jazz Club was thrumming. Every time the doors opened and closed onto the Chelsea street, Poppy could hear the driving drum beat and belting brass from a block away. Black cabs lined up along the kerb, depositing their passengers, who stepped out in fur coats, top hats and tails, for a night on the town. Although the newly opened 43 Club, on Gerrard Street, Soho, was now the hottest venue in town for London's bright young things – thanks, in part, to the American actress Tallulah Bankhead, making it her home from home – Oscar's was still the favourite haunt of much of London's more established (some would say sedate) "fast set". Unlike The 43, it kept its liquor licence up to date, so the clientele could be assured they wouldn't have to flee the premises in case of a raid. Poppy realized that for some people, that would be one of the attractions of The 43 – living on the edge of a life of crime – but she, and most of the other frequenters of Oscar's, preferred a slightly less nerve-wracking night out. Delilah, of course, visited The 43, but the young actress went out nearly every night of the week; The 43 was just one of many on her list, including Oscar's.

Poppy joined the short line waiting to get into the club. With the snow beginning to fall again, she was grateful the queue was not round the block as it had been when, only a year earlier, Oscar's had been the number one venue in town. Soon she was stepping into the foyer and checking in her fur-trimmed coat at the cloakroom. Oscar Reynolds – as dapper as ever with his slicked-back black hair, gold monocle, and white tie and tails

– spotted her from across the foyer. "Poppy! How many times have I told you to come straight in! I've told the doorman to let you, you know that?"

"I know that," said Poppy and presented each cheek for Oscar to kiss in turn. "Sorry I'm late. Is everyone here?"

"They are," he said, ushering her through the double doors into the main dance hall and dining area. "They're at the usual," he said, nodding towards the circular table to the left of the bandstand. The table was set for six. Four women – in their fifties and sixties - were already seated. Poppy's aunt, Dot Denby, wearing a vivid crepe silk fuchsia gown, with a purple feather boa and matching feather in her hair, was a former suffragette and leading lady of the West End stage. She was now in a wheelchair after being injured in a "votes for women" demonstration back in 1910. Beside her, as tall and slim as Dot was short and round, was Grace Wilson. Grace was the former bookkeeper of the militant suffragist cell, The Chelsea Six, which disbanded in 1914. She and Dot had been companions for over a decade, separated in that time only once, when Grace served a twelve-month jail term for obstruction of justice. But Grace was now out of the clanger and she and the former doyenne were off on a trip of a lifetime on the Orient Express. Grace was wearing a grey silk matching blouse and skirt. The ruffles down the front of the blouse were no longer de rigueur, but, thought Poppy, the ensemble suited Grace's quietly formal personality.

Next to Grace was the equally tall and slim Marjorie Reynolds, mother of the club owner Oscar. She had changed out of the houndstooth suit Poppy had seen her in at the museum and was now wearing a tasteful green satin gown with black velvet trim. If Poppy was not mistaken, it was an original Jacques Doucet. Marjorie raised her black lacquer fan with mother of pearl inlay and waved it at Poppy. Poppy waved back. This caught the attention of the fourth woman at the table, wearing a navy blue crêpe de Chine gown, covered with a navy blue blazer. The blazer – more daywear than evening – would have been odd on anyone other than the former leader of the Women's Suffrage and Political Union, who was so famous she could get away with just about anything. "Well, good evening, Poppy."

"Good evening, Mrs Pankhurst."

Oscar pulled out a chair for Poppy and placed a menu at her place setting. She thanked him and asked for a glass of chardonnay.

"Oh, do have some pink champers darling," cried Aunt Dot. "It's on me! In fact, can you bring a couple of bottles over, Oscar?"

The host said he would and affected an elaborate bow before withdrawing.

"Your boy's doing well, Marjorie," said Emmeline Pankhurst, peering short-sightedly at the retreating Oscar.

"Yes he is," said Marjorie. "I thought after that to-do last year he might have thrown in the towel, but I'm glad to say he's made of stronger stuff."

"Just like his mother!" trilled Aunt Dot.

"Quite," said Emmeline. "It's thanks to you that we got the suffrage bill through in Eighteen. Still a long way to go though. Votes only for women over thirty who own property is simply not good enough. You mustn't give up, Marjorie, you must never give up!"

This was met with a "hear hear!" from the other women at the table.

"Never fear, Emmie, Marjorie is the last person to give up!" Aunt Dot raised a glass to her friend; Marjorie smiled her thanks.

"So Grace, what do you think the highlights will be on your trip?" asked Marjorie, turning her attention to the quiet woman.

Grace's brown eyes stared past Marjorie to the small stage beside the bandstand. Then, in little more than a whisper, she said: "She looks so much like Gloria, doesn't she?" Poppy turned to look at what had caught Grace's attention. And there, on the bandstand, talking to the band leader and adjusting the microphone to her 5 feet 2 inches height, was Delilah Marconi, daughter of the late Gloria Marconi, another of the Chelsea Six. Gloria had died in 1913 in mysterious circumstances. Tears welled in Grace's eyes, threatening to spill over. Dot took her hand and squeezed.

"Yes she does. She's a beauty, just like her mother. Gloria would be so proud of her. And she'd be proud of you too, Grace, for finally telling the truth and putting that monster of a man away. Now, enough of this morbidity. Marjorie was asking about our trip!"

Dot turned her sparkling blue eyes towards the lady MP and gushed out their itinerary for the next three months on the Orient Express. "Well first, of course, there's Paris, and then on to Strasbourg and Salzburg – where they have the Mozart museum, you know – and then Linz and..."

Poppy had heard her aunt recite the route so many times, she could almost recite it herself. She tuned out and focused her attention instead on Delilah, who was just about to start singing. Poppy appraised her friend's ensemble with admiration – a black satin sheath dress with an embroidered bronze and gold phoenix emblazoned from hem to neckline. As Delilah opened her arms to virtually embrace the band, Poppy saw that the sleeves mimicked the phoenix's wings. The back of the dress drifted into a train of black, gold, and bronze feathers, which Delilah artfully draped across the stage as she positioned herself in front of the microphone. On her head, encasing her blunt, black-fringed bob, was an elaborate headdress, following the phoenix theme.

"Then of course there'll be Belgrade and Sofia..."

Poppy smiled to herself, wondering what her mother would think of Delilah if she came down to London next summer, as she had said she might. Last Christmas Mrs Denby had given her daughter a book on etiquette, written by a Mrs Lilian Eichler, to help her, the enclosed note said, "to know how a modest young woman should dress for each social occasion". Poppy had taken the chapter on dressing for the office to heart – hence her professional-looking Chanel suit – but the chapters entitled "The Slattern" and "The Eccentric Dresser" just made her laugh. Mrs Eichler no doubt had someone like Delilah Marconi in mind when she wrote:

> *Many men and women, in the mistaken belief that they are expressing personality, adopt certain peculiarities of dress. Eccentric dressing always attracts attention, and is therefore bordering on the vulgar. There are, of course, many men and women who enjoy attracting attention, who delight in being considered "different". In such people we are not interested. It is the people of good taste that we wish to advise against the mistake of wearing peculiar and unconventional clothes.*

"And finally we're in Istanbul. After that we'll –"

Grace put a hand on her friend's arm. "Dorothy, dear, we'll hear the rest later. Delilah is going to sing."

The band struck up the opening bars of "I'm a Jazz Vampire", which Poppy and Delilah had heard for the first time at a speakeasy in Manhattan earlier that year. The London crowd loved it! The women swayed in time to the jazzy beat, the men whistled at the titillating lyrics, and Delilah playfully reeled them in as she sang: "Wise men keep out o' my way, they know

I'll lead 'em astray, they fall the minute I sway, I insist you can't resist a jazz vampire."

As the saxophone honked out its final solo the crowd at Oscar's rose as one and applauded Delilah and her fellas. The musicians soaked up the adulation and then broke into a medley of tunes made famous by the Original Dixieland Jazz Band. When Delilah finished her set, an adoring gentleman helped her step down from the stage. He kissed her hand and then watched with open admiration as she sashayed across the dance floor, her phoenix train swishing behind her.

"Aren't you dancing, darling?" asked Dot as the Maltese girl approached the table.

"Not till I've had something to eat, Dot; I'm famished! Have you gals ordered yet?"

"Not yet," said Poppy, whose tummy was grumbling as loudly as a percussion section. "We were waiting for you!" She pulled out the seat beside her and Delilah plopped down.

"Then wait no more!"

The women perused their menus and put in their orders. Poppy decided to have Oscar's special: roast quail with fondant potatoes. It had taken her a while to discover that fondant potatoes were just a posh way of saying pan-fried potatoes, but she liked the way Oscar's chef cooked them, all buttery and golden. While they waited for their food, Poppy told Delilah all about her day and the invitation to Winterton Hall for the séance, auction, and shooting weekend. She wanted to sound her society friend out on what exactly one wore to these sorts of occasions. Mrs Eichler had a chapter on sporting wear for the hunt and the shoot, but there was nothing on auctions and séances.

"You're going to Winterton, too, Popsicle? Oh how spiffing!"

"Why?" asked Poppy, delighted and surprised. "Have you also received an invitation?"

"Sort of," answered Delilah, nodding her assent to a refill of pink champagne. "It's a work thing. They've asked me and Fox Flinton to perform a mime to narration before the séance. I'll be playing the pharaoh queen, Nee-for-something..."

"Nefertiti," supplied Poppy. "But Fox Flinton? Why him? Isn't he that dreadful ham actor from the Apollo you worked with in September? I thought you couldn't stand the man."

Delilah flapped her hands in mock outrage, nearly taking out the waiter as he delivered warm bread rolls to the table. "Sorry, sweetie!" Then to Poppy: "I can't! He couldn't keep his hands off me backstage. He's twice my age and won't take no for an answer! But he's a cousin of Lady Ursula Maddox, apparently. They asked him to suggest an actress to play Nee-for-whatever, and he said, I quote: 'There is no one more suited to play an Egyptian goddess than the delectable Delilah Marconi.' Then he offered himself to play my husband."

She grimaced, then took a roll from the waiter, breaking it open with her perfectly manicured fingers.

"Why did you agree to it, then?" asked Poppy, buttering her own bread.

"Because of the séance, of course! I've been dying to go to one of the Conan Doyle ones – excuse the pun – but I've never managed to wangle an invitation." She pouted. "I think it's because of my association with Rollo and Daniel and that article they wrote last year. No offence, darling."

Poppy smiled at her friend and took a sip of her champagne. She felt the bubbles fizz in her mouth then zing in her throat as she swallowed. *Lovely.*

"No offence taken. How are you getting down? Is your motor still off the road since that last prang?"

Delilah shook her head in despair. "They're saying it's a write-off! Can you believe it? It was only a little bump."

"With a telephone box!" laughed Poppy. "It's a miracle no one was inside."

Delilah frowned. "Yes it is. You'd swear I'd murdered someone the way the Post Office have been going on. Daddy has had to pay them an awful lot of money."

*Poor daddy*, thought Poppy. She loved Delilah dearly but sometimes she wished her friend would start to realize that money didn't grow on trees. "So, do you need a lift then? I can ask Rollo if there's space in the company motor."

"Oh, that would be spiffing of you, thank you. Otherwise I might have to take the old Fox up on his offer." She shuddered.

"Did I hear you say you needed a lift to Winterton Hall, Delilah?" It was Marjorie Reynolds.

"Yes you did."

"You can come with me, if you like?"

"Oh yes, please," answered Delilah, no doubt, thought Poppy, comparing the comfort of Marjorie's luxury vehicle with the crammed interior of the *Globe*'s old Model T.

Poppy cast Marjorie an inquiring look. *She hadn't given any indication at the museum that she was going to attend. In fact, she'd suggested the opposite, saying she would like to be a fly on the wall at the séance... hmmm...*

Poppy's newshound nose twitched. "Will that be on behalf of the Home Office, Marjorie?"

A sly smile fleshed out Marjorie's thin lips. "Oh, let's not talk shop at your aunt's special dinner, Poppy." Then she turned to Dot. "Now, Dot and Grace, tell us again about your trip."

Aunt Dot's face lit up. "Of course, Marjorie! I thought you'd be tired of hearing about it! But if you're not, well, first, of course there's Paris..."

# CHAPTER 5

The gateway to Winterton Hall – flanked on either side by two sphinxes – was as imposing as Poppy had expected it to be. The weather had cleared remarkably from the previous day and the sandstone gatehouse – built like a little mock Roman temple – was stroked with rays of mid-afternoon sun. The gravel drive wound for over a mile through parkland and gardens, interspersed with *fabriques:* garden buildings and follies imitating Classical designs from Greek, Roman, and Egyptian architecture. One could forget, for a moment, that one was on an English country estate, only forty minutes west of central London; but then a cricket oval, with its comfortingly familiar iron roller, brought one home again. The Model T Ford, with Daniel driving, Rollo in the passenger seat, and Poppy and Yasmin in the back, skirted an artificial lake with an Egyptian obelisk pointing, helpfully, to a clear winter sky.

"Looks like we might get some shooting in after all," observed Rollo.

"Spiffing," answered Yasmin, her voice dripping in sarcasm.

"What? You don't want to blast blocks of clay from the sky with the landed classes?" asked Rollo, peeking his ginger head around to look at his almost-fiancée in the back seat.

"You forget, my Yankee friend, that my father *is* one of the landed classes." Yasmin raised an exquisite eyebrow towards her hairline, and flicked her finger against the tip of her striking Egyptian nose. Poppy giggled. She was enjoying seeing the playful side of Britain's first female barrister, usually so formidable as she presented her cases at the Old Bailey. Yasmin was the daughter of a British major general and an Egyptian heiress. Her Anglo-Egyptian heritage gave her striking looks, accentuated by the most up-to-date of hairstyles: the Eton crop. Poppy, frankly, was in awe of her. She was as stylish as Delilah, and with a mind as sharp as a tack and ambitions that led all the way to Downing Street. Poppy doubted she would ever see a woman prime minister in her lifetime, but if there ever was one, she could imagine it would be someone like Yasmin Reece-Lansdale, KC.

Poppy, trying not to stare at the older woman, wondered what her brother would be like. Apparently, unlike his sister, he had identified with the Egyptian side of his heritage and now lived in Cairo. He had been at the forefront of Egypt's bid for independence from Britain's "protectorate", and thanks to his and his fellow-activists' work, the British government was in the process of passing legislation to approve the North African nation's independence within a couple of months. But Faizal Osman (who had changed his Christian name from Fitzroy and taken on his maternal grandfather's name as a surname) was not going to be at Winterton as a political activist, but in his day job as the Director of Antiquities of the Cairo Museum.

"Nearly there, folks!" said Daniel as the Model T rounded a bend. And there, on a hill, brooding over the estate like a red mother hen, was Winterton Hall. The original red-brick Tudor mansion had been added to every century since the sixteenth and was now a hodgepodge of architectural styles. A central domed hall with a Grecian facade was flanked on either side by two sprawling wings, one Georgian, one Victorian. To the left was a long bank of stables, and to the right a tennis court, bowling green, and archery range. In front of the house, bracketed on either side by the gravel drive, was a leylandii maze in need of a good trim. Poppy could see the heads of statues above the greenery, trapped forever in the labyrinth.

"More than enough room to swing a cat," chortled Rollo.

"With at least thirty bedrooms for your moggy to choose from!" agreed Daniel. "I'll have to get some snaps of the old pile while the light lasts. I'll just drop you off first and –"

Bang! Poppy and Yasmin were thrown forward against the front seats, while the men were rammed against the dashboard.

"What the deuce!" Rollo pushed himself back from the glove compartment as a large battleship-grey Chrysler pulled alongside them.

"You ladies all right?" asked Daniel, sticking his head between the seats.

Poppy righted herself and did a quick top-to-toe health check. "Yes, I think so. You Yasmin?"

Yasmin rubbed the back of her neck and muttered: "For now. But whiplash takes a while to develop."

The window of the Chrysler rolled down and the weaselly face of Lionel Saunders, entertainment editor for *The London Courier*, popped out.

"You folks all right?" and then, without waiting for an answer: "Yes? Jolly good. You should be more careful, Rokeby. You're not driving a tank now."

"You rammed us off the bloody road!" roared Daniel, struggling to open the door.

But before he could, Saunders and his photographer – Harry Gibson – sped off, scattering gravel against the Model T like shrapnel on a battlefield.

Daniel leapt out and shook his fist aftrt them. Rollo, Poppy, and Yasmin got out too. Poppy tried to calm Daniel, while Rollo examined the back of the car and Yasmin continued to rub her neck.

"You all right, toots?" asked Rollo, turning his attention from the bashed rear end of the Ford to his lady friend. Yasmin's eyes narrowed and lips tightened.

"Right as rain Rollo. At least I will be when I serve those buffoons with an injunction."

She, Poppy, and a still huffing and puffing Daniel, joined the little editor in examining the damage. The back right wing was dented and scuffed and the exhaust pipe had been knocked loose, but no obviously substantial damage had been done.

"Not too bad," muttered Daniel, calming down slightly.

"Don't say that again, Mr Rokeby," said Yasmin briskly. "As far as you're concerned the damage is significant and – as four witnesses will testify, including one Queen's Counsel – deliberately inflicted. I suggest you photograph the vehicle for the record and I shall take affidavits from you all."

"Well, to be honest, I can't say for certain it was deliberate."

*Neither can I,* thought Poppy, as Daniel continued: "I was in the middle of the road and perhaps the *Courier* boys couldn't see me when they came round the bend, and –"

Rollo stuck up a hand like a traffic warden. "Can it, Rokeby, Yasmin's right. It looked deliberate to me. But even if it wasn't, they didn't offer to help us. And this is not the first time they've done something like this. I still think it was them who sabotaged our printer last month. Don't worry toots; I'll get our solicitor onto it and then a judge can decide."

Poppy glanced at Daniel over Rollo's head. He didn't look like he was going to argue. And neither would she. Let the solicitors fight this one out.

"You all right?" he asked, gently, his grey eyes appraising her with concern.

Her heart warmed as it always did when Daniel looked at her like that.

"I am," she said.

Just then Marjorie's cream Lincoln rounded the bend and pulled up beside them. "Good heavens! What happened?" she called across Delilah, who was sitting in the passenger seat.

Yasmin told her.

"You'll be suing them, I imagine," answered the lady MP.

"You can bet your bottom dollar on it!" grinned Rollo.

Daniel knelt down and examined the undercarriage. "Looks like there may be some damage under there after all. Can't be sure till I get it up on blocks. Can we hitch a lift to the house, Mrs Reynolds? Then we can get someone to come back and tow the old motor and collect the luggage?"

"Of course!" cried Delilah on Marjorie's behalf, looking very fetching in an Isadora Duncan-style headscarf. "Hop in!"

The Lincoln joined the queue of vehicles at the entrance to Winterton Hall. There was a line of servants to help the guests disembark: the men in black suits, the women in white aprons and mop hats. Daniel spoke to a dignified-looking gentleman in butler's livery and arranged for the Ford to be towed and the luggage collected.

"I'd better go with them," he informed Poppy and the rest of the *Globe* party. "I want to take some snaps for the solicitors before they move it. Yasmin nodded her approval.

As Daniel and some of the Winterton staff drove off in one of the estate vehicles, Poppy and the other guests were ushered up the wide marble staircase and through the mock Greek portico into the main hall, adorned with holly and tinsel and dominated by a giant Christmas tree.

In the shadow of the tree, with fairy lights twinkling, they were informed by the butler – a Mr Grimes – that the lord and lady of the house apologized for not greeting them in person but they were otherwise occupied making preparations for the séance that evening. "Miss Marconi," said Grimes, turning to Delilah, "they have asked you to join them as soon as you arrive. Mr Flinton is already here. Bella here will show you to your room then take you to join them; if that is acceptable to you."

"It is," said Delilah and winked at Poppy. "I'll see you later Popsicle."

Poppy, Marjorie, Rollo, and Yasmin were then greeted by name and shown to their rooms. They were informed that predinner drinks would be at six o'clock, where Sir James and Lady Ursula would meet them. Dinner would be at seven, port and cigars at eight thirty, followed by the evening's entertainment: a dramatic re-enactment of the love story of Akhenaten and Nefertiti, followed by the first viewing of the Nefertiti mask, and then the séance. In case this was too much to remember, Grimes informed them, a written itinerary for the whole weekend, as well as a guest list, was provided in each room.

The *Globe* team, as well as Marjorie and Yasmin, were allocated rooms in the Georgian west wing. The *Courier* contingent (the only other newspaper who responded to Maddox's invitation) were billeted in the east, along with the delegates from the Berlin and New York Metropolitan museums. The delegation from the British Museum was also in the west wing, as were the representatives of the Egyptian Antiquities Department from Cairo. The Conan Doyles, Delilah, and Fox Flinton had rooms in the main house, near the Maddox family, as, Grimes reminded them, Mr Flinton was Lady Ursula's cousin. Poppy was sure Delilah would have preferred to be with her friends in the west wing – out of the clutches of the Fox. Perhaps she could arrange to swap later.

Grimes led them through an enormous domed entrance hall, dominated by a spectacular chandelier and classic nude statuary, through a number of reception rooms and a glass-walled orangery. They accessed the west wing via a long gallery lined with small taxidermied animals, cabinets of butterflies and birds, and, startlingly, a large black bear, frozen in time in its last battle with the hunter. "Lady Ursula's father shot it on holiday once," Grimes supplied. Poppy wondered whether it was Lady Ursula's father or the bear who had been on holiday, and stifled a giggle. Rollo must have been thinking the same thing because he winked at Poppy as Grimes led them out of the gallery and into the west wing.

One by one the guests were led to their bedrooms. They were told their luggage would be delivered as soon as Mr Rokeby and the men arrived back with it. In the meantime, if there was anything they needed, they should just ring and one of the maids would assist them. Poppy thanked Grimes as he withdrew with a bow and closed the door behind him.

Poppy looked around the room. It was comfortable and clean but not excessively luxurious. Poppy reminded herself that this was a private residence and not a hotel. The furniture was old and mismatched but solid and of good quality. The single bed was covered in a green satin bedspread that was slightly frayed at the edges, but still perfectly serviceable. A fire had been lit and was burning quietly in the grate. Poppy picked up a poker and gave it a stir, thankful that it didn't take long to come to life. She looked out of the second-floor window, with a view of the stable yard, and noticed preparations for the clay shooting party scheduled for the following day. Men in thick tweed coats, woollen scarves, and flat caps were cleaning an arsenal of shotguns and sporting rifles, watched over by half a dozen horses, curiously peering over their stable doors. A pair of foxhounds lay curled up in the last pool of sunlight in the far corner of the courtyard. Poppy checked her watch: it was nearly half-past three. The sun would be setting soon, and if the night remained clear, a frost might very likely settle. Poppy was glad she had brought her mink fur wrap – a cast-off of Aunt Dot's – but a warm and stylish one.

She would start getting ready at half-past four as there was no en-suite bathroom and she'd have to book a slot in the communal one down the hall. She would be sharing with Yasmin, Marjorie, and another lady from the Egyptian delegation, whom she was yet to meet.

She had an hour to spare. What should she do? She would have taken a walk around the grounds – she was keen to try out the maze – but she should probably wait for her luggage to arrive and perhaps do some preparation for the evening. As promised, there was an itinerary and guest list laid out on the oak dresser. She took it, kicked off her shoes, and propped herself up on the bed with her notebook and pencil. She scanned the itinerary and, after confirming that she had correctly memorized the Friday evening schedule – including the séance she really was not keen on attending – noted that the auction was after the shooting party on Saturday. Carriages were after breakfast on Sunday morning.

Poppy then turned her attention to the guest list, keen to get to grips with who was who. The list was helpfully divided into the areas of the house where the guests were to be accommodated.

## The Main House

- Sir James Maddox and Lady Ursula: hosts
- Sir Arthur and Lady Jean Conan Doyle: author & metaphysicist, spiritualist medium
- Mr Fox Flinton, Esquire: actor
- Miss Delilah Marconi: actress
- Mr Albert Carnaby, Esquire: auctioneer, Carnaby's Auctioneers

## THE EAST WING

- Mr Lionel Saunders, Esquire: reporter, *The London Courier*
- Mr Harry Gibson, Esquire: photographer, *The London Courier*
- Herr Dr Heinrich Stein: Director of Antiquities, Museum of Berlin
- Herr Dr Rudolf Weiner: assistant, Museum of Berlin
- Dr Jonathan Davies: Director of Antiquities, Metropolitan Museum of New York
- Miss Jennifer Philpott: assistant, Metropolitan Museum of New York

*Poor Miss Philpott,* thought Poppy. *The only lady in the east wing. Ah well, at least she'll have a bathroom to herself...* She checked her watch: a quarter to four.

## THE WEST WING

- Dr Giles Mortimer: Head Curator, Dept Egyptian & Assyrian Antiquities, the British Museum.
- Mr Howard Carter, Esquire: Archaeologist, Egyptologist, and special adviser to BM
- Dr Faizal Osman: Director, Egyptian Antiquities Service, Cairo Museum
- Miss Kamela El Farouk: assistant, Egyptian Antiquities Service, Cairo Museum
- Mrs Marjorie Reynolds, MP: Minister of State for the Home Office
- Mr Rollo Rolandson, Esquire: Owner & Editor, *The Daily Globe*

- Miss Poppy Denby: reporter, *The Daily Globe*
- Mr Daniel Rokeby, Esquire: photographer, *The Daily Globe*
- Miss Yasmin Reece-Lansdale, KC: art collector and legal counsel

Poppy made a priority list of whom she would like to interview – starting with Howard Carter, the man, according to Dr Mortimer, who would be tasked with ascertaining the authenticity of the Nefertiti mask. After that Mortimer... no, she could catch up with him in London if necessary... so Carter first, then Yasmin's brother, Faizal Osman, to find out if the Egyptians thought it had really been stolen. And perhaps he could also give her some information on the alleged murder. Poppy wrote the words "murderous circumstances" next to Osman's name and circled it. After that, Sir James Maddox; he was essential... but she'd like to be forearmed with information from Carter and Osman first. She wrote numbers next to each name in order of priority.

There was a knock at the door.

"Who is it?"

"Your luggage, miss." Poppy smiled. She knew that voice. She jumped up and opened the door to find a grinning Daniel holding her suitcase in one hand and a camera tripod in the other.

"I thought you might need this, m'lady," he said, and placed the luggage at her feet.

"Why thank you, m'lord." Poppy did a playful little curtsey and they both laughed. "Will you come in for a minute? I can ring for tea..."

Daniel looked uncertain. "Perhaps it might not be appropriate."

Was he saying that because it would be socially improper for a gentleman to enter a single lady's bedroom, or because he really didn't want to be alone with her? "Oh, all right then. Well, perhaps a walk..."

His face relaxed. "Yes, a walk will be lovely. Do you want to put some shoes on?"

Poppy looked down at her stockinged feet. "Good idea. Just a tick." She turned to retrieve her shoes, but as she did a loud blast rang out. "What on earth was that?"

"Gunshot," said Daniel and they ran together to the window.

"Keep pressure on it!" Daniel, his hands bloodied, knelt beside a young man sprawled on the cobbles of the stable yard. The photographer looked up at the gathering crowd around him. "There's no time to wait for the ambulance. Can we take him in one of the estate cars, Grimes?"

The butler said they could and shouted instructions to ready Sir James's Rolls. "It's the fastest we've got," he added.

As soon as Poppy and Daniel had seen what had happened from their second-floor window they ran down to the courtyard to help. A boy – of around fourteen – had been shot in the foot, while cleaning one of the shotguns for the following day's sporting shoot. Daniel, a former soldier, had worked as a field medic during the war and was experienced in dealing with gunshot wounds. Poppy took upon herself the role of communications coordinator and crowd control, explaining to each guest as they arrived what had happened.

"Daniel says it's a relief he was only using birdshot. But it was such close quarters he might still lose his foot."

"The poor boy!" cried Marjorie.

"What the hell was he doing with a loaded weapon?" asked Rollo.

"No one knows. His dad – the fella over there –" Poppy explained, nodding to a distraught man being comforted by his colleagues "– said it was his first time on the job. He's just learning. Something must've gone wrong."

"You can say that again," growled Rollo.

A tall, dark-haired man ran past the group of friends and knelt down beside Daniel and the other men attending to the boy. "Have you made a tourniquet?" he asked.

Daniel said he had.

"That's Faizal Osman," Rollo explained. "Yasmin's brother."

Osman looked up as the Rolls chugged into the yard. He was a darkly handsome man in his late thirties, with the same coal-dark eyes and long straight nose as his sister.

"Bring a plank!" he shouted. "Let's get him to the motor." *Clearly, he is a man used to being in charge*, thought Poppy. If Daniel had been a different sort he might have resented the newcomer taking over, but he was too intent on helping the young lad, whimpering in pain, to worry about pecking order. *That's why I love him,* thought Poppy.

A plank was brought from a nearby stable and the boy was gently lifted onto it. The boy's father, Daniel, Faizal, and another man carried him to the car and eased him onto the back seat while Mr Grimes supervised.

"Booker, you go with your boy."

"I'll go too," said Daniel. "We don't want to lose pressure on the wound."

"If it's not too much trouble, Mr Rokeby, I'm sure Sir James will be much obliged."

Sir James, Poppy noticed, had not arrived. Nor the Conan Doyles, Delilah, and Fox Flinton. She assumed that the gaggle of people emerging from the pathway to the east wing, hurriedly pulling on their coats, were the German and American museum representatives. And of course, there was the team from the *Courier*, with Lionel Saunders sucking hungrily on a cigarette.

He glared at Poppy. She glared back. If there was a story to be had, once again, the *Globe* was first on the scene. Was there a story here? She wasn't yet sure. Nonetheless, newsworthy or not, the shooting was attracting attention. On the opposite side of the courtyard, near the doorway to the west wing, were two women: Yasmin and a younger woman wearing a Mohamedan headscarf. Poppy assumed it was Faizal's assistant. She turned her attention back to the group of men helping the young boy into the Rolls Royce.

"It's no trouble at all, Mr Grimes," said Daniel, positioning himself on the back seat with the patient. "Rollo, can you handle the camera until I get back?"

"Is the pope Catholic?" answered the editor. Then, in a gentler voice: "Get that kid some help."

Faizal Osman withdrew from the vehicle, backside first, his shirtfront bloodied, and announced: "I think I'm surplus to requirements."

"Danny was a field medic," Rollo explained. "The boy's in good hands, Faizal."

Faizal nodded his agreement and immediately went up in Poppy's estimation. *A man who likes to be in charge but does not lack humility. Interesting. Very interesting.*

The Anglo-Egyptian man joined Poppy, Rollo, and Marjorie as they watched the Rolls drive out of the courtyard.

"How far is the hospital, Mr Grimes?" asked Marjorie.

"There's one in Henley-on-Thames. They should be there in about twenty minutes. I'll telephone ahead to tell them to expect a gunshot victim." He turned to head back into the house.

"And the police too," called Marjorie.

Grimes stopped in his tracks. "The police?"

"Of course," said the Minister of State for the Home Office, under whose jurisdiction the British police force fell. "They have to be alerted of any gunshot injuries. It's the law. If you don't, the hospital will."

The butler pulled back his shoulders and cleared his throat. "Of course, madam. You're right. I shall telephone the local constabulary immediately after the hospital. I shall just let Sir James know."

Grimes withdrew, shooing the gathered household staff back to work.

The newly arrived guests, however, took longer to disperse and gathered around Rollo as he informed them of what exactly had happened. Various exclamations of "by Jove!", "good golly", and "my word!" were uttered. Then, introductions were made. Poppy, who had run out without a coat, offered her apologies and said she needed to get inside before she froze to death. She would meet everyone later. Faizal offered her his coat, but she declined with thanks, and hurried back into the house.

As she passed Saunders and Gibson she heard Lionel mutter: "Off to find some smelling salts, I wager. The little lady can't take the whiff of blood."

Poppy's hackles rose.

# CHAPTER 6

The long table, seating twenty-two, was resplendent with the best silver and Yuletide decorations. Three courses had been served and removed and now the guests waited for dessert. Two seats remained empty: Lady Jean Conan Doyle had fallen ill just before dinner and sent her apologies, and Daniel, who had not yet returned from the hospital. He had, however, telephoned to say that the young lad had been stabilized and then transferred to a bigger hospital for surgery. The doctors at the local hospital were unsure whether or not they could save the foot, so arranged for a better-equipped facility in the city to take him. The Rolls was going to follow the ambulance to take the boy's father to be with his son. The drive back would take over an hour. Rollo, who had taken the telephone call, filled the guests in on the latest developments.

"You should have called me, Rolandson," said Arthur Conan Doyle. "I am a physician, you know."

"I was not responsible for 'the calling', *Sir* Arthur," drawled Rollo, putting undue emphasis on the title.

Sir James Madddox, a large, red-faced man who looked like he might have difficulty going up and down stairs at any speed, turned to his butler, who was hovering at the sideboard decanting a bottle of dessert wine. "Why didn't you call Sir Arthur, Grimes?"

"There wasn't time, Sir James. Mr Rokeby impressed upon us the need for immediate action."

"Rokeby?" asked Conan Doyle. "The photographer?"

"Yes," said Rollo, patting his stomach as a footman placed a bowl of sorbet and meringue in front of him. "The very fella who debunked your –"

"Rollo," Yasmin said sharply, putting a restraining hand on the editor's arm. "Let's not get into that."

"Quite, let's not," agreed Lady Ursula Maddox, a finely boned grey-haired woman in her fifties. "Before she became ill, Lady Jean impressed upon me the importance of weeding out any contrary vibrations before the séance."

"Weeding out?" snorted Rollo. "Then just as well Rokeby isn't here. He's an even bigger weed than I am!"

The German and American delegations chuckled; the British and Egyptian were politely impassive.

"Oh, don't be such a wet blanket, Rollo; you'll spoil it for the rest of us," chastised Delilah, cracking open a piece of meringue with her dessert spoon. "Lady Jean is right – we must all try to have positive thoughts and good vibrations or the spirits will not come."

Rollo rolled his eyes. Yasmin frowned at him.

"It's such a pity Lady Jean will not be leading the circle tonight," observed Marjorie. "A chill, you say?"

"A stomach upset," declared Conan Doyle. "It came on rather suddenly."

"Yes, we thought we might have to cancel," declared Sir James, "but fortunately Lady Ursula happened to know that the esteemed medium Madame Minette was staying with the Chapmans in Henley-on-Thames. A quick telephone call was all it took. She should be arriving any moment."

There was a polite cough from the sideboard.

"Grimes?"

"The lady arrived shortly after the fish course, Sir James."

Maddox looked blankly at his butler. "Why the deuce didn't you tell me?"

The butler put down the decanter and turned to his master. "The lady asked to be admitted discreetly. She," he cleared his throat again, "she said she wanted to prepare herself without any hullaballoo. I told Lady Ursula and she instructed me to take her to the parlour."

Maddox turned his attention to his wife. "And you didn't bother to tell me, my dear?" His voice was tight.

"You were busy discussing the mask with Dr Mortimer and I felt it was prudent not to interrupt," she answered, matching her husband's tautness.

Poppy flicked a glance at Dr Mortimer, seated between Marjorie and the archaeologist Howard Carter. Mortimer was forensically examining his pudding while Carter was pouring a glass of water for the Egyptian museum assistant, Miss El Farouk. All were assiduously pretending not to listen to the spat between the lord and lady of the house. Poppy, who was seated opposite the British Museum and Cairo delegations and next to Lionel Saunders from the *Courier*, had spent the first three courses trying to eavesdrop on the conversation across the table while simultaneously pretending not to be keeping another ear on Saunders' chitchat with the American and German delegations. Fortunately, Rollo was seated closer to them so she told herself to relax, knowing that her editor would pick up anything she missed. The *Courier* photographer, a surly man who let Saunders do all the talking, spent the time between courses sketching a diagram of the dinner party on a napkin.

On Poppy's right, the actor Fox Flinton had been eyeing up the empty seat reserved for Daniel all night. Once he had suggested to Delilah that they "shimmy up", but Delilah pointed out Daniel might arrive any minute so best to keep it open. She was, however, keen to shimmy up the other way so she could be opposite Conan Doyle. Flinton did not seem quite as keen on this idea and so the two actors stayed put. Poppy was grateful for the gap between her and the Fox. Poppy had encountered him before in her role as arts and entertainment editor. His crowning achievement had been a critically acclaimed Hamlet back before the war, but since then the Fox had never quite got the roles or the press he probably deserved. Poppy felt sorry for the fading actor but admitted that he didn't help himself by the impression he gave that no one was good enough to direct him and his insistence on casting his own leading ladies via the dressing room couch. Poppy worried a little for Delilah, but her friend assured her she could handle herself.

Poppy wished too that there was a spare seat between her and Lionel Saunders. Lady Ursula was either completely ignorant or completely mischievous when she told the two journalists she had seated them together so they could "swap notes". The two had never been friends. Ever since Poppy's first day on the newspaper, when she provided a story at the last minute to fill in for Lionel's failure to produce suitable material by deadline, the older journalist had branded her an enemy. Poppy was well aware that he considered her an upstart who only got the job because of her looks and believed she used her feminine wiles to hoodwink unsuspecting male sources. Well, Lionel could think what he wanted; the fact was she had scooped him on every big story in the last eighteen months. She wasn't quite sure how she could scoop him on this one – they were both at the same event, seated right next to each other – but Poppy knew that

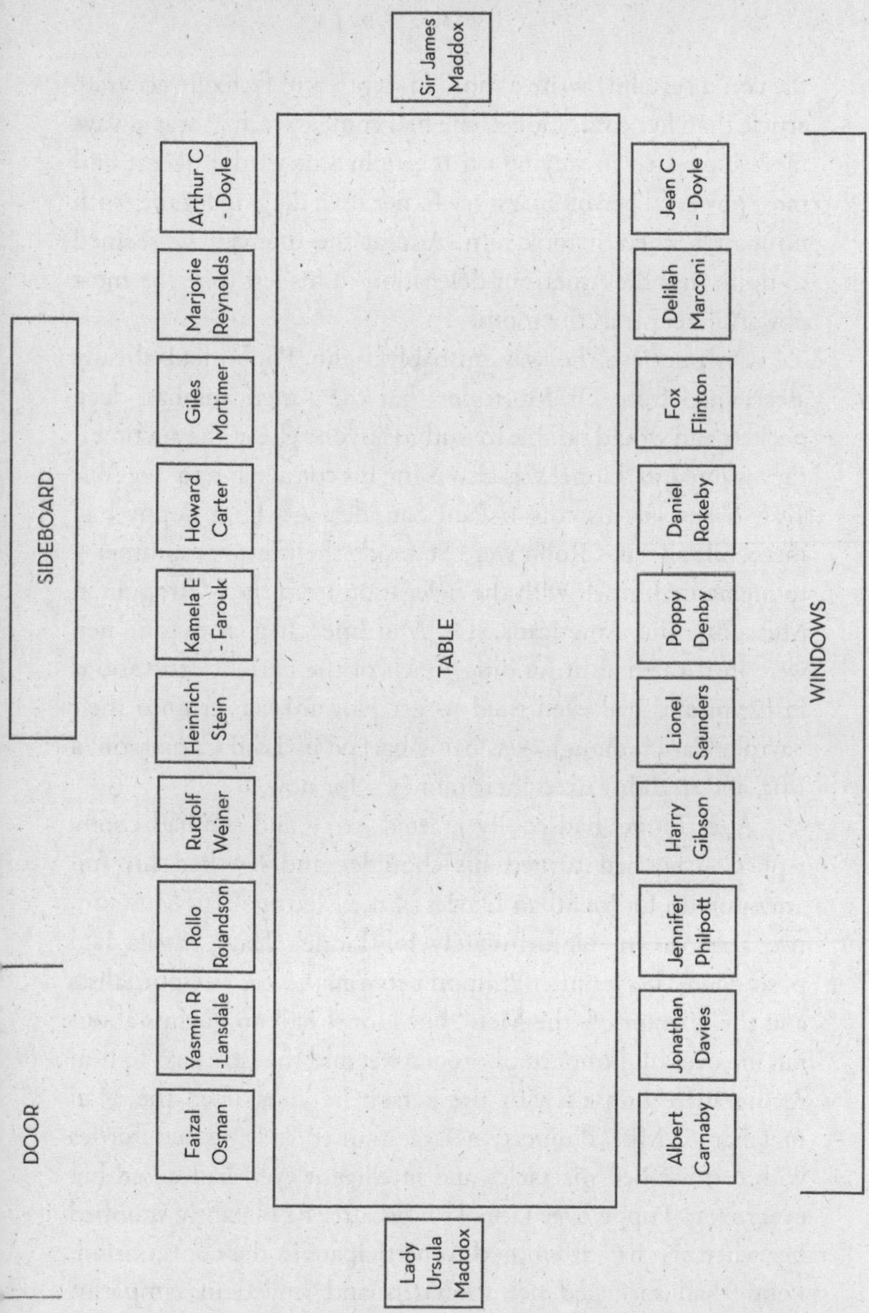

SIDEBOARD

DOOR

Sir James Maddox

TABLE

WINDOWS

**Left side (top to bottom):**
Arthur C - Doyle
Marjorie Reynolds
Giles Mortimer
Howard Carter
Kamela E - Farouk
Heinrich Stein
Rudolf Weiner
Rollo Rolandson
Yasmin R - Lansdale
Faizal Osman

**Right side (top to bottom):**
Jean C - Doyle
Delilah Marconi
Fox Flinton
Daniel Rokeby
Poppy Denby
Lionel Saunders
Harry Gibson
Jennifer Philpott
Jonathan Davies
Albert Carnaby

Lady Ursula Maddox

she could certainly write a more in-depth and factually accurate article than her rival. Lionel, she had come to realize, was always more interested in staying on the right side of the richest and most powerful person in a story rather than digging for the truth no matter where it took him. And at the moment he seemed to think that the American delegation to his left were the most powerful people in the room.

On one level he was probably right. Poppy had already ascertained from Dr Mortimer that the Americans had deep pockets and would be able to outbid anyone else at the auction if they wanted to. Lionel was also using his connection to *The New York Times*, via his cousin Paul Saunders – whom Poppy had met while she and Rollo were Stateside the previous summer – to ingratiate himself with the delegation from the Metropolitan Museum. The Americans, Dr Mortimer had also told her, were instrumental in funding much of the current excavations in Egypt and had even tried to get Howard Carter onto their payroll. Carter, though, was being backed by Lord Carnarvon, a Brit, and so didn't need their money – for now.

After Lionel had coolly greeted her – and she had coolly replied – he had turned his shoulder and lavished his full attention on Dr Jonathan Davies of the Metropolitan Museum, two seats down. Unfortunately for Lionel, Lady Ursula had positioned Miss Jennifer Philpott between the *Courier* journalists and the director of "the Met", but Lionel had no qualms about talking over his hunched photographer and the lady next to him to ingratiate himself with the person he considered the Man in Charge. Miss Philpott, a large-framed lady in her forties with tortoiseshell spectacles and intelligent eyes, had raised her eyebrow to Poppy over Lionel's head after he blatantly snubbed her when she had attempted to participate in the conversation. Poppy had shrugged her shoulders and smiled in sympathy.

In return, Miss Philpott had raised her glass to the young journalist. Lionel, as usual, was sniffing down the wrong track. Dr Mortimer had told Poppy that Miss Philpott was actually the expert in Egyptology – a veteran of three seasons in the Valley of the Kings and two at El-Amarna – and that Dr Davies was merely there as the money man.

Poppy liked the look of Miss Philpott and decided she would try to have a word with her after dinner. But for now, she was intent on listening in to the people she so far believed were the real power in the room: the Egyptians. If what she had been told by Dr Mortimer was correct, they were there not to bid for the mask but to gather substantiating evidence for their case that the artefact had been stolen. In addition, the presence of Marjorie Reynolds suggested there was something else going on other than the sale of a mask. This had more to do with diplomatic relations between Britain and its soon-to-be former protectorate. Let Lionel focus merely on the sale; she was going to dig deeper.

Rollo, meanwhile, while he wasn't goading Conan Doyle at the other end of the table, was chatting to the German delegates. They were there to try to get the Nefertiti mask as a companion to the bust of the pharaoh queen they already held in the Berlin Museum.

Next to Rollo, Yasmin was in deep conversation with her brother, while Miss El Farouk was responding to Howard Carter's questions in, what Poppy assumed, was Arabic. The lady did though speak excellent English and she and Poppy had swapped pleasantries over the soup. She appeared to be only a few years older than Poppy – twenty-five or twenty-six perhaps.

Halfway through the pudding course Mr Carter was drawn into conversation with Dr Mortimer and Marjorie to his left, who was enquiring as to how the search for King Tut's tomb was coming on, leaving Miss El Farouk without an interlocutor.

Poppy took her chance. She checked to see that Lionel was still engrossed in his conversation with Dr Davies, then asked:

"Miss El Farouk, do you perchance know anything about the 'murderous circumstances' surrounding the mask?"

The Egyptian woman, who had just finished her pudding, dabbed at her mouth with a napkin before answering. "Please, call me Kamela. And may I call you Poppy?"

"Of course," said Poppy, nodding her thanks to the footman as he took her dessert plate away. "I'm not sure if you saw the press release that Sir James sent out – it may only have come to us journalists – but in it he said the mask was found under 'murderous circumstances'." Poppy emphasized her point with quote marks in the air.

"Hmm," said Kamela, her dark eyes looking thoughtful. "I didn't know he had said that. But, it's true, there were two deaths associated with the finding of the mask."

"Two?" asked Poppy, casting a quick glance towards Lionel to see if he was listening: he wasn't, he was hanging on every word the American man uttered. Then she leaned forward. "Please tell me more."

Kamela pushed a long strand of black hair back under her white silk scarf. "All right then. There's no secret about it. The mask was found in an underground storeroom of the famous sculptor Thutmose. No doubt Sir James will tell you all about it later. The story I heard – from the local folk who lived nearby – was that two youngsters, a brother and sister, of around sixteen or seventeen, stumbled on the storeroom. But it turns out they weren't the first there. When they arrived it appeared as if someone had been there before them and had packed up the treasures for shipping."

"One of the archaeologists from the German dig?"

"Apparently not. The Germans had been unable to find the chamber – isn't that right, Herr Stein?" she acknowledged the older member of the German contingent who was listening in on the women's conversation.

Herr Stein nodded his assent. "It is. Dr Borchardt had found the main workshop, but this chamber had up until then alluded him. In fact, he was away in Cairo at the time when the incident in question took place."

"Why isn't Dr Borchardt here?" asked Poppy.

"He's currently on a dig in Heliopolis. This is more museum business. He is not actually employed by the museum; he just works with us now and then. If you don't mind, Miss Denby, I'd be very interested to hear what else Miss El Farouk has to say about this. I'm intrigued to hear the Egyptian version of events."

Kamela smiled sardonically. "You will discover, Poppy, that there are a number of different versions of this story. All I can tell you is the one I know – and believe."

Poppy nodded her understanding. "Yes, there are always a number of versions of a story. I'd be interested to hear Herr Stein's version too."

"I have already told your editor, Miss Denby. He can fill you in."

"Thank you. I'll ask him later. Do continue, Miss El – sorry, Kamela."

Kamela nodded to Herr Stein and continued. "Apparently, when the youngsters got there they discovered the bodies of the site watchman and his dog, hidden in a sarcophagus."

"A coffin?" asked Poppy, thinking back over the artefacts she'd seen at the British Museum.

"That's right," said Kamela. "But one made of stone. It was incomplete though. As you will hear from Sir James, Thutmose abandoned his workshop when the queen left the city after the king's death. No one knows why the sculptor left the things behind. Did he hope to come back for them later? Or was he leaving them behind permanently? The hidden storeroom suggests the former. But we'll never know."

Poppy feared she was being diverted into a history lesson. She gently nudged the antiquarian back on track. "So the bodies..."

Kamela chuckled. "A journalist, of course. Not to worry; I understand you need to cater to your readers. So, the bodies... yes. The brother and sister found them after they had found the mask that is going to be sold here tomorrow night."

"Were they going to steal it?" asked Poppy. It was Herr Stein's turn to smile sardonically.

Kamela tossed him a quick glance, then returned her attention to Poppy. "Possibly. But that's not the point. As I said, it looked like all the contents of the storeroom had already been packed up for shipping. Someone else – on a much larger scale – was planning on stealing the artefacts."

Poppy was puzzled. "Correct me if I'm wrong, but didn't the German archaeologist, Dr Borchardt, have permission to dig? Didn't he have a licence? Hence the goods were not being stolen."

Kamela smiled indulgently. "Actually Poppy, you'll find that this is the one thing that Herr Stein and I both agree on: Ludwig Borchardt was not the thief. Isn't that right, Herr Stein?"

Herr Stein was sipping his wine. He raised the glass to Kamela. "That is correct, Miss El Farouk. As I said, Borchardt was away at the time. Someone else was looting the site while his back was turned." He flicked his eyes to the head of the table, then made a point of returning to his wine. *Good heavens*, thought Poppy, *is he suggesting...*

"That's right," continued Kamela. "But even if it was Dr Borchardt who found the workshop and planned on shipping the artefacts, he could not do it without the permission of the Egyptian Antiquities Department. We grant licenses to excavators – particularly foreign excavators – on the condition that all finds are split evenly, fifty-fifty, between them and the Cairo Museum. For too long, Miss Denby, we have lost our cultural heritage to European nations. Like the Nefertiti bust in Berlin..."

Herr Stein inhaled sharply and put down his glass. "As you very well know, Miss El Farouk, the head of the Antiquities Department at the time gave Dr Borchardt *permission* to take the bust as part of his fifty per cent."

"Well, that's your version of the story..." Kamela folded her napkin and ran her thumbnail sharply along one edge.

Poppy feared they were going off on a tangent again. She'd heard all about the disputed Nefertiti bust from Dr Mortimer. "So, the bodies in the sarcophagus. Are those the two deaths you were referring to? The watchman and the dog?"

Kamela put the napkin onto her side plate. "No. There was another. The boy."

Poppy gasped. "The boy who found the storeroom? And discovered the watchman? Oh, how awful! Do you know who killed him? Was it the thieves?"

Kamela looked down at the empty place setting before her and then up at Poppy. There was anger in her eyes. "He died two years later. In prison. He and his sister were discovered by one of Borchardt's men who had brought a policeman with him. The man had been tipped off that someone had found the chamber and was trying to loot it. He had sent the watchman over to check it out while he went to get the local constabulary. When he returned – and this is his story – he found the brother and sister fleeing from the chamber. The boy, apparently, had blood on his hands. The man went inside, found the body of the watchman, and insisted the policeman arrest the brother and sister."

Poppy absorbed this information. There was a lot here. She'd have to write it all down as soon as she had a chance. "So," she continued, "the boy and girl were arrested. And, it seems the boy was convicted of murder… what about the girl?"

Kamela raised her hand to decline the offer of another glass of water from a hovering footman. "No, the boy was only charged as an accessory to murder. The girl served three months for looting, but was let off the accessory charge. The boy was sentenced to three years. But he died in a prison riot two years later. He was only nineteen."

*The same age as Christopher when he died. Oh, how tragic.* Poppy sighed deeply, thinking of her brother, and then asked: "And you think he was innocent?"

Kamela shrugged. "That's what the local people tell me. His story sounds plausible, don't you think? And the girl's too."

"You've met her?" asked Poppy.

"No," admitted Kamela. "No one has seen her since her brother died. Apparently she left Egypt to start a new life somewhere. She was well educated. After serving her time in prison she went back to school and got a diploma. But after that…"

Kamela spread her hands and smiled sadly.

"It's a terrible tale," said Poppy.

Just then Sir James announced that coffee would be served in the drawing room and, after that, the evening entertainment would begin. With expressions of thanks for a lovely meal, everyone got up and made their way to the door. Poppy found herself next to Kamela as they exited the dining room.

"Thank you for telling me that story," said Poppy. "There's just one more thing I'd like to know. Perhaps Sir James will mention it later, but I want to know what you think. What happened to the mask?"

Kamela tensed and then stopped. She stepped out of the line of traffic and ushered Poppy to join her. Poppy did. "Well, that's why we're here – me and Dr Osman. After the man and the policeman took the brother and sister to the police station, the man returned to – and these were his words to the judge – 'secure the artefacts'. However, he claims that when he entered the tomb, the mask was gone."

"Gone? Well, surely that exonerates the boy then! Someone else must have stolen it. Someone else must have been there!"

"That's exactly what the boy's lawyer told the judge. But the judge just took it as evidence that the siblings had not acted alone. That they had an accomplice. Still, there was enough doubt to not convict the boy of murder – just as an accessory – but it didn't exonerate him."

Poppy watched the rest of the dinner party file into the drawing room. She indicated that she and Kamela should follow. The two women started walking, side by side. "It does sound as though there was a miscarriage of justice," said Poppy, "just from what you've told me. Tell me, what happened to the man who brought the policeman to the workshop?"

Kamela stopped again and turned to Poppy, her dark eyes boring into those of the young journalist. "Well, Poppy, that may surprise you more than anything else I've told you tonight. That man was no other than Sir James Maddox."

Poppy took a step back. "You mean..."

Kamela took Poppy's elbow and ushered her towards the drawing room. "I certainly do. Now, shall we enjoy the rest of the party?"

# CHAPTER 7

The drawing room, with its roaring log fire, was so hot it might as well have been Egypt. Poppy took off her mink wrap and draped it over the back of the armchair she was sitting in. As she did, Daniel appeared and plopped himself down on the arm.

"You're back!" said Poppy. "Have you had anything to eat?"

"I have," he said, accepting a cigarette from Howard Carter, who was passing them around. "The chauffeur took me down to the kitchen. Cook had kept something for me. Splendid piece of beef."

"It was," agreed Poppy. "Delicious."

"Have I missed much?" he asked.

Poppy turned to him, her blue eyes wide, dying to tell him everything Kamela had told her. But the entertainment was about to start. "Loads," she said, "but I'll tell you later. How's the boy?"

"I think he's going to be all right. The doctors say they'll be able to save his foot. But..." Daniel lowered his voice, "...there's something funny going on with that whole shooting business."

"Oh?" said Poppy, her curiosity piqued. "Why?"

Daniel raised his finger to his mouth and whispered: "I'll tell you and Rollo later too."

"All right," agreed Poppy as Sir James stood up and shushed them with a 'simmer down' motion of his hands. The assembled guests, nursing glasses of brandy and sherry, allowed their babble of conversation to still.

Sir James stood with a brandy snifter in one hand and a cigar in the other. "Well, I hope you've all been having a splendid evening so far." This was met with a round of hear-hears. Sir James smiled, his face as round and red as a billiard ball. He raised his glass in acknowledgment. "Why, thank you. Thank you. Then you'll be pleased to know that the night is but a pup. First up – and I'm going to need to put these down –" He put down his glass and cigar, reached into a basket beside the fireplace, and took out a piece of white cloth with gold brocade. He bent his bald head and tucked it into the cloth, in an approximation of an ancient Egyptian headdress. The guests chuckled. "May I introduce to you the royal courtier Ay – father of Nefertiti." The audience applauded. He bowed, holding his headdress in place with one hand.

Poppy looked over at Kamela El Farouk, who was crammed onto a sofa with Yasmin and Rollo. Her face was impassive. Yasmin's, however, wasn't, and she rolled her eyes in disdain. Everyone else, though, seemed to be enjoying the performance – even Daniel, who chuckled beside her. Poppy turned her attention back to Sir James.

"I lived in Egypt way back before the birth of the man you call Jesus. Thirteen hundred years or so before him."

"How do you know about Jesus?" chirped Rollo. "Did you use H. G. Wells' time machine?"

"Ay" chuckled. "We Ancient Egyptians have many secrets hidden in our pyramids. And that is one of them. Who knows what your friend Carter will find next."

Carter raised his glass and grinned.

"Speaking of Carter – and his quest for the boy king – I (excuse the pun) am to become pharaoh after Tutankhamun. But –" and he grinned again "– using Mr Wells' time machine, I will now take you back to before young Tut was born and introduce you to my beautiful daughter, Nefertiti!" He gestured extravagantly with one arm to the door of the library where Delilah – dressed in a very revealing Egyptian costume that looked like it had been borrowed from the wardrobe of the moving picture *Cleopatra* – made her entrance and struck a pose. She was greeted with enthusiastic applause.

"Nefertiti," continued Sir James, "means 'the beautiful woman has come'. And no doubt you can see why she was called *that*." Delilah battered her false eyelashes seductively and was rewarded with a wolf whistle from Rollo.

"One day," continued Sir James, "my boss, the pharaoh Amenhotep IV..."

Fox Flinton stepped into the library – he too in Egyptian costume – and stopped to pose. He then affected a lascivious look at "Nefertiti" before kneeling before Sir James, his hands raised in supplication.

"He would *never* have knelt," observed Yasmin in a stage whisper and rolled her eyes again.

This was met with a few sniggers and the Fox hurriedly clambered to his feet.

Sir James ignored the heckling and continued with his narration. "Amenhotep, seeing how beautiful my daughter Nefertiti was..."

Delilah sashayed across the room, drawing admiring glances from everyone.

"... asked for my permission to marry her."

"He would *never*..."

"*Shush!*" chastised Lady Ursula. "You're spoiling it."

"Yes, Yasmin, you're spoiling it," said Rollo teasingly and winked at her.

"Sorry," said Yasmin insincerely.

Sir James cleared his throat. "Ahem, thank you. As I was saying, Amenhotep, seeing how beautiful Nefertiti was, asked to marry her. And I, of course, gave permission." He opened his arms and gestured for the young lovers to come together. They did and fell into an exaggerated stage embrace. This was accompanied by a chorus of "Ahhhhhhhhhh," from the audience.

"Now, Amenhotep and Nefertiti lived in a place called Thebes, which was the capital of the New Kingdom. If you were to go to Thebes today it wouldn't be there, but – my glimpse into the future tells me – its ruins can be found in a place called Luxor. I think some of you already know Luxor. Hands up all the archaeologists in the room who have dug there." Poppy looked around and saw Howard Carter, Miss Philpott, both Herr Stein and his assistant and – finally, with a sheepish grin – Sir James too. She noted that neither of the Egyptians had done so.

"But in the fifth year of his reign, Amenhotep had a vision..."

The Fox gave a good rendition of Saint Paul being blinded on the road to Damascus.

"Where the god Aten – otherwise known as the sun – spoke to him. Aten told Amenhotep that he, not the old gods, including the king of the gods Amen, after whom the pharaoh was named, was the true god of Egypt. Aten said that only he was to be worshipped and declared Amenhotep his official representative on earth. Amenhotep was immediately converted and changed his name to Akhenaten, which means 'devoted to Aten'."

"Ah," observed Lionel Saunders from his seat on the piano stool, and took a swig of his brandy.

"Akhenaten told his beautiful wife about his vision and she too was converted." Delilah imitated the painting of *Mary the Mother of Jesus at the Annunciation* by Botticelli, and did a very convincing version of it despite her provocative attire.

"Nefertiti renamed herself Neferneferuaten-Nefertiti – which, we can all admit, and I don't know if I've even pronounced it correctly, is a real mouthful. Which explains why everyone simply carried on calling her Nefertiti. And that, ladies and gentlemen, is what we shall do too."

The audience gave an appreciative chuckle, which was followed by a mistimed guffaw from Lionel. Poppy noted a line of empty glasses beside him on the piano.

"So," continued Sir James, "the king and queen decided to move away from the old city of Thebes to find a new capital for the religion they had started."

The Fox and Delilah mimed picking up suitcases and going on a journey, stepping over legs and climbing over footstools amid great hilarity from the guests. After two circuits of the room they stopped and mimed digging and hammering.

"They travelled all the way up the Nile to a place called Tel El-Amarna – a narrow valley between two cliffs – where they built a beautiful whitewashed city called Akhetaten, which means 'the horizon of Aten'."

The Fox and Delilah stood arm in arm and gestured with their other hands as if presenting something for approval.

"But," continued Sir James, "as you no doubt agree, the name of the city sounds far too similar to Akhenaten, and after a couple of drinks we're bound to forget it –" Lionel guffawed at this again "– so let's just call it El-Amarna, which, I believe, is what it is called today." He looked towards the Egyptian contingent. Faizal Osman nodded in agreement.

"In El-Amarna, Akhenaten and Nefertiti had six daughters."

Delilah mimed holding six babies one after another and passing them to the Fox, who hammed up almost dropping a couple of them.

"Akhenaten named Nefertiti his co-regent and together they both ruled as pharaohs. For the next twenty years they lived happily together: raising children, leading the people in the worship of Aten –" both Delilah and the Fox knelt down in prayer "– and continuing to build their city."

"Eventually, when their eldest daughter, Meritaten, was old enough, Akhenaten married her, and she became his second wife." This was met by a few titters. Sir James raised his hand. "And now, before the feminists in the room say anything –" he looked pointedly first at Marjorie Reynolds, then at Yasmin, then finally, with a patronizing smile, at Poppy "– that's what they used to do in those days."

Poppy and Marjorie's eyes met across the room and they shared a mutual, virtual sigh.

"Meritaten, in turn, gave birth to a baby boy, and his name was..." Sir James cupped his hand to his ear and leaned in towards the audience.

"Tutankhamun!" called out a number of the archaeologists.

Sir James grinned. "That's right. And before the boy stopped playing with toys his father sadly died."

The Fox clutched his heart and fell to the ground. Delilah threw herself on his chest and wept.

Sir James sighed, his voice dripping with hammed-up emotion. "And what became of Nefertiti?"

"Yes, what became of her?" slurred Lionel, adding another glass to the piano.

"No one knows, Mr Saunders. Some believe she died soon after her husband. Others that she survived him and led the people back from El-Amarna to Thebes. Her tomb, to this day, has never been found. Some people think it might still be in Amarna – but that's unlikely – it's been well excavated. Another theory is that it might be in the Valley of the Kings. Most royal tombs have already been found. But not King Tut's. And not Nefertiti's either. Perhaps Mr Carter will find them both..."

"From your mouth to God's ear!" declared Carter, followed by a "Hear-hear," from Dr Mortimer.

Sir James indicated that he wasn't quite finished. "But what we do have — thanks to the royal sculptor Thutmose and his workshop — are some beautiful statues, masks, and busts of her, the one in Berlin, of course, being the most famous..." He nodded towards the German contingent who, Poppy couldn't help thinking, were looking rather smug. "And the one that is going to be auctioned here in this very house, tomorrow night."

"Can we see it?" asked Jonathan Davies, the American.

Sir James smiled. "Not tonight, Dr Davies, no. It is currently under lock and key but will be revealed in due course at the auction."

A murmur of disappointment spread through the room. Sir James, perhaps worried he was losing his audience, then added: "But don't despair, there is more for you tonight. Lady Ursula, is Madame Minette ready?"

Lady Ursula said that she was.

"Good, then let us see if we can contact the spirit of Nefertiti."

Delilah, who was still lying on the Fox's chest, coughed loudly.

"Aren't you forgetting something?" called out the Fox.

Everyone laughed. "Of course!" said Sir James. "My apologies. Ladies and gentlemen, a big round of applause for the very talented Miss Delilah Marconi and Mr Fox Flinton!"

# CHAPTER 8

It turned out Madame Minette was not *quite* ready, so the guests were offered coffee while they waited. Rollo waved Poppy and Daniel over to him.

He leaned back on his heels, with his thumbs hooked into his cummerbund and chomped on his cigar. As his staff approached, he pulled out his cigar and held it between thumb and forefinger, and asked: "Having fun?"

Poppy said she was, but Daniel, who had spent most of the night driving back and forth to hospital, said he could do with a good night's sleep. He looked around the room at the chattering guests and observed grimly, "But it looks like they're just getting warmed up."

"Stiff upper lip old chap," grinned Rollo. "You can sleep when you're dead."

"Speaking of the dead," said Poppy, "I've heard that we're not all going into the séance. Apparently the round table can only seat twelve. You might be able to duck out of that one, Daniel."

Rollo patted the photographer on his lower back. "I think me and Danny Boy won't be invited anyway – after the job we did on the fairies. So that just leaves you, Poppy."

Poppy's stomach clenched. She wasn't as sure as Daniel and Rollo that the whole thing was a party trick. Unlike them, she did believe – to some degree – in the supernatural. She believed in God and, although she didn't believe they were behind every bush, she couldn't discount the possibility that there were evil spirits too. Didn't the Bible mention them? Hadn't her father preached on them? There were three possibilities with this séance: either it was a hoax as her male colleagues believed, or it was a demonic deception as many in the church believed, or it was just what the spiritualists said it was – the spirits of loved ones who had passed on were trying to speak to the living. But Poppy didn't have time to mull it over any further, as Rollo was steering the conversation towards other things.

"So what happened with the boy, Danny? You said there was something funny going on? Spill the beans."

Daniel took a sip of his coffee, served in the tiniest cup Poppy had ever seen. He savoured the hot liquid, absorbing its restorative power. "His name's William. William Booker. His father is the gamekeeper here at Winterton. He's just left school and started work on the estate earlier in the summer. He helps with the hounds, and today, for the first time, he helped with preparing the guns for tomorrow's shoot. He was supposed to check the mechanism of each weapon and oil them. But it seems like one of the barrels had not been discharged – or checked after the previous shoot – and still had shot in it."

"Is that unusual?" asked Poppy.

"Yes. A good huntsmaster will check each weapon before putting it away. Booker senior was beside himself, wondering how he could have missed that one at the last shoot."

"When was the last shoot?" asked Rollo.

"It was a live one – pheasant – the back end of October. About six weeks ago. But here's the funny thing… the gun was loaded with buckshot, not birdshot."

Both Poppy and Rollo appeared underwhelmed at this revelation, so Daniel went on to explain. "A bigger animal requires bigger pellets to kill it. Buckshot is bigger than birdshot and hence will do more damage."

"What's usually used for clay shooting?" asked Rollo.

"Bird."

"Hmm." Rollo stumped out his cigar in a convenient ashtray. "And what does the father say?"

"He says he swears by all that is holy that he never put buckshot in the guns. Not at the previous shoot, nor for this one. In fact, he swears that he had not loaded any of the guns for tomorrow's shoot at all. They were just at the oiling stage – they would only have loaded the barrels tomorrow, just before the shoot."

Poppy looked around the drawing room at the assembled guests, waiting for the séance to begin. They were gathered in clusters chatting, each in their national groups: German, American, Egyptian, and British. Yasmin was with her brother and Miss El Farouk, Marjorie was with Howard Carter and Dr Mortimer, and the Fox and Delilah were at the piano picking out a ditty. At the fireplace were Sir James, the auctioneer, and Arthur Conan Doyle, with Lionel Saunders, looking slightly unsteady on his feet, nearby. The *Courier* photographer was not in the room; neither was Lady Ursula, who, Poppy presumed, was trying to hurry up the tardy Madame Minette, while Lady Jean Conan Doyle was apparently still in bed. Flitting from group to group, like bees in a meadow, were three footmen, supervised by Mr Grimes, the butler, who monitored the dispensing of refreshments.

"Who else had access to the guns?" she asked, turning back to Rollo and Daniel.

"They would have been under lock and key," said Daniel, popping his empty cup on a footman's silver serving tray as he passed by.

"Then who had access to the keys?" asked Rollo.

"Booker said it was only him and senior members of the household."

"And who would that be?" asked Poppy, noticing the photographer slip back into the room and whisper something to Lionel Saunders. Saunders nodded and followed him back out.

"Sir James, of course, Lady Ursula, who apparently is a crack shot, and Mr Grimes. As the butler, he has keys to everything."

Rollo waved to a footman and mimed sipping coffee. He turned back to his staff. "The question that's begging is *why*. If this Booker fella hasn't just botched things up and is trying to cover for himself, why would someone load one of the weapons, in advance, with buckshot?"

*Yes, that is the question…* thought Poppy. "No doubt that's what the constabulary will ask when they come to make inquiries. Any idea when that will be?"

"Probably tomorrow," said Daniel. "Didn't Grimes say he would give them a ring?"

"He did," agreed Poppy. "They'll probably want to speak to you too, as a witness."

"Goodo," said Rollo. "Let us know what's said, eh Danny Boy. Now, team, let's get back to the business at hand. I had a good chat to the Germans. Nice to be exchanging words for a change instead of bullets…" He grinned, Daniel laughed, and Poppy gave a mock groan. "… and they told me some very interesting things about our host."

"Oh?" said Poppy, remembering what Herr Stein and Miss El Farouk had already told her. "What did they say?"

Rollo looked towards the fireplace. "That Maddox used to work for them. He apparently used to do the rounds of all the digs before the war. He had no formal qualifications, but he was an enthusiastic self-funded amateur who could be counted on to provide a bit of covering finance in exchange for letting him play archaeologist now and again."

"That's interesting," chipped in Poppy. "Being an amateur didn't stop him from being on the board of the Egyptian Exploration Society..."

Rollo raised a surprised eyebrow.

"It was in his jazz file," she said in way of explanation. "Sorry, carry on."

"No bother at all, Miz Denby. Glad to hear you've been doing your homework. So, where was I? Right, Maddox playing archaeologist. Well, according to Herr Stein, he was helping out on Borchardt's dig back in 1914. It was a few months before the outbreak of war and the Germans weren't sure how much longer they would be able to dig there as Egypt – as you know – was at the time a joint British/French protectorate. No one knew for sure there'd be a war, but the signs weren't good. So, they were trying to get as much done as they could. Hence, they were only too happy to take on an extra hand that didn't require a salary. That's when Maddox joined the team. However, items started going missing – just small things, but enough to be troublesome. Typically, the local guides and labourers were blamed, but no evidence was ever found. Herr Stein tells me Borchardt suspected Maddox, but couldn't prove it."

"And now they think he stole the mask too," added Poppy, in hushed tones, and went on to tell her colleagues what Miss El Farouk had told her.

When she had finished, both Daniel and Rollo were staring at her wide-eyed. "Golly, that's far worse than pilfering a few old trinkets," observed Daniel, lowering his voice to match Poppy's conspiratorial tone. "Are they suggesting Maddox was involved in the death of the watchman? And then framing the boy?"

Poppy shook her head. "He might have been, but she didn't actually say that. However, she more than hinted that he was behind the theft of the mask. What we haven't heard yet is how he claims the mask came to be in his possession."

"Actually I have," said Rollo. "Yasmin's brother told me Maddox said he came across it last year in a souk in Cairo. He said it was sold to him by a local dealer. But when Faizal asked for details of the dealer – so the Antiquities Service could follow it up – the man had apparently disappeared and his shop was boarded up."

Daniel snorted. "Convenient."

"Quite," agreed Poppy. "However, if it's clear that the mask was stolen – whether by Maddox or this mysterious Egyptian dealer – then surely the Egyptians have a right to take it back."

Rollo nodded. "Yes, that's what Faizal thinks too. Maddox, though, has a court order declaring him to be the lawful owner of the mask. He apparently produced a receipt and his solicitor presented it to a judge who declared it proof of purchase in good faith."

"A British judge?"

Rollo grinned. "Of course. Naturally, the Egyptians are contesting it, but so far they have been unable to get the case reopened. However, I think they hope to put pressure on the British government to do something about it."

Poppy looked over at Marjorie Reynolds, who was in deep conversation with Dr Mortimer. So she had been right: the presence of the Minister to the Home Office did have some significance.

"So then, let me get this straight," said Daniel. "This mask is being auctioned tomorrow night but it's not clear if the auction is even legal?"

"That about sums it up," said Rollo. "But as long as Maddox has the court order on his side, there's nothing the Egyptians can do about it. So, unless something happens between now and tomorrow night; it looks like the mask will soon find a new home in London, Berlin or New York."

"Or Cairo," added Poppy.

"Possibly," agreed Rollo, "but I don't think Faizal and Miss El Farouk will be too keen on paying for something they already believe is theirs."

"I don't blame them," said Daniel.

"Me neither," said Poppy, then chewed her lip.

Rollo looked at her curiously. "What is it?"

"I'm just thinking. In Maddox's jazz file, back at the office, there was a short article from *The Times*, written in 1914, stating that he had been relieved of his post at the Egyptian Exploration Society because of queries around the procurement of some artefacts. I wonder if that had something to do with all this. It was just a short piece and I thought underwritten. I made a note of it though. I wonder if the journalist who wrote it has any more information."

"Do you remember who it was?" asked Rollo.

Poppy thought for a moment. "It will be in my notes. But I think it was Jenson. Walter Jenson. Or Jensford. I'll have to check."

"There was a Walter Jensford at *The Times* back in '14. He's retired now, but still goes to the Press Club on occasion. Could that be him?" asked Rollo.

"Quite possibly. Do you know him?"

"In passing, yes." Rollo took out a cigarette case and offered it to Daniel, who declined. The editor paused to light his cigarette, breathed in deeply, then exhaled. "I'll see what I can find out."

Poppy nodded her appreciation. "It would be nice if we could stop the sale of the mask, wouldn't it? If it is stolen, I mean; it just doesn't seem right."

Rollo gave a paternal smile. "Always the crusader, Miz Denby. Realistically, I doubt we'll find out anything before tomorrow night. No, I think the sale will go ahead. But if evidence is later found that it was stolen, perhaps the sale could eventually be reversed. And if not, well…" he grinned "… either way, it'll make a damned good story."

Suddenly there was a loud, sonorous bong. Lady Ursula stood in the doorway, holding a little brass gong. "Ladies and gentlemen, Madame Minette and I have been going over the guest list and have selected the following people for the séance. I hope those left off the list will not be offended, but there are only twelve seats at the table. The first three seats will be filled by Madame Minette, Sir James, and myself. Sir Arthur would have most definitely been on the list, but Lady Jean has taken a turn for the worse and he thinks he needs to be with her."

"My apologies," said Conan Doyle, bowing to Lady Ursula.

"Not at all, Sir Arthur. We understand. Hopefully Lady Jean will be better in the morning and be able to join us for the rest of the weekend's entertainment."

"I'm sure she will," said the famous author, then bowed again and exited the room.

"So," said Lady Ursula, after he had left, "we have room for nine more. Would the following people care to join us: Herr Stein, Miss Philpott, Miss El Farouk, Mr Flinton, Miss Marconi, Mr Carter, Mr Saunders, Mr Carnaby, and Miss Denby. If anyone would prefer not to join…" Poppy flashed a look at Rollo. He shook his head. "… no? Everyone happy? Good, then Grimes will put on some gramophone records here in the drawing room, while the rest of us head off to the parlour." She bonged the gong again. "Let the spirits come!"

# CHAPTER 9

The gas lights in the parlour were turned down low, and a single votive candle was lit and centred on the round table. A flamboyant woman in a gold and green gown, with hennaed hair caught up in a green silk scarf, its tassels falling down one side of her face, was already seated. Her eyes were closed and her hands splayed on the table in front of her. Each finger had its own ring and on her arms a jangle of bangles. *Madame Minette,* Poppy presumed.

Lady Ursula ushered the guests in and, in a hushed voice, instructed everyone as to where they should sit. Ignoring the direction, Delilah took the seat next to Madame Minette, opened her hands as if to receive a blessing, closed her eyes, and released a meditative hum.

"Not there, Miss Marconi," hissed Lady Ursula. "That is *not* your seat."

Delilah opened her eyes and giggled. Lady Ursula sniffed and pointed sharply at the seat she expected Delilah to move to. "Madame Minette has already sought the counsel of her control spirit and he has indicated you should sit *there.*" She punctuated her instruction with a further jab of her finger to the seat next to Fox Flinton.

"Come on, Delilah, don't throw a spanner in the works. Cousin Ursula knows what she's doing," chided the Fox, patting the seat beside him.

"Thank you, cousin," said Lady Ursula, nodding at Delilah and flicking her head towards the "correct" chair.

Delilah threw up her hands in mock contrition: "Whatever the spirits declare." Then she got up and moved to her allocated seat. No one else dared to challenge "the spirits" and obediently sat where they were told.

It was then that Poppy noticed a camera had been set up on a tripod in the corner of the room and behind it was Harry Gibson, the *Courier* photographer. She sniffed. Yes, there was a smell of magnesium in the air.

"Are you going to document the séance?" asked Poppy.

"No," said Lady Ursula, "the spirits will be alarmed by the bright lights. But Mr Gibson and Mr Saunders asked if they could have a photograph of the circle before we begin."

Lionel Saunders smirked at Poppy, suggesting he believed he'd scooped his rival. Poppy shrugged. It was no skin off her nose. Without the Conan Doyles there the photograph had already lost much of its newsworthiness. Although... come to think of it... she wasn't that keen on appearing in a photograph showing she had been at a séance. Her parents would be appalled – if by chance they ever saw it. But here she was, despite her misgivings. *I suppose pretending I'm not would just compound the sin*, she thought unhappily.

"Do you have a problem with that, Miss Denby?" asked Lionel.

"No, not at all," she answered, crossing her fingers under the table, then uncrossing them quickly when she realized she was indulging in yet another unchristian act. She swallowed her guilt and crossed her legs instead.

"Is everyone comfortable?" asked Lady Ursula, taking her seat to the right of Madame Minette, while her husband sat to the medium's left.

*Is she ever going to open her eyes?* thought Poppy.

"Good. Now, let's get this photograph taken, and then I'll explain to the uninitiated how the séance will operate. Mr Gibson, you may proceed."

Gibson grunted and then in a monotone voice said: "All right then. Do something séancy."

This brought chuckles from around the table.

"Come on folks, let's do something séancy," chirped Howard Carter. "Prepare for the table to levitate…" He took hold of the edge and began to rock it.

Two bangled arms slammed down on the table, bringing it to a stop. Madame Minette's eyes – as yellow as a snake's – flashed open and bored into Carter's. "King hunter, desssissst," she whispered, "you are upsssetting the ssspiritsss," then she closed her eyes again.

The medium's hiss hung in the air with the smoke from the spluttering candle. Silence fell on the circle. It was eventually broken by the photographer: "So, are you going to do something séancy or not?"

There were no giggles this time. Everyone looked at one another, then at Madame Minette. Her eyes were still closed. Silence.

"Well, all right then," said Lady Ursula. "Perhaps we should all place our hands on the table, like Madame's, making sure our fingertips all touch. Can we do that?"

Poppy looked at Howard Carter; he had a twinkle in his eye. Was he going to rock the table again? To her disappointment, he didn't, and simply complied with the request.

Lady Ursula looked around and nodded with approval. "Good, then perhaps we can all bow our heads. Will that work, Mr Gibson?"

"It'll do," said Gibson.

*Oh good,* thought Poppy, *if our heads are bowed people might not recognize me. Hmm, but I bet Saunders will put my name in the caption...* She sighed quietly and then bowed her head.

"Right, hold that pose..." Poppy heard the clicks and creaks of a camera lens being focused as the mechanical bellows expanded, then, after a "One, two, three..." from Gibson, there was a small explosive flash, the smell of magnesium burning, and a final "Thanks folks, that'll do."

Everyone opened their eyes, blinking away the smoke from the flash, even Madame Minette. For a moment she and Poppy locked eyes. *Ah, they're more amber than yellow,* thought Poppy. Still, they gave her chills. Poppy looked away.

Lady Ursula was now standing. "Thank you, Mr Gibson. You may leave now. You can collect your camera later."

Gibson looked to object but was dismissed with a slightly slurred: "See you later, Harry. I'll keep an eye on the equipment," from Lionel.

Gibson shrugged, picked up a whisky tumbler from the sideboard behind him, took a sip, and left the room, closing the door behind him.

Lady Ursula clapped her hands three times. "Good, now we can begin. How many of you have sat in a séance circle before?"

Six hands went up: Fox Flinton, Delilah Marconi, Lionel Saunders, Howard Carter, Albert Carnaby, and Sir James Maddox. Lady Ursula smiled and raised her hand too. "So that leaves Miss El Farouk, Miss Denby, Miss Philpott, and Herr Stein who are first-timers. Is that correct?"

The newbies all said it was.

"Well then, for your sake, I shall explain what will happen. Unless..." she said, turning to the medium whose eyes were still open "... you would prefer to."

The medium twitched her lips into what Poppy assumed

was an attempt at a smile. "No, Lady Ursssula, you can explain. Although much is beyond explanation."

Lady Ursula nodded her head. "That's very true, Madame, and something we should not forget. Tonight, ladies and gentlemen, you might see and hear things that have no apparent explanation. Do not... I repeat, *do not*... try to apply a scientific mind to them. I know Sir Arthur Conan Doyle – who sadly is not with us – has tried to marry science and spiritualism, but it takes a rare mind like his to be able to do so. There are some things that you need to take on faith. The metaphysical world is one of them – although there is much scientific evidence to support it," she hastened to add.

Poppy shook her head. Either one was to use science or one was not. Lady Ursula could not have it both ways. But "faith" *was* something Poppy understood. *But not in this*, she said to herself. She looked to the door, wondering if it was too late to leave. But then, she caught Howard Carter's eye. There was that twinkle again. And she remembered what Rollo and Daniel had said about the whole thing being a hoax. No, she would see it through. Then, afterwards, try to figure out *scientifically* how it was all done.

"Righteo," continued Lady Ursula. "The aim of a séance is to connect the living with those who have passed on. We – those of us experienced in spiritualism – know that many of the spirits want to communicate with us. Sometimes there are spirits of people long dead, with no living relatives. Other times, they are people recently passed on who know they are still missed and loved. Those spirits often have unfinished business here on earth. You'll be surprised at how many of our brave boys who sacrificed their lives in the Great War are still with us. In fact, that's how I became involved in this. I was not blessed with children, but counted the children of my sister as my own. Sadly, though," she lowered her head for a moment then raised it again, "both of them were taken from us too soon. Dear Victoria was only thirteen when she died of consumption in 1912. Walter died five years later on the Western Front – he was twenty."

She sighed deeply and looked slowly around the circle, taking each guest in. "I'm sure most of you have lost someone. And you know how heart-wrenching it is."

There were murmurs of assent from around the table. Yes, Poppy knew exactly how that felt. Lady Ursula smiled gently. "So I don't have to explain to you what a joy it was when I went to my first séance and the spirit of dear Walter spoke to me. He assured me he was happy and at peace."

Before she could stop herself, Poppy raised her hand. Lady Ursula frowned. "Miss Denby, now is not the appropriate time to interview me for an article. I'm sure we can find time later –"

"No, no," Poppy assured her. "I'm not interviewing you. I just want to ask a question – for myself – so I can understand what's going to happen tonight. Just one. I promise."

Lady Ursula looked at Madame Minette. The medium nodded.

"All right, just one," said Lady Ursula, in a tone reminiscent of a school ma'am putting a precocious child in its place.

The rest of the guests were looking at Poppy expectantly; all except Lionel, who was rolling his eyes in irritation. Poppy ignored him as she usually did. "Well, I was wondering how you knew it was your nephew. That it was *really* him. Not someone pretending to be him –"

Lady Ursula took a sharp intake of breath.

"Either someone living or someone dead," Poppy hastened to add. This seemed to soothe ruffled feathers and Lady Ursula relaxed.

"A fair question, Miss Denby. And one that is easy to answer. The spirit knew something that only Walter would know. Like you, I too was sceptical, but when I heard that he remembered the colour of the dress I wore to his eighteenth birthday party, I knew it was him. Now, if you don't mind, I will quickly finish explaining the mechanics of the evening and then I will hand over to Madame Minette."

Poppy nodded her thanks while filing away the bit of information to ponder upon later.

"So, very quickly then," continued Lady Ursula, "all mediums work differently. Lady Jean – who is sadly not with us tonight – is an automatic writer. She sees which spirits arrive and then writes down messages from them. Other mediums use a Ouija board, which the spirits themselves will move to spell out their messages letter by letter. Madame Minette here receives the messages and speaks them out as the spirits take turns to possess her body."

Poppy felt a cold chill run down her spine. *Possession? Oh dear God, should I leave?*

But then she hurriedly reminded herself that people she highly respected were convinced it was a hoax. It had to be a hoax. No, she had a job to do and she would stay.

Lady Ursula continued: "Madame Minette also tells me that before full possession takes place, the spirit will knock to announce its presence. As all our hands will be flat on the table it will obviously not be us doing the knocking. The first spirit you will hear will be what is known as the control spirit. This is Madame Minette's spirit guide. It is the spirit of a man called Alexander, a Greek slave in the court of the Emperor Nero, who burned to death during the great fire of Rome. Alexander, when he comes, will then help to control the other spirits who want to speak."

*A bit like the chairman at a debate*, thought Poppy.

"In addition, there may – or may not – be physical manifestations. Flickering lights, ghostly music, moving furniture… whatever happens, do not be alarmed. Madame Minette and Alexander are in control. Is it clear how it will operate?"

Everyone said it was. There was a frisson of excitement in the room, which surged as the gas lights suddenly dimmed and then raised again.

"The ssspirits are anxiousss tonight," whispered Madame Minette in her strange, sibilant voice.

In response the guests' expressions alternated between expectant, amused, scared, and barely contained scepticism. Miss Philpott fell into the latter category. Poppy made a mental note to speak to her afterwards.

"Then let us begin before they move on," said Lady Ursula. "Hands on the table as they were before please. We need to harness the collective psychic energy of everyone here. Do not break the circle under any circumstances. Are you all ready?"

There were nods all round.

"Good. Then spirits we welcome you. Speak as you will."

"Ssssspeak assss you will," repeated Madame Minette, who then began to take long, deep breaths. Poppy pressed her palms firmly down onto the table, willing the stability of the wood to still her shaking frame. She felt sweat beads form at her temples and her tongue cleave to the roof of her mouth. She couldn't deny it – she was scared, but also curious. How were they going to rig this thing? Her eyes flitted around the room. Behind Madame Minette was a cupboard, about six feet high, draped in a black cloth. What was in the cupboard? She wondered too what might be under the table. A white cloth reached all the way to the floor, so she had been unable to look beneath it when she entered the room. What might be hidden under there?

Suddenly the room was filled with the sound of pan pipes playing a pentatonic scale – up and down and down and up. Delilah squeaked in delight. Poppy cocked her ear – there was no hiss or crackle to indicate it was a recording.

"Alexsssander is here," said Madame Minette and softened her lips as if she were a lover waiting for a kiss. "Are you here Ssssander?"

*Knock, knock, knock.* Poppy jerked in fear, her hands losing contact for a moment with Herr Stein on her right and Mr Carnaby on her left. Herr Stein reached out his little finger and re-established the connection. Mr Carnaby followed suit.

"Ah, you are welcome Sssander. You may enter." Madame Minette lowered her chin to her chest then flung back her head and shook, as if convulsed by epilepsy.

Poppy dug her fingernails into the tablecloth.

The convulsions ceased and Madame Minette's chin once more fell to her chest. The pan music was playing again as she slowly raised her head and gave the most chilling smile. "Good evening, Albert," she said, looking directly at Mr Carnaby to Poppy's left. Mr Carnaby's hand flinched. "It's so lovely to see you again, my dear boy." All trace of sibilance had left the medium's voice and, if Poppy was not mistaken, there was now a slight trace of an East Lothian accent.

"M-mother?" asked Mr Carnaby, his voice barely louder than a whisper.

"Of course it's me, my dear, dear Bertie. Have you missed mumsy?"

"Y-yes. I think of you often."

Madame Minette smiled. "That's what a mother likes to hear." Suddenly, Madame Minette began to twitch and jerk. Her chin dropped and raised again. This time her eyes were full of anger. "Get out of her, Mary! I did not give you permission to enter first!" The medium's voice had dropped an octave and she now spoke with a vaguely Italian accent.

"Who-who are you?" asked Albert Carnaby. "What have you done with my mother?"

"I am Alexander. Steward to the great Nero, emperor of Rome!"

"I'm surprised there's no fiddle music," observed Howard Carter laconically, and was hushed by Lady Ursula.

Delilah stifled a giggle.

"I'm sorry, Alexander. Please continue," said Lady Ursula, bowing her head in deference.

"Alexander" pulled back his lip into a snarl. "My master would never have permitted this insolence." He pinned his yellow gaze on Howard Carter, who met it with a single raised eyebrow.

It was Poppy's turn to stifle a giggle. Her fear was beginning to dissipate. *What a pantomime. I bet she's an out-of-work actress*, thought the young journalist, and started formulating draft intro paragraphs for her article, while trying to keep a straight face. She bit her lip and forced herself not to look at Delilah. That would be the end of them, she just knew it.

"There are only three spirits who wish to speak tonight as there is insufficient psychic energy in the room," said "Alexander". Lionel, Lady Ursula, and Sir James all shot accusing looks in Poppy's direction.

"The first is Mary Carnaby, who has already spoken." Madame Minette's head twitched to the left. "What's that Mary? All right. You may speak to your son. But if you dare speak out of turn again, you shall *not* return. Ever."

Madame Minette did the now familiar chin to the chest then flicked her head back. And lo and behold, Mary Carnaby returned with her gentle East Lothian burr. "Albert my boy. I do not have much time. Are you still there, Albert?"

"I'm here, mother," said Mr Carnaby.

"Good, good," said Mary. "I just want to ask – have you sold the Renoir yet?"

Mr Carnaby's finger twitched against Poppy's. "No mother. But I'm putting it up for auction next week. How did you know?"

Madame Minette smiled her chilling smile. "Spirits talk. The spirit of Pierre-Auguste asked me to ask you not to sell it yet. To wait for the next auction. Can you do that?"

"P-Pierre-Auguste? Pierre-Auguste Renoir?"

"Of course. What other Pierre-Auguste would I be talking about? Pierre-Auguste does not want you to sell the painting next week. He says you must wait until February. Is that clear?"

Poppy cast a furtive glance at Mr Carnaby's face. There was puzzlement but nothing to indicate the auctioneer did not believe he was talking to his mother. *Wasn't he one of the guests who had previously attended a séance? A true believer?*

"All right, mother. I'll do as you ask. You can tell – Pierre-Auguste – I'll hang onto his painting until February. But please, before you go, can you tell me if you've seen Ruthie? Can you ask her to come next time?"

Madame Minette gave her creepy smile. "I can ask but I cannot make her, Albert. I shall give her your love."

"Y-yes mother, p-please do," said Mr Carnaby, his voice cracking with emotion.

Poppy felt a surge of anger rise in her. *How dare this charlatan toy with this poor man's emotions? Ruthie must be dearly loved and missed.* She imagined for a moment stretching her hand over Albert Carnaby's and squeezing it for comfort. But she did not break the circle. She was already on thin ice with

Lady Ursula. However, it was patently obvious the medium was using information that would be easy enough to find out. Carnaby's was a world-renowned auction house. As long as there was advance notice of who would attend the séance – which there had been – it would be easy enough to find out which paintings were up for auction next month. Although, Poppy had to admit, Madame Minette had not had much notice. Hadn't Lady Jean Conan Doyle been scheduled to lead the circle? *Hmm*. But before Poppy could follow her next train of thought the medium bobbed her head down and up again and Alexander was back, only to announce, like a music hall master of ceremonies, that the next spirit who wished to speak was no less than the pharaoh queen Nefertiti herself.

*Drum roll please!*

Head down. Head up. "Who is it who summons me from my eternal sleep?" said Madame Minette in a haughty voice of indeterminable foreign accent.

Sir James cleared his throat. "It is I, your eminence, Sir James Maddox of Winterton Hall. We have spoken before, if you recall..."

The "queen" turned to look at the man seated to her left. "Ah, yes. At that séance in Giza. You wanted to know where I had been laid to rest."

"That's correct, your eminence, and you declined to tell me."

Nefertiti pulled back her lip into a snarl remarkably like that of Alexander's. *Limited range*, thought Poppy and suppressed a smirk.

"That was because I do not want to be disturbed." She flashed a look at Howard Carter. "And neither does my grandson, Tutankhamun. Be warned, king hunter, if you disturb his sleep you will be cursed. Do you hear me?"

Carter stifled a yawn.

"But you do not mind me having your mask, your eminence?" asked Sir James.

Nefertiti stuck her nose in the air, affecting a regal air. "I do not. The mask was never truly mine. It was made for me but never used by me. 'Tis not the one I am buried with."

Sir James cleared his throat again. "Good, good. That is a relief to hear, your eminence. Do you know that it is going to be sold at auction tomorrow night?"

Nefertiti nodded her assent.

"And do you have any preferences as to where it should go?"

*Oh please! Utterly transparent!*

The "queen" smiled, making her look just like Mary Carnaby. Or was it Alexander? Poppy was losing track.

"I do not. All I ask is that the highest bidder respect me and my station. I am Nefertiti, the most beautiful woman in the world. I do not want to be sold for a pittance."

Miss Philpott let out a loud snort. "Forgive me, oh queen, but do you perhaps have an acceptable figure in mind? If so, let Lady Jean know and she can write it down for us. I'm sure you know where to find her. Upstairs, turn left, third door on the right..."

"Oh, I'm sure that's not what the queen meant, is it your eminence?" said Sir James, staring intently into Madame Minette's eyes. "You did not mean monetary value, did you? Of course you didn't."

The "queen" met his gaze. "Of course I did not mean monetary value. My value is beyond money. I am the queen of the heavens, the consort of the sun. Who can put a price on me?" Nefertiti cocked her ear as if hearing something from afar. "Hark! Akhenaten is calling me. I must go."

Head down.

Poppy waited for the head to come up but nothing happened.

The guests' eyes flicked towards each other. *Is it over?*

"Is that it?" asked Miss Philpott. "Because if it is, I could do with another brandy. Anyone care to join me?"

"Hear hear," said Howard Carter and pulled his hands from the circle.

But as he did Madame Minette's head whipped up. "Poppy! Poppy Pie! Is that you?"

Poppy felt as though someone had poured a jug of ice water down her back.

There was only one person who had ever called her Poppy Pie. But no, it couldn't be. This whole thing was a hoax. A cruel hoax. She refused to play along.

Madame Minette spoke with a Northumbrian accent. "It's me, Christopher. Are you there, Poppy Pie?"

Poppy had had enough. She stood up, overturning her chair with a clatter, and pointed at the medium. "You're not going to fool me Madame Minette, or whatever you call yourself." Then, with eleven pairs of astonished eyes following her, she stormed towards the door.

"Don't go Poppy Pie! I just wanted to say I'm sorry about the magazines. I never meant to get you into trouble."

Poppy stopped in her tracks. *The magazines? The Strand magazines? How does she know about them? There's no way she could know...* Poppy felt suddenly faint. She reached out her hand to steady herself on the door frame.

"Poppy, are you all right?" It was Delilah, standing beside her, her arm around her waist.

Poppy breathed deeply, calming herself, then gave Delilah a grateful squeeze. "I'll be fine. Thank you." She looked around the room, taking in the shocked and concerned looks. "I'm sorry

I spoilt the fun, everyone. I know it's just a game. But I think what that woman is doing is cruel. And I don't want to be a part of it. Good night."

And with that, she left the room.

# CHAPTER 10

The house was still dark when Poppy buttoned up her coat, pulled on her boots, and slipped out into the icy morning air. The stable yard, where the afternoon before the young boy had had his accident, was crisp with frost. So she trod carefully over the sparkling cobbles, accompanied by the snicker and stomp of horses still snug in their stalls. She rounded the wing of the house and onto the crunchy gravel of the circular drive. To the left was the sweep of stairs leading up to the grand entrance of Winterton Hall, and to her right the stark gardens, saved from winter austerity by splashes of evergreen. And there, with its leylandii walls, was the maze she had noticed on arrival yesterday. On either side of the entrance were two matched Grecian urns, cemented to the top of fluted pedestals. She wondered if the urns were originals.

She wasn't sure what drew her to the maze, but during the long sleepless night as she tossed and turned, haunted by her brother's face and her outrage at the audacity of the medium, Madame Minette, it kept coming to mind. Perhaps because it was a puzzle, its convolutions a physical manifestation of her tumultuous thoughts.

She had left the séance last night and gone straight to bed. She'd thought about popping in to see Daniel and Rollo in the drawing room, but decided not to. She didn't feel like being lectured by Rollo about not seeing the job through. Delilah could explain what happened. No doubt Lionel would rub it in, but he always did. She could handle Lionel.

The bed had been less than comfortable. And when the fire in the hearth had burned itself out, the room, with its aged and cracked Georgian window frames, became as icy as a tomb. She was grateful for the warming pan one of the Winterton maids brought for her, but she still had to get up in the middle of the night to retrieve her dressing gown from the back of the door and climb back into bed wrapped in an extra layer. And oh, how she wished she'd packed bedsocks!

She looked up at the pre-dawn sky, hoping to find some kind of guiding light to lead her through the maze. But the moon had slipped behind a cloud and the sun had not yet risen. She would just have to find her way by instinct.

The evergreen walls sparkled with frost-encrusted spider webs, like little strings of Christmas fairy lights. That reminded her: when she got back to Chelsea she should put up Aunt Dot's Christmas tree. It was already well into Advent but the decorations hadn't gone up yet. Poppy loved Christmas in Chelsea. Back home in Morpeth her parents observed the season the way they observed everything else: with subdued moderation. But Aunt Dot – oh my! – Poppy had been gobsmacked when she came home from work last December to find the house transformed into something from *The Nutcracker*. One of Aunt Dot's theatre friends – a set designer from the Old Vic – had helped her do it. Poppy wondered if Carlos would be available this year. Probably not, as Dot and Grace were off on the Orient Express. Ah well, she'd give it a go herself when she got home. Perhaps Delilah would help her. Or Daniel...

Last year, after a string of parties at Aunt Dot's in the run-up to the big day, she had gone to Daniel's house after church to spend the afternoon with him and his family. It had been a tense time with Maggie, his sister, but the joyful exuberance of the two children eased it. This year there had been no invitation.

Although there were still two weeks to go, she doubted one would come. She didn't hold it against Daniel – she knew things were difficult with Maggie's plans to move to South Africa, and it might possibly be the last Christmas he would spend with his children for a while. The last thing he needed was to worry about how his on-off sweetheart was getting on with his sister.

*On-off sweetheart.* Poppy approached a crossroads in the maze. Who would have thought when she agreed to go out to dinner with him that very first time, back in the summer of 1920, that things would become so complicated. *Which way? Left or right?* Poppy looked up and saw that the moon had come out from behind the cloud and the morning star sparkled. She turned right towards the star.

So where would she spend Christmas? Perhaps if she let it be known she was on her own someone would invite her round. Delilah's father would be coming over from Malta, and they were going to a big shindig at his Uncle Elmo's house. Perhaps Poppy could tag along. And there was always Marjorie who lived around the block in Chelsea. Perhaps she could spend it with her and her son, Oscar. She wasn't sure what Rollo was doing either. Ike Garfield's wife, Doreen, had hosted something last year for the *Globe* staff on Christmas Eve, but she would have a full house with family coming over from Trinidad this year. *Never mind, if worst comes to worst, I can just have a quiet day at home…*

Snap! There was a short, sharp crack; as if someone had stepped on a twig. Poppy froze. She looked behind her: there was no one there. She listened again and thought she heard someone breathing behind the hedge wall on her left. "Hello? Is there anyone there?"

Silence. Poppy's heart began to thump. She hurried on, turned left, turned right, and then came face to face with a dead end. She turned around, and as she did, saw a shadowy form standing in the entrance to the cul de sac.

"Oh! You gave me a fright!" said Poppy, squaring up to the fellow maze traverser. But the figure did not speak. Poppy took a small step backwards. The shadow, which Poppy could now see had the silhouette of a man in a trench coat and fedora hat, took a step forward. She could hear him breathing, and see a cloud of white vapour form in the air between them. Poppy clenched her gloved hands, wishing she had some kind of weapon – an umbrella or walking stick.

"I – I'm meeting someone. He should be here any minute." Silence.

"I'm here Daniel!" she called. She cocked her head but didn't hear anything. "Ah! There he is! Well I think I'll go meet him. Won't be long until breakfast." Poppy turned her body sideways, intending to slip between the shadow and the hedge. "If you'll excuse me..."

The shadow opened his arms and straddled the gap, cutting off any opportunity of escape.

What the heck was he trying to do? Was he trying to intimidate her? Poppy's fear was washed away on a surge of anger. "Look, I'm not in the mood for silly games. Either introduce yourself or move on." Poppy took a step towards him, hoping to get a better look at the face under the fedora hat, but as she did he turned and walked away.

Incensed, Poppy ran to the gap in the hedge, intending to demand the stranger stop and reveal himself. But then the red mist lifted and she stopped in her tracks. *Be grateful he's gone Poppy. Let him go.* Fear settled on her again. *What if he comes back?*

Poppy pressed herself as close to the hedge as she could and peered around the corner – to the left and right. There was no one there. She listened intently but could not detect footfall.

*Has he gone? Oh Lord, I hope so.* She no longer wanted to get to the centre of the maze. She just wanted to get out – safely. But which way should she go? In her fright she'd lost her bearings; she was like Ariadne without her golden thread. She closed her eyes and took a few calming breaths. *Dear God, I know I'm being silly, but please help me. I just want to get out of here.*

After a few moments she felt calmer, more centred, and began to recall the sequence of left and right turns she'd memorized on her way in. Then, with a mental flip, she conceptualized it all in reverse and, slowly but surely, worked her way back to the Grecian urns. She stopped and took in the sweep of lawn in front of Winterton Hall, sparkling with frost in the moonlight. There was no one there. She let out a long sigh of relief. Had she just imagined the shadowy figure in the maze? It was dark. She was still a bit on edge after the séance. She hadn't had much sleep… had she allowed her imagination to run away with her? She chuckled out loud, her voice brittle in the freezing air.

But her laughter caught in her throat. On the frosty expanse there were three sets of footprints. Two sets came from the direction of the stables. One of them, she was sure, was hers. But the other… bigger, deeper; were they the footprints of the man? They hadn't been there when she arrived. Was this evidence he – whoever he was – had intentionally followed her?

She was relieved to see the stranger's footprints, leaving the maze, headed off in the opposite direction, towards the east wing of the house. Poppy peered through the darkness, scanning her limited field of vision for anything that moved. There was nothing. *I should get inside before he comes back.* She ran as fast as she could towards the stable yard, slipping and sliding as she reached the frosty cobbles. Then she lost her footing completely and fell, slap bang onto her bottom.

"Good heavens! Are you all right?" A man's voice. A shadow lumbering towards her. Poppy gathered herself to scream but then stopped as she recognized the voice. "D – Daniel?"

"Poppy! Are you hurt?" He was kneeling beside her, his gloved hands grasping her shoulders.

"Oh Daniel!" she cried and opened her arms and thrust herself into his chest.

"Steady on! Whatever's the matter? Did you hurt yourself?" he asked, pulling her more tightly into his embrace.

Poppy did a mental checklist of her body parts. Nothing seemed out of kilter, although through the thick cushioning of her winter coat she could feel a little pain in her right buttock. Best she not mention that. "No, I think I'm all right. I just had a bit of a scare, that's all."

And then she told him all about the spooky stranger in the maze as he helped her to her feet. "He *what*?" Poppy could feel Daniel tense with rage.

"He was probably just joking, but I didn't find it very funny."

"I don't blame you," he growled. "Come on, let's get you inside; then we'll find out who it was."

Poppy felt safe. Very safe. What could possibly happen when she had Daniel with her? And then her stomach grumbled: loudly and unashamedly. "All right," she said, "but do you mind if we do it after breakfast? I can't sleuth very well on an empty stomach."

Daniel chuckled as he picked up her hat which had fallen to the cobbles, placing it firmly back on her head. Then he kissed her nose. "Oh, you are a funny bunny, Miss Denby," he whispered, his lips just a fraction away from hers. Poppy glowed.

# CHAPTER 11

"All right chaps, which of you silly kippers thinks it's funny to scare a lady before breakfast?" Delilah stood in the doorway of the dining room, her cat-like eyes ranging over the other guests as they lined up for the breakfast buffet.

"Delilah, shhh. I wanted to find out who did it without them knowing," whispered Poppy behind her.

"Whoops! Sorry Popsicle," whispered Delilah over her shoulder. Then at full voice: "I heard someone say there's no coffee left! You scared the life out of me!"

The assembled guests gave Delilah curious looks, not quite sure what she was getting at, although Fox Flinton gave a supportive chuckle.

"Fear not. There's plenty coffee in the pot, Miss Marconi," said Sir James, as he accepted a cup from Grimes, the butler, and took it to his seat at the table.

"Good save, Delilah," whispered Daniel from behind Poppy. Then added, for the room's benefit: "Speaking of kippers, shimmy along ladies, I'm famished." This elicited heartier laughter from the guests.

"The kippers are top notch, Danny Boy," said Rollo, already seated with a plate piled high with a sample of everything on offer. Poppy was always amazed at how much food went into her editor's small body.

"Then that's what I'll have! With some scrambled egg and toast. After you ladies," said Daniel, gesturing for Delilah and Poppy to precede him to the serving table.

Delilah, recovered from her near faux pas, asked for a poached egg, bacon, grilled tomato, and toast. And of course coffee. Black. No sugar. "I'm sweet enough."

Poppy opted for a couple of Cumberland sausages, a fried egg (sunny-side up), some mushrooms, tomato, and toast. "Oh, and a glass of orange juice please."

"The orange juice is on the table, madam," answered Grimes in a tone as stiff as his starched collar. Poppy imagined him for a moment wearing a trench coat and a fedora. *Hmmm, possibly. But why would he bother?*

"Kippers please, Grimes!" ordered Daniel.

Poppy set aside her thoughts of the butler and the maze and moved on, giving Daniel room to pile up his plate. She took a vacant seat next to Miss Philpott. The American woman was tucking into a cheese omelette, liberally sprinkled with parsley.

"Morning Miz Denby. They are pulling out all the stops, aren't they? It's a breakfast worthy of the Ritz!"

"It is that," said Poppy, nodding her thanks to the footman, who pushed her chair in and handed her a linen napkin.

"Must be costing them a fortune." Miss Philpott nodded affirmatively to a top-up of coffee.

"Looks like they can afford it," observed Poppy, stabbing a dollop of butter and spreading it on her toast.

Miss Philpott lowered her voice and leaned in to Poppy. "Appearances can be deceptive, Miz Denby. Word is the Maddoxes are in the hock. Overextended themselves on all of Sir James' foreign expeditions. He has bankrolled half a dozen digs in the last decade. Problem is, it was never his bank to roll."

"Oh," said Poppy, casting a furtive glance at her host, hoping he hadn't heard anything. Sir James was deep in conversation with Yasmin Reece-Lansdale and her brother, Faizal. By the body language of the two men, it was not an amiable discussion.

Yasmin, as usual, in her white silk blouse, looked as cool as a cucumber, but the heightened colour on Sir James's neck and Faizal's flared nostrils suggested otherwise. Miss El Farouk had not yet come down for breakfast.

"Yes," continued Miss Philpott. "The money came from Lady Ursula's side. And by all accounts she's finally put her foot down and said he needs to start clawing some of it back. Hence the auction. If it goes well, I think we might see more of Maddox's collection coming on the market."

Poppy's newshound nose twitched. "Oh really? And does the Metropolitan Museum have its eye on anything in particular?"

Miss Philpott chuckled and tapped the side of her nose. "It might, it very much might. Actually, it's not just Sir James' collection we have our eye on. We're also here for the auction next week at Carnaby's, although that might now be scuppered."

"And why's that?" asked Poppy, cutting into her yolk and watching the yellow goo spread over the white egg.

"Because the Renoir we were hoping to bid for might not be on the bill any more. Thanks to the artist's untimely intervention last night..."

Miss Philpott paused to fork a portion of omelette into her mouth. Poppy noticed that unlike the Americans she'd met in New York earlier in the year, Miss Philpott ate the British way – with the fork in her left hand. It was oddly comforting, as Poppy had been bizarrely on edge whenever she ate in the States. Poppy cut into her sausage and dipped it into the yolk, waiting for Miss Philpott to finish her comment.

"You were there for that, weren't you? The message from Renoir?"

Poppy said she was. Then: "I'm sorry about storming out like that. I hope I didn't ruin your evening."

Miss Philpott looked at her curiously from behind her tortoiseshell spectacles. "Not at all, Miz Denby. It poured a necessary bucket of cold water over the whole silly affair. I don't blame you for it one bit. These charlatans toy with people's emotions so. It's not right."

Poppy put down her fork. "So you also think they're charlatans."

"Of course!" said Miss Philpott, another chunk of omelette poised on her fork. "I hope you've worked out by now that the entire event was put on to try to inflate the bids on the Nefertiti mask?"

"I surmised as much."

"But the Renoir intervention — I can't figure out yet what benefit it will be to the Maddoxes to delay the auction. As far as I know, it's not theirs. And they've never bid for an Impressionist before. Their interest is Classical."

Poppy hadn't thought about the motives for the "Renoir intervention" — other than to terrorize poor Mr Carnaby, who seemed to be in thrall to the "spirits" and an easy target for manipulation — but it was an intriguing thought. This story was getting better and better. She quickly scanned the room, looking for Lionel Saunders. Ah, there he was, looking a bit worse for wear, hunched over and nibbling on a slice of toast like a rodent. His partner in crime, Harry Gibson, was nowhere to be seen.

"Have you mentioned the Renoir to Mr Saunders from the *Courier*?" asked Poppy as casually as she could.

Miss Philpott smiled knowingly. "I haven't. He doesn't think I'm worth talking to. And — if it will help you — I'll ask my colleague, Dr Davies, not to mention it to him either."

Poppy took a sip of orange juice and put down the glass. "That's very kind of you, Miss Philpott. But while I don't want to look a gift horse in the mouth, may I ask why you would like to help me?"

Miss Philpott snorted with laughter, sounding very much like one of the horses in the stables outside. "Let's just say, Miz Denby, I like to see a sister getting ahead. I was fascinated to read all about your escapades in New York last spring and more than a little happy to see certain people get their comeuppance. Some people think that just because they make a donation to the museum they can act like lord or lady muck – as you Brits so charmingly put it – but you well and truly put them in their place. So, let's just say this is my way of saying thanks. Is that acceptable to you?"

Poppy smiled warmly at Miss Philpott. "Well, thank *you*. I appreciate it. Will you be staying in London before the Carnaby's auction? Or won't you be going now? It would be good to have a proper interview about all this."

Miss Philpott greeted her colleague, Dr Davies, as he took the seat next to her.

"Morning ladies."

"Ah, Jonathan, I'll fill you in on the details later, but I am just setting up an interview with Miz Denby for later this week. Yes, we'll be travelling up to London tomorrow morning. We're staying at the Hotel Russell, near the British Museum. Do you know it?"

Poppy said she did and arranged to meet Miss Philpott and Dr Davies on Tuesday. She knew she would be in the office all day on Monday typing up articles from the weekend. The Renoir was an interesting story, but it would be a separate piece from the Cairo Brief. She didn't want to muddy the waters too much. Readers would be expecting all things Egyptian, not an article on a recently deceased modern Impressionist.

Poppy was just clearing her plate of the last morsels when Sir Arthur Conan Doyle arrived. He looked tired and worried. Sir James rose to meet him. "Everything all right, Arthur?"

"I'm afraid not, James. Jean is no better. She hardly slept a wink. I'm going to take her home. I took the liberty to telephone our physician in Harley Street, if that's all right. He's going to make a house call. I'm dreadfully sorry to put a damper on your weekend, old boy. Jean and I were both looking forward to it tremendously – particularly the séance. I'm just grateful you were able to get a replacement at such short notice."

Sir James patted Conan Doyle's shoulder. "These things happen, Arthur. What do you think's caused the gastritis?" He looked around at the rest of the guests. "Nothing contagious, I hope?"

Conan Doyle lowered his chin to his chest and shook his head slowly from side to side. "I doubt it. Seems more like something she ingested. But food poisoning would normally have passed by now… this looks like it might be something else…"

Whatever the "something else" might have been, Conan Doyle did not speculate out loud. Sir James said he'd get a footman to help Sir Arthur bring Lady Jean down and that he would get his chauffeur to drive them back to London. Apparently the Conan Doyles had arrived by taxi from the station the day before.

Sir Arthur then left with a chorus of get-well wishes from the guests. However, something Conan Doyle had said sparked Poppy's interest. Last night she had wondered how on earth Madame Minette had managed to get advance information on all the guests at such short notice – that is, if her assumption were true that that's how the con was set up. But what if it was the Maddoxes' intention all along to bring Madame Minette in? It was, after all, highly convenient that she just happened to be in the neighbourhood. The Conan Doyles, of course, were the main draw card for the press. Sir James obviously knew that or he wouldn't have put it in the press release. Would they have been quite as keen to come if the famous author and his wife were not going to be here? *Probably not.* But if she was correct, and Madame Minette was the chosen medium all along, what did that mean about Lady Jean Conan Doyle's sudden "illness"? No one had actually seen her. Was she really ill? Or were the Conan Doyles in on the whole thing? Poppy shook her head. No, surely not. Sir Arthur really did look worried. *He's an author, not an actor. That didn't look put on.* Poppy glanced over at Rollo, who was going up to the serving table for seconds. When he'd finally finished she would corner him and share her suspicions.

Just then, the doorbell rang, echoing through the grand entrance hall beyond the breakfast room. "Are we expecting anyone?" asked Sir James.

"It might be the police, m'lord," said Grimes, indicating that a footman should take his place at the serving table. "About the accident yesterday. If you recall, I telephoned them after Mrs Reynolds told us that the hospital would be legally required to report any gunshot wounds."

Sir James nodded. "Yes, of course." He stood. "If you'll excuse me ladies and gentlemen, I'll just attend to this. Please feel free to take your time or finish as you please. The clay pigeon shoot will begin at eleven. Anyone who wants to join in should meet in the stable yard." And with that, he and Grimes left the room.

Rollo piped up: "Don't you think you should go too, Danny Boy? You took the lad to the hospital. No doubt the police would like to talk to you as well..."

Daniel took a sip of coffee. "I'm sure they'll call me if they need me, Rollo."

Rollo made a curious grunting noise and narrowed his eyes. Daniel put down his cup. "Of course you're right. I'll see if they need me."

He got up, winked at Poppy, and left before Lionel Saunders had a chance to react. The man from the *Courier* did not look well pleased. Poppy stifled a chuckle.

Rollo then declared: "Well, it looks like my eyes are bigger than my stomach. I won't be having seconds after all, my good man. Miz Denby, are you finished?"

"I am, yes."

"Then perhaps you'd care to join me for some fresh air..."

After working with him for eighteen months Poppy knew how her boss operated. This was not a request. "Of course, I'll just get my hat and coat."

## CHAPTER 12

On her way back down from her bedroom, Poppy paused at the closed library door, behind which the policeman was speaking with Sir James and other witnesses. She made a show of winding and rewinding her woollen scarf, while trying, unsuccessfully, to tune in to the low murmur of voices.

"You ready, Miz Denby?" Rollo received his bowler hat with thanks from the footman who had retrieved it from the hall cloakroom.

Poppy realized she had missed a trick.

"I'll just be a tick," she said to Rollo, then turned her attention to the footman. "Excuse me, could you show me where you keep the gentlemen's outdoor wear?"

If the footman thought the request curious, he hid it well. "Certainly, madam, it's in here."

He gestured to a door next to a statue of the Reclining Ariadne. *She from the maze fame*, Poppy noted. *Oh, the delicious irony! Lead me, Ariadne, with your golden thread...*

The footman opened the door and Poppy stepped into a deep closet, lined on either side by racks of hanging coats, hats, and winter boots.

"Golly, there are a lot of them," she observed. "How do you know whose is whose? You must need an awfully good memory to keep track of them all."

The footman's face lit up with pride. "I do indeed, madam. It's quite a job. And Mr Grimes does not give it to just anyone."

"I'm sure he doesn't." Poppy smiled at the servant, noting that he was around the same age as she. "It really is a remarkable gift! Would you be able to tell me, for instance, which guests wear which hats? Who, for instance, wears a fedora?"

The footman pulled back his shoulders and recited a list of names: "Well, there's Sir James, of course, then of the guests: Mr Carnaby, Dr Osman, Dr Mortimer, and the two gentlemen from the *Courier.*"

"That is very impressive indeed. What do the other gentlemen wear?"

"Well, Mr Rolandson, as you know, wears a bowler, as does Mr Rokeby and Sir Arthur Conan Doyle. Dr Davies wears a derby – which, I believe, is the American version of the bowler – and Mr Carter and the two German gentlemen all wear homburgs. Then there's Mr Flinton –" He paused, allowing the slightest of smiles to grace his lips under his moustache: "he wears a boater – in all weather."

Poppy was mentally filing this all away. Unfortunately, there were quite a few fedora wearers in the entourage, but at least she had eliminated some of the men from her enquiry. Apart from one... "And Mr Grimes? What does Mr Grimes wear?"

The footman cocked his head slightly, but then instantly regained his composure. "Mr Grimes does not keep his hat in this cloakroom. He uses the servants' entrance – which has its own cloakroom – downstairs."

"Ah, of course," said Poppy. "How silly of me. Well thank you... er... Mr..."

"Wallace. Just Wallace."

Poppy smiled. "Thank you, *Mister* Wallace."

The slight smile returned. "You're most welcome, Miss Denby."

"Ahem." It was Rollo, peeking his head into the cloakroom.

"If you've finished playing sardines, Miz Denby, perhaps you would care to join me for that walk."

She flashed a smile at the footman and then turned to join her editor. "Right away, Mr Rolandson."

"So what was all that about?" Rollo and Poppy, wrapped up warmly against the brisk winter air, descended the grand steps of the main entrance just as the Rolls – presumably carrying Sir Arthur and the stricken Lady Jean – drove off down the drive.

"I do hope she's going to be all right," observed Poppy.

"Yes, it does seem rather convenient, doesn't it? Lady Jean falling ill like that and that harpie with the hennaed hair taking over at such short notice."

"You saw her?"

Rollo shook his head. "No, but Delilah gave me a full and accurate description. That girl would make an excellent journalist if she ever chose to give up the greasepaint. She's very observant. Lacking in discretion – to say the least – but observant. She also told me about your little party trick."

Poppy's stomach tightened. He didn't sound very pleased.

"Well you see –"

Rollo raised his gloved hand. "In a moment. First I want to hear about the hat malarkey. What are you up to, Poppy?"

Poppy looked out at the expanse of lawn, towards the maze. The sun was now well up and had melted the top layer of frost from the grass. The footprints – evidence of her stalking shadow – were gone. Nonetheless, she told Rollo about her pre-dawn encounter with the man in the fedora hat.

Rollo let out a low growl. "Whoever it is, deserves a good belting."

"That's what Daniel says too."

"So who do you think it was?"

Poppy listed the fedora wearers again: Sir James, Lionel Saunders, Harry Gibson, Albert Carnaby, Faizal Osman, and Dr Giles Mortimer.

"Hmmm," said Rollo. "And you're sure it was a fedora?"

"Quite sure. It has a very distinct silhouette. The coat could have been anything, if I'm honest – although I did think it might be a trench coat – but the hat was definitely a fedora."

Rollo steered them past the maze and down a gravel pathway, leading to a walled orchard where bare branches clawed over the dry stone wall like witches' fingers.

"So it was a man. In a coat and a fedora. Are you sure it was a man?"

"You mean it could have been a woman in men's clothing?" Poppy thought for a moment, allowing the memory to form more clearly in her mind. "No. It was definitely a man. It was the way he stood, the way he held himself..."

"How tall?"

"Taller than me. I'm five-five."

"Then every man here except me. Although Lionel's not much above five-five. What about bulk. Was he fat, slim…?"

"In between. He didn't fill the entire gap in the hedge. I could have still squeezed past if he'd let me."

"So probably not Mortimer or Sir James. They're obviously bulky. That leaves the *Courier* lads – although possibly not Lionel – Carnaby, and Faizal. The question is, why?"

Rollo pushed open the wooden gate to the orchard, its hinges protesting at the unexpected intrusion, and stepped aside to let Poppy through. Inside, apple, pear, and plum trees huddled together as if for warmth. The remnants of autumn carpeted the copse: unraked foliage and rotting fruit, while a few die-hard leaves still clung to the tips of the branches above. Poppy and Rollo followed a crazy-paving footpath until they came to a wrought-iron bench that was crying out for a lick of paint.

"Shall we?"

Poppy sat, wincing slightly at the pain in her rear-end from the fall earlier. She was going to have a very large bruise there.

"So why do you think, Poppy?"

Poppy let out a long sigh, her breath clouding in the freezing air. "Perhaps they were trying to scare me. Or intimidate me. But why I don't know. I was already a bit on edge from the séance…"

Rollo raised a shaggy red eyebrow.

"Yes, yes, I'll get to that – so maybe they wanted to push me a bit more."

"They? I thought there was only one person."

"There was. In the maze. But last night I felt as if there was some collusion between Madame Minette and one, or both, of the Maddoxes."

Rollo pressed a crab-apple leaf between the palms of his gloved hands. When he opened them again, the leaf had crumbled. He brushed his gloves together to dispose of the remains. "Well, that goes without saying. It was obviously a set-up. Delilah told me about the attempts to influence the bid on the Nefertiti mask."

"Did she tell you about the Renoir?"

"Only that the great man sent a message along. Why? Is there something else?"

Poppy told him what Jennifer Philpott had told her at breakfast.

"Hmmm, very interesting. Yes, definitely follow up on that, Poppy. So, quite clearly the medium had been briefed to put pressure on Albert Carnaby. Poor blighter. I went to his wife's funeral, you know. It was about three years ago. The story the family put out was accidental death. A fall from a bridge. But everyone knew it was suicide. Albert blamed himself. He's never got over it."

"Was her name Ruthie?"

"Yes. It was all over the papers. We covered it too. So, easy enough for a medium – or someone feeding the medium information – to find out. Same with the Renoir. Albert was photographed in front of it earlier in the year when you and I were over in New York. In fact, I think Daniel took the shot. We'll have to check the jazz file when we get back to the office, but I think it was mentioned there that it would be put up for auction before Christmas."

Poppy nodded. *Yes, that rang a bell.* "So that explains the first two communications from the spirit realm, but what about the one to me? I assume Delilah has told you the medium impersonated my brother?"

"She did, yes. And that you got upset and stormed out."

Poppy bit her lip. "Yes I did. And I'm sorry. I should have stayed to the end of the séance so I could write about the whole thing."

"Yes, you should have." Rollo hugged himself and rubbed his arms with his sheepskin gloves. "Brrrrr. It's cold enough to freeze the hair off a pig's… back."

Poppy smiled to herself.

"Should we get moving again?"

Poppy looked at him. *Was that it? Was that as far as the reprimand was going to go?*

As if reading her mind, he added: "But don't do it again, Miz Denby. All right?"

"All right," she agreed, relieved. "I would have stayed, I'm sure, but it's just that my brother is a touchy subject."

"Which is probably why they raised it. They wanted to spook you."

"But how would they know? It wasn't in the papers or anything."

"Not in London, perhaps, but might it have been in the local news in Mowpeth?"

"Morpeth," she corrected. "Yes, I think it was. But that was six years ago now."

"It would still be in the archive though. And there'd be copies at the local library." Rollo got up and indicated they should carry on walking. Poppy gingerly got to her feet.

"You all right, Poppy? You look like you've got a sore... hip." Rollo grinned.

"Yes, I slipped on the cobbles this morning and hurt it. My hip. I hurt my hip."

"Do you need to see a doctor?"

"No. It's just a bit bruised. I'll be fine."

The pair of journalists continued their circuit of the orchard, heading back towards the gate. Poppy agreed that her brother's death would have been in the local news. "But they must have gone to an awful lot of trouble to get it. They would either have had to go up there themselves or paid someone to do it for them. But why would they bother? And who are 'they'? The Maddoxes? Madame Minette? This fella who tried to scare the heebie-jeebies out of me? Perhaps they want to scare me off the story?"

"Or," said Rollo, as they reached the gate, "perhaps they want to scare you *onto* the story."

Poppy stopped in her tracks. "Why on earth would they want to do that?"

"You've got a reputation, Poppy. You dig until you get to the bottom."

He unlatched the gate and ushered her through.

"You mean they *want* me to investigate? Why?"

Rollo shrugged. "Perhaps they just want publicity. The more publicity there is around the sale of this mask, the more attention they'll get for any future auctions. If Jennifer Philpott is correct, and more of the Maddox collection is going to come onto the market, then what better way to get people interested than to capture the attention of one of London's leading reporters."

"But they already had our attention! We're here, aren't we? And the *Courier* boys."

Rollo headed back up towards the house. Poppy kept pace with him.

"That's true," he conceded, "but perhaps they wanted to ensure you *remained* interested after this weekend – that you might come to the next and the next and the next. And if your brother was speaking to you from beyond the grave, that might tempt you to come."

Poppy felt her anger surge. "Well they're wrong! I'm not tempted. I'm angry. I'm angry that they have tried to use something so personal against me. But what I can't figure out is how they knew…"

"It was in the papers."

"His death was, yes, but not the magazines. There was nothing in the papers about the magazines. Why would there be? That was personal. No one else knew about that."

Rollo was looking at her curiously. "Whatever are you talking about, Poppy? What magazines?"

"Didn't Delilah tell you?"

"No."

Poppy sighed and told Rollo the story of her brother's detective story magazines that he kept under his mattress and how she had tried to stop her mother from finding them. "So you see, no one would have known about that. Unless my mother has told someone. But why would she? She's never even spoken to me about it."

The gravel of the path merged with the gravel of the driveway in front of the main house steps. The door opened and a uniformed police constable appeared alongside Mr Grimes.

"Yes, it's a mystery," agreed Rollo, "but that's what you specialize in Poppy. I suggest you get to the bottom of it. And I suggest your first port of call should be that medium. Perhaps you can pay her a visit this afternoon after the shoot. There's free time before the auction this evening. Take Danny Boy with you."

The police constable raised his hat as he passed them halfway down the steps.

"Sir, madam."

Rollo raised his hat in return. "Ah, good morning, Constable, might I have a word..."

"Of course, sir, what can I do for you?"

# CHAPTER 13

Poppy appraised herself in the mirror, turning to the left and right to see how she might look in her new trouser suit. Poppy had never dared try the new fashion of trousers for women before, but Delilah had assured her they were still perfectly feminine and completely appropriate for a shooting weekend. The trousers were in a jodhpur style, fitted at the calves but then widening above the knee to be loose fitting – even baggy – around the thighs. Under the matching jacket with brown suede trim she wore a white blouse with a flouncy cravat at the neck. It was finished off with a tweed sports hat in a trilby style, with a small pheasant feather tucked into a brown velvet band. Delilah told her she could wear the outfit for shooting, riding or rambling in the Alps. Poppy had no intention of ever going riding but a ramble in the Alps sounded rather fun. Although it was frightfully far… and could one actually *ramble* in the Alps…? Perhaps she should start with the Lake District. She smoothed the jacket over her derriere and resisted the urge to pull down her trousers and have one more look at the rather impressive bruise ripening on her right buttock. Instead she checked her watch: a quarter past ten. Yes, there would be time to do what she needed to do before the shoot.

Poppy slipped down the back stairs – where she'd observed the servants coming up and down last night – and found her way to the serving level of Winterton Hall. She had been relieved to see Mr Grimes still upstairs, not yet dressed for outdoors. Hopefully she'd be able to do what she needed to do before he came down to get his hat and coat for the eleven o'clock shoot. As quickly and unobtrusively as possible, she worked her way to where she assumed the back door would be, and after a few minutes, one wrong turn, and a quick duck into a doorway to avoid a chambermaid, she found what she was looking for: the servants' cloakroom. She slipped inside and was met with a smaller version of the room upstairs. There were about a dozen coats and hats: bowlers, flat caps, and one rather posh-looking fedora. The fedora was not really a working man's hat, but if anyone would have one, it would be the butler of a fine country estate. And there it was. A black one on the hook above a black trench coat. Could this be the attire of the morning stalker? Poppy had no real way of knowing, but it did, very firmly, place Mr Grimes on her list of suspects.

Her suspicions confirmed, Poppy turned to leave. On a whim she stopped and thrust her hands into the trench coat pockets. She felt a handkerchief, a cigarette case, and some loose change in one and in the other – *oh goodness, what is that?* – a metal cylinder. Poppy looked over her shoulder. *Good heavens, girl, what are you doing? If anyone comes in they'll assume you're stealing...* But she couldn't resist the temptation and pulled the cylinder out to have a look. She caught her breath: it was a shotgun shell. What was a shotgun shell doing in Mr Grimes' pocket? She appraised it quickly, not knowing much about weaponry and ammunition, memorizing as much as she could in order to describe it to Daniel, before slipping it back into the pocket. Suddenly, she heard voices approaching the closet. It was too late to leave without being noticed so she burrowed into the corner furthest from the door and pulled an overcoat over her.

"You got the port ready, Wallace?"

"Yes, Mr Grimes."

"Good lad. And don't forget some of the ladies might want sherry."

"I've got that ready too, Mr Grimes."

Poppy heard the men shrugging into coats, praying they wouldn't notice her. They didn't. The men left, the door closed, and Poppy let out an almighty sigh of relief.

The rest of the guests were already gathered in the courtyard by the time Poppy joined them, chattering and smoking in companionable clusters. The intrepid sleuth had had to take a convoluted route to avoid detection on her journey back from the bowels of the building, but she was not late – Sir James had not yet called the gathering to order. Tweed suits were in abundance – including the women – but only Poppy, Delilah, and Yasmin Reece-Lansdale dared to wear trousers. The older ladies – Lady Ursula, Marjorie Reynolds, and Jennifer Philpott – all wore long skirts under their tweed jackets, and Kamela El Farouk was not there. Poppy wondered why but then reminded herself that the shoot was optional. In fact, if it had been a hunt for live game, Poppy would not have joined in either. Thankfully, the use of captive birds had been outlawed back in the summer of 1921. Wild birds could still be hunted, but that was trickier to organize in the winter months, so many of the country estates were now offering clay shooting as an off-season alternative.

Poppy joined Delilah, Marjorie, Faizal, and Yasmin. Daniel was busy with his camera taking un-posed photographs: she waved, and he waved back. Rollo was in a jovial conversation with his fellow Americans – sharing gossip about New York society folk and celebrating the World Series, which had featured two local teams. The German duo were sharing cigarettes with Carter and Mortimer, while Lionel Saunders appeared to be interviewing Albert Carnaby. Poppy noted that Harry Gibson, the photographer, was absent.

"Oh Poppy, you look spiffing, doesn't she?" Delilah declared, appraising her friend from head to foot. "I told you it would suit you, didn't I?" She then went on to explain to Marjorie and Yasmin exactly where she had suggested Poppy buy her new outfit and then to interrogate the two women as to the provenance of their own. Faizal drew on his cigarette and glanced over at the group of German and British archaeologists. Poppy wondered if he would hive off when he had the chance.

However, he stuck with the ladies, and when he had an opportunity said: "Mrs Reynolds, would you mind if I walk with you to the shoot? I have something I would like to discuss with you. Is that all right?"

"Of course, Dr Osman," replied Marjorie, her tone pleasant but professional.

Sir James, with Lady Ursula and Mr Grimes at his shoulder, called them all to order. He explained that they would be walking about half a mile to a field where the shoot had been set up. If anyone felt unable to walk, transport could be arranged. He asked for a show of hands as to who wanted a lift. Only Lionel Saunders' hand went up.

Rollo's ribbing of "Come on Saunders, man up!" was met with a roar of laughter from the German and British groups. Lionel's hand went down.

"Well Saunders, if you change your mind – or any of you – Lady Ursula and Grimes will be bringing the sandwiches, port, and sherry in the motor."

"Thank heavens for that!" declared Rollo. "We Americans can't shoot on an empty stomach!"

Sir James raised his hat – a deerstalker – and replied: "Anything to make our colonial cousins feel at home."

"*Former* colonial cousins," corrected Rollo.

There were chuckles all round.

"Righto, now that we've avoided an international incident, let's get this show on the road!" With walking stick aloft, like a lightning rod conductor, he turned on his heel and led the way out of the courtyard.

In a bubble of good humour, all the guests followed, gee'd on by a "tally ho!" from Fox Flinton, emerging from one of the stables trotting like a pony.

"Oh Fox, you silly billy," laughed Delilah.

"Does my lady want a ride?" he asked, bending down. Buoyed by high spirits, Delilah jumped on his back and he gave her a piggy back around the courtyard. Poppy joined in with the corporate laughter but wondered to herself if Delilah had finally succumbed to the older man's seductive charms. She hoped not. But Delilah was Delilah and wouldn't do anything she didn't want to do.

The Rolls blasted its horn and the party stepped aside to let it pass. Mr Grimes, sitting next to the chauffeur, with Lady Ursula in the back seat, was a dark silhouette. Poppy shivered: *could it really have been him?*

"Hold on Poppy!"

Daniel, his Kodak Brownie camera case slung over one shoulder, and an unwieldy tripod on the other, caught up with her.

"You should have put that in the motor," she observed.

He grinned, his face ruddy from fresh air and exercise. "I think I'll manage half a mile. Have you seen Harry Gibson? I thought he'd be shooting the shoot."

"I thought so too," said Poppy. "Lionel's here. Perhaps he's already out there."

Poppy gestured to the treeline beyond the field through which they were traipsing.

"Could be."

"So what happened with the policeman this morning?"

"All routine, really. He asked –"

Poppy grabbed his arm and said "Shush."

"What?"

She leaned in close and whispered: "Sorry, I just heard Faizal say something to Marjorie. They're behind us, aren't they?"

Daniel looked back and confirmed that they were.

"Then give me a minute..." Poppy tuned in to the conversation behind her.

"– I'm sorry Mrs Reynolds, but that's really not good enough."

"Well, Dr Osman, there's nothing more I can say. That's the official policy of His Majesty's government. There has been a judgment by an esteemed member of the judiciary and it cannot be overruled. We are a democracy, sir, under the rule of law."

"But the judgment wasn't legally sound! Have you read Yasmin's brief?"

"I have. And if the Egyptian government feels strongly enough about it, they can bring an appeal to the Supreme Court. Your sister should have told you that already."

Faizal cleared his throat. "You know as well as I do, Mrs Reynolds, that an appeal can take years. We do not have years. The mask is being auctioned off tonight. And if it's bought by New York or Berlin it could be out of the country and beyond our reach in a matter of days. That mask has been stolen from the people of Egypt. It belongs in the Cairo Museum." He paused, then continued in a more conciliatory tone: "Come Marjorie, the British government has a chance here to show its goodwill. As we all know, with independence coming in just a few months, it's *very* important that we all remain on good terms, don't you think?"

Marjorie sighed. "I'm sorry Faizal; I really am – you know how I feel about this. But as a member of the Home Office my hands are tied. I'll tell you what, though: I will make every effort to speak to Maddox again before tonight. Perhaps I can persuade him of the diplomatic delicacy of the situation. Perhaps he will delay the auction..."

"And pigs might fly."

"It's the best I can do for now, Faizal."

"I know, Marjorie. I know."

Poppy cocked her head, hoping to hear more, but the pair behind her fell into silence.

Daniel nudged her elbow. "Did you get all that, Miss Nosey Parker?"

Poppy chuckled. "I did. Pretty much what I suspected. So sorry I interrupted; what happened with the policeman?"

A pair of crows were squabbling over a dead field mouse. They stopped and leered at the human cavalcade as it passed by, then resumed their territorial dispute.

Daniel turned his attention from the birds to his companion. "He took statements from me, Grimes, and Sir James. He said he already had a statement from the boy's father – he's the gamekeeper, the fella in charge of the arsenal – if you recall."

"Yes, I remember." Poppy looked to the treeline and could make out a couple of tents and a small group of men with shotguns waiting for them. "Who's in charge when he's away?"

Daniel shrugged. "I should imagine he has assistants – an estate this size. They've obviously not allowed his absence to stop their fun."

"No. I shouldn't imagine they would. Unless there was something suspicious going on..."

"Such as?"

"Such as what you told me and Rollo last night. About the wrong shot being in the weapon. What was it you said? It was buckshot, not birdshot?"

"That's right." Daniel switched the tripod from his left to his right shoulder.

"Need a hand there, Rokeby?" Faizal called from behind.

"I'm fine, Osman, but thanks for the offer."

Poppy waited to hear if there would be any further comments from behind before eventually continuing. "So what did the policeman say? Did he ask Maddox and Grimes about it?"

"He did. They said they weren't sure how it happened and that they would have a talk to the men to make sure it didn't happen again. They had no answer for why the gun had been left loaded. They said the policeman should ask the gamekeeper that. He said he had and that the man had sworn blind that he had emptied all the weapons of all shells before packing them away after the last hunt."

"And what did they say?"

"They suggested the fella was a bit confused. But they didn't blame him, worried about his son and all."

"And what did the policeman say?"

"He pretty much agreed with them. So the long and the short of it is, the gamekeeper is getting the blame for negligence – and will get a warning from both the police and his employer – but no further action will be taken as no one was seriously hurt."

"The boy nearly lost his foot!"

"Yes he did. But I think – because it's the gamekeeper's son – that that's punishment enough."

"Hmmm," said Poppy.

"Hmmm, what?"

"I was wondering what might have happened if the boy hadn't fired the gun yesterday. If no one had noticed there was buckshot in the barrel instead of birdshot. If someone had deliberately loaded it with more powerful ammunition. And what if that gun was shot today..."

Daniel shifted the tripod again. He was getting tired. But, Poppy knew, he'd be too proud to ask for help. "What are you suggesting, Poppy?"

Poppy wasn't really sure. But finding the shell in Mr Grimes' overcoat pocket had sparked her suspicions. That and the unnerving incident in the maze. Was she just being paranoid? Probably, but she told Daniel about it anyway.

"Hmmm, you're right; that is very odd. And you say there was a green stripe around the top of the shell?"

"Yes, green. It was definitely green. Does that mean anything?"

"It certainly does. A green stripe means it's a buckshot shell."

"Buckshot?" asked Poppy, far louder than she should have.

"Who shot a buck? Where?" cried Fox Flinton, from further forward in the procession. Delilah let out a peel of laughter.

"Just telling Miss Denby about another hunt I was on," offered Daniel.

"Quick thinking," whispered Poppy, who was relieved to hear no further ribbing from the Fox. They were almost at the end of their walk with the canvas gazebos of the shooting camp a dozen yards ahead. She stopped and then stepped aside, pulling Daniel with her. "Perhaps we can get some wide-angle shots of the camp," she said loudly. Only Rollo – and perhaps Lionel – would know that she would normally not be telling a professional photographer how to do his job. No one else seemed to think it curious, and they trudged past the pair of journalists and swarmed into the camp.

Daniel, playing along, swung down his tripod and started setting it up.

"Yes, a green stripe is buckshot, red is birdshot. So why did Mr Grimes have a buckshot shell in his pocket?"

Poppy looked over at the Rolls that had preceded the perambulating guests. Grimes, with the help of one of the assistant gamekeepers, was unpacking picnic hampers from the boot and laying out the contents on a trestle table.

"Well that, Daniel, is the question."

"Everything all right here, team?" Rollo trudged over to them, a cucumber and egg sandwich in hand. *Trust Rollo to get to the food first,* thought Poppy.

"Right as rain, boss," said Daniel, loud enough for everyone else to hear, then lowered his voice and told the editor what Poppy had discovered in Grimes' pocket.

"Jumpin' jelly fish!"

*Jumpin' jelly fish? Has he had a head start on the port as well as the sandwiches?* But no, the face that grinned up at Poppy was very much sober. Amused, but sober.

"What's so funny?"

"You are, Miz Denby. If I recall, not too long ago, you were chastising me for crossing police lines and trespassing. Now here you are, rifling through people's pockets! We'll make a proper investigative journalist out of you yet!"

Poppy narrowed her eyes and attempted a scowl. Daniel chuckled. "He's just teasing you, Poppy."

"I know. However, my dubious tactics aside, what do you think, Rollo? Do you think there might be something in it?"

"Something like..." prompted the editor.

"Oh, I don't know," said Poppy, trying to sound nonchalant. "Something like the accident yesterday might have scuppered someone's plans to stage an accident today."

Both men looked at her in surprise. But it was Rollo who replied. "You think someone – either Grimes working on his own or working for someone else – planned to *shoot* someone today? What a very interesting suggestion. Who do you think the victim was supposed to be?"

Daniel shook his head. "Whoa! Hold your horses. I think you two are going a bit too far with this. So the wrong ammunition was in the gun. The gun wasn't cleaned properly after the last shoot. It could easily happen."

"It could," agreed Poppy, "but why then did Grimes have the shell in his overcoat?"

"Yes, Danny Boy, answer the lady..."

Daniel spread his hands out wide. "I don't know. But I still think you're making a mountain out of a molehill here. Look, I've got to get on with this. All right?"

"Fine and dandy," said Rollo. "You're probably right." Then with a wink at Poppy: "But what if you're not? What if someone *was* planning on shooting someone today. The question is who and whom?"

"And why?" added Poppy, only partially in jest.

Daniel sighed. "You two are incorrigible. Even if you're right, I don't think you're going to find out anything today. With that accident yesterday, and the police aware of the incident, you would have to be a fool to try anything at this shoot."

Poppy looked over at the gazebos, filling up with fellow guests. "I do hope you're right, Daniel, I really do."

# CHAPTER 14

Daniel was right. The closest anyone got to being hurt was the pair of crows who were showered with shards from the blasted clay pigeons. And Poppy had a lot more fun than she thought she would. Not having to worry about suffering prey, Poppy relaxed into the event and enjoyed learning how to load the weapon, aim, and fire as the clay discs were catapulted from the trap. By the end of the session she had notched up two "kills" and was very proud of herself. This, though, paled in comparison with Lady Ursula who, as had been intimated the day before, was indeed a crack shot. She killed a dozen "pigeons" in succession, clearing and reloading her shotgun with the alacrity of a gunnery sergeant at the Somme.

On the way back from the shoot Poppy walked with Sir James – who, by the look of him, perhaps should have taken the motor. He was out of breath and red in the face, having to stop every fifty yards or so. "I've got a dicky ticker," he explained, when Poppy enquired if he was all right. "Bit late taking my medicine this morning... Couldn't find... it... at first. Normally stabilizes things. Probably... thrown me... a bit... off pace... Should perk up... after lunch... I take... another dose... then. Not to worry... Miss... Denby."

Poppy smiled at him and waited patiently for him to catch his breath. "My Uncle Roger has a weak heart too. He takes a little bit of digitalis powder in the morning. It's made from foxglove, apparently. Is that what you take?"

Sir James braced his lower back and pulled himself up straight. He looked a little less flustered. "It is, yes. I used to take it just once a day too, but now it's three times a day – morning, noon, and evening." He crooked his arm; Poppy put hers through it. It was more familiar than she would normally be comfortable with, with a man she barely knew, but she could help support him over the uneven ground.

"Are you enjoying yourself on the weekend, Miss Denby?"

A montage of images flashed through Poppy's mind: being run off the road by the *Courier* lads, watching the poor boy writhing in agony after he'd been shot, being upset by Madame Minette pretending to be her brother, seeing the worried look on Sir Arthur Conan Doyle's face as he reported his wife was poorly, being terrorized by the stalker this morning in the maze…

"I am, thank you," she lied, and then added, more truthfully: "The clay pigeon shooting was much more fun than I thought it would be. And the play last night about Nefertiti was tremendous!"

Sir James chuckled. "I'm so glad you enjoyed it. And – if I'm honest – a little relieved."

"Oh?"

"Yes. I was surprised – and saddened – by how upset you got last night at the séance."

Poppy's arm tightened in his but she didn't pull away. Should she challenge him on it? Should she tell him she knew the whole thing was a cruel hoax? *No, not yet*, she cautioned herself. *The job's not finished.* Besides, she didn't have any evidence yet. So she replied: "Yes, it was a bit of a shock. I still miss my brother hugely."

Hopefully that was a neutral statement – acknowledging she was upset but not accusing anyone – or absolving anyone – of responsibility. There would be time enough for that later…

once the weekend was over. The last thing she and the *Globe* needed was to be asked to leave before the auction this evening, which is what might happen if she confronted Sir James.

Sir James patted her hand. "Perfectly understandable, my dear."

However, there was some information she needed from him. She would have to tread very carefully... "Er, Sir James, I've been meaning to ask you. How is Lady Conan Doyle? Have you heard from Sir Arthur?"

Sir James paused for a moment to take a breath before responding. "Not yet. He might have telephoned when they got back to London. But as we were out on the shoot, I haven't heard yet."

"I do hope she's all right. Such bad luck to fall ill just before the séance. You were lucky you were able to get Madame Minette at such short notice. How did you know she was in the area?"

Sir James and Poppy nodded to Faizal Osman, Giles Mortimer, and Marjorie Reynolds as they overtook them on the field.

"It was a case of bad luck but good fortune," continued Sir James. "Lady Ursula bumped into Mrs Chapman – the wife of a mill owner who lives in Henley-on-Thames – at the parish fete last weekend. She mentioned that Madame Minette was staying with them for a week. She's a distant cousin of Mr Chapman, apparently."

"Good fortune indeed," observed Poppy, patiently waiting while Sir James gathered himself to walk the next few steps.

It was now the turn of Rollo and Howard Carter to overtake them. Carter raised his hat at Poppy. Rollo gave her an approving nod; she was doing her job. "Henley-on-Thames, you say?" she asked, turning her attention back to Sir James. "Do you think she's still there – with the Chapmans?"

"I should imagine so, yes. But to be honest, I don't know. She left straight after the séance last night. She asked if my chauffeur could take her. Of course I agreed, but it was a bit inconvenient. She could have stayed overnight. We'd assumed she would. But she was insistent that she wanted to leave. So poor Fitzroy – that's the chauffeur – had to take her. He'd barely got back from that hospital run! Then this morning he took Sir Arthur and Lady Jean home. That's a good hour each way. He'd only just got back from that in time for the shoot..."

"He must be exhausted."

"Well quite. Not to mention the petrol bill!"

Poppy made appropriate noises of sympathy. They were approaching the stable yard and Poppy realized that she had not yet spoken to him about the job at hand: the auction. That's what she was really there for. So she spent the last few minutes in his company asking him about the mask. In answer to her questions he declared that he didn't really mind where the mask ended up as long as it would be looked after and that he'd be appropriately reimbursed for his expenses. And no, he did not want to say exactly how much he'd paid; it would not be gentlemanly of him. He reiterated that he had bought the mask from a dealer in Cairo. Yes, it was unfortunate that the man could no longer be found, but that was hardly his fault, was it? No, he did not believe the mask had been acquired by illegal means. That was a rumour started by the Hun because they had a chip on their shoulder since they lost the war. He hoped Miss Denby would take whatever Herr Stein told her with a pinch of German salt. And, oh yes, if that Osman chap and his "little assistant" wanted to challenge the court order then that was their prerogative. And no, he did not give a hoot that Miss Reece-Lansdale was advising them on legal matters. It was time that woman decided where her loyalties lay: Egypt or England. But what else did one expect from a half-breed? Not that it was her fault that she was mixed race, of course – these things tended to happen in the colonies, you know… by gumption, he was sorry for that last comment. Not an appropriate topic of conversation for a young lady. Could Miss Denby forgive him?

Poppy assured him she could and then continued with her questions, amazed at how garrulous he was. Had he forgotten she was with the press?

So no, Mrs Reynolds had not spoken to him about it on behalf of the British government. But if she did, he'd tell her what he'd told Osman and "the girl" earlier today: they could take a running jump off the nearest cliff. Well, not literally, of course; far be it for him to wish ill on anyone…

"Like the watchman and his dog?" Even as she said it, she realized she might have gone too far. But she had to ask it now. The chips would just have to fall as they may…

Sir James stopped outside the door of the west wing of Winterton Hall. "What's that, Miss Denby?"

"The watchman and his dog at Thutmose's secret chamber. Back in 1914 when the mask was first found. That was the 'murderous circumstance' you referred to in your press release, wasn't it? I heard about it from Miss El Farouk…"

Sir James released Poppy's hand from the crook of his arm and took a moment to catch his breath. Eventually, he continued: "Yes, that was a very unpleasant business. But they got the chap who did it – or at least helped the person who did it. A local lad. Did Miss El Farouk tell you that?"

"She did," said Poppy. "But she also said that she believed the boy was innocent. And that he'd died a few years later in prison. Did you know that?"

Sir James cleared his throat. "I did not hear about his death, no. That is unfortunate. But believe me, the lad was guilty as sin. I attended his trial. And it was a fair one."

"Miss El Farouk thinks differently."

The colour rose in Sir James' face. "Well she would, wouldn't she? Have you ever been to the colonies, Miss Denby?"

Poppy said she had not.

"Well, if you had... you... you... would know... that the... natives... always stick together. The boy was... guilty. Of that... I'm sure."

"Are you all right, Sir James? Can I call someone? Or get you anything?"

Sir James summoned up a weak smile. "Thank you... no. But I... do need to... rest. Good... day to you."

And with that, he walked slowly away. Poppy watched, deeply concerned. She was just about to hurry after him and insist she accompany him, when Mr Grimes drew alongside his master, slipped a hand under his arm, and helped him into the house. As they entered, the butler cast a steely look in Poppy's direction, as if she were personally responsible for his employer's condition. *Well two can play at that game*, thought Poppy, and returned the gaze, steel for steel.

Poppy rushed upstairs, changed out of her shooting clothes into an indoor frock of navy blue, and jotted down as much of her conversation with Sir James as she could remember. She also made notes about what she had overheard of the conversation between Marjorie Reynolds and Faizal Osman. Then there was a knock at the door. It was Delilah and Kamela El Farouk.

"Are you coming down for lunch, Poppy?" asked Delilah, looking very fetching in forest green culottes and a cream blouse with a mandarin collar, embroidered with gold and green silk. Miss El Farouk wore a lilac frock with a white silk headscarf.

"Yes, I'm famished!" said Poppy. The cucumber sandwich she'd had at the shoot now seemed a long time ago. She packed her notebook into her satchel, picked up her light navy jacket with white trim, and joined the other women on their way to lunch.

"Did you have a restful morning, Kamela? I didn't see you on the shoot?"

"I did, thank you. I caught up on a bit of reading. Shooting isn't really my thing."

Poppy grimaced as they entered the corridor containing the hunting trophies, presided over by the black bear. "It's not mine either. But not having to actually kill something makes all the difference. It was really jolly good fun."

"Oh, it's not the killing that bothers me," observed Miss El Farouk. "It's killing something innocent that's the problem." She gestured to the animal heads lining the walls. "There's a difference between killing something for food and killing for sport, wouldn't you agree?"

"Yes, I would. And that's exactly how I feel about it too," said Poppy.

"So do I," agreed Delilah. "But shoots can be splendid. It's not the shooting itself, but the party around it. Such fun!"

"Will there be a party tonight?" asked Miss El Farouk. "After the auction?"

"I jolly well hope so!" said Delilah and danced a quickstep down the remainder of the corridor, ending it with a pirouette and a curtsy. Poppy and Kamela laughed.

"Oh, you girls are a breath of fresh air!" said Kamela. "I do love my job, but I seem to spend most of my days with fuddy old men."

"Dr Osman doesn't seem that fuddy – or that old. In fact, he's quite a dish," said Delilah and gave a little wink to Poppy.

"Are you and he…?"

"Good gracious no!" said Miss El Farouk. "He's nearly forty!"

"Totally ancient!" laughed Delilah, and the other girls joined in.

After lunch – a tasty spread of vegetable soup followed by venison pie, mashed potatoes, and gravy – Poppy managed to catch up with Daniel and told him that Rollo had suggested the two of them spend the afternoon trying to track down Madame Minette.

"We could take a drive into Henley-on-Thames. Just the two of us," added Poppy.

Daniel smiled at her. "I could think of no better way to spend the afternoon. The only problem is, Fitzroy hasn't had a chance to look at the Model T yet. He's been run off his feet since we all arrived. He said he was going to sort it this afternoon."

"Oh bother," said Poppy.

"Are you young people in need of a motor?" It was Marjorie, who had overheard their conversation.

"We are," said Poppy. "But the company car needs a bit of work. Thanks to the silly kippers from the *Courier* who ran us off the road."

"Why don't you borrow mine?"

"Golly, Mrs Reynolds. That's sporting of you. Are you sure you don't mind?"

"Not at all, Mr Rokeby," said Marjorie. "I'll go fetch the keys."

# CHAPTER 15

Winterton Hall was six miles east of Henley-on-Thames and Marjorie's powerful Lincoln ate up the miles far more quickly than Poppy wanted. It was a real treat to be alone with Daniel, even if it was on official business. Poppy was very conscious of his proximity, particularly when his gloved hand reached down to change gears, a mere inch from her thigh. Daniel was a very attractive man. Twenty-nine years old, six-feet tall, well-built but not bulky, he was physically exactly what Poppy would have hoped for in a man. She loved the way his brown hair was brushed smoothly to the side – so unlike her own unruly locks – and how his dark grey eyes twinkled with good humour when he looked at her.

She remembered the first time they'd met, in the summer of 1920, on platform 1 of King's Cross Station. She had just got off the Flying Scotsman, hauling her trunk behind her because the porters were on strike, when she was approached by a young man carrying a camera case. She had accidentally dropped her book – a novel by Agatha Christie – and the young man spotted it. That was the first time she'd noticed his twinkling eyes: when he had teased her about lady mystery writers. However, it was also the first time she'd seen the shadow that occasionally fell upon him, when he mentioned the war memorial he had just been photographing. The memories of the war and his fallen comrades were never far from Daniel; and the scars he'd earned trying to save some of them from a trench blaze marred his hands under the driving gloves.

It was in a field hospital in Belgium, where he was recovering from his wounds, that Daniel had first met Rollo Rolandson, who taught the young British soldier the rudiments of photography. Two years later, in 1917, Rollo won *The Daily Globe* in a poker game and offered Daniel – discharged from the army on medical grounds – a job on the London newspaper. Daniel, who at the time had a wife and two children to look after, jumped at the chance. Sadly, a year later his wife died of the Spanish flu and his sister, Maggie, took over looking after the children.

*Maggie.* Poppy sighed. If it weren't for Maggie she and Daniel might already be married. The woman had never liked Poppy. She saw her as a threat to her surrogate family and had tried on more than one occasion to drive a wedge between her brother and the young, attractive journalist. The thing that infuriated Poppy more than anything was that Maggie couldn't make up her mind if Poppy was a threat because she feared the younger woman was about to take the children away from her, or because she wasn't. Last Christmas Poppy had endured endless jibes about women who pursued careers at the expense of their children, or did not know that a woman's true place was in the home. And, to make it worse, for a while Poppy wasn't sure if Daniel shared his sister's views. Earlier in the year, in the spring, Poppy had called off their relationship when Daniel disapproved of her decision to go to New York for three months, not understanding – or seemingly caring – that this was a once-in-a-lifetime chance for her to further her career.

However, they say absence makes the heart grow fonder, and on her return he apologized and told her that he fell in love with her as a career woman and would continue to love her as one. This put Poppy's mind at rest, and for the next few months they happily renewed their courting.

This did not, however, mean that Poppy did not want children – she did – but not yet. The problem was, Daniel already had children, and if the two of them were to marry then Poppy's decision, which she hoped to put off for a few more years – of whether to stop work completely or do a bit part-time on the side until the children were older – would be brought abruptly forward. And both Daniel and she knew it.

*Perhaps that's why he still hasn't proposed...* Poppy cast a sideways glance at her beau. Clean shaven, but with a slight shadow along his jaw, his beautiful mouth was unencumbered by a fashionable moustache. Poppy closed her eyes, imagining for a moment that mouth kissing hers... Her pulse raced as she remembered the handful of times which it had, and the same number of times when either she, or Daniel, had pulled away. Despite her progressive views on women voting and working, she held to traditional views on sex before marriage. But that didn't stop her dreaming...

"Penny for your thoughts."

Poppy opened her eyes and smiled shyly. *If only he knew...*

"I was just thinking through the case."

"Really? I wasn't."

"Oh?" she asked, feeling a slight blush flush her cheeks.

He grinned. "Perhaps we can take a walk along the river after we've visited the Chapmans."

"That would be lovely."

The Lincoln powered over Henley Bridge with the dark waters of the river below. Poppy raised her eyebrows in surprise at a pair of canoes, manned by men in woolly hats and scarves, suggesting some or other university affiliation.

"Hardy souls," observed Poppy.

"No doubt they'll warm up later with a pint or two."

They drove past a beautiful medieval church and onto a

quiet high street. As it was Saturday afternoon, most of the shops – apart from one or two tea rooms – were shut. Poppy imagined just a few hours earlier the pavements would have been full of shoppers dressed up against the biting air, laden with Christmas shopping.

*Christmas shopping. Golly, I'd better get some done! I'll suggest a morning on Oxford Street with Delilah next Saturday…*

"According to the directions from Fitzroy, the Chapmans' place should be just up here…"

Daniel indicated a left-hand turn and manoeuvred the Lincoln into a smart, tree-lined street. Right at the end was a large, imposing villa of red brick with a black front door, punctuated with a big brass knocker.

A few moments later they were on the doorstep, assured they were in the right place by a small brass plaque under the house number: *Chapmanville.*

*Nouveau riche*, thought Poppy, then immediately chastised herself for such uncharitable thoughts.

"Perhaps we should have telephoned ahead," said Daniel, as he rapped the knocker then straightened his tie.

"Possibly," said Poppy, "but that would have warned Madame Minette we were coming."

He looked down at her. "Do you think she might not want to see you?"

"Let's just say we didn't exactly get on like a house on fire last night."

The door lock clunked and turned and they were greeted by a butler in a black suit and white bow tie. "Good afternoon. May I help you?"

"Ah, good afternoon. My name is Miss Denby and this is Mr Rokeby. We are looking for Madame Minette. Is she in?"

The butler looked puzzled. "Madame Minette?"

"Yes, the medium. We met her last night at Winterton Hall. She was conducting a séance. We were informed that she is staying here with Mr and Mrs Chapman. Sorry we didn't telephone ahead..."

"Ah. Perhaps you mean Mrs Hughes. Mrs Minifred Hughes."

"Mrs Hughes? Is that her real name? I'm sorry, I only know her – her – professional name. But it sounds like the same lady. Is Mrs Hughes French?"

"She is not."

*Well, that's no surprise*, thought Poppy. But she tried to keep the disdain out of her voice when she asked: "Is she in then? Mrs Hughes?"

"She is not."

It was starting to get very cold on the doorstep. Poppy wished the butler would invite them in, but he was guarding the door like Cerberus at the gates of Hades.

"Do you know when she will be back?" asked Daniel.

"I do not, sir."

The butler did not budge.

Suddenly there was a call from behind him. "Who is it, Belson?"

Belson turned and called back: "It is a lady and gentleman looking for Mrs Hughes, madam."

"Minifred? Well, have you told them she's not here?"

"I have, madam."

*Oh, this is getting annoying.* "Hello! Sorry to bother you!" Poppy called, hoping her voice would circumvent the butler and reach the lady behind. "But we were hoping to speak to Madame Minette – Mrs Hughes – about a séance. She was fabulous last night. We'd like to hire her for a little soirée we're having ourselves. Might you know when she'll be back?"

A turbaned head stuck itself around the door frame. But from the look of the pale, gaunt face under it, the scarf was for medical not fashion purposes. The butler stepped back to allow the lady through. "Hello," said the woman. "I'm Rhonda Chapman. And you are?"

Poppy smiled. "I'm Poppy Denby and this is Daniel Rokeby."

The woman screwed up her face, drawing attention to her lack of eyebrows. "Denby? Are you any relation to Dot Denby?"

"I am! She's my aunt. I'm very pleased to meet you, Mrs Chapman." Poppy stuck out her hand. Mrs Chapman took it and shook it limply.

"I used to know Dot, back in the day. You look very much like her, you know? Or at least what she looked like when she was young." Mrs Chapman smiled, wistfully. "I hope she is in better health than I am."

Poppy's heart beat in sympathy. "She is very well, thank you. She's off travelling at the moment. If she knew I was coming, I'm sure she would have passed on her regards."

Mrs Chapman nodded. "I'm sure she would have. And she might have saved you the trip. Your aunt actually knows Minifred – or used to. They were in the theatre together, back in the day."

*So she* is *an actress.*

"Would it be possible to come in and wait for Mrs Hughes?" asked Daniel.

Mrs Chapman looked up at Daniel. "I'm sorry to be rude, young man, but unfortunately not. I am waiting for the doctor to come and give me some treatment. I thought you were he."

"Oh, it's we who are rude!" said Poppy. "We should have telephoned. We didn't really think. We thought we'd just pop by while we were in Henley-on-Thames. It was a spur of the moment thing, really. Not important. We're sorry to have bothered you."

Mrs Chapman gave a tired smile. "Perhaps you and your aunt could come for tea sometime. When she returns. If I'm still here..."

Poppy's heart lurched again. She embraced the older woman with a sympathetic gaze. "We'd be delighted to. I shall let her know in my next letter. And I shall ask about Mrs Hughes too. However... that could take a while to get to her... we were hoping to book Madame Minette before Christmas. Can we drop by to see her later – when she returns – and when, of course, it is more convenient for you?"

"That won't be possible, I'm afraid. She has gone home. She left first thing this morning. Very suddenly. Barely a word of goodbye."

A motor car pulled up on the drive behind the Lincoln. A gentleman carrying a doctor's bag stepped out.

"Ah, here's Dr Rose. You must excuse me."

"Of course," said Poppy, politeness vying with urgency. "But could we bother you for Mrs Hughes' home address? We really do want to book her..."

Mrs Chapman gave a tired sigh. "Of course. Belson, will you give this young lady Mrs Hughes' address? You'll find it in my address book in the drawing room. Good afternoon doctor. It's like King's Cross Station here today."

The doctor raised his hat to Poppy and Daniel, but his look was disapproving. "You need to rest, Mrs Chapman, not receive visitors."

Chastised, Poppy and Daniel stepped away. "Sorry to have bothered you. We'll just wait for that address and be on our way," said Poppy. Then, to save Mrs Chapman having to decide whether or not to let them in, added: "We'll just wait in the motor."

Fifteen minutes later, with Madame Minette's home address – a property in Acton – successfully obtained, Poppy and Daniel set out on a walk along the river. They parked the motor near the bridge and walked down a flight of stone steps to the towpath below. Mid-afternoon in December and dusk was beginning to settle over the riverside town. Down by the river, licks of light highlighted icy patches on the bank. Poppy looked up at the darkening sky and wondered if they were going to be in for some more snow. *Those clouds look heavy…* She pulled her fur collar up to meet the edge of her hat.

"Cold?"

"A little," she smiled up at Daniel.

"Do you want to go back to the motor then?"

"No," she said, and slipped her gloved hand into the crook of his arm. She was going to savour this time with her beau.

He reached out his arm across his chest and took her hand in his. She sighed and leaned her head on his shoulder as they walked. A man with a spaniel on the opposite bank raised his hat in greeting. Daniel let go of Poppy's hand to raise his in return, but then instantly connected with her again.

"It's been a funny old weekend, hasn't it?" he said.

"It has. Lots of material gathered. Lots of angles to follow. I think we'll need a good sit-down with Rollo on Monday to work through it all."

"We will, but would you mind if we didn't talk shop for a little while? It's not often I get you all to myself these days."

Poppy glowed. "Of course."

They walked in love-charged silence, their winter boots crunching on the gravel. Beside them the Thames, dark and brooding, murmured its approval. "I'm sorry if I've been a bit unpredictable these last few months," said Daniel. "It's definitely not what I had planned when you came back from New York."

"Oh? What did you have planned?"

He squeezed her hand. "I think you know that, Poppy. I was hoping to work things out between us so that we could – we could –"

A splash. The spaniel, now off its lead, had hurled itself into the river chasing a stick, oblivious to the cold.

"Yes?"

"So that we could find a way to be together. Permanently."

Poppy's heart skipped a beat. *Is this it? Is he about to propose?*

They approached a canoe shed at the top of a frosty slipway as a few flakes of snow fell onto the sleeve of her coat.

"It's snowing," said Daniel, stating the obvious. "We should get back to the car..."

*No! Say what you were going to say!* "Let's slip in here for a bit. It might clear..."

He smiled down at her. "Good idea." He pushed open the door to reveal empty racks where the vessels were normally stored. "They really should lock these things."

"They probably do when there's something in it. Nothing to steal right now."

"No?" said Daniel, pulling the door closed enough to give them some privacy but still to allow in a bit of light. "I was hoping to steal your heart." He put both hands on her shoulders and stared boldly into her eyes.

Poppy blinked and swallowed, then softened her lips. "You don't have to steal it, Daniel. It's already yours."

A look of pure love washed over his face, visible only for the moment before his lips found hers and they kissed – a long, deep, lingering kiss. Poppy sank her chest against him, trusting he would hold her weight in his strong embrace. He did. Then, after an exquisitely indeterminable length of time, their lips parted.

"Oh Poppy," he breathed. "I'm not sure being alone with you is the wisest thing. You're intoxicating, Miss Denby."

*Then make an honest woman of me,* she thought, willing him to ask.

He took a step back and reached a hand into his pocket.

Poppy held her breath.

The door to the shed creaked. Poppy looked over Daniel's shoulder, expecting to see a canoeist. *Drat it all, why couldn't they* – but it wasn't a canoeist. Standing in the entrance, silhouetted against the setting sun, was not a young man with a woolly hat and scarf, but the shadowy outline of an older gentleman in a trench coat and fedora hat.

Poppy screamed. Daniel spun round. The shadow fled.

Poppy gabbled an explanation about the man from the maze; Daniel flew out of the shed in pursuit. Poppy followed him to the door, looked left and right, but could not see the man in the fedora. Neither, it seemed, could Daniel. A few minutes later he returned, breathing heavily from exertion and announced that the blighter had got away. "I'm sorry Poppy; he had too much of a head start."

"Did you see his face?"

"To be honest I didn't see anything of him." He looked over Poppy's shoulder. "Perhaps he went the other way. Should I –"

Poppy shook her head. "No, he'll be long gone. And you could break your neck trying to catch him in this weather."

They both looked up. The snow was now falling steadily.

"We should get back before it really sets in," said Daniel, sounding desperately disappointed.

Poppy looked at him, hoping he would continue saying what he was going to say before they were interrupted. But the moment was gone. And instead of the glow of happiness she had basked in just a few minutes earlier, there was a cold chill of foreboding. *Why was the shadow man following her?* She shivered and pulled up her collar. "Yes, let's get back to the car."

# CHAPTER 16

The snow was falling thick and fast on the drive back to Winterton Hall; even if Daniel and Poppy had wanted to steer their conversation back to more personal matters, it was not safe to do so. The Lincoln held the road well, but the tight country lanes, slippery tarmac, and decreasing visibility meant that Daniel had to concentrate only on his driving. Then, as soon as they pulled up to the front door, they were met by Rollo wanting to plan the photoshoot of the auction, and Delilah who wanted help choosing what to wear. After returning the keys to Marjorie, Daniel and Poppy exchanged a wistful glance and then went their separate ways.

Poppy noted that Grimes, the butler, hadn't answered the door. She asked the footman if he was in – she thought it was finally time to ask the man some pointed questions. But she was told that he was out for the afternoon "on estate business". He would, however, be back in time to supervise dinner.

"Out in Henley-on-Thames?" she asked the young footman.

"I have no idea, Miss Denby; he didn't say."

"Come on Poppy, I need your help!" called Delilah.

Poppy thanked the footman and joined her friend.

Poppy lay back in the steaming hot water and sighed. The bruise on her right buttock was really starting to ache, and a piping hot bath before getting dressed for the evening's festivities was just what was called for. She lowered her head under the water and then reached for the cake of shampoo. As she massaged the foam into her scalp she imagined for a moment Daniel sitting behind her, washing her hair. When they married, would he do that? *When we marry? No Poppy, if we marry.* She reminded herself that it was not a certainty that Daniel had been about to propose. After all, nothing had changed in his circumstances. His sister was still talking about taking the children with her to South Africa; Daniel was still trying to talk her out of it. Planning and organizing a wedding – or trying to figure out how she fit into his complicated domestic arrangements – would be the last thing on his mind. Or was it…?

Poppy ducked under the water again to rinse off her hair, then lay back, her head on the rim, while she worked up a lather with a bar of soap. "Most men ask: 'is she pretty?' Not 'is she clever?' Be pretty *and* clever. Buy Palmolive." Poppy recited the advertising slogan in a sing-song voice, then laughed. "What utter poppycock!"

She thanked God Daniel loved her for more than her looks. And she loved him too. They would work things out… *please God, let it work out…*

She closed her eyes and conjured up the memory of their latest kiss. She sank into the fantasy, savouring every sweet moment, and then, just as she was about to imagine what might happen next, a dark shadow filled her mind's eye. She gasped and opened her eyes, half-expecting to see the man in the fedora standing in the bathroom. But of course, he wasn't. Why couldn't she get him out of her mind? Like earlier in the boat shed, he had once again spoiled her time with Daniel. Who was he? Was it Grimes, as she suspected? And if so, what motive would he have for following her and Daniel to Henley-on-Thames? Or for scaring her in the maze? Or for having a shotgun shell in his coat pocket…? Was he acting on his own, or at the behest of someone else? Sir James? Lady Ursula? Was this all tied in to what Rollo had suggested earlier in the day – that they were trying to unnerve her and make her more interested in attending future séances in order to ensure more newspaper attention? Or was it the opposite: were they trying to scare a young, inexperienced journalist *off* the case? Perhaps they had something to hide and didn't want it to be exposed. Rollo Rolandson, no doubt, would be seen as a cynical old hack, beyond influence and manipulation. But Poppy, perhaps, was seen as the weak link in the *Globe* chain. *Ha! They obviously don't know me very well!*

But, she had to admit, she *had* been unnerved, particularly by the fact that Madame Minette seemed to know something about her brother that no one else should know. *How on earth had she known about the magazines…?* Poppy resolved to visit the medium, aka Mrs Minifred Hughes, in Acton as soon as she had an opportunity to do so on Monday. Her week ahead was already filling up: editorial meeting Monday morning; possibly a trip out to Acton in the afternoon. Then Tuesday she planned to visit the Americans – Miss Philpott and Dr Davies – at their hotel near the British Museum, to discuss the Renoir angle. And of course they would discuss whoever managed to successfully bid for the Nefertiti mask this evening.

There was a knock on the door.

"Yes?"

"Sorry to rush you, Miss Denby. It's Kamela El Farouk. I was hoping to have a bath before dinner. Would that be all right?"

"Of course! I'll be finished in two ticks."

*Oh bother!*

"Goodness me, Miss Denby, are those the Prince of Wales' pearls?"

Lady Ursula Maddox honed in on Poppy after dinner as the guests were being offered a glass of sherry or brandy before the auction started.

"They are indeed, Lady Ursula. They were a present from my Aunt Dot on my twenty-third birthday. How did you know?"

"Oh, they were all over the papers back in the day. It caused quite a stir, you know – the heir to the throne giving such an expensive gift to a mere actress. It certainly got tongues a-wagging, I can tell you."

Poppy suppressed a smile, certain her aunt would have revelled in all the attention. "They were just friends, I can assure you," she said, feeling she needed to defend Dot's honour.

"Oh, I'm sure they were," said Lady Ursula. "But the prince was known for his wandering eye. Even I caught his attention." She nodded to a portrait of a younger version of herself on the wall behind Poppy. "That was me at around the same time your aunt and the prince were – er – *friends*."

Poppy chose to ignore the implied slur against her aunt and instead appraised the painting. It was an oil painting but done with the lightness of touch of a watercolour. Ursula, wearing a light pink blouse and straw hat tied under her chin with a chiffon scarf, was sitting on the bench in the orchard she and Rollo had been in earlier that day. Beside her was a basket of apples as if just harvested. She was looking wistfully into the distance. The artist had captured a sadness in her eyes that now – twenty years on – had been replaced by something Poppy couldn't quite put her finger on... something *predatory*? Yes, that was it – Lady Ursula seemed to look on people like a sparrowhawk contemplating its prey. Poppy shuddered inwardly. "It's beautiful," she said.

"Why thank you," said Lady Ursula. "It was a gift from my cousin Fox. He was quite a gifted artist when he was a young man. In fact, he used to paint portraits when he was still an up-

and-coming actor. To pay the bills, you know. But he let it slip when the stage work started taking off."

"How interesting. You hear of lots of actors who are creatively gifted in different ways. Delilah, for instance, can sing, dance, and act."

"That's not what she's best known for though, is it?" asked Lady Ursula, tartly, directing her gaze towards the young woman who was engaging a clutch of men in conversation on the other side of the room. As per Poppy's suggestion she was wearing the Egyptian-themed gown she had worn the other evening at Oscar's, with the train of peacock feathers.

Poppy smarted. "Delilah has many gifts. But the best of them are loyalty and kindness."

Lady Ursula turned her gaze back to Poppy and offered an insincere: "I'm sure they are."

Poppy swallowed her retort, forcing herself back onto a professional track. "So, the auction… who do you expect will win the bid?"

Lady Ursula looked shrewdly at Poppy, hazel eyes meeting blue, then scanned the room. Her gaze lingered first on the Americans, then the Germans, then the Egyptians, and finally the British. "I'm not sure," she answered. "The Americans have the deepest pockets, but the British seem very motivated. Why else would Giles Mortimer have Marjorie Reynolds accompany him? If the British Museum has the backing of the British government then perhaps they might be able to compete with the New Yorkers."

Poppy looked over to Dr Mortimer, Howard Carter, and Marjorie Reynolds who were deep in conversation. Were they planning their auction strategy? Yes, perhaps Lady Ursula was right. "What about the Germans and the Egyptians?" she asked.

Lady Ursula flicked a bejewelled hand in dismissal. "Neither of them can compete financially. The Berlin Museum could have done once, but they've been a bit cash-strapped since the war. All those reparations the Weimar government has had to pay..."

"And the Egyptians?"

Lady Ursula's eyes narrowed. "They think we owe them something. We owe them *nothing*. We've agreed to let them govern themselves; let them govern themselves. Let them pay their own way. Let them compete like grown-ups and put in a proper bid instead of whining about long-dead history."

"Are you talking about their accusations that the mask was stolen?"

"I am."

"It was only eight years ago, wasn't it? Just before the war started? Hardly ancient history."

Lady Ursula's mouth narrowed, her lips compressing so tightly that all blood was driven from them. "I see you've been listening to gossip, Miss Denby."

"If you mean I've been speaking to Dr Osman and Miss El Farouk, then yes, Lady Ursula, I have. That is my job."

The older woman's lips now curled back, revealing a line of small, uneven teeth. "Let sleeping dogs lie, Miss Denby."

*Golly, is she referring to the dead dog in the tomb?* But just as she was about to question the lady further, Sir James, looking much better after an afternoon of rest, called the room to attention.

"Ladies and gentlemen, in a few moments, the auction will begin. However, before that, as per the request of all four interested parties, I have agreed that one representative from each group be allowed to examine the mask to determine its authenticity. So, without further ado, I present to you the death mask of Nefertiti!"

With a flourish he whipped a damask cloth off a table beside him to reveal – propped up against a pile of books – an exquisite visage in blue enamel, gold leaf, black ebony, and jade.

Poppy, and everyone else in the room gasped.

"Oh! My! She's beautiful!" trilled Delilah.

"She is that, Miz Marconi," agreed Jonathan Davies and then let out a long, appreciative whistle.

Sir James grinned like the Cheshire Cat. "I'm glad you appreciate her, ladies and gentlemen. I trust that will be reflected in your bids. So, if you please, Herr Stein, Dr Osman, Miss Philpott and Mr Carter – I believe you are the nominated experts..."

The four representatives stepped forward and approached the mask with a mixture of deference and curiosity. Each of them was given a pair of white cotton gloves and, one by one, they picked up and examined the mask, turning it this way and that. Both Herr Stein and Miss Philpott used eyeglasses; Carter and Osman each in turn held it up to the light, causing the encrusted jewels to sparkle. After about five minutes and a period of huddled consultation, the four experts turned to face the expectant guests.

"Well," prompted Sir James, "what is your verdict?"

Three of the experts nodded to Howard Carter, indicating he should speak on their behalf. "Well, without the benefit of a laboratory, where we could compare the mask to existing artefacts whose authenticity is beyond question, it appears that the article *may* be genuine."

A flutter of excitement twirled around the room.

Carter continued: "Herr Stein here believes it is of comparable quality to the bust of Nefertiti in Berlin, and both Dr Osman and Miss Philpott say it shows similar marks of style and craftsmanship with other works of Thutmose held in their respective museums. I believe the age of the wood under the enamelling is suggestive of the Eighteenth Dynasty – mid-1300s – and similar to other artefacts I have examined of that period. However –"

"Well, there you have it!" exclaimed a beaming Sir James. "The experts have declared the mask authentic. So let's proceed with the auction. Mr Carnaby…"

"However…" repeated Howard Carter, forcibly, backed up by three serious faces, "there are one or two – how should we say – *curious* anomalies…" Three heads nodded. "And we are all in agreement that further tests will be required under laboratory conditions, and that these should be carried out – by the four of us – post-haste, at the British Museum."

Sir James stared at him, aghast. "Good heavens, man, what are you saying?"

"I'm saying," said Carter, standing shoulder to shoulder with his fellow antiquarians, "that we are not prepared to bid on the mask until those tests have been done."

A collective groan went around the room. Every single person, apart from Kamela El Farouk and Yasmin Reece-Lansdale (whose expression could only be described as smug), looked disappointed.

"But – but – but –" spluttered Sir James, his face turning an alarming shade of puce, "the auction is scheduled for tonight!" His breathing became increasingly laboured. Grimes moved to his master's side. "Everyone is – is – here! We can – sort out – sort – it's genuine – the mask – Nefer – Nefer –" The host clutched his chest, emitted an agonized groan, and slumped towards the floor. Grimes caught him and manoeuvred him towards a footstool. Fox Flinton rushed in to help. Then Daniel, who had been behind his camera at the back of the room, charged forward.

"Put him on the floor. Loosen his clothing."

Grimes and the Fox obeyed, laying Sir James flat on the Persian rug in front of the fireplace.

Grimes ripped off his master's bow tie, frontispiece, and cummerbund while Fox unbuttoned his shirt. Lady Ursula was now on her knees at her husband's side. "James! James! Call the doctor!"

"Yes, call the doctor, now!" ordered Daniel, bending over the stricken man.

Sir James was suddenly still. Daniel put his ear to his chest and listened. Then, with a loud expletive started pumping the older man's chest. "Rollo! Help me! The kiss of life!"

Rollo bent over Sir James, pulled back his chin and started breathing over his mouth and nose, alternating breaths with Daniel's compressions.

No one else in the room breathed, as if lending their lungs to the desperate effort to save their host's life. But eventually, one by one, they resumed, and Daniel's compressions slowed and finally stopped. The only sound that could be heard was Lady Ursula's sobs and the spluttering of the fire.

# CHAPTER 17

Breakfast the next morning was a very subdued affair. Grimes was in attendance and told each guest as they arrived that Lady Ursula sent her apologies but would not be coming down. No one was told that they were expected to leave, but it was assumed. It was announced that the Winterton Rolls Royce would run anyone to the station who didn't have their own transport. It would be leaving at ten o'clock.

Poppy accepted a poached egg from Grimes, wondering how on earth she could now question him about the maze and the boat house. No doubt behind the professional façade was a man devastated by the recent death of his employer. His coal-dark eyes were fixed and staring at a point beyond Poppy when she thanked him for the egg and retreated to join her colleagues at the table.

"Morning Rollo. Morning Daniel."

"Morning Poppy," they muttered in unison. Delilah, Marjorie, and Yasmin soon joined them. The two German men had already eaten and were having coffee and cigarettes, while the Americans, Giles Mortimer, and Howard Carter were still eating. Faizal Osman arrived and said that Miss El Farouk would not be having breakfast and was busy packing. There was no sign of Fox Flinton, Albert Carnaby nor the two *Courier* journalists.

"I think Lionel and Harry left last night – after the doctor and the mortuary van left. I heard their motor," said Daniel.

"It would have been heavy going in the snow," said Rollo. "It didn't stop falling until well after midnight."

Poppy didn't ask why Rollo had been up well after midnight. She too had lain awake well into the early hours going over the events of the evening.

The general consensus was that Sir James had died of a heart attack. After the hysterical Lady Ursula was helped from the room by Fox Flinton and Marjorie Reynolds, Grimes used the cloth that had covered the Nefertiti mask as a temporary shroud and laid it over his employer's livid face. Then, with a remarkable sense of decorum, suggested the guests leave the drawing room. Drinks, he said, would be served in the dining room. Poppy followed the crowd into the dining room and accepted a glass of sherry to steady her nerves. Conversation was stilted. It would be impolite to talk about anything other than Sir James, but there wasn't much that could be said other than "shocking", "dreadful", and "tragic". Poppy did catch Howard Carter whispering to Dr Mortimer, however, that a decision still needed to be made about the mask, and Mortimer had whispered in reply that he'd make enquiries about it when it was polite to do so.

Fox Flinton returned from helping his cousin to her room. He said her maid and Mrs Reynolds would be sitting with her until the doctor arrived. Then he confirmed what Poppy already knew: Sir James had a weak heart and had been taking medication for it for a few years. That was one of the main reasons he had stopped going to archaeological digs. That and – he confided indiscreetly – Cousin Ursula had decided to draw the purse strings. Why he felt a household of strangers should know that, Poppy had no idea. But clearly the man was in shock, and perhaps that had brought on verbal diarrhoea. He did, however, have something useful to relay: Lady Ursula asked Albert Carnaby to take custody of the "cursed" mask.

"What? Now?" asked the auctioneer.

"I assume so," said Fox.

Carnaby got up and hurried away.

"*Cursed* mask?" asked Delilah. "Do you think she means that literally?"

"I'm sure she doesn't," said Poppy, but noticed Lionel's and Harry's eyes light up. She could guarantee what angle the *Courier* would be taking on this. The rival journalists exchanged some whispered remarks, and Harry left the room announcing that he needed to retrieve his photography equipment.

"Should you get yours too?" Poppy asked Daniel.

"Yes. But I'd still like to get a photograph of the mask – if it's not too awkward. I'll wait until Carnaby returns and I'll ask him. It would hardly be appropriate to take it in the room with the corpse now, would it?"

"Well..." said Rollo, stifling a grin.

"Rollo!"

"Just kidding, Miz Denby."

Soon after that, the doctor came, having fought his way through the snow from Henley-on-Thames. Poppy could hear stomping of boots and mutterings of "dreadful night" and "I'll go up to see Lady Ursula when I'm finished."

By the time the doctor had finished with both Sir James and Lady Ursula, the mortuary van had arrived, and after the guests watched their host's final departure from the dining room window, one by one, they drifted off. Most went to bed, but a few night owls decamped to the library for further drinks and cigars. Daniel, who had collared Albert Carnaby, set up a photoshoot of the mask in the hall with Rollo assisting him. As Poppy was surplus to requirements, she left them to it.

And now, the next morning, breakfast was finished. There was nothing for it but to pack up and leave. Daniel ascertained that Fitzroy had managed to repair the Model T, so with the help of a subdued Winterton staff, they packed their suitcases and said their goodbyes. Poppy, Rollo, and Daniel would return in the Ford as they had arrived. However, Yasmin asked if she could swap with Delilah and travel back with Marjorie in the Lincoln; and would the minister to the Home Office mind if Faizal and Kamela caught a lift too? Apparently there was business to be discussed between the Egyptian representatives and the British government. Delilah readily agreed.

The Americans and the Germans caught a lift with the Rolls. They would train back to London. Before they left, Poppy confirmed her appointment with Dr Davies and Miss Philpott for a breakfast meeting at the Russell Hotel on Tuesday. Fox Flinton said he'd be staying a while longer as he needed to support his cousin. Albert Carnaby, who had travelled in with Fox, said he would catch a later train back as there was not room in the Rolls at the ten o'clock departure.

And so the sad convoy, equipped with snow chains, made its way from Winterton Hall, as Grimes stood sentinel at the entrance to the house of mourning. He was wearing his black fedora and greatcoat. Poppy shuddered.

"Jake, Mary, and Jehoshaphat!" Rollo slapped down a copy of *The London Courier* into the middle of the editorial conference table. He then let off a string of expletives without bothering to apologize to Poppy. Daniel mouthed a "sorry" to Poppy, who gave a wistful shrug. But when Daniel and Poppy saw the front page of their rival, they understood exactly why Rollo was erupting like a volcano.

Underneath a photograph of the body of Sir James with the death mask of Nefertiti resting, where it had fallen, beside him, was the following article:

# EGYPTIAN ADVENTURER DIES AT DEATH MASK AUCTION

## The curse of the Pharaoh Queen strikes again

*By Lionel Saunders*

*Henley-on-Thames, Sunday, 11 December 1921 – The renowned adventurer and antiquities collector Sir James Maddox has died at his home, Winterton Hall, under mysterious circumstances.*

Sir James collapsed during an auction of the death mask of the Egyptian Queen Nefertiti, on Saturday night, in the presence of representatives from the world's leading museums. It is believed his heart stopped.

*Courier* correspondents were present to witness events as they unfolded, including an attempt by some of the guests to revive the victim, which, according to Dr Edward Vance, who examined the body soon afterwards, "might have had more effect if properly done". Dr Vance also expressed disappointment that the renowned author and physician Dr Sir Arthur Conan Doyle, who had been at Winterton Hall earlier in the day, had not been there to save the life of his friend.

"If Sir Arthur had been at the auction he would have known how to properly do heart massage and the Kiss of Life," said Dr Vance.

Dr Vance confirmed that Sir James died of a heart attack brought on by shock. The *Courier* can reveal that the shock was the result of the unjustified suggestion by archaeologist Howard Carter (best known for his quest to find the tomb of the boy king Tutankhamun) that the priceless bejewelled mask might be a fake.

It was after this ungrounded accusation had been made – in the presence of representatives from the British, Berlin, Cairo, and New York Metropolitan Museums respectively – that Sir James clutched his chest and fell to the ground in the throes of a heart attack. His wife, Lady Ursula Maddox, rushed to his side and held him as he died. According to Dr Vance the lady is suffering from acute shock but is likely to make a full recovery.

Auctioneer Mr Albert Carnaby told the *Courier* that he believed Mr Carter had been put under duress by the delegation from the Cairo Museum "to make the preposterous allegation that the mask was a fake in order to prevent a museum from a civilized white nation adding the priceless artefact to their collections."

"As Egypt moves towards independence and beyond I think we are going to see more of these groundless accusations as the former colony seeks to humiliate the very nations and institutions that have saved its art and culture from disappearing into the Sahara Desert," Mr Carnaby added.

Mr Carnaby also said that, at the request of Lady Ursula Maddox, the mask is to be kept at Carnaby's Auction House until further notice.

The auction took place as the culmination of a weekend of activities at Winterton Hall, including a clay shooting party and a séance. It was at the séance, on Friday 9 December, that the curse of the pharaoh queen was first mentioned and which guests at the weekend believe might have played a role in Sir James' death.

Mr Fox Flinton, the actor, who is a cousin of Lady Ursula, told the *Courier* he believes it was the Curse of Nefertiti that killed Sir James. Mr Flinton also told the *Courier* that it is not the first time the curse has struck and that a man was found dead, "in much the same way as Sir James", back in 1914 in the tomb where the mask was first found.

The *Courier* is currently investigating the details of this first death and will bring them – and any further developments regarding the mask – to its readers as soon as they are revealed.

"It's utter codswallop! The whole bloody thing!" Rollo was pacing up and down the conference room, gesticulating wildly. "But what really gets my goat is that they've brought out a Sunday edition! The *Courier never* have a Sunday edition. If I could get my hands on that snake Saunders I'd wring his scrawny neck!" He mimed the action to punctuate his point.

Poppy too was furious. Not about the Sunday edition – hats off to them for taking the initiative and getting the scoop – but for maligning Daniel and Rollo, who had desperately tried to save Sir James' life. "How dare they!" she spluttered. "I didn't see them lift a finger to do anything. At least you two tried! And from what I could see, you did everything properly. I've worked at a hospital, remember? It's outrageous! Completely outrageous!"

Daniel reached across the desk and squeezed her hand. He was the only one in the room who didn't appear to be affected by the article. "All right you two, calm down. There's no use crying over spilt milk. The question is, what are we going to do now?"

Rollo stopped pacing and slumped into a chair. "You're right Danny Boy. What's done is done – now we need to plot our revenge."

Daniel shook his head. "Not *revenge*, Rollo, and as soon as Poppy calms down I'm sure she'll say the same. But we can get back by scooping them. However, we should do it with the truth, not a pack of lies. Here, have a cigar." Daniel plucked a cigar out of Rollo's breast pocket and offered it to his employer.

Rollo took a deep breath, smiled wryly, and took the cigar from Daniel. "Thanks Danny Boy. You're right. We can turn this around." He picked up the *Courier* again, skimmed through it, and circled a couple of paragraphs. "We can't do anything about the Kiss of Life comments as it will appear petty trying to defend ourselves, but we can do something about the rest of it. I can probably pull together a more detailed article on the séance – they've only just mentioned it briefly, although they do have a photograph. But from what I recall Delilah telling me – I'll formally interview her for it, as well as a couple of the others who were there – the curse mentioned was in relation to King Tut's tomb, not Nefertiti's mask. Is that right?"

Rollo was back into management mode. Whatever anger Poppy felt would need to be set aside for a while. There was a job to do.

"Yes, as far as I recall, that's the case. I actually suggest you speak to Howard Carter, as he is the one who Madame Minette directed her comments to."

"Good idea, I'll see what I can do. And you managed to get hold of Madame Minette's address, didn't you? Do you think you could drop around there sometime soon?"

Poppy had intended to do so on Monday. It was now just after lunch on Sunday. The newspaper office was usually closed on a Sunday, but the three journalists had agreed in the car that they should try to get something together to put into the Monday edition (which was normally printed on a Saturday night) because of the sudden and dramatic end to Sir James. They knew the *Courier* would be doing something, but hadn't been prepared for them to bring out an emergency edition overnight. So it was even more imperative that they put in some hours now to get back into the running. Although the Monday edition had been printed, there would still be time to reprint the front page if they worked through the afternoon and into the evening. But would there be time if she went to Madame Minette's?

She mentioned her concerns to Rollo who, after making a few notes regarding the proposed schedule, agreed that it could wait for Monday.

"That way you could also ask her about the Renoir angle. Would you be able to bring your meeting with Davies and Philpott forward though?"

Poppy nodded. "Yes, I'll give it a go. I can put in a call to the Hotel Russell and ask them. And while I'm at it I'll see if I can speak to Yasmin and her brother. And perhaps Marjorie. There's another angle in the Egyptians trying to delay or stop the sale of the mask. I don't think it's the way the *Courier* made it out to be, but there is something in it. I think Yasmin was the one who advised her brother to suggest that tests be conducted on the mask. I think she's trying to buy time for her to orchestrate a legal intervention."

Rollo nodded in agreement. "Yes, I think you're right. She did say to me that she was 'on the case'. I'll tell you what – leave Yasmin to me. But you can handle Faizal and Miz El Farouk. They're staying at the Hotel Russell too. You might also get a bit more on this 1914 murder – I see the *Courier* botched that story up too; it certainly wasn't 'in a similar way' to Sir James, was it?"

"No, it wasn't."

"Good. Then flesh that out a bit more. See what you can pull together this afternoon."

Poppy had been making notes. "All right, I'll see what I can do."

Rollo was now chewing on the unlit cigar. "Good, good. This is coming together very nicely. Danny, what pics do you have?"

"None of the séance, unfortunately. But I've got some of Delilah as Nefertiti, plus one of the mask. A lovely close-up. Better than the *Courier*'s. I've also got some of the shoot, but they won't help..."

Rollo unplugged the cigar from his mouth and jabbed it at Daniel. "Not that shoot, no. But what about the shooting accident the day before?"

Daniel shook his head. "Sorry, nothing."

"Doesn't matter," said Rollo. "We've still got the information. The *Courier* didn't even mention the shooting of the boy. We can scoop them on that. A weekend of tragedy! Which hospital was he taken to?"

"The Royal Chelsea."

"Not too far, then. Good. Get your pics developed first, then head over there. Try to get a picture of the boy in bed looking sorry for himself. I'll give Ike a ring and fill him in. We'll need his help. He can meet you there. I'm not sure what the story is behind the shooting but there definitely is one. Maybe the boy and his father will be able to tell you more, now that the immediate shock is over. And then perhaps Ike can ring the butler at Winterton and question him about why there was a shell in his pocket."

"B-but then he'll know I was snooping!"

"There were three of us there, Poppy. Ike won't have to say which of his colleagues told him, just that one of us did. Besides," he grinned, "you *were* snooping."

Poppy bit her lip. "Yes, I was."

Rollo chuckled. "And I'm so glad you were. Right team, off you go! Let's show those *Courier* boys what *real* journalists can do."

# CHAPTER 18

The Hotel Russell on Russell Square was a monstrous red terracotta affair of arches, towers, and domes, now made doubly garish by an explosion of Christmas decorations. The main entrance was guarded by life-sized statues of the four British queens Elizabeth, Anne, Mary, and Victoria, after whom the hotel's palatial suites were named. The foyer was dominated by a Pyrenean marble staircase, and the dining room – which led to an indoor sunken garden, twinkling with festive baubles – had been designed by the same man who had created the dining rooms of the sister ships *Titanic*, *Atlantic*, and *Olympic*. Poppy read all of this on an information card as she waited to be helped at the reception desk. She decided that she would have to pop into the dining room before she left – for old times' sake – as she had just recently travelled on the *Olympic* and had spent some delightful evenings eating and dancing in that room.

Eventually Poppy caught the attention of the receptionist and asked him to let Miss Philpott and Dr Davies know she was there. She had telephoned ahead and Miss Philpott, Dr Davies, and Miss El Farouk had agreed to see her. Dr Osman was not in as he was spending some time with his sister. Poppy thought she would speak to the Americans first, then the Egyptian lady. Fifteen minutes later she and Jennifer Philpott were sitting at a table on a patio off the sunken garden sharing a pot of tea. Dr Davies, it turned out, sent his apologies – he had been called out suddenly to another meeting.

But Poppy didn't mind. She liked Miss Philpott and felt she had already made a connection with her. Dr Davies was an unknown quantity and she might have had to spend valuable time establishing a rapport with him instead of getting straight down to business.

The ladies spent a few minutes going over the events of the previous evening, expressing their shock and sadness before getting to the point of the meeting: the Renoir.

Miss Philpott reached into her handbag and brought out a catalogue for Carnaby's Auction House. "I dug this out for you. Thought it might be useful. It's for the pre-Christmas auction," she explained. She turned to a bookmarked page and opened it in front of Poppy. "Here's the Renoir in question." She pushed the book towards the young journalist, pointing to a black and white photograph of a painting entitled *Yachts on the Seine*. "That's the painting Madame Minette – pretending to be Albert Carnaby's mother – asked him to withdraw from auction."

"Why?" asked Poppy, looking at the typical Impressionist-style painting, bleached of colour.

"I'm not sure," said Miss Philpott. "The owner of the painting is listed as 'a private collector' and the guide price is £1,000."

"Is that a lot for one of these?"

"It's at the top end, yes, but his work has gone up in price since he died last year. However, what makes this painting special is that it's one of a pair of companion paintings Renoir did with his pal Claude Monet. The two of them often used to paint the same scenes together."

"Hmmm," said Poppy. "Do you know who has the companion piece?"

"I don't," said Miss Philpott. "But… if the two were to be sold as a pair, that would inflate the price considerably."

"Really?" asked Poppy, her mind ticking over all sorts of scenarios. "I wonder if that's got something to do with the request to withdraw it. Perhaps it's someone's way of stalling until the companion piece can be auctioned at the same time."

"Good thinking," said Miss Philpott as she popped a sugar cube into her tea. "Do you think there's a story in this for the paper?"

Poppy stirred her own tea and took a sip. "There might be. The whole thing was very odd, wasn't it, shoehorning it into a set-piece about Nefertiti? I mean it's obvious why the Maddoxes would want to create some mystique around the mask, but why muddy the waters with the Renoir?"

Miss Philpott pushed her spectacles up onto the bridge of her nose. "You think the Maddoxes orchestrated the whole thing?"

Poppy nodded. "I do. Who else could it be? But there's nothing illegal about what they've done. Some would say it was all just part of the party fun. But the Renoir – that just doesn't fit, and it's troubling me."

Miss Philpott looked at Poppy shrewdly. "I heard from Judson Quinn at *The New York Times* that you had a first-class newshound nose, and it looks like he's right."

Poppy flushed. "Why thank you, Miss Philpott. That's very kind."

"Please, call me Jenny. I think you're right about this Poppy. And even though on the surface there doesn't seem anything illegal about it – just a little curious – I too have my instincts. I've been around the art and antiquities business long enough to tell you that crime is rife."

Poppy's ears pricked up. "Are you saying there might very well be a crime here, Jenny?"

Miss Philpott nodded. "It's a real possibility. It would be

very helpful if we knew who has the Monet companion piece and who the 'private collector' who owns this one is."

Poppy nodded her agreement. "Yes it would. Any idea how we could find that out?"

Miss Philpott sipped her tea and put the cup back on the porcelain saucer with a tinkle. "Let me make some enquiries. I have a friend here in London at the National Gallery who is an expert in the Impressionists. He's a personal friend of Monet – who of course is still very much alive – and he may know who he sold the painting to. Just leave it to me. I'll see what I can find out."

"Oh, that will be spiffing! When are you going back to New York?"

"Not until after the auction so there's still time. I'll drop by the gallery after our meeting with Carnaby at the British Museum tomorrow."

Poppy's eyes widened. "You're meeting him tomorrow? About the mask?"

"Yes. We collared him before we left Winterton this morning. There's one thing not to harass Lady Ursula in her time of grief, but Albert Carnaby doesn't fall into the same category. We didn't come all this way not to have a chance to bid on that mask. So, we've arranged for the mask to undergo tests on Monday morning, then to have a meeting with him in the afternoon to discuss the results and, if it's authentic, reschedule the auction as soon as possible. Dr Davies and I can extend our stay here by a couple of weeks if necessary. Obviously we can't expect Lady Ursula to have another auction before the funeral, but we don't see why Carnaby can't do it on her behalf as soon as possible afterwards."

"When is the funeral? Do you know? I'd like to pay my respects."

"I'm not sure. I'll try to find out tomorrow."

Poppy nodded. "Yes, and I'll ask our receptionist who deals with death and funeral notices to keep an eye out too."

Just then, Kamela El Farouk joined them. She looked quite fetching, Poppy noticed, in a peppermint green frock and matching headscarf, with wisps of long dark hair visible around her face. She was apologetic as she joined the other two women. "I'm sorry I'm a little early Poppy. I can wait until you've finished speaking with Miss Philpott, if you like."

"No, not at all," said Poppy. "I think we're finished here. Miss Philpott has been most helpful. Can you give me a ring tomorrow, Jenny? About what we spoke about? I'll be at the office in the morning." She handed a calling card to the American lady, embossed with: *Poppy Denby, journalist, The Daily Globe, London* and an accompanying telephone number and address. Miss Philpott slipped it into her handbag. Poppy handed her the auction brochure too.

"No, you keep that; Dr Davies has another copy."

"Thank you." Poppy slipped it into her satchel then, as Miss Philpott left, called over the waiter to ask for a fresh pot of tea and a clean cup and saucer for Miss El Farouk.

"Oh, and would you like a bite to eat? I'm feeling peckish."

Miss El Farouk said she would and she and Poppy chose something each from the cake trolley.

Suitably served, Poppy got down to business. "Thanks for seeing me at such short notice, Kamela. By any chance, have you seen the *Courier* today?"

"Unfortunately yes."

"Then you'll know that they have got the wrong story about what happened in 1914. It wasn't in a tomb and the watchman didn't die in the same way as Sir James – at least not from what you told me on Friday night."

Miss El Farouk nodded, chewing on a piece of lemon

drizzle cake. When she had finished, she dabbed at her mouth with a linen napkin and said: "I think they must have got their information from eavesdropping on us at dinner. I never actually spoke to either of them. Neither did Dr Osman. Not surprising with their clearly anti-Egyptian stance, is it?"

Poppy, embarrassed on behalf of her more jingoistic countrymen, apologized.

"Not your fault at all, Poppy. I'm sure the *Globe* will do a much better job."

"We'll certainly try," agreed Poppy and then proceeded, pencil in hand, to clarify the story Miss El Farouk had first told her.

"So to summarize, a pair of local youngsters, whose father worked for Dr Ludwig Borchardt, the eminent German archaeologist who found the original Nefertiti bust, stumbled on a hidden chamber near to the site of Thutmose's workshop. We will have to do a little sidebar on who Thutmose was, and his connection to Nefertiti and Akhenaten, but that's easily done. But the main story will be the murderous circumstances surrounding the discovery of the mask that may or may not be on auction again soon."

"Yes, that's right. The youngsters –"

"Do you know their names?"

"Unfortunately I don't recall. I'm sure they will be in the trial transcript, but that will be back in Cairo… does it matter?"

"Not really. But I do like to be as complete as I can. Never mind. But what we do know – if you're prepared to go on record –"

Miss El Farouk said that she was.

"– is that the watchman – known as Mohammed, you say? – was murdered. Beaten to death. And his dog too. You are sure about that?"

"Yes. Definitely. It was all over the papers at the time. The Egyptian papers, that is..."

"Of course, although I wonder if it got any coverage here... or in Germany... but I won't have time to follow that up. Again, never mind. I think I've got a lot to put in the article already, particularly the bit about Sir James finding the body and helping to apprehend the suspects."

"Helping to *frame* the suspects."

"Yes, but that's not official. It's not on record."

"I can go on record. You can quote me accusing him of killing Mohammed."

Poppy opened her eyes wide. "You think Sir James is guilty of *murder*?"

Miss El Farouk's eyes flitted from side to side. "Possibly. He's certainly one of the likely suspects. No one else apart from the policeman could have done it. And that's a bit of a stretch. So can you quote me on that?"

Poppy frowned, wondering how that would go down with the *Globe* readers. They might see it as uncouthly digging up dirt on the deceased and adding unnecessary upset to an already grieving widow. On the other hand, it was a juicy accusation... She made a note and circled it, saying: "I will have to pass that with my editor first. My feeling though is that he would require a corroborating source. Do you have one?"

Miss El Farouk shook her head glumly. "I don't. But what about the mask being stolen? Herr Stein could corroborate that."

"He could corroborate the accusation, yes."

"Can you use it?"

Poppy nodded. "I think we can, because it's linked to the dispute around the sale of the mask – as long as we don't say Maddox definitely stole the mask, only that accusations have been made that the mask was stolen. The readers can infer for themselves whether or not Sir James is being accused. Can you just clarify though why you believe it was stolen?"

Miss El Farouk finished her cake and dusted the crumbs from her fingertips. "Yes. That's easy. Despite all the witnesses to the mask's discovery, it was not listed in the manifest of the contents of the chamber. However, because of all the drama surrounding the murder of the watchman and the arrest of the youngsters, this only came to light a few weeks later."

Poppy tapped her pad with her pencil. "And what did Sir James say?"

"Well, as he wasn't responsible for drawing up the manifest or packing up the contents of the storeroom, he claimed it wasn't his responsibility, and he has no idea what happened to the mask – between it being found and then resurfacing in the shop in Cairo years later."

"Who was responsible?"

"An assistant of Borchardt."

"Name?"

"Unfortunately I can't remember. Herr Stein might know."

Poppy made another note. "Thanks, I'll ask him. But you can definitely say that the mask disappeared soon after the body was found?"

"Well I can't say *how* soon afterwards..."

"No, of course. Perhaps we could just say 'afterwards'."

"Is that a problem?"

Poppy smiled. "Not at all. We've got lots to go on. Thanks so much for your help, Kamela."

"You're welcome. However..."

"Yes?"

Miss El Farouk offered to pour Poppy another cup of tea. Poppy declined. The Egyptian woman continued as she filled her own cup: "I do hope you can manage to write something about the Egyptian side of the story. And why we believe the mask was stolen and that, as it didn't go through the proper channels via the Egyptian Antiquities Service, it should *not* have been taken out of Egypt."

Poppy nodded her understanding. "Yes I can, in passing. But don't worry. Rollo, my boss, is working that angle with Yasmin Reece-Lansdale. She'll be sure to give him the full story."

Miss El Farouk chuckled. "I'm sure she will."

Poppy made her way across Russell Square Park towards the back of the British Museum on Montague Street. She had arranged to meet Daniel there, as it was easier for him to find parking than outside the busy hotel where he would have to jostle for space with taxis picking up or dropping off clients. The snow that had covered the countryside around Henley-on-Thames, turning it into a Christmas card scene, had been pummelled by millions of pairs of London shoes and London wheels into dirty puddles of slush. Fortunately, this time she had remembered her galoshes and had slipped them on before stepping out of the hotel.

She made a quick, huddled dash through the park – not wanting to linger as it was now dusk – and breathed more easily when she reached the relative safety of Montague Street. She chastised herself for being so silly, but she couldn't quite shake the unnerving events of the weekend. She checked her watch: it was five to four. Daniel had said he would meet her at four o'clock on his way back from the hospital. Poppy would ordinarily have got the tube or bus back to Fleet Street, but as it was Sunday, service was intermittent. Besides, it was another opportunity to be with Daniel.

Poppy crossed the street and stood under a lamp post, beside a gate in the wrought iron railings of the museum. This wasn't the grand public entrance, just a service gate, and with the museum closed for the day, it was, unsurprisingly, locked. She thought about what Jenny Philpott had told her about the meeting with Albert Carnaby tomorrow. If it was at the museum, no doubt reps from the British delegation – definitely Dr Mortimer, possibly Howard Carter – would be in attendance. She hadn't mentioned anything about the Germans and the Egyptians, but Poppy wouldn't be surprised if they too would be there. *Hmmm, I wonder if I can wangle an invite... or at least be on hand to interview them when they come out of the meeting.* She wished she had asked Miss Philpott what time the meeting would occur. She made a mental note to telephone Jenny at the hotel when she got back to the office. It was too late to backtrack now. She checked her watch again. Two minutes to four. *Daniel should be here any minute...*

Suddenly some movement in the museum grounds caught her eye. Striding purposefully along the side of the building was a man in a black fedora and trench coat. Her hackles rose. It was time to confront this man and find out what he was jolly well up to. She clutched the railings with her gloved hands and called out: "Hello! You sir! Can I have a word?"

The man turned and stared at Poppy. It was too far away and too dark to see his face, but his body language was clear to see: he tensed, stared, then turned on his heel and stalked off.

Poppy ran along the railings parallel to his path, calling out: "You sir! Stop! Why have you been following me?"

The man put down his head and continued to ignore her until he came to a short flight of steps, which he hurried down. Poppy could not tell where the steps led, but as he did not return she assumed they led to a door into the basement of the museum. She called again. The man did not emerge. She grabbed the railings and shook them in frustration. *Oh bother that the gates are locked!*

A horn honked behind her. Poppy turned to see the *Globe*'s Model T Ford pull up at the kerb. Daniel rolled down the window to greet her while his passenger – Ike Garfield – jumped out and opened the back door for her. "Your carriage awaits, m'lady."

"Poppy, what is it?" asked Ike, looking into her pale face.

Poppy explained to the two men what had just happened and pointed to where the man in the fedora hat had disappeared.

"Are you sure it was him?" asked Daniel, still in the motor and keeping the engine running.

"Yes," said Poppy.

"A fedora hat and overcoat you say? Like I'm wearing?" asked Ike.

Poppy looked at her fellow journalist and realized that he was wearing the same attire as her stalker. But that was not unusual. Fedora hats and trench coats were not uncommon... could the man in the museum just have been some innocent employee?

Ike asked the same question.

"It could have been, yes," said Poppy. "But then why did he ignore me when I called?"

Ike shrugged. "Perhaps he thought you were a member of the public trying to get into the museum when it was closed. He didn't want to deal with you so he scarpered. Rude, yes, but not criminal."

Poppy frowned at Ike. He was annoyingly right. She turned her attention to Daniel. "What do you think?"

Daniel looked at her sympathetically. "I don't know. I didn't see him. But you're obviously unnerved. Look, why don't you get into the motor. It's freezing out there. I don't think we'd be able to get into the museum now to check anyway. So why don't we go back to the office and see if we can get hold of Dr

Mortimer? We can tell him what's happened and ask him who might be at the museum at this time of day on a Sunday. That could narrow it down for us. Does that sound like a plan?"

Poppy took one last look at the museum. There was no sign of the stalker. "I suppose it does," she agreed, and got into the car.

# CHAPTER 19

Rollo staggered into the editorial office carrying a huge platter of sandwiches, followed by Poppy with a tray of coffee cups. Ike cleared some space on the conference table – moving photographs, flat plans, and jazz files – while Daniel shut the door behind them to keep the heat in.

"Where did you get all those on a Sunday, Rollo? Made with your own fine hand?" jibed Ike.

Rollo grinned. "Not on your nelly. I twisted someone's arm over at my club."

"Speaking of your club," said Poppy, distributing the mugs of brew to the four assembled journalists, "did you remember to follow up that reporter from *The Times*? What's his name? Walter Jensford?"

Rollo accepted his cup from Poppy with thanks. "That's the fella. Wally Jensford. And as a matter of fact, I did remember, Miz Denby. This old stallion isn't ready to go out to pasture yet."

"Oh, I didn't mean –"

Rollo gave a look of mock outrage. "Forty-five isn't *that* old."

Before Poppy could renew her halting apology, Rollo continued: "He's still a club member. But as I thought, retired from the biz. He's been unwell, apparently, and has moved into a nursing home out in Shepherd's Bush. But I think we can visit him. Are you up for it, Miz Denby?"

"Of course! When?"

"I'll try to arrange something for tomorrow. Didn't you say Madame Minette lives out that way somewhere?"

Poppy checked her notebook. "Yes, Acton."

Rollo made a note. "Good. We can do them on the same trip."

"Will that be before or after the meeting at the British Museum?"

Rollo looked at her in surprise. "Are we invited to that?"

Poppy shook her head. "Not that I know of. Nothing stopping us waiting outside for news though, is there? Either way, Jenny Philpott said she'd tell me what happened afterwards. And remember, I told you she's also going to speak to her friend at the National Gallery about the Renoir – to see if he knows anything about it or a companion piece."

Rollo took a sip of coffee. "Ah! That hits the spot. Thanks Poppy. I've spoken to Yazzie and she's told me reps from all four museums will be present. If they can get Carnaby and Lady Ursula to agree, they'll schedule a new auction as soon as possible. She's also promised to telephone me the outcome immediately. We'll stop press if we have to, but I think we can still make the Tuesday morning edition."

Ike grinned. "And unless the *Courier* has someone on the payroll at the museum, we could beat them to it."

Poppy picked out a cheese and tomato sandwich from the pile. "Actually, I think they might. Or if not on the payroll, then at least in their pocket. Albert Carnaby seemed all too happy to give them the type of quotes that their readers like – jingoistic, anti-Egyptian, ungrateful natives, and the like. So it might be a race to see which of us gets it out first."

Rollo growled. "You're right. Damn it. They'll get it from Carnaby. We'll just have to make sure we write the better story. I'll do it myself. Danny Boy, can you stake out the meeting and see if you can get some pics as soon as the news is released?"

"How will I know when it's released?"

"Liaise with Yazzie." The editor wrote something down on a scrap of paper and passed it to the photographer. "Here's her number."

"So," said Ike, "I assume you and Poppy will be heading out west in the morning then. I can drop you off if you like. Save you the cab or train fare – at least one way. I'm thinking of paying a visit to Winterton Hall."

Three pairs of eyes turned to the West Indian journalist. "Why's that?" asked Rollo.

"Danny and I haven't had a chance to fill you all in on what happened at the hospital yet."

"How's the boy?" asked Poppy.

"He's all right," answered Daniel. "Recovering from the operation. In a fair bit of pain, but the doctors think they've saved his foot and he'll be able to use it again."

"Oh, that's a relief!" said Poppy.

"So what's the story?" asked Rollo.

"Well, the father was so grateful to Danny for helping out that he was happy to let us talk to the lad," said Ike. "And a very interesting tale he had to tell too."

Both Poppy and Rollo leaned forward.

Ike grinned, enjoying being centre stage for a change. "Turns out the boy had been bribed to put a deer cartridge in one of the shotguns."

"Bribed?" gasped Poppy. "By whom?"

"Well, bribed wasn't the word he used. But that's what it amounts to. He was given a pound to load one of the guns with deer cartridge and to keep quiet about it."

"And who gave him the money?"

"The butler," Ike consulted his notes. "A Mr Grimes."

Rollo winked at Poppy. "So you were right, Miz Denby; it was the butler who did it in the courtyard."

"But why?" asked Poppy, delighted that her suspicions about Grimes had been right, but confused as to motive. "What did he intend to be done with buckshot?"

"Ah, well, that's where it gets even more curious. Grimes didn't actually say it to him; it was written in a note which was in a sealed envelope. Grimes said he had been instructed to give it to the boy, but didn't say who it was from. The note was unsigned. But it instructed him to fill a particular weapon with buckshot."

"Which one?" asked Rollo. "They all looked the same to me."

Daniel shook his head. "Not exactly. I noticed most of the guns were standard Purdeys. But one of them was a spanking new Browning."

Rollo and Poppy – neither of them knowing anything about weaponry – gave him a "do you really have to go into such detail" look. Then Rollo said: "Get to the point, Danny."

Daniel and Ike exchanged a conspiratorial look. Poppy could tell they were excited.

Daniel took a deep breath, then played his trump card: "Do you know who was the only person to shoot with the Browning yesterday?"

"Who?" asked Poppy and Rollo in unison.

"Lady Ursula Maddox!"

Rollo's jaw dropped. "Grimes paid the kid to put more powerful bullets in the old dame's gun?"

"Cartridges, not bullets, but yes," said Daniel.

"But why?" asked Poppy again.

"That's what the boy didn't know. Nor did his father. And that's what I'm going to try to find out at Winterton tomorrow. I've already made an appointment," said Ike.

"You have?" asked Rollo. "On what pretence?"

Ike grinned at his boss. "No pretence. I'm going to write Sir James' obituary and have asked Lady Ursula if she will meet with me to discuss it. I called just after we got back to the office, after picking Poppy up at the museum."

*The museum!* Poppy suddenly remembered the man in the fedora. She had wanted to ring Dr Mortimer but then realized the museum wasn't open... and if the museum wasn't open...

"Who answered the telephone at Winterton?" she asked.

"The butler. Grimes. Initially he didn't want to bother Lady Ursula, but when I told him I would go ahead and write the obituary anyway, and that if she didn't speak to me she would lose the opportunity to have some input, he changed his mind. So he called her to the phone and –"

"What time was this?" Poppy interrupted.

Ike looked surprised. Poppy wasn't usually this rude. "Half past four. Why?"

Poppy bit her lip then puffed out her frustration. "Because then the man at the museum couldn't have been Grimes. It would have been impossible for him to get from Bloomsbury all the way out to Winterton in half an hour."

Daniel gave Poppy a sympathetic look. "Well, that should make you feel better, Poppy. It was just a coincidence then. Just another man wearing a fedora and a trench coat. No one's following you."

Was that true? Was no one following her? Had she just imagined it? But before Poppy could explore those thoughts further Rollo interrupted.

"Can we please get back on track here?"

"Sorry Rollo, yes."

"Thank you, Ike. Good work, old sport – I'll buy you a pint for that once we've put this edition to bed. So, tomorrow you'll head out to Winterton in the morning, dropping me and Poppy in Shepherd's Bush to speak to the old *Times* reporter. Poppy, when we're finished there we can get a cab to Acton – it's not that far – to see if we can catch Madame Minette at home. Then we should be able to get the train back from Acton sometime in the early afternoon. That should give us time to write up before deadline and still leave some time to cover whatever comes out of the museum meeting. Good, good. And now –" he looked at his pocket watch then slipped it back into his waistcoat pocket "– we've got two hours to write up the front-page copy for tomorrow's edition. Poppy, you flesh out the Nefertiti mask story and whatever you have so far on the 1914 murder. Ike, can you put something together on the boy? Just go with the 'another accident on a tragic weekend angle' for now – you can write a follow-up on it tomorrow. As it stands, it will be enough to scoop the *Courier*, who failed to mention it at all..." He grinned at Poppy; she grinned back, relishing the thought of one-upping Lionel.

"Then, Danny Boy, get the front-page pics ready. I've already written the lead – a more fleshed out account of Sir James' death, pointedly correcting some of the inaccuracies of the *Courier* report – so I'll typeset that. And then I'll get the press rolling." He slammed down his palms onto the table, making the coffee cups and sandwich platter rattle. "Go to it team! We're on deadline!"

# CHAPTER 20

It was nearly eight o'clock when Poppy's cab pulled up outside Aunt Dot's Chelsea townhouse. She stifled a yawn as she paid the cabbie his fare then let herself into the dark, cold house, carrying her weekend case with her. Daniel had offered to see her home, but Poppy had declined, knowing that he wanted to get back to see his children before their bedtime. Poppy flicked the light switch in the hall and picked up Saturday morning's post from the mat. There were a couple of bills plus a telegram. She tore open the envelope and read:

> *Dear Poppy STOP Greetings from Paris STOP*
> *Grace & I about to board Orient Ex for grand*
> *adventure STOP Hope Winterton fun STOP*
> *Next stop Prague STOP Bon voyage to us STOP*

Poppy smiled as she refolded the telegram and slipped it back into the envelope. It was lovely to hear Aunt Dot sounding so chipper. After the stressful last eighteen months, separated from Grace, the two women deserved some happiness.

Poppy took off her hat and placed it on the rack. She started unbuttoning her coat but thought better of it. Having not had a fire lit all weekend, the house was freezing. She kept it on as she made her way to the sitting room, knelt down, and lit the fire that Aunt Dot's charlady Violet had very kindly prepared. After a few minutes the kindling was nicely ablaze and licking the coals. Poppy got up, brushed the coal dust from her hands, and then headed towards the kitchen to make herself something to eat.

The kitchen was down a short flight of steps at the end of the hall. It was even colder down there than upstairs, with the stone flag floor not providing the insulation of the carpeting in the rest of the house. In addition, there was a door that led out into a small courtyard where the coal shed was kept, and Violet had forgotten to put the draught dampener across the bottom. Poppy found the sausage-shaped sack and pushed it in place with her foot. Then she lit the gas cooker and put a kettle on to boil. It had been a while since Rollo's sandwiches and she was hungry, so she checked the larder to see what she could find. There was bread – a couple of days old but still edible – and, in Aunt Dot's fancy new gas-run refrigerator, some sausages. *Hmmm, sausage sandwiches. Nice.*

Poppy carried her wares out of the larder, put them down on the bench, then selected a heavy cast-iron pan for the sausages. The kettle was beginning to bubble and hiss. Poppy reached for a tea towel that hung from a peg on the back of the door. But as she did the door knob turned... Poppy froze. The knob wiggled. Poppy grabbed the frying pan and held it in both hands, like a rounders bat. Then she called out: "Who's there?" The wiggling stopped. "V – Violet?" Poppy asked, knowing as she did that it wasn't the charlady who only worked weekdays, and never at night. Then the knocking began: *knock, knock, knock* in three steady raps, then a pause, then the three raps again. Hell would freeze over before Poppy answered that! The kettle whistled, loud and shrill, a hysterical descant over the percussive rap.

She put down the frying pan, grabbed the tea towel, then lifted the kettle off the flame, her mind racing through self-defence possibilities involving boiling water and kitchen utensils. The rapping continued. She picked up the frying pan and bashed it against the wooden door, screaming: "I'm calling the police! They'll be here any minute!"

The rapping stopped. Silence. The telephone was in the hall. Poppy would have to run to make the call. But what if he tried to break in when she was away? She looked to the kitchen window. The curtains were drawn, and she was too scared to open them in case the intruder saw her. With the light behind her, she wouldn't be able to see him as easily. And he might try to smash his way through... Poppy tried to remember what kind of catch was on the window. From what she recalled it was a strong one, as was the one on the door. But a determined intruder might be able to force his way in...

She ran up the stairs into the hall, still carrying her frying pan. She grabbed the receiver and dialled the operator, her hands shaking. "Police please! Hurry!" The operator sounded annoyingly calm as she asked: "Which area?"

"137 King's Road Chelsea! Hurry! There's someone trying to get in."

"One moment please. Connecting..."

As Poppy listened with one ear to the whirrs and clicks, she tuned in with the other to sounds from the kitchen: *knock, knock, knock* had now become *bang, bang, bang*. Surely the neighbours would start complaining soon. Wouldn't they...?

"Hello, police, what is your emergency?"

Poppy, still clutching the frying pan, gabbled out an explanation.

The policeman remained calm. "Are you sure it's not a friend or family member who has forgotten his key?"

Poppy took a deep breath, swallowing her anger, and explained why that could not be the case. It was the back door... friends would come to the front. All of her family were out of town... and besides, someone had been following her yesterday... No, she hadn't reported it... *sigh*.

"Is there someone you can call? A male friend? A neighbour?"

Was there? She didn't know the telephone numbers of any of the neighbours. There was Delilah who lived down the street, and Marjorie around the block, but would they be any help? Should she call Daniel? Daniel, who was on the other side of the city. Daniel, who had been away from his children all weekend...

"No," she said. "There's no one."

The policeman told her that he would send someone round right away. She should keep the doors locked and check from an upstairs window to see if it was the policeman at the door before she answered it. Poppy thanked him and put the phone down. The banging had stopped. Dare she go back into the kitchen?

She edged along the hall, telling herself that if "he" had broken in she would have heard it, and tentatively stuck her head around the kitchen door. The draught-dampener was still in place... no one had come in. Suddenly she heard the doorbell ring – someone was at the front door. She hurried back up the stairs. Was that the policeman already? She should go upstairs to look...

She ran upstairs and into the spare bedroom that overlooked the front door. She looked down to see there was no one on the front step. Over the road patrons were emerging from the Electric Cinema. It was now half-past eight and the six o'clock feature show was coming out. She scanned the cinema-goers in their winter coats and hats, but couldn't see the now-familiar figure of the man in the fedora and trench coat. There were some fedoras, yes, but they were on the heads of men with ladies on their arm. She doubted her stalker was one of them. No, he wasn't there.

But there *was* a policeman. He was crossing the road, heading towards her front door. "Oh thank God!" she said out loud and ran downstairs in time to respond to the constable's knock.

For the next fifteen minutes the policeman searched the house, went around the back and checked out the coal shed, ascertained that all windows and doors were locked, knocked on the neighbours to ask if they had seen anything (they hadn't), and finally gave Poppy a paternal talking to about how natural it was to imagine things when staying alone at night.

Poppy firmly but calmly told him she hadn't imagined it, thanked him for his time, and then locked the door behind her. She thought she might call a cab and ask to spend the night at Delilah's flat. But a call to her friend established that no one was at home. She then thought she might try Marjorie, but decided against it. The neighbours had now been alerted that there might be funny goings-on next door, and would no doubt come to her aid if she screamed for help. In fact, one of them, a gentleman, had given her his telephone number, wondering why Miss Denby Snr hadn't already done so. No, Poppy decided, she would be brave and stay home. And cook those sausages.

The sausages eaten and the dishes washed, Poppy went into the sitting room and poured herself a sherry. The fire she'd lit earlier was blazing nicely and she finally felt warm enough to take off her coat. Then she slipped off her shoes, curled her feet under her in the armchair, and sipped her sherry.

*What a night. What a weekend.*

Who was the stalker and why was he harassing her?

If she had been right, and it was him at the museum, then her suspicion that it was Grimes the butler could not be true. He could not have made it back to Winterton in time to talk to Ike Garfield on the telephone. However, what if it wasn't him at the museum? What if Ike was right and it was just an innocent stranger wearing the same common outdoor attire? If that was the case, then the person knocking at her door could still have been Grimes. He could have made it from Winterton to Chelsea between half-past four and half-past eight. Poppy looked at her watch. It was a quarter to ten. Should she ring Winterton now and ask to speak to Grimes? If he wasn't in she would know it was him… but would they answer the telephone at this time of night? Poppy reminded herself that it was a house in mourning. She didn't want to upset Lady Ursula any further. In fact, the more she thought of it, the more it did not seem feasible that Grimes would have left his mistress at a time like this to drive all the way to London to harass a young journalist. No, despite her dislike for the man, Poppy was beginning to dismiss him from her list of suspects. Who, then, did it leave?

Poppy got up and went into the hall – checking to left and right as she did – then quickly retrieved her satchel. Safely back in the sitting room, she took out her notebook and pencil and turned to the list of names she had jotted down in Winterton when she first contemplated the identity of the stalker.

She had narrowed the list down to Sir James, Lionel Saunders, Harry Gibson, Albert Carnaby, Faizal Osman, Dr Giles Mortimer, and Mr Grimes the butler. With a regretful sigh she crossed Sir James off the list, then, after a pause, crossed out Grimes too. So that left the two *Courier* boys, the auctioneer, and the two museum representatives. All, as far as she knew, were currently in London. She asked herself why she had discounted the other men at Winterton and remembered it was to do with their choice of hats: the two German gentlemen wore homburgs; Jonathan Davies, the American, a derby; Sir Arthur Conan Doyle, a bowler; and Fox Flinton, a boater. There was, of course, also the possibility that Mr Fedora had borrowed someone else's hat… but why would he feel the need to do that?

A fedora was a very common hat that in itself would help disguise the identity of the stalker… And then of course there were all the male staff… but, as with Grimes, she found it difficult to accept that they had commuted to London. Difficult, but not impossible… She made a note to ask Ike to look into it when he visited Winterton tomorrow. Perhaps one of them had taken the afternoon and evening off…

She now had four lists:

1. Known fedora-wearers who were definitely or might be in London:
- Lionel Saunders
- Harry Gibson
- Albert Carnaby
- Faizal Osman
- Dr Giles Mortimer

(She then remembered that Rollo had pointed out that Lionel was considerably shorter than the height Poppy had described. She put a question mark next to him.)

2. Non-fedora wearers who definitely were or might be in London (and might have borrowed a fedora as a disguise):
- Fox Flinton (boater)
- Jonathan Davies (derby)
- Herr Stein (homburg)
- Herr Weiner (homburg)
- Howard Carter (homburg)
- Arthur Conan Doyle (bowler)

(She put a question mark against Fox Flinton's name – as far as she knew he had stayed at Winterton to support his cousin Ursula. Then, on reflection, she crossed out Sir Arthur's name. Surely he had been far too busy seeing to his wife to play silly games.)

3. Other males of unknown hats and unknown location:
- The Winterton staff – ask Ike to get staff list if possible.

- 4. Males who are definitely innocent:
- Rollo
- Sir James Maddox
- Daniel

(She put a smiley face next to Rollo, a sad face next to Sir James, and a heart next to Daniel.)

She reread her notes and decided that on the evidence to hand, four men had obvious means (wearing fedoras) and opportunity (being at both Winterton and in London): Albert Carnaby, Harry Gibson, Faizal Osman, and Giles Mortimer. The question that was less clear was motive.

Albert Carnaby was an odd fish, she had to admit. On the basis of what she'd seen at the séance, she would go as far as to say "emotionally disturbed". Yes, he was a very strong candidate. Harry Gibson she'd known for nearly two years. Like his colleague Lionel Saunders, he was a nasty piece of work and she wouldn't put it past him to have decided to terrorize her just for the fun of it. It was he, after all, who had been driving the car when the *Globe* Model T had been pushed off the road. Faizal Osman she'd met just once, but she could not for the life of her fathom why Yasmin Reece-Lansdale's brother would want to toy with her in such a cruel way. So that just left Giles Mortimer. Again, she had no idea why he might want to do it, but she didn't know enough about him to discount him, and, she reminded herself, he did work at the British Museum...

A coal dropped onto the hearth. Poppy unfurled herself from the armchair, picked up a pair of tongs, and popped it back into the fire. As she did, the mantelpiece clock struck eleven. *Golly, is it that time already?*

# CHAPTER 21

Poppy was swimming in the sea at Whitley Bay. Her brother was with her. The waves lifted them up and down, their legs kicking frantically under the water to keep them afloat. Their mother called to them from the shore: "Be careful! Don't go too far out!" and their father waved to them, a pease pudding and ham sandwich in hand. It was getting dark and a light swept over them in a wide arc: it was coming from St Mary's Lighthouse.

Suddenly her brother cried out and disappeared under the waves. Poppy waited for him to pop back up or to grab her ankle and pull her down, pretending he was a shark. She waited. And she waited. The light from St Mary's was sweeping from left to right faster and faster. She looked to shore but could no longer see her parents. She thought she could still hear her mother's voice, distantly calling: "Come back Poppy; come back!" But she couldn't leave without her brother. She dived under the water to find him.

As her eyes adjusted to the murk, she saw him below her, face down, his arms and legs splayed like a tortoise in his red-and-white striped bathers. His blond hair was spread out like a halo. She dived down further and grabbed his collar and pulled him up. His body rotated until he faced her – wearing the death mask of Nefertiti. The beautiful jet eyes bored into Poppy's. She tore off the mask to reveal the face of her nine-year-old brother, his blue eyes lifeless.

She took a fistful of bathing suit and dragged Christopher upwards, towards the sweeping light. But as she burst through the surface she lost her grip and he drifted away from her, back below the waves. She flipped herself over to dive again but then someone grabbed her shoulders and pulled her upwards. She fought, she screamed, then she stared into the face of the man in the fedora hat. He too was wearing Nefertiti's death mask. She clawed at the artefact, trying to tear it from her stalker's face. He laughed and pushed her under the water until her lungs were about to burst.

She screamed. She woke. She cried.

It was eight o'clock when Poppy got off the bus on the Victoria Embankment and walked the short distance to New Scotland Yard. She strode with purpose, utterly incensed with what she had found half an hour earlier on her doormat, and was determined to show it to the police. In her mind it was proof that she had not imagined the events of the previous evening. It was a letter, with her name on it, and no stamp, hand-delivered before the morning post, possibly sometime during the night. She had torn it open.

In a sloping, cursive hand was the following:

*Dearest Poppy,*

*I was so happy to speak to you again after all these years through Madame Minette. However, it hurt me that you ran out of the room. I understand that you have questions – you were always a curious child – but if you come to another séance I will explain everything. I have so much I want to say. And messages to send to Mam and Dad too. I came to your house last night but you would not let me in. I hope one day you will. It is cold and lonely in the spirit realm without you.*

*I look forward to the day you will join me.*
*With all my love and deepest affection,*

*Your brother,*
*Christopher*

Poppy strode into the charge office and slapped the letter down on the desk. But her heart sank when she saw who was manning it: a sergeant with a handlebar moustache. Poppy had had run-ins with this man before. She braced herself for his derision and was surprised when he greeted her with a smile and a "Good morning, Miss Denby. It is Miss Denby, isn't it?"

"It is. Yes." She noticed a copy of *The Daily Globe* open on the counter.

"I see you know Sir Arthur Conan Doyle." The sergeant cocked a thumb toward the paper.

"Er, yes. Well, I've met him. Just this weekend."

The sergeant chuckled. "Pity he didn't stick around for the death of old Maddox, eh?"

Poppy wasn't quite sure where this was going, but she played along. The last time she'd tried to lay a charge at this station the sergeant had prevented her from doing so. "It was a tragic death. I doubt Sir Arthur could have prevented it."

"Not if it was poison, no."

"It wasn't poison. It was a heart attack."

The policeman twirled an end of his moustache around his finger. "Oh no, it was poison. Someone murdered him. The autopsy report's just come in. But listen, I want to ask you a favour… my missus is a Sherlock Holmes fan, and I was wanting to give her a signed copy for Christmas. I was wondering if you could ask Sir Arthur for me, as a special favour, eh? We coppers and you reporters can help each other out from time to time... isn't that so?"

Poppy was stunned. *Poisoned? Sir James was poisoned?* The sergeant was looking at her expectantly. "So can you?"

"Can I what?"

"Ask Sir Arthur to sign a book for my missus."

"I – er – yes, of course," said Poppy, not knowing how exactly she would get to see Conan Doyle, but deciding she'd figure that out later. "I'll see what I can do. What's your wife's name?"

The man smiled, his moustache lifting like a set of dumbbells at the gymnasium. "It's Gladys. Ask him to sign it to Gladys. Thank you, Miss Denby. Good fortune for both of us that you came in today now isn't it?"

"It is," agreed Poppy, now wondering how she could get her hands on the medical report. Rollo would know. She'd best get to the office.

"Was there a reason you came in today? Is there something else I can help you with?"

Yes there was, but the news about Sir James' poisoning had taken the wind out of her sails. Now that she thought of it, perhaps the poisoning gave it a new significance. *It is cold and lonely in the spirit realm without you. I look forward to the day you will join me.* Was that a death threat? Was she to be the killer's next victim? Or was she just being hysterical? She needed to give this some more thought. And talk to Rollo about it. And tell him about Sir James' murder, before the *Courier* got wind of it. Perhaps now was not the time to give the note to the police...

"Er no, nothing. I just came in to thank you for sending someone around to my house last night."

The sergeant frowned. "There was trouble at your house last night?"

"Someone kept knocking on my door. But the constable who came scared him away."

The sergeant nodded. "Good. It was probably just a drunk at the wrong door. Happens more often than you'd think. But you be careful, Miss Denby. And if there's anything I can do, just let me know. Sergeant Barnes it is. And don't forget my missus, Gladys – with a 'y'."

"Stop the press!" Poppy burst into the newsroom, then dished out her astonishing information about the murder of Sir James Maddox. All hell broke loose. Rollo got on the blower, confirming Poppy's story with his contact at Scotland Yard, and then jotted down details of the medical examiner's report. The poison was digitalis – common foxglove – but also used in heart medication. The examiner discounted a mere accidental overdose, as crystallized remnants of the digitalis, found in Sir James' moustache, proved to be of a different grade and composition than that used in the medicinal preparations. Either Sir James had been given additional digitalis, or his usual supply had been tampered with. A telephone call to Sir James' usual physician confirmed that he had not been prescribed anything more than or different to his usual dose, so the medical examiner's conclusion was that unless it was suicide it was "probably" foul play. It was now up to the police to prove it one way or the other.

Poppy suddenly remembered what Sir James had told her on the walk back from the shoot – he had been late taking his dose that morning because he couldn't at first find it. Rollo was delighted to hear it and swore the journalists to secrecy. "The *Courier* will no doubt hear about the ME's report, but they won't have that little morsel. Well done Poppy! Ike, Poppy, I think we all need to go to Winterton now."

"My appointment is at ten o'clock. You won't have time to do the other two interviews first," observed Ike.

"Not to worry. I'll call the nursing home and see if I can reschedule old Wally for later – or another day if needs be. We don't have an appointment with Madame Minette anyway. If she's there she's there and if she's not she's not. We can drop in on the way back. Agreed?"

"Agreed," said Ike.

Poppy and Rollo climbed into the company car as Ike inserted the crank into the front of the motor. As Ike put his back into getting the old vehicle started, Daniel arrived on his motorbike.

Rollo pushed open his window and briefly told the photographer what had happened and that he should find out if the meeting at the museum was still going to go ahead. "We should be back mid-afternoon at the latest, probably earlier."

Daniel saluted Rollo, winked at Ike, and smiled, lovingly, at Poppy. Her heart skipped a beat, and she wondered when they would next have a chance to be alone together...

"Tallyho!" cried Rollo as the engine caught and Ike jumped into the driving seat.

The old Model T chundled westwards, winding its way from Fleet Street towards West Cromwell Road, which would take them out of the city. Ike observed that perhaps it might be time for Rollo to invest in a new vehicle. The editor just grunted. He was far more interested in thrashing out various scenarios of who could have "dunnit".

"So Poppy, who's top of your list?"

Poppy turned her attention from the passing London streets and the Monday morning commuters to her editor in the front seat. She mulled over the question for a moment, then answered.

"I think Grimes is involved in some way. There's something about him that bothers me. He might not be my stalker, but he's shifty, definitely shifty."

"I agree," said Rollo, "but what evidence do you have that it's him?"

"Nothing definitive," Poppy admitted, "but there's something about the buckshot cartridge. Daniel told me that buckshot would be able to kill a man, whereas birdshot would just injure. Perhaps the shot was intended for Sir James on the day of the clay shooting outing. Perhaps that was Plan A, and when that failed – when the boy accidentally shot himself in the foot and drew attention to the weaponry – it had to be abandoned. Hence Plan B – the digitalis."

"Hmmm," observed Rollo. "I think that's got some legs. But to me, having a different grade of digitalis on hand suggests forward planning."

"Might the two plans have been prepared in advance?" suggested Ike as he negotiated a bend. "The digitalis could have been bought just in case the shooting failed."

Poppy thought about this. "Yes, I think that's very plausible. But the thing that confuses me is, why two very different types of murder? One is quiet, silent, and perhaps might even have gone undetected; the other loud, overt and very, very public."

"A shooting could still have been put down to being an accident though. Shooting accidents are an occupational hazard for the British upper classes, aren't they?" Rollo laughed.

Ike joined in then added: "I think you Americans have the prize for that, Rollo!"

But Poppy wasn't listening. She was still trying to puzzle out the shooting and poisoning plots.

"What I'd like to know is motive. What would Grimes have to gain?"

"A very good question, Poppy," observed Rollo, suddenly serious again. "My money's actually on Lady Ursula, because of that very thing: the almighty dollar. It's common knowledge that she held the purse strings and that she'd called time on her husband's extravagant hobby. Yazzie also told me that there is a mortgage out on Winterton and some debtors are taking legal action against the Maddoxes."

"How would Sir James' death help her then?" asked Poppy.

Rollo shrugged. "I'm not sure yet. We'll have to do a bit of digging. Perhaps there's a life insurance policy... I'll ask Yazzie if she knows anything."

They drove past a sign that declared they were now on the main road to Henley-on-Thames. They should be at Winterton in under an hour.

"Well, that would be a good motive for murder," agreed Poppy, "but I'm not ready to let Grimes off the hook yet. He did after all deliver the note to the boy. And he had the cartridge in his coat pocket so he obviously knew about the contents of the letter. Perhaps he and Lady Ursula are in cahoots."

"I'd go along with that," agreed Rollo. "I'm sure the police will get to the bottom of it. My contact at Scotland Yard told me Henley-upon-Thames have requested help from the Met. Our old friend DCI Jasper Martin will be on the case."

An image of the short, round, detective came to mind. DCI Martin was an excellent detective – although he had blind spots. With a previous case he had been determined to follow a line of enquiry that would have convicted an innocent person. It was only when Poppy and her colleagues unearthed some crucial information that he was able to redirect his enquiries in the right direction. But between DCI Martin and the *Globe* team, no doubt the truth would eventually come out. The question was, would they find the killer before he or she struck again? *If* they were going to strike again. Poppy remembered the note from her stalker. She took it out and showed it to Rollo, describing the events of the previous night and how she had ended up at the police station earlier this morning in time to hear the news about Sir James' murder.

Both men chastised her for not calling someone to come and stay with her the previous evening. "Don't make the same mistake tonight Poppy," warned Rollo.

"I won't."

# CHAPTER 22

As the Model T left the London city limits behind, the snow lay more thickly on fields and dry stone walls. West Cromwell Road became the Great West Road, wending its way along the River Thames, which looked breathtakingly beautiful cloaked in frost. But the old car was not built for such inclement weather, and at one point they got stuck in a dip in the road. Rollo and Poppy had to get out and push until Ike caught traction again. It was with some relief that they eventually turned into the grounds of Winterton Hall, watched by the two sphinxes wearing fluffy white wigs of snow. A few minutes later they pulled up behind a Black Mariah police van, already a quarter of an hour late for Ike's appointment with Lady Ursula.

They rang the doorbell and didn't have to wait long for it to be answered by a sombre-faced Grimes. He greeted Poppy and Rollo by name, expressing surprise that they had not telephoned in advance to say they were coming.

"Ah, but I did. I'm Ike Garfield. We spoke yesterday afternoon. Lady Ursula agreed to see me at ten o'clock today. My colleagues here asked if they could catch a lift as they have work to do out this way."

Grimes assessed Ike, his gaze lingering for a moment longer than was polite on the West Indian gentleman's dark face. Then he looked at his pocket watch. "It is a quarter *past* ten."

Ike agreed that it was and explained about getting stuck in the snow.

Grimes grunted and said he would see if Lady Ursula could still see him. She was currently speaking to a police officer.

"DCI Martin from the Met?" asked Rollo.

Grimes' upper lip twitched under his moustache. "I am not at liberty to say, Mr Rolandson."

Grimes turned and looked as though he were about to shut the door – to leave them waiting outside while he went to speak to his mistress – when Rollo stepped boldly across the threshold. "We'll wait inside, eh Grimes? It's freezing out here. Miz Denby?" With a melodramatic flourish, Rollo stepped aside, bowed, and ushered Poppy in with a twirl of his hand. Poppy chuckled to herself as she walked past the stiff shadow of the butler, followed by Ike who added insult to injury by taking off his bowler hat and giving it to Grimes with a "thank you, my good man".

Grimes held the hat as if it were the corpse of a dead rat then summoned the footman who was lurking uncertainly near the cloakroom.

The young man hurried across the hall and took coats, hats, and scarves from the three journalists as Grimes retreated. Poppy smiled at him. "Thank you, Mr Wallace."

"You're welcome, Miss Denby. Would you and the gentlemen care to take a seat in the library? I'm sure Mr Grimes won't be long..."

But before they could be ushered away a door opened off the hall and Grimes stood aside to let Lady Ursula, accompanied by DCI Jasper Martin and the police constable from Henley-on-Thames, pass. The officers appraised the team from the *Globe*.

"Look what the north wind has blown in," observed DCI Martin. "Rolandson, Garfield, Miss Denby..."

"Mr Garfield says he has an appointment, ma'am," intoned the butler.

Lady Ursula, looking pale and drawn in her mourning attire, nodded and said quietly: "He does, but the other two do not. Show Mr Garfield into the drawing room, Grimes."

Grimes bowed, stiffly. "This way, Mr Garfield."

Ike and the policemen swapped places and Lady Ursula followed the journalist into the room. "Grimes," said the lady of the house, "will you chaperone us please?"

*Chaperone? Why does she need a chaperone?* wondered Poppy, but then reminded herself that some people were fearful of black folk.

In all the comings and goings, neither Grimes nor Lady Ursula had indicated what Poppy and Rollo were to do. "Perhaps you would still like to wait in the library, Miss Denby and Mr Rolandson," said the footman, and pointed the way.

But Rollo ignored him, positioning himself directly in the path of the two police officers. "Good morning, Constable Jones. It's good to see you again, I'm just sorry it's under such tragic circumstances."

"It is that, Mr Rolandson. Everyone's had quite a shock. Do you know Detective Chief Inspector Martin from the Metropolitan Police?"

Rollo nodded. "I do. DCI Martin and I are old pals, aren't we sir?"

Martin grunted. "Bosom buddies."

"Would you like your coats sir?" asked the footman.

"Yes," said Martin, then paused, looking shrewdly at Rollo and Poppy. "Actually, on second thoughts, I'm glad you're both here."

Rollo cocked his head in surprise. "And why's that?"

The detective hooked his thumbs into his braces. "Witness statements. You were both here for the duration of the weekend and were present as Sir James died, weren't you?"

"We were," said Rollo. "My photographer and I – that's Dan Rokeby – tried to save him with the kiss of life and heart compressions. But unfortunately we weren't able to. It was very distressing for everyone concerned."

"I'm sure. But very useful from a press point of view, no doubt."

Rollo shrugged. "I won't deny that."

DCI Martin turned to Constable Jones and said: "Can you take a deposition for us, Jones? I think we'll speak to Mr Rolandson first, then Miss Denby. Let's do it in the library. You boy, get us some more tea."

The footman bowed, then caught the eye of a maid who was carrying a pile of tablecloths towards the dining room. "Bella, tea for four in the library please."

Martin held up his hand. "That will just be for three. I would like to speak to Miss Denby and Mr Rolandson separately. Would you care to wait, Miss Denby?"

*Wait where?* "Of course," said Poppy.

The flustered footman revised his instructions to the maid, showed the three gentlemen to the library, then hovered in front of Poppy like a nervous puppy. "Erm, sorry about that Miss Denby. I think that the – er – the conservatory is free. Would you like some tea?"

Poppy smiled at him in sympathy. "Some tea would be lovely, thank you, Mr Wallace."

Five minutes later and Poppy was seated in a wicker chair in the conservatory near a potted lemon tree, heavily laden with fruit.

Wallace came in carrying a tray. He still looked ill-at-ease. Poppy felt terribly sorry for him. "How is everyone doing, Mr Wallace? I'm sure it's all come as a terrible shock to you. First Sir James' death, then news that it might be murder."

Wallace stopped in his tracks: the tea tray rattled; his face drained of blood. Poppy thought he might faint. She jumped up and took the tray from him.

"M-murder?"

"You didn't know? No one has told you yet?"

Wallace shook his head and reached out a hand to steady himself on the back of a chair. "Here, sit down." Poppy took his arm and eased him into the chair. The young man was too shocked to question the impropriety of it.

"H-how do you know it's murder, miss? Who told you?"

Poppy sat down in the chair opposite, poured him a cup of tea which he accepted with awkward thanks, then proceeded to tell him what she'd heard at the police station that morning. She hadn't realized Lady Ursula had not yet told the staff. But why would she? She'd probably only just heard herself – perhaps that's what DCI Martin had been speaking to her about. Perhaps he had only just delivered the news.

By the time he had finished his tea, the footman's hands had stopped shaking.

"Do you feel better, now?"

"I do, thank you, Miss Denby. I – I suppose I should go get you a fresh cup. And then wait to hear what Lady Ursula has to say about Sir James. Once the police have left I should imagine there'll be some sort of announcement."

Poppy said there probably would. But then added: "I would also prepare yourselves for a whole lot of questioning."

The footman, who had started to stand, sat back down again. "Oh? I hadn't thought of that. Do you think they suspect it's one of us?"

"Well," said Poppy, "I don't suppose any of us are off the hook. Every guest and staff member who was here on the weekend will no doubt have to account for their whereabouts.

And they'll also be digging into any feelings of bad blood towards Sir James – from the staff, family, and guests."

The footman flicked the nails of his thumb and forefinger together in a nervous gesture. "Is that right? You as a lady of the press have been involved in a few murder investigations, haven't you? You'll know what you're talking about. In fact, I heard it said you've got a nose for murder, miss."

Poppy straightened up in surprise. "Really? Who said that?"

"I heard Mr Flinton say it to Mr Grimes after young Willie was shot in the foot the other day. He said just as well there was nothing suspicious going on, or Miss Denby would be on the case."

"Golly," said Poppy, quite taken aback. *What do I say to that?* She had to think quickly. Wallace was opening up to her; this might be the one and only chance she would have to speak to a member of staff before they were told to close ranks by Lady Ursula and the butler. Even if the pair were innocent of any wrongdoing in this case, they still wouldn't want it splayed across the front pages of the papers. She smiled gently at Wallace, re-establishing the connection she first made when she insisted on addressing him as "Mr" on Saturday morning. He returned her gaze, his eyes earnest and respectful.

"Well, I don't know about me having a nose for murder, but I do dispute Mr Flinton's opinion that there was nothing suspicious going on with the shooting. I –" Poppy looked to the door, checking that no one was about to interrupt them. "– I actually suspect there might be a little bit more to that. And it might – just might – be linked to what eventually happened to Sir James."

"Oh my." The footman continued clicking his nails, then abruptly stopped. He leaned forward. "You know what, Miss Denby, I think you might be right. What would you do if I showed you something that might be evidence?"

Poppy leaned forward too. "Oh? What might that be, Mr Wallace?"

"With all due respect, miss, I'd like to know what you would do with it, before I show you."

Poppy leaned back and folded her hands in her lap. "Fair enough. Well, I'd examine it, show it to my colleagues for their opinion, and then we'd hand it over to the police."

"So you won't give it to the police immediately?"

"No. Not until we've assessed it first. It might turn out to be nothing."

The footman looked relieved, then reached into his pocket and pulled out an envelope. "That's good. You see, I've found something, but I don't really know if it *is* important. I was trying to decide what to do with it – in light of what happened to young Willie – but wasn't sure. Up until now, it just seemed a little curious, but now that you've told me what's happened to Sir James – and you think the shooting might be tied into it all somehow – perhaps I should give it to you."

Poppy took the envelope from Wallace. On the outside was written one word: "Willie". Inside was a single sheet of paper. In handwriting that differed in style from that on the outside it said:

*Young Man,*

*Lady Ursula wants to play a little prank on Sir James at the clay shoot tomorrow. Please load her weapon with buckshot instead of birdshot. For your trouble I have enclosed a pound. Do not tell anyone about this. We do not want to spoil the surprise. Once the game has been played I will give you another pound.*

There was no signature.

A chill ran down Poppy's spine. The handwriting on the note was familiar: it looked very much like the one left by her stalker last night. She would have to compare the two, but she was almost certain it was written by the same person. The writing on the envelope, however, was different.

She looked up into the frightened eyes of Wallace. "Is it important, miss?"

"It might, be, yes. Where did you get this?"

"One of the maids from the big house found it when she was cleaning the gamekeeper's cottage. His wife died, you see, and it's just him and the boy. She found this on Saturday morning and gave it to me. She said it was lying on the boy's bed, open, beside the envelope. That's how she could read it."

"Why didn't she give it to the boy's father?"

"He hasn't come home yet, miss. He's staying with family in London while his boy's in hospital."

Poppy nodded. That made sense. But something else didn't. The little she knew about the hierarchy of a grand house told her that a maid would very well report to a footman, but a footman would report to a butler, who in turn would report to the master of the house. "Why didn't you give this to Mr Grimes? There's been plenty of time since Saturday morning, even if you did just think it was curious – and it certainly is that."

It was the footman's turn to look nervously towards the door. "Because miss, you see, I recognise the handwriting..."

Poppy jerked to attention. "Whose is it?"

"Well, I don't know about the letter itself – but, you've probably noticed there is different handwriting on the envelope than inside..."

"Yes, I saw that. So you don't know who wrote the actual letter?"

"I don't. No."

Poppy willed herself to keep the disappointment off her face. "But you said you recognized the handwriting."

"I do miss. Not the writing in the note, but the name on the envelope. That was written by Mr Grimes. I know his writing. He writes up duties and such in a daily log book which we have to check. So you see, that's why I didn't give it to him straight away. He seems to be somehow, somehow –"

"Implicated?" offered Poppy.

The footman pursed his lips and nodded. "Yes miss. That's the word. Implicated. But I'm not sure in what. The letter said it was going to be a prank. But I can't for the life of me figure out what kind of prank would use guns."

"Neither can I," agreed Poppy, grimly. "But I think your instincts are right. There is something in this note and I'll get my colleagues to look at it. Then, if we think there's any more in it, we'll give it to the police. Is that acceptable to you?"

Wallace nodded, looking relieved to have finally got his secret off his chest.

Poppy, however, wasn't quite finished. "You say you don't recognize the inner handwriting."

"That's right. Never seen it before."

"And it's not Lady Ursula's? Would you know her handwriting if you saw it?"

"I would, miss. It's not hers. Even though it mentions her name."

"That is indeed very curious."

Voices sounded from outside the door. Wallace jumped up. "Please don't mention to Mr Grimes that I gave this to you, please miss? I don't want him to think I'm snooping around."

*Snooping* – there was that word again. "Of course not. However, now that you mention Mr Grimes, can you tell me one more thing?"

"If I can miss," said Wallace, clearing away the tea things.

"Was he here all day yesterday? And last night?"

"Yes miss. He didn't leave Lady Ursula's side."

So, her stalker wasn't Grimes after all. It wasn't his handwriting and he wasn't in London. *Then whose was it?*

There was a knock on the door. Wallace opened it to reveal Constable Jones, the Henley-on-Thames policeman. "Miss Denby, DCI Martin will see you now."

# CHAPTER 23

The fire in the library hearth roared with false jollity, while the holly and mistletoe draped along the mantlepiece whispered of happier times. Through the window, on the lawn in front of the maze, Poppy saw Rollo pacing up and down, smoking a cigar. He was in thinking mode, Poppy noted, no doubt planning his team's next move. She wished she had had a chance to speak to him before she was ushered in for her deposition. She would certainly tell the truth, but it might have been useful to know which version of the truth Rollo had told. From past stories she'd worked on with him, she knew that he was not averse to withholding information from the police so that he could scoop rival newspapers. All relevant evidence was eventually handed over, but not before the story hit the news stand.

Poppy had known that the note to young Willie would be something Rollo would not want her to hand over until Daniel had had a chance to photograph it – and it burned a hole in her pocket. Untruths did not come easily to Poppy, so she hoped she would not have to dilute her testimony too much. Rollo was far more fluid with facts, and she feared she might unwittingly contradict him in her testimony. *Dear God, help me to speak wisely.*

The detective had taken off his jacket in front of the warm fire, but his waistcoat was still firmly buttoned up. "So, Miss Denby," he said, after pouring her a cup of tea, "Mr Rolandson has taken me through the broad sweep of events, Friday afternoon to Sunday morning, as well as informing me that you are both aware of the allegation of murder. Is that correct?"

"It is, yes."

"Right, good. So you will forgive me then if I just hone in on a few details. From my previous dealings with you I recall that you are a woman who notices the small things, while Mr Rolandson, despite his size, does not."

Poppy didn't think that was a fair assessment of her editor's stature or skill, but she declined to say so. She stirred her tea while she waited for DCI Martin to continue. He checked his notes and conferred briefly and quietly with Constable Jones, pointing to this and that in the written transcript Jones had in front of him. Eventually he turned to Poppy and said: "Both Lady Ursula and Mr Rolandson say that you walked back with Sir James from the shoot and that the gentleman did not appear to be too well. Is that correct?"

"It is."

"Did he say what was bothering him?"

"He said he had a dicky ticker. And..." Poppy paused, wondering whether or not Rollo had told the detective what she had told him about Sir James' medication being misplaced. She doubted it, as her editor had been tickled pink that this would scoop the *Courier*. However, she felt it was too important to withhold. Unlike the note, which so far only had a tenuous connection to Sir James' death, the information about the digitalis was central.

DCI Martin looked at her expectantly. "And?"

"And he also told me that he had been late that morning in taking his medication, because, he said, someone had moved it – or it had been misplaced. He eventually found it, but it was considerably later than he normally took it. He believed that was why he was feeling unwell."

DCI Martin raised an eyebrow. "Did he now? Did he say how many times a day he took it?"

"Yes he did. Three times a day."

"Have you got all that Constable Jones?"

"I have sir."

"Good. That's very helpful, thank you Miss Denby. Did Sir James say who had moved the medicine? Or where it normally was and where he eventually found it?"

"He did not."

"All right. Fine. Did he say anything else you think may have pertinence?"

Poppy scanned her memory of her conversation with Sir James. She remembered that he had got quite upset when he spoke about the Egyptian delegation's efforts to legally overturn the auction as well as how defensive he became when she mentioned the murderous circumstances in which the mask of Nefertiti had originally been found. Should she mention that to Martin? She worried that if she did she would unfairly implicate Faizal Osman and Miss El Farouk. There was already a surge of anti-Egyptian feeling in the press; she didn't want to fan the flames unnecessarily. Besides, the press release about the "murderous circumstances" would be common knowledge and Martin could see that for himself. No, she decided not to go into detail about that. Instead she said: "He was getting a bit worked up about the auction, wondering who would bid for the mask."

"Did he say who he wanted the mask to go to?"

"Just to the highest bidder, whoever that might be."

"And he didn't mind if it was the Egyptians?"

*Ah, Martin was already on the case.* "I think he made it clear that he would prefer that the Egyptians did not get the mask. But I don't think he believed they would."

"No? And why's that?"

Again, it was probably already common knowledge. "Because of the court case they brought and the injunction they were trying to get. They would not be likely to pay for something they believed was already legally theirs. Although, of course Sir James disputed that. The legality, that is."

Martin nodded and tapped his pen against his notepad. "Yes, I've heard about that. Thank you, Miss Denby. And the Germans? Did he give any opinion on them?"

Poppy thought about this then said: "Only that he felt the 'Huns' – as he called them – were spreading rumours reinforcing the idea that the mask had not been legally procured." She stopped. Had she said too much there? Possibly, but he would find out anyway. So she continued: "If you don't know already, the German delegation believe the mask might have been stolen from the original dig – which was German-run. No doubt you'll be interviewing Herr Stein and his colleague in due course and they'll fill you in on the details."

DCI Martin nodded. "Thank you, Miss Denby, I will." He perused his notes again, then asked: "Do you recall if anyone did *not* attend the clay shoot that morning? Or if anyone was late arriving for it?"

Poppy thought about it a moment then replied: "Yes, as a matter of fact I do. Miss El Farouk said she spent the morning catching up on some reading. And Harry Gibson – from the *Courier* – didn't come either. I have no idea what his excuse was."

A mental image of Harry Gibson came to mind: he was wearing a fedora and a trench coat. Poppy pursed her lips. Yes, now that Grimes was clear, Gibson was very much at the top of her list of stalker suspects. And she'd just been reminded: his whereabouts during much of the weekend were uncertain. "Now that I think of it, I don't recall him being at breakfast either."

"Oh?" asked DCI Martin.

"No. He didn't make an appearance. Lionel Saunders was there, but not Gibson. Oh, and of course the Conan Doyles. Sir Arthur made a brief appearance to tell us he was taking Lady Jean home. I'm sure you've heard that she was taken ill on the Friday, before the séance."

"Yes, I'd heard that. I shall be speaking to Sir Arthur when I get back to London. He has already been informed of Sir James' death."

Poppy remembered how worried the poor man had been about his wife. And then, it suddenly occurred to her that she'd read somewhere that small doses of poison could cause gastritis. What was the poison? Digitalis? No, not that. Arsenic? Yes, that rang a bell... should she mention it?

But DCI Martin had moved on. "Anyone else? Anyone else who missed a meal?"

"Hmm, for breakfast on the Saturday I don't recall seeing Lady Ursula either – but I think she was tending to Lady Jean. And also Miss El Farouk had a meal sent up to her room – something to do with not wanting her food to be contaminated by pork sausages and bacon, perhaps. Oh! And then the evening before, Daniel Rokeby missed the dinner as he accompanied a boy to hospital." She turned to the Henley-on-Thames officer and said: "But I'm sure Constable Jones has filled you in on all that."

Martin nodded. "He has. So back to the shoot. Was there anyone else who missed it apart from Mr Gibson and Miss El Farouk? Or perhaps arrived late?"

Poppy cast her mind back and remembered Fox Flinton galloping like a horse out of one of the stables. "Only Mr Flinton, I think. Although I'm not sure he was late or just hiding, waiting to play a prank on us." She described the actor's antics.

DCI Martin's face was impassive. He checked his notes.

"Right then, moving forward to Saturday night. Did anyone disappear afterwards?"

"Disappear?"

"After Sir James died. Did anyone remove themselves suddenly?"

Poppy recalled that everyone apart from Lady Ursula, Fox Flinton, and Marjorie Reynolds retired to the library while they waited for the doctor to come.

"Everyone?" Martin prompted.

Poppy went through a mental checklist. "Yes, I think so… oh, hang on! Harry Gibson slipped out when Fox Flinton came back to tell Albert Carnaby that he should take custody of the mask. I think that's when he took the photograph that appeared on the front of the *Courier* on Sunday morning. He and Lionel hightailed it back to London on Saturday night."

"Hightailed? When was that?"

"Mr Rokeby – our photographer – said he heard their motor soon after the doctor had left."

DCI Martin made a note. "And did Gibson come back into the library after he slipped out?"

"He did not."

"Right, thank you. And before that, at the auction? Did anyone not attend?"

"No, everyone was there. All the guests, anyway. I can't account for the staff."

"Of course not, no. So everyone was there apart from the Conan Doyles – who had left that morning – and the medium who had left the night before? Madame Minette, was it?"

Poppy felt uncomfortable. Was Martin about to dig into her behaviour at the séance?

"Yes, that's right, Madame Minette. A last-minute replacement for Lady Jean Conan Doyle."

Martin stopped writing and met Poppy's gaze. "So I've been told. Is there anything you want to tell me about the séance?"

Poppy's stomach tightened. "Not unless you have something specific you want to know," she countered.

"Not really. Although Mr Rolandson tells me that you felt the medium was deliberately trying to influence the price that might be paid for the Nefertiti mask. Is that correct?"

"It is, yes." Should she mention her and Jenny Philpott's theory about the Renoir? No, too tenuous. There was more that needed to be fleshed out there. Instead she said: "I felt that she was also trying to manipulate Albert Carnaby, the auctioneer. She appeared to deliberately target him – bringing him a message from his dead mother and wife. It was most unkind."

Poppy did not try to disguise the anger in her voice.

Martin looked at her pointedly. "Just Mr Carnaby?"

"No, she also tried to push Howard Carter's buttons too – but he just laughed it off. He didn't appear to take the whole séance thing seriously, unlike poor Mr Carnaby, who was quite taken in by it."

"Hmm, Lady Ursula told me Mr Carnaby was not the only person who was upset. She said you made a bit of a scene and stormed out of the room. Is that correct?"

Poppy met Martin's gaze. "I hardly stormed out. But yes, I did leave. I did not want to be subject to a cruel game."

"Cruel?"

Poppy let out an exasperated sigh. "She pretended to be my dead brother. It was in poor taste. That's all."

Martin looked over at Constable Jones who made a note. "Quite," said the Met Detective. "These séances usually are."

As Poppy regained her composure, he perused his notes again. "What did you do when you left the séance?"

"I went straight to bed."

"Straight?"

"Yes. I was too upset to see anyone."

Martin raised an eyebrow. "Ah, so you don't know who was where while the séance was going on without you?"

"I do not, no. I'm sure Lady Ursula has told you that only a few of us were actually involved. I don't know where everyone else was. As far as I know they were listening to gramophone records. Mr Rolandson was with that crowd; he'd be able to tell you."

Martin smiled tightly. "He has, thank you. But tell me, Miss Denby, on the way to bed might you perhaps have stopped by Sir James' bedroom?"

Poppy was taken aback. "I did not! I have no idea where it is even. Apparently somewhere in the central part of the house. I was in the west wing. Or did Lady Ursula fail to tell you that?"

The detective and journalist held each other's gaze, neither giving way until a pine cone fell off the fire and sent sparks flying. Jones jumped up and gave the fire a poke.

DCI Martin closed his notebook. "Well Miss Denby, you've been a great help, thank you. If there is anything else I need to ask I know where to find you. You *will* be going directly back to London after this, won't you?"

"Yes, of course." He did not need to know she was hoping to track down Madame Minette on the way back. If something came of that – linked to his enquiry – she would let him know.

"Then I'll be in touch."

Poppy put down her tea cup and stood up. Jones stood too. But Martin did not. "Actually, I might see you at the British Museum."

"The museum?"

"Yes, I think I might just drop in on the meeting this afternoon. Quite a few birds with one stone there, methinks, eh? Will you be going?"

"The press aren't invited to the actual meeting. But I expect there will be some sort of press statement or announcement afterwards. One of our journalists is going to be covering it."

"Not you?"

"I wasn't planning on it, no."

"Then I suggest you change your plans, Miss Denby. Thank you. That will be all."

# CHAPTER 24.

The drive back from Winterton was abuzz with conversation as all three journalists shared their stories. Ike had had a difficult interview with Lady Ursula, interrupted periodically by Grimes reminding him that the lady had had a terrible shock lately. When she did speak it was to present her husband in glowing terms as a Renaissance Man, an internationally renowned explorer and a saviour of Classical culture. No mention of the well-known tensions in the marriage about money.

"Did you ask her what she thought of the accusations that he had stolen many of the antiquities he had purported to save – including the mask?" asked Poppy.

"I did, yes. She flatly denied it, putting it down to 'colonial types' wanting to have their cake and eat it. She said if it hadn't been for people like her husband the artefacts would still be under Egyptian sand or pilfered away by 'the natives'. She was a bit hesitant to use the word, seeing she was being interviewed by a 'native'," Ike chuckled, " but she did."

"What did she have to say about the future of the mask? Will the auction still go ahead?"

Ike slowed the Model T to negotiate a bend then answered: "She said it would. I suggested that it might be delayed until after the funeral – or investigations into her husband's murder had been completed – but she said there was no need for that. It would have been what Sir James wanted. He'd died as the mask was about to be auctioned; she wanted him to rest knowing it had gone to a good home."

"How would he know?" asked Poppy.

"She's a spiritualist, remember?" said Ike. "She'll be setting up a meeting with him soon."

Rollo laughed. "Then she can ask him who killed him. I wonder if a ghost brief has any legal standing?" He laughed again. "Seriously, though, did she indicate whom she might suspect of killing her husband? Or –" he chuckled "– why she and the butler did it?"

Ike snorted with mirth. "Unfortunately, I didn't get a confession, no. She said she had absolutely no idea who would want to hurt James. He was so well loved by everyone. But she was keen to steer the interview towards what she referred to as 'the ghostly goings on'." Ike paused as he slowed to avoid a fallen tree branch near the edge of the road, then continued: "She told me about Nefertiti's appearance at the séance and her mention of the so-called curse of the pharaohs. She also referred to the terrible accident with the boy. She asked me if I thought it strange that there had been a near death and then an actual death on the same weekend. I said I absolutely did. I think she was trying to imply it was all part of the curse, but I said I think the police will be pursuing the theory that the same real-life killer was involved in both. And you know what?"

"What?" said Poppy and Rollo in unison.

"Well, you won't believe it, but when I said that, she went even paler than she already was and looked at the butler in shock. She said: 'Good gracious, so *they* think it's linked too!' Then she said: 'Grimes, do you want to tell Mr Garfield what you told me?' And Grimes said..." Ike paused as a faster vehicle overtook them. "... He said 'if madam thinks it's a good idea', then went on to tell me that he had found a buckshot cartridge lying on a pouffe in the drawing room after he supervised the clean up on Friday night. He had no idea where it had come from. But he wondered if it was connected to the boy's accident on Friday afternoon."

"Ha!" said Rollo. "Either they suspect that we already know about the cartridge and are trying to pre-empt us with a plausible alibi, or they genuinely aren't involved. I am reluctant to accept the latter option without further proof. What about you, Poppy?"

Poppy leaned between the gap in the two front seats to be better heard. "I agree. I do think there's something up with those two. However, it might not be murder."

She told Ike and Rollo that when she and Daniel got back from Henley-on-Thames she had asked the footman if Mr Grimes was around. He had said he wasn't – that he'd left on some business. "Perhaps he was taking the cartridge to the police station. Like you suggest though, Rollo, it might have been deliberate misdirection. But perhaps not. I wonder if he also told them about the note."

"The note?" asked Ike, gearing down to negotiate a bend.

"Yes, the note the boy told you and Daniel about." She grinned. "And you won't believe it gents, but here it is!" She presented the note to Rollo with a flourish. Rollo read it out loud to Ike. Both men were delighted and congratulated her on not giving it to the police.

"I will give it to them," said Poppy, smarting slightly that her colleagues might think she was losing her moral compass, "but Daniel should photograph it first."

"Quite right," agreed Rollo, then braced himself against the dashboard as the Model T rattled over a pothole. Poppy felt as though every bone in her body had been shaken in a tin can. She sat back into the relative ease of the rear upholstery.

"I did mention the note to Ursula and Grimes," said Ike. "That the boy had said Grimes had given one to him telling him to load Lady U's gun with the shot. I suggested that that might implicate them both and wondered if they had anything to say about it. I didn't know at that stage that the note had been found."

"Oh? What did they say?" asked Poppy, leaning forward again.

"Lady U was astounded – or at least appeared to be. She turned on Grimes and asked him to explain. He said he had been given a sealed envelope to give to the boy and had no idea what was in it. He said he had written the boy's name on it as it was blank."

"Well that's true – about him writing the name – the footman identified the handwriting on the outside," said Poppy.

"Did he say who had given it to him?" asked Rollo.

Ike sighed. "Unfortunately not. He said he would tell her in private and as this was a police investigation he didn't think it was appropriate to tell the press something before he'd told the authorities."

"So he hadn't told the police yet, about the note. I wonder why?" asked Poppy.

"Well, he'll have to now," added Rollo. "He'll know that we know. And that the boy has told us. He'll look as guilty as sin if he doesn't."

"He already looks as guilty as sin," observed Ike.

"Perhaps," said Poppy. "The thing is, Grimes does not strike me as a stupid man. And only a stupid man would deliver a note orchestrating a shooting – accidental or otherwise – and then not try to retrieve it afterwards. It obviously implicates him. The only thing I can think of is that he genuinely didn't know what was in the note, or that he's trying to cover for whoever wrote it."

"Lady Ursula? She's a cool customer. She could quite easily have been putting on an act for you, Ike," said Rollo.

Ike agreed. "Quite easily. I definitely felt as though there was an undercurrent between them. I would love to have been a fly on the wall after I left."

The old car careered over a series of three potholes.

"Steady on!" shouted Rollo. "We're not in Monte Carlo, Ike!"

Ike grinned at his editor. "Sorry, unavoidable. A motor with a better suspension wouldn't have such problems, eh, Poppy?"

Poppy agreed that it wouldn't, thinking back to the luxury of Marjorie's Lincoln. But before she could slip into further reverie, Rollo prompted her to continue with her thoughts on the story at hand. "What do you think, Poppy? Do you believe Ursula knows more about the note than she's letting on?"

"I do, yes. I don't have any evidence of that yet, but I think Grimes might be covering for her. On the other hand, the footman said it wasn't her handwriting…"

"She could have got someone else to write it for her," offered Ike.

"That's possible," agreed Poppy. "But whoever it was, it was the same person who came to my house on Sunday night." She reached into her satchel and took out the second note, passing it forward to Rollo.

He perused it, nodded to Ike, and said: "I agree. They're written by the same person. If I get my hands on the scoundrel who's trying to scare you…" He made a wringing gesture with his hands.

"So who's top of your list for the stalker?" asked Ike, this time managing to successfully avoid a pothole.

"Harry Gibson," said Poppy, bracing herself for the impact that didn't come. She went on to tell the men about Harry's various comings and goings relating to the shooting and the death of Sir James.

"Harry?" said Rollo. "The man's a snake, without a doubt, but I'm not sure he's a killer. I could very easily believe he was stalking you, just for kicks, but why would he kill Sir James?"

"I don't know," answered Poppy grimly, "but he was absent quite a bit over the weekend – he and Lady Ursula at the same time. He could have written the note for her. I think I need to come clean with DCI Martin about this as quickly as possible. I'll take the notes over to Scotland Yard as soon as we've got them photographed."

Rollo was twirling an unlit cigar between thumb and forefinger. *Oh, I do hope he's not going to light that up*, thought Poppy.

"What is it, Rollo?" asked Ike.

"I'm just trying to piece this all together. Now, correct me if I'm wrong, but we're assuming here that Poppy's stalker is the same person who arranged for the shooting accident and is the same person who murdered Sir James. Is that correct?"

"That's what I'm thinking, yes," said Ike. "Poppy?"

Poppy pondered this for a minute, then said: "It does seem like the most plausible explanation, yes. But the most plausible solution isn't always how these investigations turn out, is it? For me, it all comes down to motive. So far we have sniffed out a monetary motive for Lady Ursula, and a 'just because he's a nasty bloke' motive for Harry as my stalker. But, Rollo's right, what motive would Harry have to murder Sir James?"

"Maybe he was paid to do it?" offered Ike, then tossed out a "Hold on, folks!" as he swerved to avoid two large crows eating the remains of an unfortunate badger.

Poppy pursed her lips in sympathy for the victim, then returned to the conversation. "Maybe he was paid. But by whom? Lady Ursula? Very possibly. On the other hand, if it is connected to the mask – which it does seem to be – who would have the most to gain by Sir James dying before the auction could go ahead?"

"Well, Lady Ursula seems very keen on getting the auction underway as soon as possible," said Ike. "So the idea that the murder took place to stop the auction doesn't hold much water for me. I can accept that she might have wanted to delay it – so that she would be the sole beneficiary of the proceeds – but not to stop it completely."

"Agreed," said Poppy. "But we're just focusing on Lady Ursula here. And while I think she is still our top suspect – and that it's highly possible Harry Gibson is working with her – let's not ignore the other candidates."

"Such as?"

"The people who didn't want the mask to be sold in the first place," offered Rollo with a jab of his still unlit cigar.

"Exactly," said Poppy. "And as far as I can tell, that would be the German and Egyptian delegations... but... it's just a theory."

"It's a good theory," said Rollo. He grinned and lifted his bowler. "I'll keep it under my hat, Miz Denby. But I think we need a lot more to go on before we start pointing fingers as Yazzie's brother – or for that matter the Krauts - don't you think?"

"Yes Rollo, I agree. And..." she took a deep breath "... would you mind awfully, not lighting up that cigar in the motor?"

Rollo grinned again and once more lifted his hat. "I'll put that under here too then."

Fifteen minutes later – with Poppy's watch approaching twelve – the Model T pulled up to a semi-detached house in Acton. This was the address that Mrs Chapman from Henley-on-Thames had given for her husband's cousin, Minifred Hughes, aka Madame Minette. Ike stayed in the car to write up some notes on his interview; Rollo and Poppy went to knock on the door. After a few moments it was opened by a boy of around twelve, wearing a dressing gown. He had dishevelled ginger hair, red-rimmed eyes, and a raw-looking nose. There was something familiar about the lad, Poppy thought. She smiled at the boy and asked if Mrs Minifred Hughes was home. The boy shook his head and croaked: "She's out."

"Are you off school with a sore throat?" she asked sympathetically.

"Yes, miss."

"Is Mrs Hughes your mother?"

"She is, miss."

"And when will she be home?"

"Four o'clock."

"Oh," said Poppy, "never mind. Can you give her a message for me please?"

The boy shrugged. He didn't look well. There was no guarantee he would remember a message.

Poppy smiled again. "Don't worry; I'll write it down. Can I use your hall table?" she asked, spotting a semi-circular table with a telephone on it just behind the boy. The boy nodded and stepped aside to allow Poppy in. Rollo moved to follow her, but the boy blocked him. "Mother says I'm not to let anyone in. I'll let the lady write the note, but that's it."

Rollo nodded his understanding. "And rightly so, young man. You can't be too careful." Rollo took a step back and waited for Poppy.

Poppy took out her notebook and leaned on the table, then wrote a note explaining how she came to have Madame Minette's address and repeated the story that she wanted to book her for a séance. She also apologized for her rude behaviour on Friday night. She left a telephone number and asked Madame Minette to give her a call. Then she folded up the note and handed it to the boy. As she did, she looked up and noticed a watercolour painting on the wall above the telephone. Her heart skipped a beat. It looked very much like the painting she had seen in the Carnaby auction catalogue: *Yachts on the Seine*. No, correction, it looked *just* like it, except with colour. She fixed a benevolent smile on her face and said: "What a lovely painting. My mother would love something like that for Christmas. Do you know where your mother got it?"

The boy coughed and sniffed. "Uncle Fox gave it to her."

"Uncle *Fox*?"

"Yeah, he's not my real uncle, just a friend of my mum. But they've been friends for ever – from before I was born. He's a famous actor you know. And an artist."

Poppy remembered the beautiful portrait of Lady Ursula hanging at Winterton. Then everything began to fall into place. "Did he paint that?"

The boy coughed again. Then croaked: "Yeah, I think so. Look miss, I feel proper poorly. I'll give mum the note." He gestured for Poppy to leave.

Poppy smiled at him and patted him on the shoulder. "Yes, of course. Go back to bed. We're sorry to have bothered you. Hope you get better soon."

The ginger-haired boy croaked his thanks, then shut the door behind Poppy. As Poppy and Rollo walked back to the car she could hardly contain her excitement. "Rollo," she said, "I think we've just met a fox cub – and he might have solved part of our case."

# CHAPTER 25

Poppy, Rollo, and Ike grabbed a quick bite to eat at a pub in Acton before heading back to the office. They decided that there was too much to do to try to fit in a visit to the retired journalist from *The Times* and would try to do it tomorrow instead. The new lead with "Uncle Fox" and the painting had propelled the Renoir story up their list of priorities. While they were waiting for their takeaway pies to be served, Poppy used the pub telephone and contacted Jenny Philpott at the Hotel Russell. She asked for her to meet the journalists at the *Globe* office on Fleet Street before she went to the meeting at the museum. Poppy offered to pay the taxi fare – as it would be out of Jenny's way – but the American lady declined. She said she'd meet them there in half an hour.

Just over half an hour later Poppy and her two male colleagues arrived in the newsroom to find Daniel chatting to Miss Philpott over a cup of coffee.

"Golly, sorry to keep you waiting, Jenny," said Poppy.

"The old Model T wasn't built for racing," added Ike.

"There is *nothing* wrong with the company car. However, if you and Poppy would like to donate three months' salary each, I'll be happy to get a new one. No? I thought not. Miss Philpott, this is Ike Garfield, senior journalist here at the *Globe*. Ike, Miss Jennifer Philpott from the Metropolitan Museum of New York."

Ike shook the American woman's hand. "A pleasure to meet you ma'am."

"Trinidadian?" asked Jenny.

The West Indian journalist smiled widely. "You've got a good ear, Miss Philpott. Yes, I'm from Trinidad. But happily living here in London now."

"Please, call me Jenny." She pushed her spectacles up her nose as she turned to Poppy and Rollo. "I've only got about twenty minutes before I have to leave for the museum – sorry to rush you – but I'm intrigued to hear about this new development."

"No problem," said Rollo. "Thanks for coming over. Shall we?" He indicated that they should all go into his office. "Danny Boy, can you arrange to have some more coffee sent in, then join us?"

Five minutes later they were all seated in Rollo's office nursing mugs of coffee. "Good heavens, are you sure it was the same Renoir?" asked Jenny.

"It was identical, yes. But the boy said his Uncle Fox had painted it."

"Did you see the signature? Bottom right-hand corner?"

"Unfortunately I didn't manage to get that close. There was a signature, yes, but what it was I couldn't say."

"So what are you thinking?"

Poppy put down her cup on top of a pile of files on Rollo's desk, hoping it wouldn't spill; it was easier than trying to find a clear spot. "I'm thinking forgery, that's what. The boy seemed certain it was Fox who painted it. It could have been an original, of course, but then we'd be looking at theft – either way it's a crime."

"Why theft?" asked Daniel. "Couldn't Fox have bought it and given it to his friend? Correct me if I'm wrong but some of these artists don't start selling at high cost until after they've died. Like that Van Gogh chappy. Perhaps this was one of Renoir's earlier works so wasn't too expensive."

Jenny shook her head. "You're right about Van Gogh, Mr Rokeby, but Pierre Auguste Renoir has been a big seller since around the 1870s. Durand-Ruel – probably the biggest art dealer in the world – gave him his first exhibition here in London in 1874. So in this case, if it was the original painting that Poppy saw, it would be very surprising to see it hanging in a semi in Acton."

"And the boy did say Fox had painted it," added Poppy.

"He's a boy. Fox could just have told him that," argued Daniel, continuing to play devil's advocate.

Poppy nodded. "Yes, that's true. But if you recall at the séance on Friday night, Albert Carnaby said he had the painting and it was going to be put up for auction." She reached into her satchel, took out the catalogue that Jenny had given her the previous day, and turned to the page she'd marked showing *Yachts on the Seine*. "See, here it is, listed in the official catalogue." She jabbed her finger at the photograph. "And that – I promise you – is the painting I saw. So either the painting on the wall is the original or this is. My feeling is the latter."

Rollo templed his fingers. "So, to follow your line of thinking, this is all linked in to why the medium – pretending to be Carnaby's mother – insisted he withdraw the painting from auction until next year."

"Exactly!" Poppy flicked through her notebook until she came to the interview she'd had with Jenny Philpott the previous day. She ran her finger down the page until she came to a note for the National Gallery. "Jenny suggested that the reason it was withdrawn was to give someone time to procure a companion piece to it. Renoir, it seems, used to often paint the same scenes as Claude Monet. If the two works were sold together it would inflate the price. Have you found out any more about that, Jenny?"

"I have," said the American woman. "I met with my friend – the Impressionist expert – for breakfast this morning. He said as far as he was aware there was no companion piece. So that's a lame duck."

Rollo flicked his templed fingers together. "Which makes forgery seem increasingly likely. Madame Minette wanted to delay the sale of the original in order perhaps to – to – to what?"

"To replace it with a forgery. Then she'd have the original which would be worth a packet," suggested Poppy. "That's my theory."

"Madame Minette and Fox Flinton – seems like the two are in cahoots," observed Ike.

"Agreed," said Rollo, "but at this stage it's all a theory. And no crime has actually been committed yet. All there is is a painting on a wall. It's not illegal to copy a painting – as far as I know, as long as it isn't passed off as the original for financial gain. So there's not much we can do yet. I think it's a bit too flimsy to give to the police. And we have no idea how, if at all, this fits in with Sir James' murder… Jenny, would your friend be able to tell if a painting was an original or not?"

Jenny nodded. "He would, yes. That's part of his job at the gallery. To authenticate originals."

"Good. Then we'll have to figure out a way to get him and the painting – or paintings – together."

Jenny looked at her watch. "I'm sorry Rollo, but I have to go. I'll speak to my friend as soon as I can. But for now I've got the Nefertiti mask to deal with. Can you call me a cab?"

Rollo grinned. "Better than that, Ike here can drive you over. Then, when he's there he might be able to wangle his way in. Is that all right with you Ike? Driving the old jalopy again?"

Ike laughed. "I'll give it the old crank."

Poppy and Daniel were alone in his dark room. The small room, at the back of the art and photography department on the second floor, was known as the Lion's Den – a pun on Daniel's Den, rather than a warning about dangers that might lie within. Poppy never felt unsafe with Daniel.

The room smelled of chemicals – acetates, nitrates, bromides – and a diffused red light gave it an other-worldly quality. Although there was no need to do so, people who entered the room felt compelled to whisper, in awe of the alchemy that took place within. Emulsified paper floated in metal trays; and if one watched for long enough, images would form and then be hung out to dry.

Two images were forming now: one of the letter from Poppy's stalker, and the other the note to the gamekeeper's son. Daniel plucked out each in turn with a set of tongs and pegged them to the washing line strung across the room. "Right, that's done. Now we can take the originals to the police station."

"We?" asked Poppy.

"Yes, if you don't mind the company. I've got nothing to do until the meeting at the museum comes out and that's not for another hour. I'll give you a lift on the motorbike. Not quite the comfort of the old Model T but I'll wrap you up snug and warm."

Daniel tapped the tip of Poppy's nose with his finger.

She smiled at him and he put his arms around her, pulling her close. She felt the roughness of his canvas apron against her cheek, the smell of hessian sweetening the acridity of the air. "As soon as this story's over, Poppy, we need to have some time alone. I need to talk to you."

Poppy had a flashback to the romance-charged moment in the boat house when she thought he'd been about to propose.

"No time like the present," she murmured.

She felt him tense against her. "No, not now. I've got some things to say. Some things to explain. We need some time to process it all."

*Process? What do we need to process?*

She pulled away from him and looked into his face. He looked sad – terribly, terribly sad. "Oh Daniel, what is it?"

He blinked a few times and then forced a smile onto his face. "Nothing."

"It's not nothing. I can tell. Yes, we've got a job to do, but it can wait a few minutes more, because now you've got me worried. What's wrong?"

He pulled away from her and busied himself straightening pegs on the line. "I don't want to get into it now. I shouldn't have said anything. It's just that..."

"What?" She took his hands in hers and held them, resisting the urge to run her thumbs over the scars.

He sighed. "You know Maggie is getting married, right?"

"Yes. To the South African mine manager. Don't tell me: she doesn't want to invite me to the wedding. No surprise there."

He tried to smile but failed. "No, it's not that. It's to do with the children. Last evening when I got home she was waiting for me. After I'd said goodnight to Amy and Arthur she told me that she still wants to take the children with her – to South Africa."

"I know she wants to do that – she's said it before. But that's simply not possible, is it? They're your children, not hers. I hope you told her that."

Daniel squeezed Poppy's hands. "It's not as easy as that. She may not be their natural mother, but she's been the only mother they've known since Lydia died."

"Well yes, but she can't expect you to let her take them away from you."

"She isn't. That's not what she was asking."

"What was she asking then?"

Daniel paused, the tension thickening between them. "She wants me to move to South Africa with her and Charles. After they're married. He has a daughter here in boarding school who they'll be taking home with them too. Maggie wants to look after her – and Amy and Arthur. But she doesn't want them to be separated from me either."

"Well, that's good of her," said Poppy, caustically.

"Don't be like that, Poppy; she's trying to compromise. This is her chance at happiness. I can't take that away from her. And I don't want to deprive my children of her either."

Poppy's heart felt like a late-autumn rosebud, frosted then crushed. "But what about me?" she whispered, knowing she sounded childish but unable to stop herself.

"Oh Poppy, Poppy!" He pulled her back into his arms and kissed her head. "That's what I wanted to talk to you about. To see if we can find a solution to this. Charles says there's a newspaper in Kimberley – the town where he works – and he can get me a job there. Perhaps when I'm there I can see if they can give you a job too."

"In South Africa? You want me to move to South Africa?"

"I want you to marry me!"

Poppy felt faint. She had waited so long to hear those words. *But not like this…* She did not want to leave London. She did not want to leave her job at the *Globe*. She did not want to be separated from her family and friends. Her parents were up north, yes, but it was just a half-day's train ride, not the weeks and weeks and weeks it would take on a boat to Africa. She'd never see them, nor Aunt Dot. And what about Rollo and Ike and Delilah? What about the career she was building in one of the most exciting cities in the world? Could she give all that up for love? And what if things didn't work out in South Africa in that small town with the diamond mine? Maggie didn't like her one bit; how long until that all blew up? And yet... and yet... she understood why Daniel would want to go. His children were his life, long before she had come into it...

She started to cry, her tears soaking into the hessian. "Oh Daniel. I don't know what to say. I – I –"

There was a rap on the door. "Oi! Love birds. Rollo says you need to get a move on."

"Let's talk about this later. When we have more time," said Daniel.

"Yes, let's." The words were like a mouthful of broken glass.

# CHAPTER 26

The tears were still spilling down Poppy's cheeks as the motorbike zig-zagged from Fleet Street to Scotland Yard, the rivulets freezing to mini glaciers in the biting winter air. Outside the police station Daniel helped Poppy out of the sidecar, folding the blanket and avoiding meeting her eyes. She took a moment to readjust her hat and wipe her face with the end of her scarf.

Inside the charge office they were greeted by an uncharacteristically friendly Sergeant Barnes, the ends of his handlebar moustache waxed to a rapier point. "Miss Denby! I didn't expect you back so soon. Have you got the Sherlock Holmes book yet?"

Poppy forced a smile. "Not yet, but it's near the top of my list. I'll get it done by the end of the week, I promise." *I'm not sure how... perhaps I can arrange to interview him to get comment on Sir James' death.*

Barnes' half-scowl suggested she damn well better live up to her promise, or else! Meanwhile, as she had not yet proven to be completely unfaithful, he still made an effort to be helpful. "What can I do for you then, miss? Anyone bothering you again?" He cast a watchful eye over Daniel.

"Well, sort of. It's actually related to what happened last night. This morning I meant to bring in this note, but when you told me about the poisoning of Sir James, I – well – I – anyway, here it is now." She spread out the note on the counter.

Barnes took out a pair of pince-nez spectacles and read the note. He grunted.

"You should have given this to me this morning, Miss Denby. This puts last night's incident in another light. It's not likely a drunk who has gone to the wrong house would take the time to write a note to the occupant before scarpering, is it?"

"No, it isn't," said Poppy, adopting a chastised schoolgirl look. "You're right, sergeant, I should have given it to you earlier. However, I'm giving it to you now. Along with this." She spread the second note on the counter and placed both envelopes next to it. She explained the background to the note and drew the sergeant's attention to the different handwriting on one of the envelopes. "So you see, as soon as I saw this second note – at Winterton Hall this morning – I realized that my note might not just be a harmless prank, but tied into the goings-on over the weekend."

"You mean Sir James Maddox's murder?"

"I do sergeant, yes. Can you give these to DCI Martin, please? I'm sure he'll want to take some handwriting samples from the Winterton guests."

Barnes screwed up his nose to secure the pince-nez. "Why didn't you give them to him yourself, Miss Denby? He's just been out there. You must have seen him."

Poppy blinked her bluebell eyes, doubting that the tactic would have any impact on the doughty Barnes, but willing to give it a go. "I did. But – well – I wanted to compare the two to make sure they were written by the same person, and to hand them in together – which I'm doing now."

Barnes made a guttural sound at the back of his throat and jabbed a thick finger at the second note. "Who gave it to you?"

"Someone at Winterton."

"Someone?"

"A member of staff."

"You'll have to do better than that."

Poppy remembered the promise she'd given to the footman that she would only hand the letters over if she and her colleagues thought there might be something in it. They did. But had she promised not to say it was him? She had implied it, yes, but she hadn't actually *said* it. Nonetheless, she decided to stretch the truth a little, to protect young Mr Wallace for as long as she could. "It was a footman. I don't know his name. It's only the butler that introduces himself by name at these posh houses, you know. There are quite a few male servants at Winterton – and they all dress the same." The last comment was accompanied with a cock of the head and a wry smile. Barnes' face remained impassive.

"You should have given it to DCI Martin as soon as you got it."

Poppy nodded, the chastised schoolgirl look back. "I should have, yes, and I'm sorry. Can you still give it to him though? And I'll pop in later in the week as soon as I've got that Sherlock Holmes book for you. 'To Gladys', with a 'y'." She smiled.

Behind the pince-nez were the eyes of a conflicted man: the police officer and the husband. Fortunately for Poppy, the husband won. "All right, I'll give them to him. But don't be surprised if he wants to interview you about it. And maybe even caution you for withholding evidence."

"I wasn't *withholding* evidence, Sergeant Barnes. I've brought them to you!"

Barnes made the guttural sound at the back of his throat again, then bent down under the desk to retrieve a brown evidence envelope. "Do it earlier next time."

Poppy promised that she would, thanked the sergeant, and, with Daniel in tow, left the charge office. Outside it was starting to snow again.

Daniel looked up at the brooding sky. "I'll call you a taxi to get to the museum. Not the best weather to be in a motorbike sidecar."

"I don't mind," said Poppy.

"But I do," said Daniel.

Poppy bit her lip. Under ordinary circumstances she would have challenged Daniel about wrapping her up – unnecessarily – in cotton wool. But one look at his wretchedly sad face told her not to. The conversation in the dark room fell like a sleet curtain between them. They needed to talk more, but it would have to wait until the job was done. And the job for now entailed getting to the British Museum to find out what had happened at the meeting about the Nefertiti mask.

Daniel hailed a black cab. Poppy got in and gave instructions, while out of the corner of her eye and with a heavy heart, she saw Daniel kick-start the motorbike and drive away at top speed.

When the cab – a contraption even slower than the *Globe*'s Model T – eventually dropped Poppy on Great Russell Street, she could see there was already a press huddle waiting in the Greek portico outside the grand entrance to the museum. But instead of facing the doors of the museum, waiting for the official delegation to emerge, their attention was drawn to the foot of the marble steps, where two men were brawling, and two other men were trying to prise them apart.

Poppy recognized one of the men trying to break up the scrap as Ike. She rushed through the gates, slipping and sliding on the slushy gravel. She steadied herself, not wanting a matching bruise to the one she already sported, then trudged doggedly on towards the kerfuffle. As she drew closer she recognized the second man trying to act as peacemaker – shorter, slimmer and fairer-skinned – as Lionel Saunders from the *Courier*. And on the ground, legs and arms flailing, were the men's respective photographers: Harry Gibson and Daniel Rokeby.

"Daniel!" cried Poppy. "What are you doing? Stop it! Stop it!"

With the combined efforts of Ike, Poppy, and Lionel, the brawling duo were finally wrenched apart. Both had bloodied noses. Both were spitting venom.

"What the hell's your problem, Rokeby?"

"You're my problem, Gibson, that's what. Scaring women for kicks! You stay away from Poppy Denby!"

"Are you drunk, man?" This was Lionel, his slight frame not likely to hold Gibson back if he chose to re-engage.

Fortunately, Ike Garfield was a stronger specimen; and just as well, because from what Poppy could tell, Daniel had been – and still was – the aggressor.

"What's going on, Daniel?" she asked as he strained against Ike's forearm.

"He was insulting you, Poppy, suggesting you and I had done something improper. The man is a cad and a reprobate. I wouldn't be surprised at all if he was the stalker."

"Stalker?" asked Lionel. "What are you on about?"

"Ask him!" bellowed Daniel.

"I'm asking you!" retorted Lionel, looking as if he was about to let Gibson back into the ring.

"Calm it! All of you!" ordered Ike. But it didn't look as if anyone was listening to him.

Poppy stood between the two groups, her arms outstretched. "Ike's right, calm down, everyone."

She turned to Harry Gibson, who was wiping his nose on his sleeve. "Mr Gibson, did you come to my house last night; around eight o'clock?"

"Why would I do that?"

"Did you?"

"My whereabouts have got nothing to do with you, Miss Denby." He spat out the word "miss".

"Answer her!" It was Ike, and this time it was he who looked like he might let his charge go. Man for man, it was obvious to all – including the gallery of pressmen above them in the portico – that if they teamed up, Ike and Daniel would wipe the floor with the *Courier* journos. Lionel Saunders seemed to realize the same thing.

"Tell her, Harry. We've wasted enough time on this."

"Well, if you must know, we were at Sir Arthur Conan Doyle's last night interviewing him about his response to the death of James Maddox – not that it's any of your business. Like everyone else, you can read about it in the morning edition." He grinned, the blood from his nose pooling in the cracks of his teeth. "Scooped you! Ha!"

"What time was that?" demanded Daniel.

"Between seven and nine. And by the way, Lady Jean is doing much better, thanks for asking," smirked Lionel. "Now, let's call a truce. We've all got a job to do here."

"Write something down, then we will." Poppy retrieved a notebook and pencil from her satchel and thrust it towards Harry Gibson.

"What are you going on about?" asked Harry, swatting at the notebook.

"Write: 'my name is Harry Gibson and I am not a stalker'. If you do that, we'll call it quits. Agreed?"

"Are you mad?"

"Yes, Miss Denby, are you mad?" Poppy spun around to see the disapproving face of DCI Jasper Martin, arms folded across his barrel chest. Behind him was his team from the Metropolitan Police Murder Squad.

"I – I –"

Martin put up his hand like a traffic warden. "I'm assuming this has something to do with the notes you dropped off at Scotland Yard. If so, then I too would like a writing sample from Mr Gibson… and," he spun his head like a hooded viper, "from Mr Rokeby."

"Daniel? It wasn't Daniel!"

"Be quiet, Miss Denby! Do *not* interrupt me. If you're not careful I will have you arrested for obstruction of justice."

"Obstruction of justice? What on earth have I done to obstruct justice?"

"Poppy…" Ike let go of Daniel and put a restraining hand on her shoulder. She willed herself to calm down.

"Sorry."

Martin waited a moment to see if she was truly compliant, then continued: "Actually, I will need a writing sample from everyone who was at Winterton Hall from Friday through Sunday, men and women included. And ah, it looks like I've arrived just at the right time."

Martin looked up to see the delegation from the Berlin, Cairo, New York Met, and British museums – as well as Marjorie Reynolds, Albert Carnaby, and Yasmin Reece-Lansdale – emerge from the museum. They stepped out onto the portico and were met with a barrage of flashes from the assembled press photographers, minus those of the *Globe* and *Courier.*

"What did I tell you, Miss Denby? Plenty of birds with only one stone."

He scanned the group above him. "Hmm, no Fox Flinton." He turned to the policemen behind him. "You, find Fox Flinton and get a sample from him. And you, round up Delilah Marconi and then drop by the Conan Doyles."

"What about Rollo Rolandson?" asked one of the policemen.

"Don't worry about him. We've already got a sample on file from the last time he was in the clanger. Oh, and when we're finished here, take Rokeby and Gibson to the Yard and charge them with disturbing the peace."

"But – but –"

"Be *quiet* Miss Denby!"

# CHAPTER 27

The basement of the British Museum was an Aladdin's cave of historic treasure. Lumps of stone, crudely carved by ancient men, were piled high next to crates of mosaic pieces and shards of pottery, waiting to be reassembled. On one wall hung exquisite silk hangings with motifs from the Far East, while on another were papyri and wood panels adorned with hieroglyphics. Statues from Egypt, Italy, Greece, Babylon, and South America glowered at the assembled archaeologists, politicians, and journalists as they were compelled to provide writing samples and fingerprints to the police.

Yasmin Reece-Lansdale – to DCI Martin's annoyance – made it clear to all present that they did not have to comply with his request as he did not have a court order and that none of them were under arrest. Despite this, most of the assembled "suspects" begrudgingly obliged, muttering that they might as well get it over and done with. Only Yasmin, Marjorie Reynolds, Dr Giles Mortimer, and Faizal Osman refused and huddled between the legs of the Bull of Nineveh that had been brought into the basement for repairs. They made it clear that they were not refusing as an admission of guilt, but rather as a statement of principle. Martin assured them that they were doing nothing more than wasting time and that he would get a judge to compel them by the end of the day. "You do that, DCI Martin, and we'll be happy to comply," said Yasmin.

"Bloody difficult woman," muttered Martin as he left the rebels under the bull to supervise the compliance of the rest of the rabble.

Once Poppy had provided her own writing sample – to prove, Martin said, that she had not just written the notes herself to cause trouble – she joined her friends under the bull.

"You didn't have to do that," Yasmin told her primly.

"I know," said Poppy, "but sometimes standing on principle is just cutting off one's nose to spite one's face."

"Standing on principle is *never* the wrong thing to do," cut in Faizal Osman tartly.

"I never said it was *wrong*, Dr Osman; I just don't see the point when a judge will make us do it later anyway. And besides, I want the person who wrote those notes to be caught as soon as possible." She went on to tell her friends about the disquieting events at the maze, the boat house, and Aunt Dot's house.

"Good gracious, Poppy, that's terrifying! You should have called me. I would have come around immediately."

Poppy smiled at Marjorie Reynolds, just imagining her and her elderly butler – Mr Samuels – arriving at the town house brandishing umbrellas and walking sticks. "Thank you, Marjorie. But I think the policeman scared him away and the next door neighbour said he'd be able to come if I needed him."

"Nonetheless," said Marjorie, "I think you should stay at my house until this stalker – and the murderer – are caught." She gave Poppy her best "don't argue with me I'm a Member of Parliament" look and Poppy had no choice but to give in.

"Thank you, Marjorie."

"I wonder if the murderer and the stalker are the same person?" mused Miss El Farouk as she joined the group after submitting her writing sample.

"Interesting question," observed Dr Mortimer. "What do you think, Miss Denby?"

Poppy swallowed hard. She decided not to tell him that he – and for that matter Faizal Osman – were on her "might possibly be the stalker" list, due to their hat choices and location – although, she admitted to herself, neither of them was very likely. "Well, it does seem as if there is some link, yes – at least between the shooting on Friday and the stalker. The notes were written by the same person. I'd be very interested to see those writing samples." She craned her neck to see one of Martin's men gathering up the sheets of paper. "What do you think my chances are of getting a look at them?"

"About the same as a snowball's chance in hell," observed Yasmin. "However, if you do get arrested for obstruction of justice, I could subpoena them for your defence..."

"Oh, I doubt he'll really arrest me! Or do you think he will?" Poppy bit her lip, then noticed a twinkle in Yasmin's eye. "You're just pulling my leg, aren't you?"

Yasmin laughed, softening her fiercely beautiful Egyptian features.

"Yes, I am. And all this hoo-ha about withholding writing samples is just to remind DCI Martin that procedures need to be followed. There might not be anything wrong with him asking for this today, but there have been times when evidence in cases I've worked on has been collected illegally and miscarriages of justice have taken place."

"So you're just flexing your muscles, then?" observed her brother.

"You could say that."

"So," said Poppy, "what's the decision with the mask? I missed the announcement while dealing with the fisticuffs earlier."

"Which also reminds me," Yasmin interrupted, "I'll go over to the station when they take Daniel in. Will you ask Rollo to drop by when you get back to the office, Poppy? Someone will have to pay bail if I can't convince them to release him without charge."

Poppy tried to catch a glimpse of Daniel, but two burly policemen obscured her view. "Thanks Yasmin. I appreciate that."

Giles Mortimer cleared his throat. "So, yes, the mask. Well, the good news is that the experts who examined it and performed some tests all believe it is the genuine article. And it has been agreed – after a brief telephone call to Lady Ursula – that the auction will take place here, at the museum, at eight o'clock tonight. She and her butler will be coming into town for the evening."

"Tonight?" asked Poppy. "That's rather soon – and, if I may say so, rather crass. Her husband has just died."

"I couldn't agree with you more, Poppy," said Marjorie.

"Then why so soon?" Poppy looked at each of her friends in turn.

"Probably to get the thing out of the country before the court case I'm bringing on behalf of the Egyptian government," said Yasmin. "I've put in a request for a judicial stay on sale. It could come through as soon as tomorrow. I had to notify both Lady Ursula's and Albert Carnaby's solicitors that I was doing it. Hence, I believe, this shameless attempt to flog it tonight."

Dr Mortimer pursed his lips and thrust his hands into his pockets. "I'm sorry you feel that way, Miss Reece-Lansdale, but as far as the British Museum is concerned, it is a legitimate sale. And, don't count your chickens before they hatch; *we* might be the highest bidder."

"With all due respect, Dr Mortimer, I doubt that." Yasmin and Mortimer held each other's gaze, she as tall as he.

However, before Anglo-Egyptian relations could deteriorate any further, DCI Martin announced everyone was free to go. Poppy rushed over to say goodbye to a morose-looking Daniel and told him Yasmin would be getting him out.

"I'm sorry, Poppy," he said, "but I couldn't have him saying those things about you."

"I know you couldn't. And thank you." She wanted to say, *thank you for loving me*, but the sight of two burly policemen on either side of her beau put her off doing so. Instead she smiled at him and said: "We'll have dinner as soon as you get out." *And then we'll have that talk...*

She held back tears as the policemen led him and a truculent Harry Gibson away.

"Are you coming Poppy?" called Marjorie Reynolds.

The older woman reached out her hand and took Poppy's, squeezing it warmly. "Don't worry, sweetheart, everything will work out."

Poppy wanted to throw her arms around Marjorie and pour out her heart. Perhaps she would later tonight. But not now. There was work still to be done.

Marjorie led her back into the basement.

"Where are we going?" asked Poppy. "The exit's that way."

"Giles said we can all go out the service entrance. It's closer."

A few moments later and Marjorie and Poppy, still holding hands, walked out of a door and up a short flight of steps. They emerged at the back of the British Museum at the very spot, Poppy realized, where she had seen the man in the fedora hat the day before. And there, walking ahead of them through the snow, were two men in fedora hats: Dr Giles Mortimer and Faizal Osman, neither of whom had agreed to give a writing sample. Poppy's eyes narrowed.

Back at the office Poppy waited impatiently for Rollo to return from the police station. He had caught a taxi over as soon as she had told him about Daniel's arrest. She spent the time – along with Ike – writing up copy for the morning edition. He did a write-up of his interview with the grieving widow; she did an update of the Nefertiti mask story. The result of the auction would come in too late for the Tuesday edition so would have to wait for Wednesday. Rollo, Ike, and Poppy agreed that the "fake Renoir" story needed to develop more before they could go to press with it. Rollo had already written up the lead article, which was that Sir James Maddox's death had now been declared as murder. *Golly*, thought Poppy, *it's going to be a busy edition!* Poppy typed ENDS at the end of her article and whisked it out of the Remington. She sat down with a cup of tea to read it over before submitting it to the sub-editor.

**Bloomsbury, London, Monday 12 December 1921 –**
*The death mask of Nefertiti, owned by the late Sir James Maddox, has been declared legitimate today by experts at the British Museum. The mask will now be put up for auction at the museum in an ad hoc sale organized by the widow of Sir James, Lady Ursula Maddox.*

According to Dr Giles Mortimer of the British Museum, Lady Ursula said she wanted to honour her late husband's wishes "to see the mask go to a good home". It was at a previous attempt to auction the mask – on Saturday 10 December – that Sir James collapsed and died of what, at the time, was thought to be a natural heart attack, but now has been declared murder. (See page 1 – Murder most Foul! – for further details.)

The same representatives of four internationally renowned museums who attended the first aborted auction will gather at the British Museum to bid for the mysterious mask. The *Globe* will bring you the results of the auction as soon as we know them.

The museums are: the British Museum, the Berlin Museum, the Cairo Museum, and the Metropolitan Museum of New York. However, it is unclear if the Cairo Museum will be putting in a bid as they are currently trying to have the mask returned to them by the British courts.

Miss Yasmin Reece-Landsdale, KC, acting on behalf of the Egyptians, has expressed her and her clients' belief that that is the real reason for the rushed second auction. She said: "I have submitted an application for the sale to be halted until its legality can be ascertained by a judge." However, Miss Reece-Lansdale has told the Globe that she will not be able to get a hearing for her application until Tuesday morning – which will be after the sale has gone ahead.

"We are not giving up, however, and will ask for the halt on the sale to be applied retrospectively if the judge finds in my client's favour," she said. She went on to explain that the mask would then be confiscated by the authorities and the sale put on hold until a "proper legal process" had been fulfilled. She told the *Globe* that the process could go on for months.

However, Dr Giles Mortimer of the British Museum has expressed his doubt that a judge will find in favour of the Egyptians. "They've attempted this before and failed," he said. "I think it's time they accepted that and just put in a bid like the rest of us."

Miss Kamela El-Farouk, assistant to the director of the Department of Antiquities at the Cairo Museum, said that she hopes the British judiciary will live up to its reputation of independence and give an honest hearing to the case. "We believe the mask was stolen from the people of Egypt," she said. "It should not be sold tonight, nor any other time."

This view is partially shared by Herr Dr Heinrich Stein, Director of Antiquities at the Museum of Berlin. However, Herr Stein believes that the mask was stolen from German archaeologists who had a licence from the Cairo Museum to excavate the site where it was found in 1914. "The mask disappeared from the dig before the artefacts could properly be processed. The death mask of Nefertiti rightfully belongs to the Museum of Berlin."

Asked whether or not he would be putting in a bid for the mask, he said he would. "Unfortunately we have no proof that the mask was stolen, as it did not appear in the original manifest of the contents of the site. And as it did not appear in the manifest we cannot prove that the mask was actually found on our licensed dig. We only have anecdotal evidence of its existence," Herr Stein explained.

Poppy paused, pencil in hand, and tapped the words "no proof". The article went on to explain that Sir James Maddox had been present at the dig – and confirmed that the mask had indeed been found – but that he had claimed ever since that he did not know what happened to it and why it had not been recorded in the manifest.

*This is where there's a gap in the story*, Poppy thought. *Borchardt's assistant who recorded the manifest should know what happened.* But she had not had a chance to ask Herr Stein about it yet. She reached for the gooseneck telephone and asked the operator to put her through to the Hotel Russell. Then to Herr Stein. Herr Stein answered. "Hello, Miss Denby. You just caught us. We're all about to go down for tea – the Germans, the Americans, and the Egyptians," he chuckled. "We'll be trying to figure out each other's strategy before the auction tonight. I assume that's why you're calling, to get a comment about the auction."

"Actually, not. I think I've got all I need for that. What I would like to know, though, is the name of Professor Borchardt's assistant – back in 1914 – and what he said about the mask. That part of the story is still a little unclear to me."

"Funny you should ask about that. I had a phone call earlier from another journalist wanting to talk about Waltaub too. Frederick Waltaub – that was his name. We called him Freddie."

"Oh," asked Poppy, gripped by a pang of anxiety, but trying to keep her voice casual, "was it Lionel Saunders from the *Courier*?"

Herr Stein laughed. "Scared he's going to scoop you? No, it wasn't, it was someone from *The Times* – at least he said he was from *The Times*. When I called their office afterwards to check up on him, they told me he had retired."

Poppy gripped the receiver. "By any chance was his name Walter Jensford?"

"It was, yes. He didn't sound too healthy though. Kept breaking off the call to cough. I asked him if he would be at the auction later – this was before I knew that he was no longer officially on the payroll – and he said no. He wouldn't be there but was following up on the 1914 angle. He wanted to confirm something about Freddie."

"Oh? What was that?"

"That his murderer had never been found."

Poppy gasped and nearly dropped the receiver. "F – F – Freddie was murdered?"

"Well, possibly. We don't really know. It looked like it was suicide – that he'd shot himself – but his family never believed it. The official cause of death was suicide, which is what I told *The Times* journalist – or the man who said he was from *The Times*. I thought him a little suspicious, which is why I called the paper to check on him. His editor said I should just ignore him. Apparently he's lost his marbles and forgets that he no longer works for them. Poor old chap. Not sure how he knew I was at the Russell... anyway, back to old Freddie. Yes, the family had wanted the case reopened, but had failed. As far as the police – and the Berlin Museum are concerned – the poor man killed himself."

Poppy made frantic notes. "When was this?"

"Freddie's death? Hmm, let me think… last year sometime. Summer of 1920. In Cairo. He had been there to meet James Maddox, as a matter of fact."

The lead of Poppy's pencil snapped. She tossed it aside and grabbed another one. "Oh? Do you know why?"

"Yes. Maddox had told him that he had something the museum might be interested in, a companion piece to our Nefertiti bust – the one we already have. So, as Freddie was already in Cairo – at a meeting with the Antiquities Department – we said he should go along to see what Maddox had to say. But Freddie never met him. His wife had left him. Run off with another man. He got a telegram about it when he was in Cairo. We assume that's what pushed him over the edge. He'd been drinking heavily. Tragic. Totally tragic."

"Yes it is," observed Poppy. "And did you find out what Sir James was going to offer him?"

"We did, yes. It was the death mask. The one that's going to be auctioned tonight. After Freddie's death Maddox telegraphed us to say that he had it but that he'd now changed his mind about it. That was the last we heard until the invitation to Winterton last week."

"Golly!" said Poppy. "Have you told the police about this? DCI Jasper Martin?"

"Not yet. But he's sent word that he wants to interview me and my assistant at Scotland Yard – Weiner this evening, me first thing in the morning. I should imagine he's working his way down the list, starting with those who didn't give a writing sample earlier today. Have you been interviewed by him yet?"

"I have, yes."

Poppy heard a knock on the door from Herr Stein's side of the line. "Sorry, Miss Denby, there's someone here. I'll see you later at the auction."

"Yes, I'll see you there, Herr Stein. And thank you for speaking to me. You've been most helpful."

Poppy put down the phone and circled the name Walter Jensford on her notepad. *Most helpful indeed.*

# CHAPTER 28

The station clock struck six o'clock as Poppy stepped off the Central Line train at Shepherd's Bush. It would be a tight fit to get to see Walter Jensford at the nursing home, then get back in time for the auction at the British Museum, but it was doable. Poppy would have been here earlier if she hadn't been delayed by a most unpleasant phone call.

At five o'clock she decided she had waited as long as she could for Rollo and, in consultation with Ike, had decided to visit Walter Jensford on her own. She had filled her colleague in on her conversation with Herr Stein about the death of the German archaeologist in Cairo. Both agreed that whether or not the man's death had been murder – or, as official reports claimed, merely suicide – there was more to the story that needed to be unearthed. Here was a third death linked, in some way, to the Nefertiti mask. Or perhaps fourth, if the boy's death in prison was added to the number. Neither Ike nor Poppy was keen to use the word "curse", but they both knew that the *Courier* would have no qualms in doing so. She had rung the nursing home and arranged an early evening visit with Mr Jensford. Mr Jensford had been reluctant at first to agree, saying he had been looking forward to speaking to "the dwarf", but Poppy promised him that Rollo would drop by as soon as he could; in the meantime he had asked her to speak to the retired journalist on his behalf.

"I'm afraid Mr Rolandson is currently tied up at Scotland Yard."

This appeared to amuse Jensford no end and they ended the conversation as his laughter turned to a rib-rattling cough and his nurse took the phone from him. "Mr Jensford is not well, miss. So I will expect you to keep your visit short. Is that understood?"

Poppy assured the woman that it was. However, just as she was readying herself to leave, Mavis Bradshaw, the receptionist, called to say that a Mrs Minifred Hughes was waiting on the line to speak to Poppy. Could she put her through?

*Minifred Hughes! Madame Minette!* Poppy took the call and within half a minute regretted that she had. Madame Minette – all traces of a French accent gone – had called to give Poppy a piece of her mind. How dare the sneaky little reporter try to take advantage of a sick child? How dare she force her way into a private home? How dare she interview a minor without the presence of a guardian? "You'd better watch your back, missy. I was paid fair and square to run that séance. Just 'cos you didn't like what was said, don't take it out on me. There is nothing unlawful about what happened. The spirits have told me things about you, Poppy Denby. And they don't like that you're mocking them in the papers – saying it's all a con. So leave me and my family alone or you might just get a visitor you don't want either."

"Is that a threat, Mrs Hughes?" asked Poppy, having a flashback to the previous night and the terrifying knocking on the kitchen door.

"Call it what you like. Watch your back missy; that's all I'm going to say."

With Madame Minette's threatening call echoing in her ears, Poppy left the office to catch a train to Shepherd's Bush. And now, forty minutes later, here she was. According to the station master the nursing home was only a five-minute walk away. It was already dark, but Poppy didn't want to waste money on a cab ride for such a short journey.

Poppy left the station with other commuters, following the station master's directions. Soon the crowd thinned as people veered off left and right, until she was on her own. The street lights cast an eerie glow in the quiet street, and the sound of her heels clicking on the pavement was muffled by a thin blanket of snow. "Not far now..." she said out loud, so she wouldn't feel so alone. She chastised herself for being so jittery. She had been like this since that ridiculous séance on Friday night and the pantomime apparition of her ghostly brother.

The nursing home was only a few hundred yards away on the opposite side of the road. She stepped between two parked cars to cross. As she did the door of one of the cars opened and someone climbed out – someone in a trench coat and a fedora hat.

"Miss Denby, I'm glad I've caught you. I need to talk to you."

Poppy gasped and stepped back.

"Wait, I'm not going to hurt you." The man reached out his hand towards her.

Poppy spun on her heel, ready to run hell for leather back to the station. A firm hand gripped her arm.

"Wait!"

"Let go of me or I'll scream!" Poppy scanned the street. Lights behind curtains told her people were home. Someone will come if she screamed.

She opened her mouth to do so when suddenly she felt something hard press against her ribs.

"Don't scream, Miss Denby. I have a gun. I would prefer not to use it, but if I must I must."

Poppy turned around, slowly, and looked into the face of Fox Flinton.

"Why? Why are you doing this?"

"I will explain in the car. Now please get in. He pulled her by the arm towards the vehicle and pushed her towards the open door. "Get in, then shimmy across."

"Why? Where are you taking me?"

"Just get in, then we can talk." Fox gestured with his hand and Poppy saw that he did indeed have a gun. She did not have a choice.

Poppy climbed into the driver's seat, thinking for one mad moment that she could kick Fox over then drive off. But she didn't know if the keys were in the ignition or whether, instead, this was the type of car that needed a crank start. A quick getaway was not on the cards. She then considered shimmying across and escaping out of the passenger seat door. But Fox was one step ahead of her.

"Don't try to escape, Miss Denby. The door is locked and even if you do manage to get out, you won't get far." He brandished the gun to emphasize his point.

Poppy swallowed hard and moved across to the passenger seat, crossing her arms tightly across her chest.

Fox closed the door behind him and turned to Poppy, the gun still trained on her. "I'm sorry, Miss Denby, for all these theatrics but it is imperative that I speak to you. Delilah told me the police are looking for me to get a writing sample. I knew immediately it was to do with the two notes I wrote."

"So, it was you who wrote the notes!"

"Yes, it was all part of a silly game. And now the police seem to think that it's to do with James' murder! Oh my! That's the last thing that it is! And I need you to tell them that!"

A man and a dog walked past the car. Poppy was sorely tempted to call out to him for help – but the gun in Fox Flinton's hand put paid to that.

"You want me to tell them that you've got nothing to do with a murder and yet here you are threatening to kill me?"

"Good heavens, no!"

"And yet you have a gun..."

"Well yes, but that is only because I didn't think you'd speak to me without it. You seem to have the wrong end of the stick. And it's partially my fault, I understand that, but –"

"If you just wanted to speak to me, why didn't you simply come to the office?"

"I did! But you'd left already. Your receptionist told me you were heading out this way before going to the museum later. I told her it was imperative that I spoke to you, that I had some crucial evidence to help with your story. So she told me that you were going to this nursing home. I said I could meet you here and then give you a lift to the museum afterwards."

"Well, that was jolly good of her," said Poppy caustically, making a note to speak to Mavis about not disclosing her whereabouts to folk. However, in Mavis' favour, she had not mentioned Fox Flinton as a possible suspect in all of this. She had discounted him because of the footman's comment that Mr Flinton always wore a boater.

And there was the boater on the back seat.

"Why are you wearing a fedora, Mr Flinton?" she asked.

Fox raised his eyebrows. "What a strange question, Miss Denby."

*Not half as strange as holding a lady at gunpoint.* "If you wrote the note, then you are the man who has been following me – first at the maze at Winterton, then at the boat house in Henley-on-Thames, then at the British Museum, then at my house last night. Do you deny it?"

"I do not, no. Although it wasn't me at the British Museum... nor was it technically me at the boat house. However, why my headgear should be of any concern is rather puzzling. I would have thought you would want to know why I did it all."

"Well I do, of course. But I also want to know about the hat. The footman at Winterton told me you only ever wear a boater, and I've only seen you in a boater."

He grinned, wryly, and despite herself Poppy couldn't help thinking that he was a devilishly handsome man. "Ah, well, that's all part of the image. When I'm out and about as Fox Flinton, actor extraordinaire, I wear my boater. It's like my trademark. But when I want a bit of anonymity I wear a fedora – like half the men in London."

"But you didn't hand your fedora in to the footman. Why's that?"

Fox shrugged. "I wanted to retain a little mystery."

"Why did you need to do that?"

Fox sighed and took his hat off, tossing it onto the back seat. "It was all part of the game. Let me explain."

"Please do," said Poppy tartly.

Fox raised a sardonic eyebrow and cleared his throat. "When Delilah told me you were going to be at the Winterton weekend, I thought it would be the perfect opportunity to create a bit of mystery. I've heard all about you, Miss Denby, and everyone knows you have a nose for murder."

There was that phrase again, the one the footman had used: *a nose for murder*. And hadn't he said he had overheard Fox saying that very thing to Mr Grimes the butler?

She mentioned this to Fox. Fox nodded. "Yes, that's exactly what I said. You see, I was trying to create a bit of a buzz about the weekend, to make sure there would be extensive press coverage. You see, me and Minny –"

"Minny?"

"Madame Minette. Minifred Hughes. The medium. I know you know who she is; the boy told me you'd been around earlier. And that you'd been asking about the painting..."

"The forged Renoir, you mean."

Fox cleared his throat again. "Well, yes, that. But that too is not what it appears on the surface. I'll explain about that later. For now, I want to tell you why I had nothing to do with James' murder so you can back me up when we go to the police."

"Assuming I believe you."

"I'm sure you will if you give me an honest hearing."

Poppy looked down at the gun still trained at her and swallowed hard. "Go on."

Fox nodded earnestly. "Thank you. You see, I'm not getting the roles I used to and so to earn a little extra I've started helping Minny out in her business. In fact, I'm looking at ways of expanding it. A weekend with the auction of the death mask of an Egyptian queen, attended by the world's foremost mystery writer and an up-and-coming sleuth like you seemed to me the perfect opportunity to get a bit of publicity. But first I had to get you interested."

"Well, you certainly achieved that. But why did you remove Conan Doyle from the picture if he was so important?"

Fox shrugged. "Just having his name attached to the weekend was enough. But his wife needed to be removed in order for Minny to take her place. I'd tried, unsuccessfully, to get Cousin James to have Madame Minette as the medium from the beginning. But he felt that the 'big name' Conan Doyles would attract more press interest."

"And he was right," observed Poppy, remembering that that was one of the main reasons she and Rollo had decided to go.

"Ursula, however, was more inclined to listen, particularly when I told her that I could get some dirt on some of the attendees and create a bit more excitement."

Poppy raised her eyebrows. "Ursula was in on it? I thought she was a true believer. I thought it was James who had set up Madame Minette to target Howard Carter, Albert Carnaby, and me."

"No, that was Ursula. James just wanted rid of the mask. He genuinely seemed to believe there was a curse attached to it. Ursula wanted to ensure they got the best price for it. She was always the one who worried about money. James was like a child in that sense; he didn't seem to know or care how much things cost. He just wanted to possess beautiful and mysterious things."

Poppy nodded. Yes, she'd gathered that. "So, you fed Lady Jean Conan Doyle something to make her ill."

"That was Ursula too. I must say I think she overdid it a bit. I just suggested some prune juice or something, but Ursula used the strong stuff."

"The strong stuff?"

"A little arsenic. Just enough to make her sick, nothing more. In small, single doses it's not lethal." Fox laughed. "Ironically, she got the idea from one of Conan Doyle's stories. So with Lady Jean out of the picture we were able to bring in Minny. And a jolly good job she did too, I thought. The only thing that didn't work, as planned, was that you were angry about your brother rather than moved that he'd tried to contact you. From what Delilah had told me, unlike Rollo Rolandson, you were open to the idea that spirits might be real, and you were still desperately sad that your brother had died. She also said you were excited that the Conan Doyles were there as your brother had been a Sherlock Holmes enthusiast."

"How on earth did she know that?"

"She said you'd told her. At Oscar's one night?"

Suddenly Poppy remembered the conversation she'd had with her friend at the jazz club; and that she'd told her about her brother's magazines! Good golly, how could she have forgotten?

A glass of champagne too many…? "Why on earth did she tell you? Did she know you were in on the séance?"

"No, no, of course not. It was just chit-chat. She didn't realize that I would use it against you. You hadn't said it was top secret or anything, had you?"

Poppy had to admit that she had not.

"But it didn't go to plan. We had expected a different reaction at the séance, a bit more like Albert Carnaby's. People who have lost someone are usually more susceptible to this sort of thing."

"Then you obviously don't know me very well, Mr Flinton."

Fox grimaced. "No, I'm afraid we misjudged you. But we didn't realize that at the time, which is why I decided to give it another go. I was up early on Saturday and saw you heading over to the maze. So I followed you, hoping to give you a little fright. I wanted you to think your brother was trying to speak to you. I had hoped you might think I was his ghost. I did the same at your house last night. Look, I'm dreadfully sorry, I realize it wasn't a nice thing to do, but I didn't think you'd take it the way you did. I thought you'd just want to try to speak to him again, and that you'd then give some publicity to our séances. We need to get the business on a stronger footing you see, for the sake of the boy…"

"Your son."

"How did you know?"

Poppy smiled wryly. "He looks just like you."

Fox grinned. "He doesn't know yet that I'm his father. I didn't until just recently. But Minny and I are going to tell him. Once we're married."

"You're getting married?"

"We are. Finally, after all these years."

"Well… congratulations." Poppy didn't know what else to say. She eyed the gun again. *What a bizarre conversation.* "Look

Fox, now that we've got the pleasantries out of the way, would you mind putting that gun away? I won't run, I promise."

Fox shrugged in apology. "I'm sorry Poppy – may I call you Poppy? – but I need you to hear the rest of what I've got to tell you, and no offence, I don't have any reason to trust you."

Poppy shrugged in reply. "Fair enough. All right, so it was you at the maze, the boat house, and Aunt Dot's house, but –"

"Oh no, not the boat house. That wasn't me; it was Grimes. He told me about it afterwards. He said he saw the two of you sneaking off to do a bit of canoodling. He thought I might want to know. You see, he's fiercely loyal to Ursula. He was in on the whole séance switcheroo. He's just as keen as my cousin to save the family from penury – his job depends on it, after all. He knew we were trying to get a bit of information on you, so he followed you. He had to go into town that day anyway."

Poppy grimaced. Her instincts had been right – Grimes was in on it. "But why would he take the cartridge into the police?"

Fox looked at her curiously. "The cartridge?"

"From the shooting."

"Oh that. No, he didn't take the cartridge in. That would have pointed old Bill's finger directly at us."

"But surely the finger was already pointing. The boy would have told the police that Grimes gave him the note."

Fox sighed. "Well yes, that has backfired a bit too. Not that well-thought through, I'm afraid. We did offer the lad and his father a good pay-off to keep quiet and not tell the police about it. But they never quite realized that that also extended to your photographer friend. I believe the lad mentioned it to him."

"He did. And the police have got the note. I gave it to them. One of the staff at Winterton passed it onto me – another thing that wasn't well thought through," she said sarcastically.

Fox lowered his chin to his chest, chagrined. "No. We didn't think the lad would leave the note just lying around like that."

*Not exactly the criminal mastermind*, thought Poppy. "Tell me Fox, what exactly did you, Ursula, and Grimes hope to achieve by the shooting charade?"

"Oh, that was Ursula's idea as well. She thought switched cartridges and an accidental shooting might add to the whole 'curse of the pharaoh' thing we were trying to set up. More fodder for the press."

Poppy was incredulous. "You mean she actually meant for someone to get shot?"

"Good grief no! She was going to discharge the gun, then notice that buckshot had been used. She was going to suggest loudly and mysteriously – in the earshot of all you journalists – that something fishy was afoot. That someone could very easily have been killed, that perhaps the pharaoh's curse ... etcetera, etcetera. But then the stupid boy went and shot himself in the foot instead. Scuppered all our plans."

Poppy's mind was racing. It was a lot to take in, but despite its stupidity, Fox's confession was making sense. "And the Renoir? How did that fit into it all? You said you would tell me."

"And I will. That was also Ursula's idea. You see, *Yachts on the Seine* was one of her private collection. She hadn't wanted James to know that she owned it in case he tried to flog it to finance his foreign travels. When Renoir died last year, the price went up. That's when she thought she'd auction it. She used an agent so it was listed as a 'private collector'. I don't think Carnaby knew it was hers. Anyway, I'd kept it for her for a while before that – to keep it out of James' sight – and while I did, I did a spot of painting. It's a hobby of mine, you see."

"You're very good."

"Thank you. Unfortunately, never been able to make much money from it. However, last week when Ursula came around to speak to me and Minny about our plans for the séance, she saw my copy of it. She suggested we try to switch it at the auction house – and then sell off the real one privately, elsewhere. You know, sort of on the black market. Apparently there are people who do that sort of thing."

"Apparently. So you agreed?"

"Well, to be honest, I didn't think we'd get away with it. For people like Minny and Ursula who don't know anything about painting, they think it's identical. But it's not. And I'm sure an expert would be able to spot the difference. But Minny and Ursula wouldn't be deterred and hence went ahead with the charade at the séance, putting pressure on Albert Carnaby to withdraw it from auction to give us time to replace the original with the fake. I let them. But I would not have let them go through with the real switch. I swear to you."

*Swear it to a judge.* "Why are you telling me all this, Fox? You are implicating yourself in some shady goings on."

"Shady, yes, but a far cry from murder. And I need you to convince the police of that. You've cleared innocent people before, Poppy. I hope you'll do the same for me."

"Why would I do that?"

"Because it's who you are. Delilah told me that too. You never stop until you get the truth, all of it. And if the police arrest me for James' murder, the real killer might get away."

"And who is the real killer, Fox? Do you know?"

Fox shook his head. He looked miserable. "I don't. I was just as shocked as you were when James collapsed. And even more so when the news came out that it was poison. I have no idea who would do that, or why." He looked at her imploringly. "Do you?"

Poppy looked across the road at the care home, then at her watch. It was half-past six. She would not have time to interview Walter Jensford and get back in time for the auction. Not using public transport. Unless...

"Fox, you said earlier that you could give me a lift back to the museum. Does that offer still stand?"

He nodded. "Of course."

"Good, then I'll take you up on it. And I'll do my best to straighten things out with the police. On one condition."

"What's that?"

"That you finally put away that gun. You've told me what you need to tell me. I'm not going to run away. You don't really need it any more, do you?"

"No, I don't. It's done its job." He slipped the weapon into his coat pocket. "I borrowed it from the prop department at the theatre."

Poppy's mouth dropped open. "You mean it isn't real?"

"Good heavens, no. Do you really think I'd hold a lady up at gunpoint?" He flashed his most dashing smile.

# CHAPTER 29

Poppy and Fox were ushered into the waiting room of the Shepherd's Bush Nursing Home by a disapproving matron who tapped her watch and pursed her lips. Poppy apologized for the lateness of the visit but hoped Mr Jensford would still be able to receive her. The matron left and then returned a few minutes later to say that Poppy – and only Poppy – could have half an hour with Mr Jensford. The gentleman would just have to wait.

Fox gave his most charming thespian smile – which had melted many a female heart over the years – and said he'd be happy to wait if the lovely lady would get him a cup of tea. The matron's heart was not melted.

The matron led Poppy past a sitting room where the residents were playing cards, chatting, or just nodding off in their chairs. One elderly lady tinkled on the piano – "Great is Thy Faithfulness", if Poppy was not mistaken – a good old Methodist hymn.

The matron knocked on a door and entered. Poppy followed. On one side of the room there was a bed and a dressing table with a wash bowl, jug, and chamber pot. On the other, a desk, piled high with newspapers and files, on either side of a typewriter. In one of two armchairs, set into a window alcove, was an emaciated elderly man, his skin too loose for his frame. His bald head perched on the end of a skinny neck reminded Poppy of a turkey. On one arm of his chair was an ashtray and on the other the Monday morning edition of *The Daily Globe*.

"I'll be back in half an hour," the matron said. "Don't tire yourself out, Mr Jensford."

Mr Jensford grinned, revealing a sparsely toothed mouth. "I'd rather be tired out by an interesting young lady than by those boring old codgers downstairs."

The matron humphed and withdrew.

"Miss Denby, I assume. Forgive me for not getting up. I'm not quite the man I used to be. Please, have a seat."

Poppy smiled and sat down. "I believe you were a top-class journalist, Mr Jensford. Mr Rolandson speaks very highly of you." That was not entirely true. The only time Rollo had ever mentioned Jensford was to confirm that he used to work for *The Times* and that he was a member of the Press Club. Nonetheless, the compliment had the desired effect. Jensford's turkey neck grew at least an inch.

"Well I was that, back in the day. And I haven't entirely given up the job either." He indicated the piles of papers and typewriter on the desk. "Doing a bit of freelance work, even from here. The wonders of the modern age, you know. I've been trying to get them to install a telephone in here, but they're resisting. I have to use the one in the nurses' station."

"Ah, so that's how you called Herr Stein earlier today. He was wondering how you knew he was there."

Jensford tapped his nose. "I still have my sources, Miss Denby." Then he picked up *The Daily Globe* and laid it on his lap. "Great work you fellas at the *Globe* have done on the Maddox story so far. I assume his murder will be front-page news in the morning."

"It will be, yes. We only got the news of the autopsy this morning, after the paper had come out. Unlike *The Times,* we don't have an evening edition."

"Then you'll have to work twice as hard to scoop them. And

I think I might be able to help you with that."

"Oh, really? Do you have some information for us?"

Jensford picked up his pipe from the ashtray and banged out the old tobacco. "I might. That depends."

"On what?"

"On whether or not I can get a byline. Or a joint byline. That's why I was hoping Rolandson would come. He could authorize that. No offence, Miss Denby, but you are too junior to be of much help."

Poppy was not offended. "You're right, I can't authorize that. But I'm sure Mr Rolandson will if the information you give us helps us scoop *The Times* – and the *Courier*."

Jensford took a pouch from his dressing gown pocket, opened it, and extracted a pinch of fresh tobacco. "What guarantee do I have?"

"Just my word, I'm afraid. I know that Mr Rolandson is an honourable man."

"Hmmm," said Jensford and plugged the tobacco into the bowl of his pipe using his knuckle. "Well, as this is a fast-moving story, I won't have time to approach anyone else. *The Times* of course will always print my stories – my name still carries a lot of weight, you know – but I haven't been able to get hold of my editor there."

From what Poppy recalled of her conversation with Herr Stein, Jensford was no longer held in high regard at *The Times*. What was it they said? He'd lost his marbles? Poppy looked at the crumpled man before her. *No, he hasn't lost his marbles. He's just old and ignored.* She smiled encouragingly. "I'm sure they'd be happy to run a story from you. No doubt there's just been a bit of confusion, but it's probably too late to fix that tonight. And *I* am here. I'd be honoured to share a byline with such an experienced journalist if you don't mind helping a young up-and-comer like me."

Jensford grinned. "They didn't hire women in my day."

*They hardly hire women now*, thought Poppy. She took out her notebook, aware that her allocated half-hour was quickly ticking away. "So, Mr Jensford, what do you have to tell me?"

Jensford struck a match and lit the tobacco, sucking like a baby on a teat until the strands caught alight. Then exhaled, contentedly.

"All right, Miss Denby. I hope your shorthand is up to it. I've got a lot to tell..."

And indeed he did. In 1914 Jensford was a foreign correspondent for *The Times* in Egypt. Ever since Professor Ludwig Borchardt from the Berlin Museum had found the famous bust of Nefertiti at El-Amarna, British archaeologists had hoped to equal his find. Nefertiti's body had not been unearthed, and men like Howard Carter and Lord George Herbert Carnarvon were convinced that there was another royal tomb somewhere in the Egyptian desert. Nefertiti's husband had died at El-Amarna – and his tomb had been found in the cliffs above the old city – but the queen and her grandson, Tutankhamun, lived and died elsewhere. The British Egyptian Exploration Society funded a number of expeditions at the time, and Sir James Maddox, as a financial contributor, was allowed to tag along. He was even a member of the society's board for a while. But he was never taken seriously by the professional archaeologists and this irked him.

Jensford had interviewed him at the time – he gave a clipping of the original article to Poppy – and Maddox's bitterness at the way he was treated by people he considered his peers was glaringly obvious. Maddox told Jensford that he was on the brink of a major discovery that would finally give him the respect that he deserved.

"What was this discovery?" asked Poppy.

"I wasn't sure. But Maddox told me to meet him in El-Amarna and that I would be given a scoop. He claimed that it would rival that of the Nefertiti bust – which was the gold standard at the time."

"Did you go?"

"Yes. I knew that Maddox wasn't much of an archaeologist, but he did have the knack of being in the right place at the right time. And whatever scientific talent he lacked, he made up for it with theatricality."

Poppy remembered Sir James' swan song – the mime of Nefertiti and Akhenaten – at Winterton Hall. "Yes, he certainly knew how to put on a show."

"The bottom line was: he was likely to produce something newsworthy, even it was only his own humiliation. So yes, I went. It was 10 April 1914 – Good Friday. I got there early evening but when I got to his lodgings, I was told he was out. So I waited. He eventually came home – after midnight. I wasn't too pleased – it was a 300-mile journey from Cairo. But the man was clearly disturbed about something so I held my peace."

"What was he distressed about?"

"He said there'd been a murder. A watchman and his dog had been killed. Beaten to death. Horrible business."

"Did he say who had done it?"

"He said he didn't know. He said that he'd dropped by the dig to see Freddie Waltaub. Waltaub was German, an assistant to the big man, Borchardt. Borchardt was away in Cairo for the Easter weekend. I think it was a matter of 'while the cat's away the mice would pillage the dig'."

"How do you know that?"

Jensford sucked on his pipe then exhaled. "Maddox was carrying a sack. He didn't show me what was in it, but I could see enough to tell they were artefacts."

Poppy's heart beat faster. "Did you see the death mask of Nefertiti?"

Jensford shook his head. "No. As I say, he didn't show me what was in it. Although in retrospect I assume that was what he was going to show me. That was why he'd asked me to come."

"Then why didn't he?"

Jensford shrugged. "I think the death of the watchman really shook him. Either that, or he didn't have the mask."

Poppy stopped and flicked back in her notebook. "Yes, that's what he originally claimed, wasn't it? That he had seen the mask but that it disappeared. And that it wasn't in the manifest. Do you think he might have been telling the truth? Herr Stein doesn't think he was."

Jensford smiled. "I see you've been doing some digging of your own, Miss Denby. The honest truth is that I don't know. I wish now I'd demanded to see the contents of the sack, but I didn't. At that stage I didn't know about the mask, so I wouldn't have known to ask about it specifically." He picked up the newspaper and pointed to her article from this morning. "But when I read your article about it in the *Globe* I realized that sometime between 10 April 1914 and now, James Maddox had in fact got his hands on the mask."

"He claims he got it last year in Cairo – that he bought it from a dealer. But when the Egyptian Antiquities Department went to investigate, apparently the dealer's shop was closed and the man had done a runner."

"Or he never existed," observed Jensford.

Jensford's elbow knocked the ashtray. Poppy quickly reached out a hand to steady it. "Are you suggesting, Mr Jensford, that Sir James had kept the mask hidden all this time? If that's the case, why did he wait?"

Jensford tapped his pipe to loosen the tobacco. "Well, if he had revealed that he had it back then, it might have linked him to the death of the watchman. The police were all over the scene. Without the murder they might have got away with it quietly."

"True," said Poppy, remembering what Miss El Farouk had told her about the incident. "However, one of my sources tells me it was Maddox himself who called the policeman to the crime scene. Why would he do that if he wanted to slip away quietly?"

Jensford pulled the pipe from his mouth and jabbed it in Poppy's direction. "A very astute observation, Miss Denby, which is pretty much the conclusion that I came to. So then, that leaves only one person who could have taken the mask..."

"And who could have killed the watchman."

"You don't believe the local boy did it, Miss Denby?"

"My sources don't seem to. Do you?"

"No. I think the lad was just a convenient patsy. For me there is only one person who could have taken the mask, and perhaps killed the watchman who was about to raise the alarm. And that person was..."

"Freddie Waltaub."

"Exactly!" said Jensford and popped the pipe back in his mouth. "Although he claimed in court he had an alibi – that he wasn't there. Looks like the judge believed him, but I never did."

"Did you know that Freddie Waltaub died in Cairo last year? Around the same time James Maddox said he found the mask in the shop in Cairo?"

Jensford's eyes twinkled. "I did, yes. Pass me that file, Miss Denby. The blue one, next to the typewriter. That's the one, thank you." He opened the file and pulled out a telegram. "This is from one of my sources on *The Cairo Post*. He sent it to me last year, telling me Waltaub had committed suicide. Thought I might be interested. Then later he sent me his article which fleshed out the story a bit." Jensford flicked through the file and pulled out a news clipping, then handed it to Poppy. She skimmed it. It confirmed the story Herr Stein had told her about Waltaub's apparent suicide after he had received news of his wife leaving him. However, there was something Stein had not told her: Freddie Waltaub had died in his hotel room only an hour after having dinner with a group of archaeologists in the downstairs restaurant. Those archaeologists named were: Jonathan Davies and Jennifer Philpott from New York, Heinrich Stein and Rudolf Weiner from Berlin, and Howard Carter and Giles Mortimer from London. Also present at the dinner were representatives for the Egyptian Antiquities Department, Faizal Osman and Kamela El Farouk.

"Good heavens! That's the exact crowd that was at Sir James Maddox's house the night he died."

Jensford leaned back in his armchair and grinned. "So, Miss Denby, do you think that's worth a byline?"

Poppy wanted to jump up and give the old man a cuddle. But she managed to control herself – just. "Oh yes, Mr Jensford, it most definitely does."

By the time Poppy left Walter Jensford and then convinced the matron to let her use the telephone to call Ike Garfield at the *Globe*, it was nearly half-past seven. They could just about manage to get to the British Museum in time for eight o'clock – assuming no other near-kidnappings or other mishaps occurred along the way.

Ike told her that Rollo had called from Scotland Yard. He said he would meet her at the museum.

"Did he say anything about Daniel?"

"Only that he was still working on getting him out. One thing he did say though was that Lady Ursula and Grimes the butler had been brought in for questioning when he was there. She apparently was spitting nails, saying she had no intention of missing the auction."

"Have they arrested her?"

"Rollo didn't think so. Not yet, anyway. But they were questioning her and the butler in relation to the murder of her husband."

"Golly! They think Ursula and Grimes did it?"

"I think they're very near the top of the list. Motive: money. Rollo said Yasmin told him there was a life insurance policy in Sir James' name. Kill him off, pay off the Winterton mortgage, live happily ever after. Means and opportunity: well, plenty – access to pills and so forth."

Despite what Poppy had just heard about the same archaeologists being present at both murders, she had to admit that Ursula still seemed to be the prime suspect. Perhaps Ursula was working with one – or a number – of the archaeologists. What was it she'd said to Rollo earlier – that the Germans and Egyptians both had good motives for stopping the auction? However, she had no other evidence on any of them… yet. But with Ursula it was beginning to stack up…

"*And* Lady Ursula had been reading up on poisoning," Poppy went on to tell Ike, briefly relaying what Fox had told her about Lady Ursula reading about poisoning methods in Sherlock Holmes stories – and what she'd done to Lady Jean Conan Doyle. Time was running short, so she said she'd fill him in on the rest of it later. However, there was one thing that absolutely *must* get into the paper by tonight's deadline for tomorrow's edition. Could Ike type it up? She gave him a summary of her conversation with Jensford, the headline being: the same archaeologists who were present at the death of James Maddox were also present when Freddie Waltaub died.

"Obviously phrase it a bit better than that, but that's the gist of it. Oh, and I promised him a shared byline. I'm sure Rollo won't mind. If it goes to press tonight we will scoop all the papers in London. *And* we won't be accused of withholding evidence from the police, as I shall tell DCI Martin as soon as I see him at the museum. I'm assuming he *will* be at the museum. But if not, I'll stop by Scotland Yard afterwards."

So, with Ike on the job at the office and Rollo on the job at Scotland Yard, all that was left for Poppy to do was to get to the British Museum in time for the auction. *Thank heavens for Fox Flinton. I would never have made it without him.*

As it turned out, Fox Flinton's motorcar was a crank-starter: an ageing, once-fashionable model, much like himself. It was an apple-red 1914 Star Torpedo Tourer with a retractable canvas roof. But it was still in good working order and handled the snowy streets between Shepherd's Bush and Bloomsbury far better than the *Globe*'s old Model T.

They travelled the most direct route, which took them through Kensington, along Bayswater Road, and past Kensington Palace and Hyde Park. Then they passed through Marble Arch and into Oxford Street, finally turning left into Bloomsbury Place and right into Great Russell Street. After seven o'clock on a snowy Monday evening the streets were fairly quiet.

She used the half-hour journey to question Fox further about his cousin. She decided not to tell him Ursula had been taken into Scotland Yard; no doubt he'd find that out for himself. He had told Poppy that he would turn himself into the police after the auction, as long as she accompanied him. She said that she would. He told her that he didn't think he *had* actually committed a crime and once he and Poppy had explained everything, no charges would be laid. Poppy doubted that. For his role in encouraging the boy to load the shotgun with more dangerous ammunition, she suspected a charge of criminal negligence might be in order. And as for the "stalking", perhaps some kind of criminal harassment. But that would only be if she laid a formal complaint. She probably wouldn't do so. As for the forgery of the Renoir, he had said that that had not been his intention, and he wouldn't have gone along with it in the end. But it had been his girlfriend's and his cousin's – and that made him an accessory, didn't it? The same with the poisoning of Lady Jean. Yes, he said he thought Ursula was only going to use prune juice, but he *did* find out that arsenic had been used and he hadn't reported it. Poppy cast a sideways glance at her chauffeur. *Sorry Fox, but I think there very well* might *be some charges*. But she didn't say it out loud. She needed to get to the museum and she didn't want to spook him.

It was five past eight when Fox parked the Torpedo Tourer on Great Russell Street. There was a line of vehicles, but from what Poppy could tell, none of them were police cars – yet. The lights in the museum were on, but the main front gate was shut. However, a security guard emerged from his little hut and directed them to a side gate.

As a fresh fall of snow billowed down they crossed the courtyard, hurried up the stairs into the portico, and were ushered through the main doors by a museum employee. In the foyer to the grand hall they stomped off the snow and deposited their coats and hats – Fox had swapped the fedora for his trademark boater – at the cloakroom. They were then directed to the Egyptian Gallery.

As they entered they were greeted by music from a live band and the hubbub of conversation. Marjorie Reynolds was the first to spot them. "Poppy! Fox! How – er – lovely to see you together." She raised an eyebrow at Poppy. Poppy gave a wry smile.

# CHAPTER 30

"Golly, Ursula's done a good job pulling this all together in such a short space of time," said Fox as he whipped two glasses of champagne off a passing tray and gave one to Poppy.

"She rang me earlier," said Marjorie, "and asked if I could twist Oscar's arm to do some last-minute catering. And look what he's managed to throw together!" She beamed.

Poppy spotted Oscar Reynolds behind a makeshift bar sandwiched between the statues of two pharaohs. She waved to him; the jazz club owner waved back.

"I think I'll head over to see him," said Poppy, and zipped away before Fox had a chance to follow her. She needed to shake him off. She had a lot of work to do tonight and she did not need the cousin of one of the main suspects tagging along with her. Speaking of which, where was Ursula? She scanned the gallery.

Delilah was chatting to Kamela El Farouk to the left of the four-piece band. As it was only two days after the death of Sir James, the tuxedoed musicians were playing a suitably subdued repertoire. However, Delilah had still managed to dress to the nines and Kamela was wearing an evening gown too. Poppy felt very dowdy in her grey skirt and white blouse, which she'd worn all day as she trudged around London. *Hmmm, Kamela. She was one of the archaeologists present at both murders...* Poppy needed to give that some more thought. She would try to speak to the Egyptian woman about it as soon as she had a chance, but not in front of Delilah. Poppy was still a little cross with her friend for gossiping about her to Fox Flinton.

Next to the glass-fronted cabinet containing the hieroglyphic parchments known as the Book of the Dead, Howard Carter and Dr Giles Mortimer were in conversation with Albert Carnaby. On the other side of the room, near a collection of mummies in colourful coffins, were Jonathan Davies, Jennifer Philpott, and Herr Stein. So, all of the archaeologists who, according to Walter Jensford, had been in the same hotel as the German fellow, Freddie Waltaub, were here tonight. All except Herr Stein's assistant, Weiner, and Faizal Osman ... She still thought the Germans and the Egyptians were the most likely to be involved in it, and now two of them were missing from the auction. Why? Were they trying to make a getaway?

*Ah, no, there's Faizal getting something to eat.* As she spotted the Egyptian man at the buffet, her tummy grumbled. It had been a long time since she'd last eaten. She headed over to join him. He was wearing a tuxedo.

"Good evening, Miss Denby. Not a bad show, what?"

"Not at all. But I'm feeling a tad underdressed."

Faizal smiled. "Oh, don't worry about that. I don't think everyone will have had time to change." He nodded towards the entrance as his sister, Yasmin, Lady Ursula Maddox, Lionel Saunders, and Rollo arrived. All three of them were wearing day clothes. "I believe some people spent the afternoon at the police station."

Poppy craned her neck to see beyond the group, hoping to see Daniel. He wasn't there. She bit her lip and brought her emotions under control. She pasted a smile on her face and turned back to her companion.

"Actually, Dr Osman, I'm glad I've caught you. There's something I've been meaning to ask you."

"Please, call me Faizal."

"Of course, Faizal. In my background research about the mask I've come across the name of a German man called Freddie Waltaub. Have you heard of him?"

"From the Berlin Museum? Yes. He was Professor Borchardt's assistant back in 1914 when the mask was first found."

"I believe so, yes. I also heard that he died last year in Cairo, sometime in the summer. Did you know about that?"

Faizal offered Poppy a plate of sandwiches. She took one while waiting for his answer.

"I did, yes. Very tragic. He killed himself in his room at the Grand Continental."

"Yes, I heard that. And I also heard that he had just had dinner with you and some archaeologists beforehand."

Faizal lowered his voice. "Where did you hear that?"

"Oh, it was in a news clipping from *The Cairo Post*," she said truthfully.

"My, my, you have done your research. Yes, I was at the dinner. And I probably don't have to tell you that a number of people here tonight were also there."

"I believe so, yes. I was just wondering why it never came up in conversation at Winterton. In fact, when I asked Kamela she said she couldn't remember Borchardt's assistant's name."

Faizal picked up a celery stick and dipped it into some cream cheese. "No, I doubt she would. She had just joined the department and didn't really know who was who. And he wasn't at the dinner long. In fact, to say he had dinner with us was not technically correct. He made a brief, drunken appearance, then at the suggestion of Herr Stein, withdrew to his room. Stein accompanied him and returned. He was very apologetic, particularly to Miss El Farouk, and told us that Freddie had received some upsetting news earlier that day and was not quite himself. And that was the last of it. And as for why it never came up at Winterton..." he shrugged "... why would it?"

Poppy finished chewing then brushed the crumbs away from her lips. "A lot of other things came up – but not that. I find that strange."

"Do you? Why? Lots of things weren't mentioned, including a host of other meetings and associations between the museums. Not to mention conferences..."

"So Herr Stein was at this particular meeting? The one in Cairo?"

"Yes."

"Strange that he didn't mention to me that he was there. In fact, I had the impression that Freddie was in Egypt on his own."

"Well laying aside, for a moment, the issue of 'why should he have told you' what gave you that impression? Did Stein say he was back in Berlin?"

Poppy thought about it for a moment, recalling her conversation with the German man. "No, actually he didn't. Sorry, my mistake, it's been a busy day. He said Freddie was in Cairo at a meeting with the Egyptian Antiquities Service. He didn't say he was there too. But he didn't say he wasn't, either."

"Well, he was. Representatives from the Met, Berlin, and British museums were all there. There were reps from Paris as well, but none of them were at that dinner. We were having a series of meetings to thrash out new guidelines for excavation licences. It had nothing to do with the Nefertiti mask."

"Nothing?"

"No. It didn't even come up. The first I heard that the mask had resurfaced was when Maddox brought it into the British Museum to be valued a few months ago. Dr Mortimer contacted me and asked if I knew about it. I didn't. But that's when we put in our first court appeal to have the mask returned to us. As you know, the judgment went against us and then this whole auction malarkey was set up."

"Did you know that Maddox contacted Freddie when he was there to tell him he had something the Berlin Museum might be interested in? And that Freddie believed it was the mask?"

Faizal stopped, celery stick poised. "I did not, no. Who told you that?"

"Herr Stein."

"Well, well. I wonder why he kept quiet about it? Stein, that is."

Poppy glanced over at the man in question, who was now at the bar. "I have no idea. Do you? What might his motivation have been?"

Faizal took a bite of his celery stick as he pondered his answer. Eventually, he said: "I gather you're aware that the Germans think that Maddox stole the mask from the dig, and as such they did not have a chance at the time to claim it as part of their fifty per cent of proceeds. You may recall, according to their licence, they were able to keep half the artefacts they found, and the other half was to remain in Egypt. How the cache was split was supposed to be negotiated between the two parties. That's what happened with the Nefertiti bust they already have, although we dispute how legitimately the proceeds of the 1912 dig were declared. Anyway, that's a different story. But as far as the 1914 mask goes, they did not even have a chance to negotiate that with us, as it did not appear in the original manifest. Freddie Waltaub claimed that James Maddox stole it. Maddox, as you know, denied it, and said that he found it in a shop in Cairo. He says that local thieves took it – which to his credit sometimes happened. He claimed he went to the dig to check that everything was in order, while Professor Borchardt was away. He saw that there were looters inside. He rushed off to call the police. When he and the policeman returned, they found the body of the guard in a sarcophagus and the young thieves nearby. He reckons their accomplices got away with the mask before he and the police officer arrived. And that they'd killed the guard before he got there."

"Why didn't the youngsters get away at the same time then?"

"I have no idea."

"You would have thought that would have cast doubt on their guilt in the subsequent trial."

"Oh it did," said Faizal. "The boy was not convicted of murder, just as an accessory. And the girl just got a few months for looting. I don't think anyone thought either of them was involved to a great degree – perhaps they were just paid to be look-outs, or were simply local guides."

"Did the youngsters ever say who their so-called accomplices were?"

Faizal shook his head. "No, they denied any involvement whatsoever. However, they were from a family of known antiquity thieves. That's what convicted them. They were guilty by association and for being in the wrong place at the wrong time."

"Did Maddox – or anyone – ever suggest that Freddie Waltaub might have been the thief? And that he had been the one who killed the guard?"

"No, never. You see Waltaub wasn't there that night, and he had a witness to prove it."

"A credible witness?"

"He was supposedly drinking with another archaeologist in Al Minya – that's about five miles away, across the river from El-Amarna – where the dig was. The archaeologist – a French fellow, if my memory serves me correctly – said he was there. The court didn't doubt it."

"And you?"

"I have had no reason not to. Not until now… Is that the theory you're working on, Poppy?"

Poppy shrugged. "Someone has suggested it as a possibility."

"Someone?"

Poppy was not about to give away her source. "Yes, someone. So, you were saying, what Herr Stein's motivation might have been for not mentioning the mask last year…"

Faizal looked at her curiously and took a sip of mineral water. "Yes, I was. The bottom line is that the Germans think they missed the chance to get the mask back in 1914, so it wouldn't surprise me if they were in secret discussions with Maddox to arrange a private sale – at a discount, of course." He gestured to the assembled guests. "But that obviously failed, and hence the auction. Herr Stein has made no secret of the fact that he is not happy to have to bid against other museums. But he's a pragmatist – as most Germans are – and has bitten the bullet, so to speak."

Poppy absorbed this for a moment, watching as Rollo worked the room. He caught her eye and raised his finger. *He wants to speak to me.* She nodded her acknowledgment. She'd just finish with Faizal first…

"Was James Maddox at the dinner last year?"

"He wasn't invited, no."

"But did you know he was in Cairo at the time?"

"I did, yes. I think everyone at the table knew."

"Including Herr Stein?"

Faizal smirked. "Especially Herr Stein."

Poppy nodded. Yes, she was beginning to realize that the German archaeologist was a very shrewd man. "You say he left the table with Freddie?"

"Yes, Freddie was drunk. Stein helped him to his room."

"How long was he gone?"

Faizal shrugged. "About fifteen minutes."

"Long enough to meet with James Maddox?"

Faizal took another sip of mineral water. "Briefly, yes."

"Interesting," said Poppy, then selected a celery stick from the platter and chomped thoughtfully.

Just then they were joined by Rollo. "Evening Faizal. Mind if I borrow Miz Denby for a while?"

Faizal raised his glass to his sister's beau. "Of course not, Rollo. I need to catch up with Yasmin anyway, to see if she's made any progress with the court order." Faizal made his way towards his sister and ushered Kamela El Farouk to join them. Ursula Maddox was in conversation with Albert Carnaby, who produced the Nefertiti mask from a suitcase. Was the auction going to begin?

"So Poppy, fill me in. What have you found out? Oh, and pass me that platter please."

Poppy passed Rollo a plate of sausage rolls. He took four and placed them on a napkin on the side of the table.

"Where's Daniel? Couldn't you get him out?"

"I could, yes. Martin eventually dropped the charges. He was just flexing his muscles. But he used the time to interview us all again about the Winterton weekend. He was particularly interested in –"

"So where is he?"

"Who?"

"Daniel. Where's Daniel?"

"Oh, he asked if he could go home. He needed to see the children. He asked me to tell you he'd see you tomorrow. He said he hoped you'd understand." Rollo popped a sausage roll into his mouth.

Poppy felt tears sting the back of her eyes. Yes, she understood. Daniel needed to put his children first – and he always would. She blinked a few times to get her emotions under control. "So you were saying, DCI Martin was going over the details of Winterton again..."

"Yes, in fine detail. Who was where when. Who wasn't at each event, etcetera. And then, at the end of it, he arrested Grimes for murder."

Poppy, who was taking a sip of champagne, spluttered it down the front of her blouse. Rollo grinned and passed her a napkin.

"Yes, I thought you'd enjoy that little titbit."

"On what grounds? Did you find out?"

"I did. Apparently they searched the house and found some digitalis powder in Grimes' room. The same grade of digitalis that killed Sir James."

"Good Lord!"

"Quite," said Rollo and popped another sausage roll into his mouth.

"And what about Ursula? Ike told me about the insurance policy. *And* Fox told me she'd been researching poisons. Surely that's enough to put her under suspicion."

"Yes, it is. But DCI Martin didn't arrest her. Either she's got some kind of alibi that I'm not aware of – and she's really innocent – or Martin simply hasn't managed to get all his ducks in a row yet. If Grimes did do it on her behalf, he'll be squealing any time now."

The lady in question called the room to order. *Is she about to announce that the butler did it?* Poppy wondered. No, as it turned out, she wasn't. She just wanted to apologize to everyone for the delay. They were waiting for Herr Weiner, Herr Stein's assistant, to arrive. He had been inadvertently delayed. It wasn't clear why, possibly the snow… At Herr Stein's request they would give him another ten minutes. If he hadn't arrived then, they would start without him. "Apologies, everyone, the auction will soon begin. Please, enjoy the refreshments."

The band struck up again and Rollo piled up his napkin with some more food. "Righto, fill me in with what else you've learned, Poppy."

Rollo was down to his last sausage roll by the time she was finished. "Good job, Miz Denby! I'd say there are a raft of other suspects – on top of Ursula – we could hand to the police."

"I think we should," said Poppy. "What if Grimes and/or Ursula were not acting alone? Or perhaps he, she or both of them are being framed. It would have been easy enough to plant the digitalis on him."

Rollo swallowed what he was chewing. "Yes, that's what I think too. They could all be in cahoots. As I was saying before, DCI Martin was asking us to go over *everyone's* coming and goings. And after what you've just told me now, it's quite possible that one of the crowd that was in Cairo last summer might have something to do with it. It's just too much of a coincidence, otherwise. Perhaps Ursula has been working with one of them all along, and all of the shenanigans with the gullible Fox Flinton have merely been a smokescreen. Besides, if Grimes wanted to off his boss, he had plenty of opportunity to do so quietly. Why do it at such a high-profile event with the press in attendance? It would be like he was asking to be caught. And he doesn't strike me as a stupid man."

"I agree," said Poppy.

She scanned the room again, wondering who it could be. Neither of the Americans seemed likely candidates – what motive could they possibly have? Nor Howard Carter and Giles Mortimer. So, she was once again back to the Germans and the Egyptians. Both groups believed James Maddox had ripped them off. Was that enough of a motive for murder, or was there another reason? And what about Freddie Waltaub's death in Cairo? If it wasn't suicide, then had one of the archaeologists killed him? If so, which one? She didn't know enough about the dinner to figure it out – other than that Freddie had arrived briefly and then left, accompanied by Herr Stein. Could Herr Stein have killed him and then returned to the dinner party? Poppy went over in her mind what Jensford and Faizal told her about the dinner – it wasn't much. But she remembered that Freddie had been killed "an hour after the dinner". *After* the dinner. So, Herr Stein could not have popped him off quickly during the meal. She wished she knew what happened *after* the meal, where everyone had gone. She would try to ask Faizal for some more information if she could. Or any of the others who were there, if she had the chance.

However, what she did know more about was the weekend at Winterton Hall. As Rollo headed over to chat to Lady Ursula, Poppy went over the comings and goings of the various guests in her mind. Yes, DCI Martin had been particularly interested in that. If she recalled correctly, there were two people who, on more than one occasion, were *not* with the group: Harry Gibson and Kamela El Farouk. Would that have given either of them an opportunity to switch Sir James' medication and then plant the evidence on Grimes? Come to think of it, where was Harry Gibson now? If he'd been released with Daniel, surely he would have come here... He didn't have a family, as far as she was aware... But she no longer believed it mattered. Now that Fox Flinton had confessed to being the stalker, the unpleasant *Courier* photographer was no longer on her suspect list. So that, Poppy realized, with dawning clarity, only left Kamela El Farouk.

Just then, Herr Stein's assistant, Weiner, arrived, and with him was DCI Martin and two uniformed policemen. Were they about to arrest Lady Ursula? Or stop the auction? That must have been what Lady Ursula thought too, as she stormed across the room, demanding to know what the trouble was now.

DCI Martin crossed his arms across his barrel chest and declared: "Oh, you'll find out soon enough. But do carry on, Lady Ursula, I think it's about time this mask finally went under the hammer." He scanned the room, like an eagle selecting his prey. "Righto, Mr Carnaby, over to you."

Carnaby nodded and scurried to the lectern that had been set up. Beside it was an object draped in a velvet cloth. He whipped back the cloth to reveal the mask. Every eye in the room turned to appraise the dazzling artefact. But as they did, something caught Poppy's eye. To her right, behind a six-foot stele, was a doorway leading to the next gallery – and through it, slipping away, was Kamela El Farouk.

# CHAPTER 31

## CAIRO, 27 JUNE 1920

Kamela El Farouk stepped out of the taxi outside the Grand Continental Hotel and stood for a moment to take in its colonial splendour. The whitewashed four-storey building with its iconic wrought-iron arch over the entrance dominated Cairo's Opera Square. And although the three flags on its roof were Egyptian, Kamela knew that the vast majority of the 300 rooms would be occupied by Europeans. Her new boss, Dr Faizal Osman, escorted her past the line of bowing porters – uniformly attired in white robes and red fezzes – and up the steps of the grandiose entrance.

Dr Osman held a degree in Classical Civilization and the History of Art from Oxford University. Of mixed race, his father was a British Major General, and his mother the daughter of one of Egypt's wealthiest men. She'd been told that he had changed his name from Reece-Lansdale to Osman – his maternal grandfather's surname – when he took up the job of Director of Antiquities at the Cairo Museum, just before the war. He was a good man who shared her view that Egyptian art belonged to the people of Egypt. However, he was also a pragmatist who realized that the past could not be undone, and a diplomat who knew how to engage with the Europeans and their various museums.

Which was the reason they were here today. In light of Britain's intention to withdraw from its administration of Egypt, Dr Osman was trying to renegotiate the decades-old system of licences that allowed European archaeologists to work in Egypt. Their expertise – and money – was still needed by the Egyptians, but Dr Osman wanted to ensure that the power balance shifted more favourably towards the locals. If anyone could do it, it would be him.

Kamela was proud to work for such a man – and proud to get such a good job so soon after graduating from the Sorbonne in Paris. Despite being top of her class in Archaeology and Near Eastern Studies, she had doubted that she would get the nod ahead of the other, all-male, candidates for the job of Assistant to the Director of the Department of Antiquities. But it seemed that Dr Osman did not hold her gender against her. He told her his sister was a lawyer in England and he believed in equal rights for women. Although younger, he reminded her in some ways of her late father. He too had taken a chance on her – a mere girl – by giving her the same educational opportunities as her male siblings, although she, and she alone, had gone to university – due to the support of an anonymous benefactor. Sadly, her father had died without divulging the identity – or motivation – of the person who had paid for her to study in Paris.

Now here she was, back in her home country, ready to start a new chapter in her life. Inside the hotel, she and Dr Osman were ushered into the dining room, where obsequious waiters fawned over colonial diners. Here and there were members of Egypt's upper classes, so she did not feel completely out of place – although she was the only woman wearing a hijab. Kamela was not devoutly religious, but she wore the scarf out of respect for her mother and because it set her apart from Europeans. For Kamela it was important that – despite her European education

– people knew she had not been assimilated into the foreign culture. For her it was as much a sign of nationalism as it was of faith.

At the table she was introduced to people who, up until now, had been merely names in textbooks. They were among the elite of the world of archaeology and Egyptology: Howard Carter, Giles Mortimer, Jonathan Davies, Jennifer Philpott, Heinrich Stein, and Rudolf Weiner. They were a warm, intelligent group of people with a shared interest in preserving Egyptian culture – although they differed, at times, as to how that was to be achieved.

They were halfway through the soup course when there was a commotion at the entrance to the restaurant. A large, unkempt European man forced his way past the maître d', dodged a couple of waiters, and approached their table. He was unsteady on his feet and red in face. He demanded another place be set for him – even though there was no room – and, in a booming voice, wanted to know why he hadn't been invited. Heinrich Stein stood up and addressed him in German. Kamela, whose father had worked with Germans, knew enough of the language to follow the gist of it. His name was Freddie. He hadn't been snubbed; Herr Stein had assumed he wouldn't be coming due to the upsetting news he'd received earlier today.

"Freddie" reached for a bottle of wine on the table. Herr Stein intervened and took the bottle from him, saying in English, for the benefit of everyone else at the table and in the restaurant: "I think you've had enough, old man. Let me take you to your room. What's your number?"

"Two one seven," he slurred as Weiner stood to offer his support. Stein and Weiner each took an arm and helped him out, to the visible relief of the maître d', who apologized profusely – in French – to the diners. A few moments later Weiner returned and said that Herr Stein was able to handle it on his own.

"Poor old Waltaub," observed Howard Carter.

"Waltaub?" asked Kamela, her throat suddenly dry.

"Yes, Freddie Waltaub. He was once a great archaeologist. But after that business in El-Amarna, he's never been the same."

Kamela took a sip of water, her hand quivering. "What business is that?"

"Back in 1914," Dr Osman explained. "I was new on the job. Ludwig Borchardt was still busy on the Amarna dig – Thutmose's workshop. Then a new chamber was found. One weekend, when Borchardt was away in Cairo, some looters broke in. They were disturbed by a guard. They killed him. Freddie Waltaub was supposed to be in charge, but he was off drinking somewhere. He never forgave himself. He's never been the same since."

Kamela steadied her hand on the stem of her glass. "Did they catch the killer?"

"No," said Dr Osman, "but two local youngsters were convicted of looting. They never divulged who their accomplices were."

Kamela cleared her throat. "Did you attend the trial?" she asked.

"I didn't. But Borchardt filled me in on it. I also read the official transcripts."

"Do you recall the names of the young people who were convicted?"

"I don't, no. Have you finished with your soup?" A waiter was hovering. Kamela said she was, and her plate was taken away.

After dinner, the archaeologists retired to the bar. Kamela waited until everyone had drinks and lit cigarettes and then announced that she needed to powder her nose. She hoped that the only other woman in the group – Jennifer Philpott – would not offer to join her. But Miss Philpott was comfortably nursing a tumbler of whiskey and in animated discussion with Howard Carter about the possible whereabouts of King Tutankhamun's tomb. Kamela slipped quietly away.

Room 217 was on the second floor. The corridor was deserted as she stepped out of the elevator and knocked on the door. There was no answer. She tried the handle – it was unlocked. She entered the dimly lit room and closed the door behind her. "Herr Waltaub!" she called out.

"Go away. I didn't call for room service." The voice was thick with tears. She turned towards it and saw Freddie sitting in a wicker chair near the window. On the table beside him was a bottle of whisky, and in his hand a revolver. She froze in her tracks.

"I'm sorry. I didn't mean to disturb you."

"You're Osman's new girl, aren't you?"

Kamela swallowed hard. "I am, yes. I was just coming to see if you were all right. And to apologize for not inviting you to the dinner. It was obviously just an oversight."

Freddie sniffed, loudly. He had been crying. "No it wasn't. No one wants me any more. Not Stein, not Osman, not – not – my wife."

"I'm sure that's not true."

He sniffed again and gestured with the barrel of the gun to something on the table. "Look for yourself."

She approached, gingerly, not certain of his intent, and saw what he was pointing at. It was a telegram, in German, from someone called Helga telling him not to bother coming home because she and the children were leaving.

"I'm sorry," she said. The wreck of a man in front of her was not the man she remembered from her trial – cocksure and confident, announcing that he couldn't possibly have killed the native because he was drinking with an old friend. The old friend – a French archaeologist – duly backed up his account. At the time Kamela had no reason to disbelieve him. She had no idea who had killed Mohammed and his dog, only that neither she nor her brother had done it. In the end, the judge believed her. But she was still given three months in jail as an object lesson for other looters. Her brother was given three years. Despite Borchardt himself asking for clemency, the judge declared that a message needed to be sent, and that as long as the boy did not divulge the names of his collaborators, a murderer was getting away scot free. However, if the lad gave their names, his sentence would be reduced to the same as his sister. Sadly, he had no names to give. Two years later, a month before he was due to be released on good behaviour, there was a prison riot. Azar Abbas was killed. He was only nineteen. It was at his funeral that her father told her – Kamela Abbas – that an anonymous benefactor had offered to pay for her to study in Paris. But as she had a criminal conviction against her, it was decided that she would apply in her mother's name: El Farouk.

Kamela sat down in the chair opposite Freddie. She had dreamt of this moment for two years, ever since she had overheard a conversation in the post-graduate common room at the Sorbonne. One of her archaeology professors, a man named Chirac, was discussing a paper with a fellow academic.

"Waltaub's not up to the job any more," he'd said. "This is utter twaddle. No wonder Borchardt let him go. Stein should do the same."

"You knew him, didn't you?" said his companion.

"I did, yes. I vouched for him during that El-Amarna scandal."

"That's right… you gave him an alibi, didn't you?"

"I did, yes. But to be honest, I wasn't sure what time he left. I'd had a lot to drink and fell asleep. When I woke, he was gone. He had been with me, yes, but he could have left before he said he did."

"Good grief man, why did you back him up then?"

"I had no reason to doubt him. I still don't, really."

"But he could have been lying. He could have gone back to the dig and killed that native. And stole the Nefertiti mask."

"It's possible, yes. But not likely, surely. Waltaub's a good fellow. Sad how he's gone to seed..."

And that was it. Kamela made an appointment to see the professor. She questioned him about his conversation. When he asked why she wanted to know, she said she had known the family of the young people who were jailed. She asked him why he didn't go to the police now and tell the truth – that an innocent boy had gone to jail.

"Is he still in jail?" the professor asked.

"No, he's dead."

The professor shrugged and said, "Well it's too late then." And brought their conversation to an end.

Kamela had thought of going to the police herself when she got back to Egypt, but realized that without the French professor's cooperation she would get nowhere. She sent him a telegram asking him if he would testify to what he'd told her. She received a telegram in reply saying: "No".

And now, here she was, in front of the man who might have killed the watchman and was ultimately responsible for the death of her brother. She had been over the events of that night so many times. There were only two possible suspects: James Maddox and Freddie Waltaub. Maddox's defence was that he would not have called the police if he had been involved – a tenuous argument, but one the judge seemed to accept. But after what she'd learned from the French professor, she leaned towards the theory that it was Waltaub who had done it and Maddox who helped cover it up.

"Herr Waltaub, do you remember that night back in 1914 when the watchman at Thutmose's workshop was killed?"

Freddie, still holding the gun with one hand, poured himself another drink. He offered one to Kamela. She declined.

"I thought you would want to ask me why I've got this gun. You don't seem frightened, Miss El Farouk. Why's that?"

"I don't think you intend to harm me, do you?"

"N – no I don't. I – I don't want to harm anyone – I never wanted to. It was an a – accident." He started crying again.

"The watchman? You killed the watchman?"

"He misunderstood what was going on. He thought I was stealing artefacts. I wasn't. I was just packaging them up for shipment."

"Was Maddox there with you?"

"Not then, no. But he came later. And stole the mask. When they took those children away. He came back and took the mask. It was there when the watchman came in and got the wrong end of the stick. I saw it there myself. Maddox swears blind he didn't steal it, but he did."

"What about the watchman? What happened?"

"It was an accident; I didn't mean to." He took a swig of whisky.

"But you did, didn't you? You left Chirac's earlier than you said you did. And went to the dig when you thought no one was there. Then you killed Mohammed and his dog when they found you."

"I told you. I didn't mean to." He took another gulp from his glass then stared at her, bleary eyed. "H – how did you know about Chirac?"

"I know everything Freddie, everything." She said the last with such venom it surprised her. Years of hurt, anger, and injustice welled up inside her. She had a fleeting thought of going to the police, but then recalled the way she and her brother had been treated. No, the police were not the answer. There was no justice, only what she herself would make.

"You were about to shoot yourself, weren't you? When I came in? That's why you have the gun."

Freddie was now sobbing. "I was, yes, but now God has sent an angel to save me."

"Yes," said Kamela, "I am an angel. The Angel of Death." She wrapped her hands around his and held the gun to his temple."

"Do it," she whispered. "Do it now."

And he did.

# CHAPTER 32

As opening bids on the death mask of Nefertiti were called out, Poppy followed Kamela into the next gallery. The Egyptian woman had reached a dead end at the far end of the room, near a display of ancient weaponry. There was no thoroughfare through this gallery and the only way out was back the way she'd come.

Albert Carnaby's voice droned from the other room. *"That's two thousand pounds, ladies and gentlemen. Can I see three?"*

"The auction's started, Kamela; you'll miss it."

*"Three thousand, thank you. Three thousand pounds with Dr Davies."*

Kamela spun around, a look on her face that reminded Poppy of a hunted animal. "Oh, Poppy. I was looking for the lavatory. Couldn't hold it in any longer."

Poppy gestured over her shoulder. The nearest ones are back through there, near the museum entrance. I know, it's a bit of a maze in here. Dr Mortimer gave me the tour last week."

Kamela smiled tightly.

*"Is that four thousand? Yes? Four thousand pounds with Herr Stein."*

"Will Faizal be putting in a bid?"

Kamela was edging around the room, holding something behind her back. "On something that already belongs to us? No." Her voice was hard. This was not the charming young woman Poppy had spent time with over the weekend.

Poppy's mind was spinning. What should she do? Kamela was trapped in here and the only way out was past her. Poppy had no doubt that Kamela was trying to get out. And the reason was not the lavatory.

*"Five thousand pounds! Thank you, Dr Mortimer. The British Museum must be feeling flush."*

Kamela continued to edge towards the entrance. Poppy wondered how long it would take for someone to notice they were gone. Had anyone else seen them slip out? And if so, would they too assume it was something as benign as a trip to the lavatory? Kamela would have to stay here or go back in. She would never make it through the next gallery and past the police. There was no way to escape.

*"Six thousand pounds? Is that six thousand, Herr Stein? Ja!"*

Kamela edged closer. There was a cold glint in her eyes. "Dr Osman was telling me you've been asking questions about last year in Cairo."

*"Any advances on six thousand pounds? Come now, ladies and gentlemen, an artefact like this will have people queuing around the block to see it. And let's not forget Sir James. He deserves more than that, surely?"*

Kamela's lip curled.

Poppy bit her own. "Did he Kamela? Did Sir James deserve more than that?"

Kamela let out a growl. All pretence gone. "You'll find he got exactly what he deserved, Poppy."

"Unlike your brother."

Kamela stopped edging and turned fully towards Poppy.

"Exactly." She whipped her hand from behind her back to reveal an ornate ceremonial dagger and pointed it towards Poppy's throat. Poppy gasped. "What are you doing?"

"You've got it all worked out, haven't you?"

Poppy swallowed, hard. "Most of it, yes. You switched the digitalis in Sir James' medication, then planted it in the butler's room. I'm not sure how you killed Waltaub, but I'm sure you did."

*"Ten thousand pounds! That's more like it, thank you Dr Davies. New York is calling!"*

Poppy sensed some movement behind her. But she dared not look. Had Kamela seen it?

No, her dark eyes were glued on Poppy. "I did not kill either of them – technically – just like they did not kill my brother – technically – with their own hands. Waltaub pulled the trigger himself – I just helped him do it. And Maddox took his own poison. Both of them would have died anyway. Waltaub was about to commit suicide when I found him. Maddox's heart was giving in. He wouldn't have lived much longer."

"That was not for you to decide." DCI Martin's gruff voice sent a wave of relief through Poppy. "Now, put that knife down and let Miss Denby go."

"DCI Martin. I was wondering how long it would take the police to figure out the truth. Seems you're a little better at doing it than those fools in Cairo."

"Those fools in Cairo are busy reopening the case, Miss El Farouk. I sent them a telegram this evening after Herr Weiner very kindly walked me through the comings and goings of everyone at the dinner last year. He thought it curious, you see, that Waltaub and Maddox both died when the same group of archaeologists was assembled. I hadn't been aware of it until he mentioned it. He's been most helpful."

*"Fourteen thousand pounds! And it's back to Berlin! Nothing from Cairo, Dr Osman? Surely your pharaoh queen deserves to be fought over. Dr Osman, Dr Osman, where are you going? Nothing from Cairo then. Do I hear fifteen from London?"*

"What the hell's going on here?" Rollo, closely followed by Faizal Osman, came up behind DCI Martin.

"Kamela!" Faizal lunged forward. Kamela pressed the point of the blade into Poppy's throat.

He stopped, his hands outstretched, placating. "Let her go Kamela, please. I shouldn't have let this go so far."

"What do you mean, Osman? You knew about this?" Martin pinned Faizal with his gaze.

"Not Maddox, no. I genuinely thought it was a heart attack. I was just as shocked as the rest of you to find out it wasn't. But I did suspect Kamela knew more than she was letting on about Waltaub. I saw you leave the bar, Kamela. And you took a long time coming back. The police said it was suicide, but I had my suspicions."

"Why didn't you say anything?" said Kamela. She looked at her boss as if she and he were the only two people in the room.

"Because I thought you'd been through enough. You'd already been to prison. Your brother had died."

Kamela's eyes opened wide. She eased the blade away from Poppy's throat very, very slightly. Poppy watched carefully, waiting for a moment to break away.

"You knew? You knew who I was?"

"Kamela Abbas, yes. I never went to the trial but I read the transcript months later. By then you were already out. I felt a miscarriage of justice had been done, but I couldn't prove it. Then when your brother died I offered your father money so you could go to Paris. Then gave you the job when you came home.

I wanted to make amends for what had happened. I wanted to give you another chance."

Tears welled in Kamela's eyes and spilled onto her cheeks. "Why didn't you say before?" She lowered the knife and dropped it to the ground. In an instant Martin had her pinned down.

"Don't hurt her, Inspector. Please, don't hurt her." Faizal's voice cracked.

Rollo ran to Poppy and put his arm around her waist. She was shaking. At that moment Lionel Saunders appeared in the doorway, his eyes wide, his mouth agape. "What the hell's going on here?"

"We've scooped you!" said Rollo, and Poppy just had to smile.

*"Twenty thousand pounds! Is that the final offer from New York? Dr Mortimer? Herr Stein? No? All right then, for twenty thousand pounds the death mask of Nefertiti is going... going... gone!"*

# CHAPTER 33

## SUNDAY 16 DECEMBER 1921

Poppy forced herself out of the armchair in front of the coal fire to answer the doorbell. She had had a quiet day after going to church that morning – sitting at the back on her own – and trying to keep up with the unfamiliar Church of England order of service. She had listened to a sermon about God sending his son to bring peace to all people, then prayed, quietly, for the people she knew were not at peace. Back home she'd spoken to her parents on the telephone and arranged to visit them for a week in the New Year. Christmas was always a busy time for them at the Morpeth Methodist Chapel, so even if she had tried to get there for the 25th she wouldn't have seen much of them. Better to go when the decorations were down and the children were all back at school. She would go into King's Cross at lunchtime tomorrow and book her ticket on the Flying Scotsman.

The doorbell rang again. "I'm coming!" she called, feeling the cold tiles of the hall through her stockings. She peered through the peephole Daniel had installed earlier in the week. Her stalker had turned out to be a prankster, he said, but she still needed to be careful. Then he tried, unsuccessfully, to encourage her to move in with Delilah while Aunt Dot and Grace were away, saying he would worry about her no end if he was not there to protect her...

After things at the museum were finally wrapped up, the police interviews conducted, and enough column inches written to fill a dozen newspapers, Daniel and Poppy managed to carve out some time together. She cooked him dinner; he installed the peephole. He told her that Maggie and her fiancé would be getting married on 20 January and then sailing to South Africa the week after – a three-week journey down the West Coast of Africa. He was going with them. He had asked Rollo for six months' unpaid leave. "I can't make a decision like this without seeing what it's like there first. I want to see where my children will be living. I want to see if it's safe. And I can't ask you to come with me until I know what I'll be taking you to."

Poppy managed to hold back the tears as she cleared away the dinner plates and found Aunt Dot's dessert bowls. She had made a sticky toffee pudding – one of her mother's recipes. She served them each a portion, then drenched it in piping hot custard.

"I understand, Daniel. I always knew you would put your children first. And that's as it should be." Poppy had come to this realization on Monday night at the museum when he had gone home instead of coming to see her. That night in bed, as she tossed and turned, working through all that had happened with Kamela and Faizal, she had allowed herself one brief fantasy in which Daniel rushed into her room, swept her into his arms, and told her that he could not live without her – not even for his children. But she knew it was a selfish dream. She knew too that she could not and would not drop everything to go with him. That was his selfish dream.

So, later in the week, after dinner, she told him she had decided to call things off. Who knew what the future might hold? Love might indeed conquer all. They might have their fairy tale ending, they might not; but for now they both knew they had to live in the real world. They had both cried then,

Daniel, holding her, as if he would never let her go. But he did. And then he went home to his children.

Through the peephole Poppy saw the smiling face of Delilah. "Open up Popsicle, it's freezing out here!"

Poppy unhitched the security chain – another of Daniel's additions – unlocked the door, and opened it to see not just Delilah but Rollo, Ike, his wife Doreen, Marjorie, her son Oscar, and Yasmin. Ike was carrying a Christmas tree and grinning from ear to ear. Oscar had a sack over one shoulder and Rollo was carrying a crate.

"Well, don't just leave us standing here, Miz Denby, or I'll be forced to give you my rendition of 'Joy to the World'. And I'd rather be inside eating mince pies and drinking mulled wine than torturing the neighbours." He nodded to the crate.

Delilah pushed forward, carrying a box of decorations. "We've come to decorate the house!"

Poppy laughed, warmed by her friends' kind gesture, and let them all in.

Two hours later, with all the pies eaten and the wine drunk, the house was transformed into a set from *The Nutcracker*. With Ike's help Poppy had dug around in the attic and found Aunt Dot's spectacular collection of Christmas paraphernalia to add to the decorations her friends had brought. With much laughter and singing, the three-storey townhouse was decked with lights and garlands to rival any display on Oxford Street. And finally, with Ike's support, Poppy stood on a chair and placed the star on the top of the tree as Delilah led them all in a chorus of "Silent Night":

*Silent Night, holy night,*
*All is calm, all is bright,*
*Round yon virgin, mother and child,*

*Holy infant so tender and mild,*
*Sleep in heavenly peace,*
*Sleep in heavenly peace.*

As the last notes settled with the coals in the fireplace Poppy noticed Rollo and Yasmin exchange a glance then hold hands.

"Ahem," he said, clearing his throat. "Me and Yazzie have got an announcement to make."

Delilah yelped in delight and clapped her hands.

"Hold your horses, Miz Marconi, we haven't said anything yet!" Everyone laughed, knowing what was about to come.

"We'd like to tell you that we've decided to tie the knot. And of course, you're all invited to the wedding."

Ike clapped Rollo so hard on the back that he nearly fell over. Marjorie, Oscar, Doreen, and Delilah added their congratulations, with Delilah demanding to see the ring. Yasmin duly obliged, thrusting out her hand to show an emerald in a nest of diamonds. As everyone gathered round, Poppy stepped back and took in the scene, smiling wistfully. *So, some people do get their fairy tale ending after all.*

# The World of Poppy Denby:
## A Historical Note

From the very start of the Poppy Denby Investigates books I had in mind to send Poppy to Egypt around the time of the discovery of King Tut's tomb. I had a marvellous vision of Poppy running through a pyramid, clutching her cloche hat, pursued by a villain with evil intent. So when I came to write Book 4 I felt the time had finally come to get Poppy on a boat across the Mediterranean. But things didn't work out that way.

The main problem was that Howard Carter and Lord Carnarvon only discovered the opening to King Tutankhamun's tomb in February 1922. The previous Poppy book, *The Death Beat*, ended in July 1921. I needed to leave some time between that and the start of the next book but I couldn't leave it too long, as Poppy and Daniel's relationship was hanging in limbo. Also, I didn't think the tight-fisted Rollo would be prepared to cough up on another international trip for his reporter so soon after returning from New York. So I faced the choice of either brushing over an important period in Poppy's personal life or abandoning the Egyptian idea.

But then, in my background reading, I came across a juicy little titbit: Howard Carter had been in London in late 1921 to have his gall bladder removed (Tyldesley, 2008). I then began to wonder if Poppy could meet him in London *before* the famous discovery. That would give me an excuse to connect with Egypt but still stay within the constraints of Poppy and Daniel's personal timeline – and save Rollo a bit of money.

I toyed with the idea of then having Poppy return with Carter to Egypt as part of a press corps – funded by a third party – but couldn't really make it work. How, and why, would her friends and colleagues go there too? So, I decided to keep the Egyptian theme but not to set the main story in Egypt. However, glimmers of that original story concept remain. The opening scene of *The Cairo Brief* is set on an archaeological dig, and one of the murders in the book is set in the Grand Continental Hotel in Cairo, the same hotel where Lord Carnarvon died from an infected mosquito bite in 1923, giving rise to the legend of the Curse of Tutankhamun's Tomb (aka the Mummy's Curse, which became the subject of popular books and films throughout the 1920s and 30s).

I kept the idea of the Mummy's Curse but transferred it instead to the death mask of Nefertiti. The mask in my book – along with the auction and Howard Carter's involvement – are completely fictitious. However, the bust of Nefertiti (kept in the Egyptian Museum of Berlin), and the controversial circumstances in which it was found by Ludwig Borchardt, are historical facts. You can read Borchardt's own account of the dig of Thutmose's workshop in 1912, listed in the "further reading" section at the end of this book. The discovery of the second chamber of the workshop in 1914 – and the murderous events that accompanied it – are a figment of my imagination.

So, one has a "cursed" Egyptian artefact, a number of unexplained deaths, an auction on a country estate, and a group of guests who need to be entertained… it didn't take me long to come up with the idea of a séance. From the mid-1800s to the early decades of the twentieth century, the spiritualist movement was in its heyday. For some it took the place of conventional religion, with spiritualist churches (starting in the USA) soon spreading around the world. Academics and leading literary figures – like Arthur Conan Doyle – attempted to prove the existence of the paranormal, using quasi-scientific methodologies. Then there were those – particularly in the 1920s – who didn't take it very seriously, but went along with the "fashion" of dabbling with the occult.

Now I'm not going to discuss the rights and wrongs or perceived "dangers" of spiritualism here – Poppy does a good job of that herself in the pages of the story – but I would like to mention my rationale for including Conan Doyle and his wife as characters, and what is and isn't "historical".

As avid readers of the Poppy Denby books might have picked up, I like to include a homage to a famous Golden Age Detective Fiction author in each story. In *The Jazz Files*, Poppy is reading an Agatha Christie novel when she first arrives in London. Then, in *The Kill Fee*, Poppy remembers a scene from Christie's *The Mysterious Affair at Styles* to help her deal with the victim of a poisoning. In *The Death Beat*, my favourite Golden Age author, Dorothy L. Sayers, makes a cameo appearance on board *The Olympic* on the way to New York. So in this book, I decided to feature the father of detective fiction, Arthur Conan Doyle. Like Poppy – and many others of the time – he had lost loved ones during the war. It was as a result of that that he started trying to contact the dead. This was useful for me, as one of the recurring themes of the Poppy Denby books is the dark shadow cast by the First World War and how individuals and society have been cut to the core by the horrors it unleashed.

The weekend at Winterton Hall, including the auction and the séance, was completely made up. However, Sir Arthur and Lady Jean Conan Doyle did regularly lead séances. I decided, however, to not have them ultimately lead this one, as it was important for the plot that the medium was a con-artist. There is no indication whatsoever that the Conan Doyles did not believe fully in what they were doing. As such, I removed them from centre stage and brought in Madame Minette as the shameless charlatan.

I hope you have enjoyed reading Poppy's latest adventure as much as I have enjoyed writing it. Ta-ta for now!

# BOOK CLUB QUESTIONS

1. In *The Cairo Brief* there is a rivalry between the staff of the *Globe* and the *Courier* to "scoop" the other. Have you ever been involved in a rivalry?

2. The two newspapers have different approaches to journalism. What are these? What ethical issues about the media are raised in this book?

3. Poppy and Delilah come from different backgrounds. They have contrasting personalities, different tastes in clothes, and differing financial circumstances. And yet they are still friends. Why do you think this is? What is it that holds their friendship together?

4. The background to the story involves the acquisition of ancient artefacts by European archaeologists. To this day, some of the artefacts held in Western museums – such as the Elgin Marbles and the bust of Nefertiti – are the subject of dispute. What are your views on this? Should the artefacts be returned?

5. There are two main romances in this book: Poppy and Daniel, and Rollo and Yasmin. One ends happily, the other not. Why do you think this is? Do you agree with Poppy and Daniel's decision?

6. When Poppy first hears there is going to be a séance at Winterton Hall she does not want to go. Why is this? Would you have gone to the séance?

7. When Poppy is alone at home someone knocks on her door in a way intended to scare her. Have you ever been in a similar situation? How did it turn out?

8.    At the police station Sergeant Barnes asks Poppy to try to get Arthur Conan Doyle to sign a book for him in exchange for him giving her information about the case. Poppy agrees to do it without actually knowing whether or not she will be able to deliver the goods. Have you ever agreed to do something you weren't sure you could achieve?

9.    In the historical notes the author mentions that she likes to pay homage to Golden Age Detective Fiction authors in her books. What elements of *The Cairo Brief* reminded you of stories from the Golden Age?

10.   Is there anything you would like to ask the author? If so, tweet her at @fionaveitchsmit or send a message through her website www.poppydenby.com

# FOR FURTHER READING...

Visit www.poppydenby.com for more historical information on the period, gorgeous pictures of 1920s fashion and décor, audio and video links to 1920s music and news clips, a link to the author's website, as well as news about upcoming titles in the Poppy Denby Investigates series.

Borchardt, Ludwig. *Excavations at Tell el-Amarna, Egypt, in 1913–1914* (from the Smithsonian Report for 1915). Washington Government Printing Office, Washington, 1916.

Department of Egyptian Antiquities. *Introductory Guide to the Egyptian Collections*. Trustees of the British Museum, London, 1964.

Eichler, Lilian. *Book of Etiquette*. Nelson Doubleday, New York, 1921.

Kemp, Barry. *The City of Akhenaten & Nefertiti: Amarna & its people*. Thames & Hudson, London, 2012.

Miller, Edward. *That Noble Cabinet: a history of the British Museum*. Andre' Deutsch Ltd, London, 1973.

Shepherd, Janet and Shepherd, John. *1920s Britain*. Shire Living Histories, Shire Publications, Oxford, 2010.

Shrimpton, Jayne. *Fashion in the 1920s*. Shire Publications, Oxford, 2013.

Tyldesley, Joyce. *Egypt: how a lost civilization was rediscovered.* BBC Books, London, 2008.

Vercouter, Jean (Trans. Sharman, Ruth). *The Search for Ancient Egypt.* Thames & Hudson, London, 1992.

Waugh, Evelyn. *Scoop.* (1938) Penguin Classics, Penguin, London, 2000.

Wingett, Matt. *Conan Doyle and the Mysterious World of Light: 1887–1920 (Sir Arthur Conan Doyle and the Paranormal).* Life is Amazing, Portsmouth, 2016.

For more information and fun photos about
Poppy and her world go to:
www.poppydenby.com

# THE JAZZ FILES

## POPPY DENBY INVESTIGATES

"It stands for Jazz Files," said Rollo. "It's what
we call any story that has a whiff of high society
scandal but can't yet be proven... you never know
when a skeleton in the closet might prove useful."

Set in 1920, *The Jazz Files* introduces aspiring journalist Poppy
Denby, who arrives in London to look after her ailing Aunt
Dot, an infamous suffragette. Dot encourages Poppy to apply
for a job at *The Daily Globe*, but on her first day a senior
reporter is killed and Poppy is tasked with finishing his story.
It involves the mysterious death of a suffragette seven years
earlier, about which some powerful people would prefer that
nothing be said...

Through her friend Delilah Marconi, Poppy is introduced
to the giddy world of London in the Roaring Twenties, with
its flappers, jazz clubs, and romance. Will she make it as an
investigative journalist, in this fast-paced new city? And will
she be able to unearth the truth before more people die?

ISBN: 978-1-78264-175-9 | e-ISBN: 978-1-78264-176-6

# THE KILL FEE

## POPPY DENBY INVESTIGATES

"Do you know who that is, Poppy?" asked Delilah.
"I do indeed."
"So what does it feel like to dance in the arms of
an assassin?"

Poppy Denby's star is on the rise. Now the Arts and Entertainment Editor at *The Daily Globe*, she covers an exhibition of Russian Art at the Crystal Palace. A shot rings out, leaving a guard injured and an empty pedestal in the place of the largest Fabergé Egg in the collection.

The egg itself is valuable, but more so are the secrets it contains within – secrets that could threaten major political powers. Suspects are aplenty and Poppy is delighted to be once again in the middle of a sensational story.

But, soon the investigation takes a dark turn when someone connected with the exhibition is murdered and an employee of the newspaper becomes a suspect. The race is on to find the egg before the killer strikes again...

ISBN: 978-1-78264-218-3 | e-ISBN: 978-1-78264-219-0

# THE DEATH BEAT

## POPPY DENBY INVESTIGATES

Poppy looked up, her face pale, her hands shaking.
"What is it, Poppy?"
"Oh my, Rollo, oh my. I think we've just struck gold."

Frances Brody, author of the Kate Shackleton mysteries Poppy
Denby is furious with Rollo, who has gambled away his position a
*The Daily Globe* and is being banished to New York. That is, unti
she discovers he plans to take her with him to work at *The New Yor*
*Times!*

Poppy can't wait to report on the Manhattan arts scene, but he
hopes are crushed when she is allocated The Death Beat – writin
obituaries. But Poppy has a nose for a story, and when a body i
found in a luxury penthouse apartment she starts to investigate
She unravels a sordid trail of illegal immigrants, forced labour, se
scandals, and an unexpected ghost from her past.

Poppy is determined to help the victims, but can she find th
evidence to bring the perpetrators to justice without putting her ow
life in danger...

ISBN: 978-1-78264-247-3 | e-ISBN: 978-1-78264-248-0

# DEATH OF A JESTER

## DEB RICHARDSON-MOORE

*"This is going to sound crazy. But there was a clown back there trying to lure a kid into the woods."*

The police cannot decide if the clown sightings reported around Grambling pose a threat or are just a hoax. That is, until a young homeless boy is lured away from his parents in the dead of night. Malachi's past is haunting him: he is pulled between the deep need to drink and drown his memories and his desire to try and find the little boy who was snatched from Tent City, right under his nose.

Then a man dressed in a clown's outfit is found bludgeoned to death. Can reporter Branigan Powers and Malachi help to bring the truth to light before the little boy is harmed, and before the wrong person is convicted of murder?

ISBN: 978-1-78264-264-0 | e-ISBN: 978-1-78264-265-7

# CHAPTER ONE

Malachi Ezekiel Martin didn't know where he was. The dream placed him in the desert in Kuwait or Iraq – he had never known where he was over there either.

He tasted grit in his mouth and saw the canvas roof of a tent overhead. Yeah, that would be the desert.

*The boy*, he thought, looking around wildly. *Where is the boy?*

He groped for the tent flap, fully expecting to look onto a barren, forsaken landscape, where everything, everything, was the color of sand – the tents, the uniforms, the rations always liberally sanded, impossible to keep out of your teeth. His head pounded, whether from the dream or from the crumpled empties of King Cobra, it was hard to say. He counted five of the forty-ounce malt liquor cans beside his sleeping bag.

He peered outside now, squinting, anticipating rows of tents and buzz-cut men headed for chow; he braced for the impaling of the desert sun. Instead, he saw cool shadow and a single man, gray hair pulled into a ponytail, hunched over a fire pit with a teetering grill rack on top, coaxing a battered coffeepot to boil. Malachi shook his head, clearing the cobwebs, involuntarily looking around the campsite for the boy, though his brain was catching up, telling him there was no boy.

Slick turned. "Coffee?" he offered.

"Soon's I pee." Malachi stumbled from his tent, past the picnic table that held two-liter Cokes and cereal bars, cans of ravioli and chicken noodle soup, all the sugars and starches those church do-gooders thought homeless people wanted to eat. He shuffled past the river birch, its lime-green leaves newly sprouted to provide lacy shade over the entrance to Tent City. It reminded him of his granny's doilies.

By the time he rezipped his camo pants – dark green and darker green, not the sand and khaki of his Desert Storm uniform – he was back to himself, back home in northeast Georgia where the red clay beneath his feet was as familiar as the honeysuckled air. He shook a clean Styrofoam cup from a package on the picnic table, and let Slick fill it with his thick bitter brew. He dragged a rusting lawn chair to sit across the fire pit from his neighbor.

"Where Elise?"

"Aw, she in jail again."

Malachi knew better than to ask why. It could be drunk and disorderly or possession of crack or even assault, but most likely a prostitution charge was in there somewhere. He didn't want to rub Slick's nose in it.

"Sixty days?"

Slick shrugged. "Dunno. Guess we see her when we see her."

Malachi changed the subject. "Today Friday, right?" He didn't wait for an answer. "Farmers' Market should be open soon. I'm ready for me some 'maters and cantaloupes."

Slick grunted. "Nah, too early. But Jericho Road be giving out that stuff, too. Pastor Liam said last Sunday."

Malachi thought of his grandparents' farm, of the okra and beans and squash and tomatoes and corn and cantaloupes and watermelons and pecans and peaches it had produced so plentifully they'd sold the bulk of it at a vegetable stand. That was his job, sitting on a stool at the end of the driveway, welcoming visitors, talking up the produce, collecting money, counting change. Between customers, he got to read, which was fine with his granny. She was quite a reader herself and they'd swapped library books back and forth.

That's a job he'd like, sitting on a stool at the Grambling Farmers' Market, ringing up produce. But he guessed those folks were all family members of the farms they sold from. They looked it, anyway, those farm-fed ladies with their tight perms and sleeveless flowered-y blouses from the Walmart. Not much call for outside help.

He took a swallow of coffee and felt a grain of something on his tongue. He spit it out. "Slick, you got grounds in there. Or dirt." He spit again. The dream of the desert resurfaced. There was always sand in his mouth in those days. That was probably why his mind had gone there.

He looked around, wondering what he wanted to do today. It was chilly here under the bridge but it was warming up out in the sun. He heard a rustle in the tangle of brush at the edge of camp and watched as a bird shot up.

Slick spoke again but his voice was lower, and Malachi had to lean into the fire to hear him.

"Family moved in last night." He nodded at the railroad tracks atop the hill that divided their section of Tent City from the unimaginatively named Tent City 2. A towering bridge spanned acres of these woods, and small encampments could be found wherever it crossed flat ground. It wasn't much, but the bridge did provide shelter from spring rains and summer's brutal sun.

"A family?" echoed Malachi. "You mean, with kids?" He hadn't ever seen kids living out here. These inner-city woods hid tents for the lucky ones, cardboard and blankets for the not-so-lucky. But they didn't hide kids.

Slick nodded. "Look like a mom and dad and teenage boy and a passel of littl'uns. I think they been staying in a old VW bus and it broke down. Somebody give 'em a big tent."

"How you know they had a bus?"

"Just what I heard."

"Aw, man."

Slick shook his head. "I know."

Malachi settled back in his rickety chair, taking another sip of coffee and getting another piece of grit. He put a finger in his mouth to snare it. It'd be worth a walk to Jericho Road to get a decent cup of coffee.

As he rose, his eye fell on the bursting undergrowth crowding the far side of the camp, where the shade from the bridge gave way to the morning sun. Deeper in the woods, he saw a flash of white, billowing white. It looked for all the world like a flowing Kuwaiti robe, but surely that was one more remnant of his dream.